OUTSTANDING PRAISE FOR
DAVID SHOBIN'S MEDICAL THRILLERS

THE UNBORN

"I've been waiting for someone who really knows medicine to write an all-out, go-for-broke medical horror story. The waiting is finally over."   —Stephen King

"Marvelous . . . the best of its kind since *Rosemary's Baby*."
                                                                —Mary Higgins Clark

"The scariest novel we've seen in years . . . lock your door . . . and start reading."   —*Cosmopolitan*

THE PROVIDER

"David Shobin's *The Provider* is one to relish—fast-paced, scary, suspenseful, and with enough shocking insider medical detail to keep you away from hospitals for the rest of your life."   —Glenn Meade

THE CENTER

"A non-stop roller-coaster ride into medical terror! David Shobin has written a winner. *The Center* is top-notch edge-of-your-seat entertainment—a thriller that only a great writer who is also a physician could have written. My pulse was still pounding hours after I finished it. This is one scary book."   —Michael Palmer

THE
CURE

DAVID
SHOBIN

St. Martin's Paperbacks

THE CURE

Copyright © 2001 by David Shobin.

All rights reserved. No part of this book may be used or reproduced in any manner whatsoever without written permission except in the case of brief quotations embodied in critical articles or reviews. For information address St. Martin's Press, 175 Fifth Avenue, New York, N.Y. 10010.

Library of Congress Catalog Card Number: 00-045923

ISBN: 0-312-97920-7

Printed in the United States of America

St. Martin's Press hardcover edition / February 2001
St. Martin's Paperbacks edition / January 2002

10 9 8 7 6 5 4 3 2 1

For Tova Shobin

My mother is a remarkable woman. During her life, she has endured adversity and tragedy with a courageous grace and an inner strength admired by all those who know her. When I was young, she inculcated my passion for reading and gardening, pursuits for which I'm forever grateful. I love you, Mom. I'm proud to be your son.

ACKNOWLEDGMENTS

Many people deserve thanks for their help in researching this book. For technical assistance regarding hormonal matters and scuba diving, I'm grateful to Joanne Smith of Wyeth Labs and to Renee Duncan Westerfield and Joel Dovenberger of Divers Alert network. A hats-off to Allison Dunton for her knowledge of Indonesia and to John McElhone for advice on police procedures. I'm very appreciative of Sam Goldberg's comments on governmental operations. Finally, thanks to Gail Shobin for her working knowledge of Larchmont.

On a personal note, thanks to Linda Price and Joe Veltre of St. Martin's Press and to my literary agent, Henry Morrison. I continue to be grateful to Drs. Steve Palumbo and John Franco for professional excellence, and to my friends Bob Riley and Jim Byrne.

THE
CURE

PROLOGUE

THE SOUTH PACIFIC

Twenty feet down, the man hovered over the reef and took the container of cyanide from his swim trunks. The clear, plastic, palm-size squeeze bottle of poison had a pointed nozzle. Removing the cap, he held the bottle at arm's length and squeezed out the contents in a steady stream, moving his hand in a wide arc from side to side. The concentrated cyanide was colorless. But it was more viscous than seawater, slightly denser. The dispersed solution shimmered in an undulating, oily wave, then slowly sank to the coral.

He capped the bottle and returned it to his trunks, remaining motionless for a moment, finning with his hands to stay in place, peering toward the bottom. The diluted cyanide slowly reached the hapless fish below. Then the man lifted his head and kicked lazily to the surface, where his small boat was waiting. He started to exhale just before his head broke through the water. Grabbing the side of his boat, he took several deep breaths and pulled himself aboard.

His name was Suranto Soedarsono, and he was known as "Pak" Suranto, a diminutive term of respect and endearment for elders. Yet at forty, he didn't consider himself particularly old. He'd been collecting marine fish for twenty-five years, and the regular diving had left him in excellent physical condition. He could effortlessly hold his breath for over three minutes. Settling onto a bench seat in the center of his craft, he looked at the shallow holding tanks and studied the dozen fish he'd already collected.

Pak Suranto specialized in the larger, more exotic specimens, like brilliant fuchsia anthias fish, dazzling orange lionfish, and long-finned Banggai cardinalfish. Such prized oddities were highly sought-after by tropical fish fanciers from the Orient to the Americas. He regularly transferred his catch to a large-masted *prahu* bound for the Philippines. Several days of specimen collecting would fetch him around two hundred dollars. Leaning over the tanks, he watched the fish struggle to recover.

Cyanide was a double-edged sword. While the goal was to stun the fish with the diluted poison, in higher concentrations it was lethal. Underwater, half of the poisoned fish died after exposure. Another half succumbed shortly after collection, and half of the remaining fish died en route to distant shores. Overall, it was a highly inefficient process. Pak Suranto stirred the water with his fingers. Most of the fish swam erratically, or not at all. Two were obviously dead, and he tossed them overboard.

It would take ten minutes for the dispersed cyanide to achieve its goal. In the meantime, he was hungry. He leaned back and stretched, briefly looking into the midmorning sun. Then he unpacked the supply basket containing his food. He was Minahassan, and like most of his brethren, he was a gourmand. He hoped his wife had packed *bakpiah*, his favorite meat-and-egg-filled dumpling. He still had a lot of work ahead of him, and he needed the nourishment. Gazing landward, he began to eat.

He was a quarter mile offshore in a remote, nearly uninhabited locale a hundred miles west of Manado. The region was a fertile, snakelike volcanic peninsula that wandered through the vast Maluku Sea. It was an area with few dwellings and even fewer people. Just beyond the distant beach, unending coconut plantations stretched for miles along the coast. To Pak Suranto, it was paradise. Finishing his meal, he covered his basket and put his goggles back on.

He fell effortlessly over the gunwale, carrying a handheld net. Then he inhaled, exhaled sharply, and took a second deep breath, which he held. He broke the water's surface and jackknifed, swimming slowly toward the bottom. The reefs in this area were pristine, alive with a rich diversity of underwater life. He thought it unfortunate that many marine creatures, including the coral itself, would be destroyed by what he was doing, but it couldn't be helped. A man and his family had to survive.

His quarry was the elusive Merlet's scorpion fish, a shoe-size, sharp-spined, emerald-and-gold creature. He'd noticed an excellent specimen hiding in a crevice in the coral, where it awaited unsuspecting prey. Pak breast-stroked into the uppermost coral head. Ten feet below, he spotted the scorpion fish in the sand, still concealed in its crevice, resplendent in its camouflage. He spread his net and moved gracefully downward, poised for the capture. But just before he struck, he noticed that the fish's pectoral fins were still, and its gills no longer moved. He cautiously reached out to touch it, mindful of the dangerous spines. The fish was dead.

Too bad, he thought. It was magnificent, and he hadn't seen one like it in weeks. But that was the price one paid for this method of collection. He lowered himself to the sandy seafloor, searching for other specimens. Out of the corner of his eye, he noticed a splash of color. Several mantis shrimp with spectacular turquoise and fire-red coloring wobbled in their burrows, obviously stunned. A handful of banded orange hermit crabs were scuttling away from them. He thought it unusual that such creatures should be found together. They were generally solitary scavengers who rarely associated outside their species unless there was an unanticipated feast. He slowly kicked in their direction.

And then he saw the foot.

He recoiled, jerking upright, his eyes going wide. The foot was very real, very human. And judging from the ragged strands of gray flesh plucked from its ankles, very dead. The crustaceans had evidently been at work. Pak felt a momentary panic, but he resisted the impulse to bolt. He returned to a sitting position and hovered motionless, feeling his heart pound as he considered what to do.

His first thought was that he'd inadvertently poisoned someone. An unsuspecting diver, perhaps, who'd accidentally strayed into his fishing area. But Pak thought that impossible. The day was clear, his vision was excellent, and he could see for miles. He was certain no one had approached the area. Besides, although he was no expert, he'd seen dead bodies before. And judging from the appearance of the skin, this one had been dead a while. Calming his fears, he inched closer.

The cadaver lay supine beneath a limestone overhang that served as the roof of a small cave in the coral. Such dark recesses were highly sought after by scavengers and other predators, like eels. He thought it possible that the victim had been dragged here for culinary safekeeping, to be slowly consumed as time went by. But by what? And more importantly, dragged from where? Pak thought it more likely that the victim had drowned. Carried by the current, a waterlogged body could be swept anywhere, and the reefs provided a kind of natural depository. It wasn't unheard-of to find bodies trapped underwater.

Pak's mind was racing, but his heart had slowed, and he knew he had about a minute of air remaining. Of equal importance was where the body had come from. He'd fished this area for months, and aside from the occasional land-based plantation worker, he hadn't seen another soul, and certainly no swimmers. It was possible that the victim had fallen overboard from a passing ship, but he considered that unlikely. He recalled seeing the brackish mouth of a river about a mile away. Was it conceivable that someone had been swept into the ocean from there?

For Pak, the commonsense solution was to flee—to swim back to his boat, leave the area, and forget what he'd seen. But although he lived in a predominantly Muslim country, Pak was a Christian, and his conscience wouldn't allow him to do that. He kicked up to the surface, refilled his lungs, and returned to the bottom. Hands trembling, he reached for the cadaver's ankle.

The cold skin beneath his fingers felt slimy. He gave a little tug, pulling the body toward him. The taut, swollen skin suddenly cracked in his grasp, sliding off the underlying tissue like a freed sausage casing. Pak felt the food rise up in his gorge. Steeling himself, he swallowed hard, resisting the impulse to vomit. He resumed his steady pull. The body slowly emerged from beneath the overhang, and the other ankle came into view. It had a foot-long piece of rope knotted about the skin.

The rope puzzled him. Its free end was frayed, as if slowly severed over time. Pak presumed that at one point it had been tied to something. The body was now visible to the thighs, and it slid weightlessly across the sand. Here and there, slivers of detached skin floated in the current, picked at by the crabs. To Pak's confusion, the corpse was naked. It wore no shoes, and he saw no shorts. And then the cadaver emerged to the groin, and he was even more surprised. It was a woman.

She was slender, with the sparse pubic hair of a Pacific Islander. His eyes strayed to her vulva, and he was repulsed. Her labia were virtually gone. Consumed by the crustaceans, only ragged strands of flesh remained. Pak's entire arm was now shaking. The trunk emerged, gray and swollen, the color of fish flesh. The woman had small, sagging breasts whose dark nipples were nearly gone. Now only the head remained hidden. The cadaver's chin hit an obstruction, and he paused for a moment.

For the first time, he noticed a piece of masonry in the sand, the size of a cinder block. He hadn't recognized it before, since its off-white color resembled ordinary coral. But now he saw that it was manmade and, more important, the other end of the rope was attached to it. The woman had obviously been weighted down and dumped here. He prayed she was already dead when she hit the water.

He returned to work with both hands, pulling the cadaver by the knees, trying to get the head clear of the obstruction. The chin dislodged, and the lower jaw came into view. The lips of the corpse were gone, the rows of teeth bared in a macabre rictus. The woman's beautiful, long black hair seemed strangely out of place. The fine strands shimmered weightlessly, gently bobbing in the current. Then, finally, the entire head emerged.

As it was pulled from the cave, the back of the skull hit the sand. It bounced, rising up slowly, as if to greet its liberator. Pak looked at what remained of the bloated face, and he was terrified. The eyes had been completely devoured. Their empty sockets stared at him, come to greet him in death.

1

THE HAMPTONS
MAY TWENTY-FIRST

The Long Island winters had recently been mild, and nowhere was this more evident than on the twin forks of the
island's East End, a lobster claw of land reaching into the
Atlantic. Aided by global warming and gentled by the Gulf
Stream, the last frosts now arrived a week earlier than
usual, and ocean temperatures were proportionately milder,
although at fifty-nine degrees, only the hardiest would
brave the water. By the third week in May, balmy days
with temperatures into the seventies were common. On this
last Saturday before the long Memorial Day weekend—the
official start of the summer season—the locals awaited arrival of the hundreds of thousands of visitors that would
swell their ranks through Labor Day.

The South Fork was a particular tourist magnet, owing
to its superb stretches of broad, white beach, a perfect mat-
ing of land and sea. But before the Hamptons became a
mecca for partygoers and celebrities, they were home to
generations of descendants of English settlers who began
moving into the area not long after the Pilgrims stepped
ashore at Plymouth. Long home to farmers and fishermen,
year-round residents were now an amalgam of writers, so-
cialites, working folk, and those simply fleeing the pressures of Manhattan, less than seventy-five miles away.

Alyssa would have liked to spend the morning outdoors
with her friends. The early day seemed enchanted, sparkling, promising adventure. She'd finished her homework
last night, and with no tests on Monday, she had the weekend to herself. But then her mom had spoiled it by making
a doctor's appointment.

"Alyssa, are you ready? We have to be there in fifteen
minutes."

"Just about."

She moped in her room clad in her nightdress, not sure

what to wear. She took it off and then changed her underpants. The sanitary pad was soaked, and she quickly removed it and stuck on a new one. The fact was, she *did* feel very tired, and her energy was nearly gone. And her cramps were pretty horrible. Maybe it wasn't such a bad idea to get checked out after all.

Wearing only her underpants, she looked at her reflection in the full-length mirror. Lately, she'd been looking at herself every day. She'd always been straight as sticks, devoid of curves; but as she touched the tiny buds of her breasts, she thought they *might* be slightly more prominent. She sighed. When almost nothing was there, it was very hard to tell.

Somewhere Alyssa had heard that the teenage years were supposed to be outrageously fun-filled, yet if this first year was anything to go by, they were destined to be pretty miserable. Everyone told her she had a pretty face, but she knew what the boys were interested in. She simply *had* to do something about it, and right now, she was doing everything she could.

Karl Müller's ancestors came to the Hamptons two hundred years ago, abandoning their region along the North Sea for the nutrient-rich water of the western Atlantic. Their imprint endured in their offspring, a taciturn lot who spoke in the slow tempo of the fortunes of fishing, where it wasn't unusual to starve during the winter and prosper in the summer, where a good haul consisted of ten thousand pounds of bluefish, weakfish, and stripers. Karl had fished the ocean from Montauk Point to Westhampton Beach for fifty of his sixty years. It was arduous, backbreaking work, with days that started before dawn and ended long after sunset.

The physical toll on Karl was marked. His face was corrugated, weathered by salt and spray. The back of his thick neck was deeply lined by the brutal summer sun. But of greater importance was the strain on his heart. For several months, Karl had endured worsening chest pain, suffering in silence. Now, however, the discomfort was etched into his face. During the past twenty-four hours, Karl's normally ruddy complexion had grown progressively more cyanotic, to the point where it resembled the pale flesh of the fish he caught. The change in his appearance was accompanied by a noticeable shortness of breath. Finally submitting to the urging of his close-knit family, Karl agreed to see the doctor. He stubbornly refused to let anyone drive him.

Accompanied by his ten-year-old grandson Josh, Karl arrived at the doctor's office in Quogue, an inland area of the town of Southampton. Family practitioner Steven McLaren was a down-to-earth physician whose patients ranged from local townsfolk to beachgoing glitterati. Although not a native of the area, Dr. McLaren was liked and respected for his constant availability, long hours, and the generous donation of his time to area fund-raisers. His office was always crowded, even at eight forty-five on a Saturday morning.

The waiting room was cramped, lined with wall-mounted bench seats bordered by plants. Next to the magazine rack was a table display of popular herbal supplements. Above it, a sign asked, Are You Maximizing Your Nutritional Potential?

In the waiting room, Josh found a seat among the half-dozen patients, while his grandfather registered with the receptionist.

"I don't have an appointment," Müller said, "but the family wants me checked out. Think he can see me today?"

Looking up, the receptionist quickly took in Karl's pallor and the beads of sweat dotting his face. "What's wrong, Mr. Müller? You don't look too good."

"In here," he said, thumping his chest. "Feels like someone's standin' on my breastbone."

Receptionist Rebecca Clausen quickly got up and opened the door separating the waiting room from the examination areas. "Come this way, Mr. Müller. I'm going to put you right in and have Dr. McLaren see you next." She held the door ajar, watching his suddenly halting steps as a grimace came over his face. "Take your time, Karl," she said, supporting his elbow. "We're headed for the first room on the right."

Müller looked over his shoulder and gave Josh a reassuring wave. Karl had always looked after himself. He disliked giving an impression of weakness, and he hated needing assistance. But with each step, the pain worsened. "Hold on," he said. "Lemme just . . ."

"If you can't make it, just lie down on the floor, okay?"

His face suddenly contorted. "Can't breathe," he managed. "I—" Then his eyes rolled upward in their sockets, and he sunk to his knees, collapsing heavily onto his side.

"Dr. McLaren!" Becky shouted. "Dr. McLaren, right away!"

The door to the waiting room was still open, and several patients got up uncertainly. Josh leapt to his feet, eyes wide and face white with fear.

"Grandpa!" he screamed.

"Stay there, Josh!" the receptionist said. "Grandpa's going to be okay."

The door to another exam room swung open, and a man in a white lab coat emerged. In his early forties, McLaren had slate gray eyes and light brown hair going gray at the temples. He took one look at the prostrate patient and dashed into the hall. Kneeling, he checked for a pulse.

"Did he say anything, Becky?" he asked.

"It's his heart. He said he had chest pain and couldn't breathe."

"This guy's too damn stubborn to take his medication." He paused, frowning. "And now I'm not getting a pulse. Donna! Drop what you're doing and get over here!"

The nurse, who'd been in the small rear lab drawing blood from a patient, appeared within seconds, a concerned look on her face. "What *happened*?"

"He's arrested. Let's get him onto the table, okay? Quick, get his feet," McLaren said, rolling Müller onto his back and grasping him under the armpits. "Becky, call for help!"

As Becky dashed to the phone, doctor and nurse lifted the stricken man, grunting from the strain. Once they placed him on the table, Donna quickly removed Müller's work shirt, while McLaren put his stethoscope in his ears. Listening to the man's chest, he quickly confirmed the absence of a heartbeat.

"Get the crash cart while I pump him!"

The two of them had been down this road a month before, and the patient had expired. CPR was something that required continual practice, and their skills had grown stale. Recognizing their shortcomings, the pair drilled repeatedly, until they functioned like a well-oiled machine. Now, McLaren leaned into Müller's chest, trying to reestablish cardiac rhythm, while Donna retrieved the crash cart.

McLaren's mind was awhirl, establishing medical priorities. His patient wasn't breathing, and getting air to his oxygen-starved tissues was paramount. "Tilt his head back, and put that oral airway in," he ordered. "Then bag him."

Donna complied, tilting Müller's chin upward, inserting a curved piece of molded plastic into his pharynx. From the cart, she removed an ambu bag, a football-size black latex cylinder with an attached rubberized mask. Squaring the mask over Müller's mouth with one hand, she squeezed the bag with the other, forcing oxygen into his lungs.

"Ambulance is on its way!" Becky shouted, poking her head into the room. "Oh God, not again," she groaned. "Is he going to make it?"

"That's the general idea, Beck," he tersely replied. "Close the waiting-room door; then get in here and plug in the defibrillator."

Becky was out and back in an instant, inserting the defibrillator's plug and turning on the power.

McLaren needed an electrocardiogram. "Turn on the EKG, and throw on the limb leads," he told Becky. "Have an IV ready in case we're lucky enough to get that far."

Becky's hands were trembling as she placed the four electrodes on Müller's wrists and ankles. His mottled skin remained frighteningly gray. As Becky carefully attached the wires, McLaren continued rhythmic cardiac compressions in sync with Donna's respirations. When Becky finally signaled that everything was ready, McLaren and Donna momentarily stopped working. Everyone eyed the EKG pens.

"Nothing," McLaren said, eyeing the meaningless squiggles. He grabbed the defibrillator paddles. "Set it at a hundred and fifty joules."

Donna continued bagging as Becky set the power, calling out when the panel light blinked from standby to ready. McLaren quickly positioned the paddles on Müller's chest and told Donna to get back. Then he pressed the button.

The unit fired, sending a powerful electrical jolt through Müller's dying heart. His body stiffened, back arching upward before falling back heavily. McLaren removed the paddles and stared defiantly at the EKG, holding his breath.

To his surprise and relief, the random pattern was replaced by sharp, recognizable waveforms. "That's more like it," he said.

"It's beating again?" Becky asked.

"It is for now. If it stays that way until he gets to the ER, he's got a chance." McLaren replaced the paddles in their cradles and put the stethoscope back in his ears. Motioning for Donna to stop bagging, he listened to Müller's chest once more, allowing himself a cautious smile when he heard coarse respirations. "Good man, Karl. Becky, get the oxygen. Donna, put up the IV."

Aware that Müller's damaged heart could stop at any minute, McLaren quickly rolled up the unconscious patient's shirtsleeve and attached a tourniquet above the elbow, searching for prominent vessels. But Müller's blood pressure was too low to distend the veins. Without hesitation, McLaren slapped the man's skin to make them stand out. Ever so slowly, the sluggish vessels swelled to the surface.

Having attached the IV tubing, Donna inverted the liter of five-percent dextrose and Ringer's lactate, hanging it from a hook on the IV pole. McLaren wiped a vein close to Müller's wrist with alcohol, steadied the man's hand, and plunged a twenty-gauge catheter into the vessel. When he removed the stylet, dark venous blood flowed back, and he quickly attached the tubing. McLaren and the two women worked smoothly together, anticipating the other's needs. As McLaren taped the catheter to the skin, Donna adjusted the flow rate, and Becky wheeled a green oxygen tank to the head of the table. Finally, McLaren adjusted the oxygen cannula around Müller's head, and Donna cranked open the tank to a six-liter-per-minute flow rate.

With Müller's vital functions restored, there was nothing to do but wait. Further tests would have to await his arrival at the hospital. There the staff could further stabilize him, begin diagnostic studies, and administer more sophisticated cardiac medications. Keeping one eye on his patient,

McLaren hastily began scribbling notes for the EMTs. A minute later, they heard the wail of an ambulance siren.

Becky opened the rear emergency entrance. The ambulance backed up beside the wheelchair ramp, and its doors burst open. Removing a stretcher, the attendants wheeled it up the ramp and into the office, proceeding down the corridor until they spotted McLaren.

"Where we headed, Doc?"

"In here," he indicated. "Sixty-year-old white male with a long history of hypertension. He came to the office this morning—"

"Isn't this Karl Müller?" interrupted the other EMT. "Stubborn old guy, he used to fish with my dad."

"*Stubborn* is right. He's probably had worsening angina for a long time. Collapsed right here in the hall, complete asystole. Looks like an anterior wall MI. We shocked him, and luckily, he came right back."

"Luck, huh?" said the first EMT, locking the stretcher's wheels in place beside the exam table. "With you, Doc, luck's got nothing to do with it. You never leave us anything to do."

On a count of three, the EMTs smoothly transferred their patient from the table to the stretcher. McLaren filled them in on everything that had happened, handing them the notes that summarized events, times, and procedures. He walked them down the hall, watching as they lifted the stretcher into the ambulance.

"You guys want me to ride along?"

"Are you kidding, Doc? We hang around you, and we'll never get a chance to practice a damn thing!"

McLaren watched the ambulance drive away. Taking a deep breath, he glanced up into the eastern sun, warm on his face. Then he looked down at his hands, which were trembling. He shoved them in his pockets and returned inside.

"Good job, you two," he said to the staff. "I think we got it right this time. Donna, see if you can get the room cleaned up. Did Müller come in with anyone?"

"His grandson's in the waiting room," Becky said. "I think he saw everything."

"Jesus. Call the Müller home, and tell them what happened. I'll talk with the kid."

Opening the door to the waiting room, he was greeted by a sea of inquisitive eyes. "I know a lot of you are aware of what happened. Mr. Müller had a heart attack," he said in soft, measured tones. "He's on his way to the hospital now, and I think he'll be all right. We're going to take a short break for a while. If anyone wants to reschedule, just tell Becky." Looking around, he found Karl's grandson huddled in a corner, being hugged protectively by a large black woman. Tears streamed down the boy's cheeks.

He slowly walked over and stroked the boy's head. Then he took his hand. "Come with me, Josh. Let's you and I have a little talk." He led Josh inside, past the reception desk.

Becky was hanging up the phone. "I just spoke with Josh's mom," she said. "She'll be by to pick him up after she drops Mrs. Müller off at the hospital."

"Thanks, Beck."

In the consultation room, he threw open the blinds, letting the room fill with sunlight. Josh sat in a chair in front of McLaren's desk. Rather than sit across from the boy, McLaren brought another chair over and sat at Josh's side.

"Are you scared, Josh?"

"No."

"Not even a little?"

Josh fell silent, chin quivering. The boy was only five years younger than his daughter, and McLaren's heart went out to him. "When I was a little younger than you, my grandma was in a car crash. It was my birthday, and she was driving over to our house when it happened. She was hurt real bad. For a while, we didn't know if she was going to make it."

"Did she die?" Josh asked.

"No, she didn't. But she was in the hospital a long time."

"Is my grandpa going to die?"

McLaren looked him in the eye. "I honestly don't know, Josh. I know he's real sick, but I think he's got a real good chance once he gets to the hospital. And I also know he's very lucky to have a grandson who loves him as much as you do." He went to his desk, opened the top drawer, and removed two Tootsie Pops, covered with brown and orange wrappers. Then he returned to Josh and held them out. "Which one do you want?"

"Chocolate."

McLaren unwrapped them both, giving one to the boy and putting the other in his mouth. "Come on, let's go outside for a walk until your mom gets here."

Twenty minutes later, Josh was gone, and the office pace returned to a semblance of normal. Only two patients rescheduled, and as more arrived, it was standing room only. Becky signed them in, while Donna cleaned up. McLaren felt that talking with Josh had helped the boy, but it had been cathartic for him as well. CPR, even when successful, was a high-stress procedure, and it often took a while for the rescuers to unwind. This was especially true for McLaren who, more than most physicians, suffered from repeated crises of confidence.

Among both patients and colleagues, he was considered a skillful practitioner. But for decades he'd felt that no matter what he did, it wasn't quite good enough. Intellectually, McLaren understood that this was the voice of his father, whose incessant carping to do better remained with McLaren long after the man had died. Yet that logical insight didn't translate into emotional understanding, or lead to a change in behavior. He remained plagued by self-doubt.

This sense of inadequacy began in childhood. In high school, he excelled academically because he felt he couldn't compete in other arenas. One of the reasons he went to med school was that he believed the prestige of being a physician would bolster his shaky sense of self-worth. But while he was a med student, he became haunted by a fear of being unprepared for crises and of being subsequently exposed. Once he was in practice, even when he succeeded, as he did today, the thought of being considered an imposter was never far from his mind. In his heart, he felt he was repeatedly flirting with being a fraud—and worse, considering himself one.

Taking a breather before they resumed work, the staff poured cups of coffee in the small employee lounge.

"Today, it was one for the good guys," Becky said.

"Amen to that," seconded McLaren. "We were lucky. Remind me to bill Mr. Müller for our drill time."

"You really think we were lucky in there?" Donna asked.

"Just my perspective. I'd rather be lucky than smart any day."

"Why can't you just give yourself a pat on the back?" Becky asked.

"Don't get me wrong," said McLaren. "I'm pretty damn glad we came out on top this time. It's just that . . . did I ever tell you about this recurring dream I have?"

"The one with the naked models and the whipped cream?" asked Becky.

"Get real," McLaren laughed. "In this dream, I'm back in med school. It's finals. As I walk in to take my seat, it suddenly dawns on me that I haven't been in class all semester. I'm completely unprepared, and I'm about to get my academic ass handed to me."

The two women exchanged looks. Finally, Becky laughed. "I never realized what a sick puppy you were, Dr. McLaren."

"Do me a favor, boss," said Donna. "Try not to dwell on that the next time one of our patients decides to keel over."

As McLaren walked back to his office, Becky said, "He confuses the hell out of me, Donna. Everyone knows what a fantastic doctor he is. That's why we're not at the beach on Saturday but sitting here with wall-to-wall patients up our behind."

"Maybe it's something psychological—you know, like when some people become almost perfect trying to make up for an ego problem?"

"I don't buy all that Freudian double-talk," Becky said. "Frankly, I don't care *what* you call it. All I know is, if anyone in my family has a serious medical problem, we head for Dr. Steven McLaren."

Thirty-two-year-old Julia Hagen stood in the waiting room with her daughter Alyssa. At thirteen, Alyssa was fast developing her mother's good looks, although today she appeared frighteningly pale. Leaning against the wall, Alyssa kept her palms pressed to her lower abdomen. Her brow was knitted in pain.

"I really have to sit down, Mom."

"It won't be long, sweetie. I think we're next."

"I think I'm going to pass out."

Julia looked at her daughter with mounting concern. Perspiration dotted the child's upper lip, and her complexion had grown waxy. Yet Alyssa had endured a lot in the past two years, and she generally did so without complaining. Julia knew that when her daughter complained, the pain was bad. Quickly walking to the reception window, she explained what was going on. Becky took one look at the adolescent and ushered both of them inside. Soon Alyssa was lying on an exam table with her feet propped up.

Alyssa was perspiring, though her face was pale. Julia wiped her daughter's forehead with a tissue. What in the world was going on? God knows Alyssa had health problems aplenty, but hadn't she been through enough? Her daughter's skin felt terribly cold. Julia was very worried, and she prayed Dr. McLaren would know what to do.

Minutes later, McLaren came in. He glanced at Julia, then at his young patient. If he was worried about Alyssa's appearance, he tried not to show it. Giving her a welcome smile, he walked over and took her wrist, checking the pulse.

"I know, I know," he said casually. "You didn't have an appointment, but you couldn't keep away from me, right?"

"My stomach really hurts, Steve." Thinking it would make their relationship easier, McLaren had encouraged his adolescent patient to call him by his first name.

"When did it start?"

"A couple of days ago, when I got my period."

"You've been having your period for over a year, kiddo," he said, imperceptibly shifting his hand to her lower abdomen, where he gently probed. "Did you get it on time this month?"

"Uh-huh," she nodded. "But it's just so *heavy.*"

"How heavy is that?"

"She went through more than a box of pads yesterday,

Dr. McLaren," said Julia. "This morning, she was changing them every half hour."

"I see," he slowly said, no longer smiling. "Alyssa, I'm going to send Donna in for a blood test. Step outside a minute, Julia."

Taking her elbow, he steered her into the hall and down the corridor. "Her pulse is pretty rapid," he said. "It wouldn't surprise me if her hematocrit's very low. But whatever it is, this bleeding's got to stop. Has she ever been to a gynecologist?"

"A gynecologist? She's only thirteen, Dr. McLaren!"

"What's this 'Doctor' stuff? I've known you since before she was born, Julia. And if Alyssa can call me Steve, so can you. Don't misunderstand what I'm saying. Even children should see a gynecologist when there's a problem, and it seems there's a problem now. I have somebody in mind."

"You don't think it's related to her tumor?"

"I doubt it. She's susceptible to all kinds of hematological problems, but not heavy bleeding. When was her last radiation treatment? Three months ago?"

"Eleven weeks."

"Eleven weeks . . . I'll give her oncologist a call. Before this bleeding started, how was she doing in general?"

Julia told him. Alyssa suffered from a cancer called a malignant thymoma—very unusual in adults, and even rarer in children. The thymus gland, located behind the breastbone and above the heart, was a small, poorly understood organ that reached its maximum size at puberty and was thought to play a role in immunity. Although it rarely caused problems, in Alyssa, the thymus had become a matter of life and death.

Slightly more than two years earlier, Alyssa's persistent cough had prompted McLaren to order a chest X-ray. The film revealed an anterior mediastinal mass that was at the root of her problem. McLaren referred her to a chest surgeon, who biopsied the mass and provided a diagnosis. Alyssa's thymoma was of the highly aggressive, fibroendothelial type, a lesion that carried a five-year survival rate of only twenty percent. Considering the patient's age,

McLaren and the surgeon promptly referred Alyssa to Memorial Sloan-Kettering in Manhattan.

The approach to Alyssa's disease was multidisciplinary, involving pediatrics, oncology, surgery, and radiation medicine. Distressed by the dismal prognosis, the doctors wanted to begin treatment immediately. Alyssa was given a course of preoperative chemotherapy with cisplatin and Adriamycin, followed by a thoracotomy for removal of the cancer. But their worst fears were confirmed at surgery. Unfortunately, the operative team could only partially resect the tumor, whose outer margins had already invaded the heart's pericardium and the outer trachea.

"Does she have a boyfriend?" McLaren asked.

"No, she's still very shy around boys. She never completely recovered socially from the months she missed at school."

"Boys that age can be very cruel."

"At this point," Julia said, "it's probably a blessing in disguise."

Although everyone had been troubled by the surgical findings, they knew miracles were possible. As soon as Alyssa could tolerate it, she was started on radiotherapy. Through it all—the loss of her hair, the painful convalescence, the side effects of radiation—Alyssa remained cheerful and upbeat. She was a model patient, and her spirits buoyed everyone. To all of them, she was just a terrific kid.

Despite her disease, Alyssa's pre-adolescent growth continued. She got her period a year after her first radiation treatment. At five-four and one hundred pounds, she was long-legged and slender, with blue eyes, straight, light brown hair, and a nuance of prepubertal breasts. Not surprisingly, Alyssa's winning personality earned her a long list of girlfriends. But around boys, she was painfully shy. Embarrassed by the long pink scar going from her neck to her abdomen, she wore one-piece bathing suits to the beach, something that made her appear even more flat-chested than she was.

* * *

"When's her next appointment with the oncologist?" McLaren asked.

"In two weeks." Julia paused, looking away. "I'm so tired of this, Dr. . . . Steve. All the running around, the tests, the treatments. What makes me feel even worse is that while all I do is bitch, her attitude is unbelievable."

"You feel guilty?"

"I suppose. Wouldn't you?"

"Yeah, I probably would."

A year after her surgery, Alyssa had undergone extensive reevaluation, with full blood work, CT scans, and ultrasounds. According to the imaging studies, Alyssa's tumor had recurred, and it was now the same size as it had been before surgery. The depressing clinical situation was apparent to everyone. It was now a waiting game, just a matter of time. Although no one spelled things out for Alyssa, she was a bright child. She knew what the score was. Yet she endured the seemingly endless, palliative radiation treatments with a ready smile and a kind word for her caregivers.

For a while, it seemed the therapy was successful. Three months ago, however, metastases to her bones and liver were discovered. Alyssa began to experience daily pain.

Donna approached, looking glum. "Her 'crit's seventeen, Dr. McLaren."

"What was it the last time we checked?"

"Thirty-three."

He looked at Julia. "That's a pretty significant drop. She'll have to be transfused. I'm going to admit her."

Julia looked away, shaking her head wearily, the strain etched into her expression. "The poor kid's been through so much lately, Dr. Mc—"

"Steve."

She nodded. "Steve. I know she won't bat an eyelash, but I don't know how much more of this I can take."

"I'm sure she'll be in and out of the hospital in a day or two."

"That's not the point," she continued, chin quivering. "What I'm saying is, we both know she doesn't have much more time left. Alyssa needs someone strong, and right now I feel so emotionally battered, I don't know if I'll be there for her when the time comes."

McLaren reached out and grasped her shoulder. "I think you will, Julia. But you have my word. On the off chance you're not, I promise I will be."

2

THE SOUTH PACIFIC

After hauling the dead body aboard, Pak Suranto studied the cadaver. Seen in the bright glare of day, the body appeared more bloated than it had underwater. Distended by internal gases, where the skin wasn't split or detached, it was stretched tight. And then there was the odor. Naturally, he couldn't smell it underwater; yet he'd smelled much worse before.

But as the overhead sun beat down on the decomposing flesh, the stench of decay and corruption became much more noticeable. The question remained, what should he do now? Bringing in the body meant losing the rest of the day's catch, but given the smell, Pak couldn't sit in the boat for any length of time.

Pak wrapped a bandana around his lower face and breathed through his mouth. He started the boat's small motor and headed for shore. The nearest police facility was twenty miles to the west, and he had no intention of motoring there beside a reeking cadaver.

When he beached his craft, he pulled it higher onto the sand, and headed inland. The heavily planted grove of coconut palms was a winding green thicket that stretched as far as the eye could see. Pak slowly walked between the tall trees. It was dark. The dense canopy overhead filtered the sunlight. Underfoot, the decomposing brown debris of fallen palm fronds made a crunching noise. He moved the dried leaves aside, making a small clearing. Then he returned to the boat.

On the ocean, the gentle sea breezes kept the flies away. But on shore, a swarm of buzzing creatures had already descended on the corpse in the boat. It was futile to try swatting them away; the flies knew food when they smelled it. Holding his breath, Pak lifted the dead woman over the gunnel. He realized the woman's rotten flesh was leaving a malodorous trail on his skin, but there was nothing he could do about it. Her rancid skin was slippery, and as he stepped back onto the sand, she slid from his arms and fell heavily onto the beach.

Just as well, he thought. He had no desire to carry the smelly cadaver over even the shortest stretch of beach. Grasping the dead woman's wrists, he dragged the body toward the woods. The flies pursued in a dark wave, following the scent. Soon Pak was straining, and he began to sweat. With each passing step, slivers of rotting flesh fell off the body and stuck to the hot, dry sand.

When he reached the clearing, he stopped and let go of the arms. He quickly covered the cadaver with palm debris. The debris didn't keep the flies away, but it made him feel better. Returning to the boat, he first dove into the surf, rinsing his body and scrubbing his hands with wet sand. When he finished, he pulled the boat back into the ocean, guiding it through the breakers before jumping on board. Then he once more started the engine, turned west, and gunned the motor.

"Turn a little more to the right, Doctor," said the set director. "Comfortable?"

"I don't think I'll ever feel comfortable here," said McLaren. Never fully relaxed under the klieg lights, he still had the faintest squint.

"Ready on the set, everyone," the director said. Then, pointing his finger at McLaren, "Action."

"Hi, I'm Dr. Steven McLaren, and I'd like to have a word with you about nutritional supplements. A generation ago, good nutrition meant eating your spinach and taking a multivitamin. But with each day that goes by, medical science reveals just how hard it is to maintain dietary balance."

Smiling confidently, he gestured to a wall-mounted shelf display. The shelves contained dozens of popular nutritional products, each with an eye-catching, easy-to-read label. McLaren paused and picked out two bottles, seemingly at random. Then he turned back to the camera.

"With Ecolabs supplements, you can be sure of getting the very best. For over a decade, millions of Americans have turned to the leader in herbal products to enhance their health and well-being. Give Ecolabs a try, and maximize your nutritional potential!"

"Cut," said the director. McLaren put the bottles down and turned away from the lights' glare. "That was good, Doctor, but you were holding the echinacea around your waist. Let's run through it once more, and bring it up a few inches."

McLaren looked at his watch. "This is taking longer than I thought. I'm going to have to duck out of here soon. Are we almost there?"

"Remember where to hold that bottle, and this'll be the last take."

A young woman poked her head into the studio. "Call for you on two, Dr. McLaren. And Mr. DiGiorgio wants you to call him when you're done. He left the number."

McLaren thanked her and walked into the control room. Pressing the phone's blinking light, he picked up the receiver. It was his ex-wife, Lorraine. In terse, concise tones, she informed him that his most recent child support payment was late. Also, she was canceling his afternoon visitation with their 15-year-old daughter, Andie. When he started to protest, she interrupted.

"Look, Steve, get off my case. It was Andie's decision, okay?"

"Don't throw guilt my way and make me out to be the bad guy."

"You want me to tell her you refuse to let her spend the afternoon with her friends?"

"Damn right I do! It's not her decision to make. That was part of our agreement!"

"Fine," she said bitterly. "Take it up with your lawyer." Then she hung up.

McLaren put the phone down with a defeated sigh. In the last few months, his relationship with his former wife had gone from bearable to nearly intolerable. Although he felt he could deal with that, he knew it had to be as hard on their daughter as it was on him. He was now upset, and it required more than three takes to finish the commercial. When he was done, he called Ted DiGiorgio, the CEO of Ecolabs.

DiGiorgio was an American success story. One of

McLaren's college roommates, DiGiorgio considered partying more of an obligation than schoolwork. Not unexpectedly, he flunked out in his junior year. But the two men remained close. Steve knew Ted was very bright, and once the revelry grew tiresome, Steve encouraged his friend to get a job. By then, Steve was in med school. With his help, Ted landed a job as a pharmaceutical company representative.

Ted was an instant success. Energetic and outgoing, he worked his territory with skill and enthusiasm, schmoozing with the physicians, learning how to read them, anticipating their needs. After only two years, he was his company's eastern regional rep of the year. Coming into the industry at a time when managed care was on the rise, he understood physician disenchantment with the business aspects of medicine. He also appreciated the slow growth of alternative and complementary medicine, an arena many doctors considered a possible source of additional revenue.

At the age of twenty-seven, loaned to the hilt, Ted bought a small generic vitamin manufacturing company. Owing to nonexistent marketing, the plant had fallen on hard times. Ted quickly added a line of herbal products to the company's inventory. American consumers had just begun to learn about ginseng and Saint-John's-wort, and Ted was in the right place at the right time. Given his effervescence and drive, the company's earnings skyrocketed, and within two years, he was a leader in the field. Seeing which way the wind was blowing, he added even more herbals to his line. Stressing the "natural, environmentally safe" source of his raw materials, he changed the company's name to Ecolabs.

Ecolabs was an instant success. DiGiorgio used slick, creative marketing to tout his company's wares, selling through trendy boutiques and setting up his own retail outlets. But beyond intelligent marketing, Ted did his utmost to add authenticity to the company's name. He hired the best and brightest to make sure the company was ecologically sensitive. Suppliers of raw materials were carefully screened to include only those whose collection methods were consistent with environmental preservation. Ted's social conscience was not just the lip-service variety.

And then, sounding out his long list of physician contacts, he seized upon an untapped source of market share: direct physician marketing. Before long, doctors from coast to coast were selling the Ecolabs line through their offices, increasing both their own bottom lines and the company's revenue.

In some circles, the idea of turning doctors' offices into salesrooms was met with skepticism, even disdain. Some proclaimed it downright unethical. Not everyone was willing to concede that medicine had an overtly entrepreneurial side. But although battle lines were quickly drawn, opponents of the concept waged a losing skirmish. Physician incomes had become so squeezed by managed care that an alternative financial source was not only acceptable, but in some cases mandatory. Before long, those opposing office sales conceded defeat. When money became tight, ethics were no longer an issue.

McLaren became a physician distributor with reluctance. After his divorce, although he felt the financial pinch, the idea of office marketing didn't appeal to him. He hadn't gone to med school to become a salesman. Ted repeatedly tried to persuade him. Office sales were a sign of the times, he argued. Although some physicians wished the concept would disappear, it wouldn't. But McLaren wasn't convinced. He respected the fact that Ecolabs was truly interested in environmental issues, and he knew DiGiorgio to be a man of integrity. In fact, McLaren took to calling Ted "the Herbalist." Yet what finally converted him were his own patients.

As herbal remedies grew more and more popular, many patients sought McLaren's nutritional advice, and he became concerned about what they were taking. The supplement market now had many players, and he worried about the safety of the products his patients consumed. Not all companies insisted on quality control. Also, although McLaren wasn't a tree-hugger, he was concerned about the environment. For most manufacturers, where herbal products came from and how they were harvested weren't the high priority they were with Ecolabs.

Finally, some patients suggested that they'd feel more comfortable purchasing supplements directly from Mc-

Laren. Ultimately, he decided to have a go at it, on the smallest scale possible. Introduction of Ecolabs products was greeted with such patient enthusiasm that he decided to become fully involved.

DiGiorgio was thrilled. As far as he was concerned, the smart move was to come on board, and his friend Steve was nothing if not smart. But DiGiorgio had another reason to be elated. Steve McLaren was a good-looking man, who, despite certain insecurities, had undeniable poise and charm. Ecolabs was about to launch a campaign of personal endorsements, and their advertising firm thought a practicing physician would add a level of authenticity. Ted considered Steve to be the ideal man for the job. Several months ago, in a studio midway between Manhattan and the Hamptons, they began the commercial shoots.

Today, when Steve reached Ted on the phone, the lingering annoyance over the conversation with his ex-wife was apparent in his voice.

"You sound pissed," said Ted. "What gives? Trouble with the shoot?"

"No, it went fine. The problem's with Lorraine," he said, exasperated. "She's bitching about her money again. And once we were finished here, I was supposed to spend the afternoon with Andie, but Lorraine came up with another bullshit excuse."

"Seems to me you've been down that road before. What're you going to do about it?"

"She'll get her damn money. It'll just take a little longer."

"Come on, buddy, we've talked about that," said Ted. "Everyone knows you're in a financial bind, what with the divorce and managed care. I keep offering you money, but you're so fuckin' proud."

"You know how I feel about handouts."

"I'm not talking about a handout, for Chrissake. I'm talking about a salary for being a distributor."

"You're splitting hairs, Ted. Same difference."

"Then think about this," said his friend. "You know how hard it's going to be to save for Andie's college education. I hear a good school goes for thirty-five K a year. If you won't take money, what about stock options? Christ, for my friends, I almost give the damn things away!"

"That's very generous. I'll think about it."

"You do that," said Ted. "So you've given up on trying to see your daughter today?"

"I guess," Steve said. He truly loved his daughter, who'd always been the light of his life. The hardest part of his divorce was not being able to see her every day, to talk with her, to be a father to her. "All I'm really sure of is that I don't want Andie to get caught in the middle of a tug-of-war."

"Concerned papa to the end," said Ted. "Sounds like you could enjoy a break. Seeing how you're off this afternoon, why not come out to the beach?"

"What beach?"

"Didn't I tell you? I rented a house for the season not far from you, in Southampton. What do you say?"

Steve thought about it a moment. Between takes, he'd checked on his most recently hospitalized patients. Mr. Müller was stable in the coronary care unit, though hardly out of the woods. Alyssa had been admitted to the pediatrics ward and was already receiving her first unit of blood. A gynecologist was coming in soon to see her. Steve could afford to relax. Maybe fresh air and a sea breeze were indeed just what he needed.

He implied he was having a midlife crisis. He told her he needed space, needed to reassess his priorities, needed to find his direction in life. But forty-nine-year-old Karen Trent wasn't born yesterday. She was immediately suspicious. Thus, when Jared, her husband of twenty-seven years, proposed a trial separation, Karen did a little digging. She soon learned that her husband's midlife crisis was the two-legged variety, a divorced, willowy blond twenty years his junior.

At first, the shock of discovery was monumental. She felt as if she'd been punched in the stomach, that life as she'd known it was coming to an end. Her husband had been the center of her universe. She'd doted on him, devoted her life to him, waited on him hand and foot. And perhaps, Karen thought, her selflessness had been her undoing. The bastard certainly hadn't deserved it. Her mel-

ancholy soon gave way to anger, and anger to resentment.
Yet after two weeks of fantasy-filled days and sleepless
nights, she came full circle, and depression returned.

Dr. McLaren put her on antidepressants, which, in time,
helped a little. She attended support groups and developed
coping skills. But it was a patchwork solution, for her heart
wasn't in it. What Karen Trent really wanted was her husband back. Deep inside, she was desperate for him to return, and she would go to any length to accomplish her
goal.

Food soothed her, introducing a little love into her love-
less life. Karen was sitting in the kitchen serving herself a
slice of cheesecake when the photos arrived by FedEx. She
signed for the package and carried it back to the kitchen,
where she opened it and removed the contents. The private
investigator had been thorough. There were a dozen pictures, most taken with a telephoto lens. Karen studied them
carefully. The blond was certainly attractive enough.
Cheap-looking, but attractive. She had a cute figure and full
breasts that doubtless brought her husband to his knees.

She put the last picture down, snapping its edge like a
playing card. Then she pushed the cheesecake away, got
up from the table, and went to her bedroom, where she
took off her clothes. Standing in front of her full-length
mirror, Karen inspected her appearance.

Jared had been gone five weeks now, and she'd been
taking the tablets for four. She was no stranger to herbal
supplements. She'd taken gingko biloba for years, ever
since she first heard it might improve memory and concentration, and she also regularly used echinacea, garlic, and
ginger. She had some reservation about the products until
Dr. McLaren began displaying them in his office. After that,
she was a believer. She hadn't told the doctor, however,
that she'd begun doubling the recommended dose almost
immediately.

Karen narrowed her eyes, scrutinizing her reflection.
Wearing only a bra and panties, she put her hands under
her breasts, lifting them slightly. She couldn't be certain,
but she thought they were fuller, and a little rounder. Then
she gazed at her face. She still had bags under her eyes
from lack of sleep, but they seemed not quite as pro-

nounced, and the fine meshwork of crow's-feet atop her cheeks had become almost unnoticeable. Her weight hadn't changed, and nearly everything else in her life was the same. She doubted the antidepressant could cause these effects. She therefore concluded it had to be the Restore-Tabs, the only new variable in her life.

And if two per day worked well, Karen Trent thought, three or four would be even better. Her husband always claimed to like her looks, and if a more youthful face and figure were what he wanted, that's what he would get. But she was reluctant to buy more of the product from Dr. McLaren. She'd already purchased several bottles, and if she bought too many, she was afraid his staff would cut her off. But several of the higher-end nutrition shops also stocked the tablets.

While Karen Trent was looking at herself in the mirror, Andie McLaren was doing the same thing. Earlier, while Andie was trying on a two-piece bathing suit, her mother had walked into the bedroom and told Andie to forget it. Not because it looked inappropriate, but because she thought Andie looked fat. Problem was, Andie knew her mother was right. Andie hated the way she looked.

Now, as she squeezed into the new one-piece Speedo, she found little consolation. The straps bit deeply into her shoulders, her middle and upper thighs touched, and the flesh pouted under her bra line like raw cookie dough. God, she was a mess. It was at times like this that she missed her father's unfailing love and support.

She loved both her parents, yet they were so different. Her mom was always there for her, but she was a hoverer. She was forever in the background, offering her opinion and making suggestions. Her mom could criticize, too, which she did all too often, not always constructively. Her dad, on the other hand, rarely gave unsolicited advice, except on medical matters. He was nonjudgmental, his support unconditional. Andie missed him. She wondered what he would think of the way she looked now.

He'd always been honest with her. Yet her friends were, too, and what they said wasn't very encouraging. One of her male friends said she was starting to look like Monica

Lewinsky. Andie couldn't remember who Monica Lewinsky was, but the way he said it made her chin start to quiver. When her best friend told her she was getting a little porky, Andie cried all the way home.

Her mother said the teenage years would be the best years of her life. What a joke that was. So far, they were depressing as hell. Still, she knew what she had to do. It was like her mom said: lose thirty pounds, and you'll be the most popular girl in school. Well, she didn't know about that, but she did know that she'd look and feel a lot better. Maybe then people would stop talking about her.

Eyes brimming with tears, Andie pulled off the suit, threw it into her closet, and put on a pair of jeans. Her father knew what to do. She'd always trusted him, especially about medical issues, but she was too embarrassed to ask him. Still, she'd seen him on TV, and if what he talked about was good enough for strangers, it was certainly good enough for his own daughter.

Going to her bathroom's medicine cabinet, she opened the bottle of Restore-Tabs and poured one into her palm. It was a horse pill, large, oblong, and brown, with a dappled surface like tree bark. She filled a cup with water, popped the pill into her mouth, and swallowed. She was up front with her father about a lot of things, but not when it came to this. There was no *way* she could tell him that she was already taking them.

SOUTH PACIFIC

When Pak returned, it was late afternoon. He was a passenger in an old Nissan driven by Sergeant Atmosaputro, a wiry man in his late thirties and a fifteen-year veteran of the police force. The sergeant had been only visiting the nearby police station, but as the senior man there, he personally took Pak Suranto's report. As differences in wealth grew in the populous island nation, dead bodies were becoming rather commonplace. In his career, the sergeant had encountered hundreds of deceased—victims of natural causes, murders, auto accidents, and drownings. But he'd never come across someone thrown overboard and tied to a cement block. That sort of Western mayhem was decidedly unusual.

They exited the main road and drove down a fifteen-foot-wide clearing between the palms used by the plantation workers. Reaching the beach, the sergeant turned left and carefully followed the edge of the groves. The Nissan lacked four-wheel drive, and he had to drive slowly. A mile further on, Pak Suranto spotted the floating red marker he'd anchored on the seafloor. The sergeant parked, immediately knowing they were in the right spot. He could smell it.

The drag marks in the sand were clearly visible. Atmosaputro unwrapped a new air freshener and hung it from the rearview mirror. Before heading into the thicket, the sergeant took two cloth masks and two pairs of latex gloves from his pockets, giving a pair to Pak Suranto. Then he unlocked the car's trunk and removed a folded black body bag. Giving a nod, he followed the fisherman into the woods.

As they approached, the high-pitched buzzing grew louder. Soon they reached the small clearing, where a brownish mound of desiccated leaves covered the cadaver. Atmosaputro grunted as he moved away the palm leaves. Even through their masks, the smell that rose up was overpowering.

"Ripe," said the sergeant. "Looks like she's been dead a few days."

"Do you think she drowned?"

The sergeant squatted, examining the body as carefully as his nostrils would allow. "Hard to say. No signs of penetrating trauma. No ligature marks or obviously broken bones. I suppose she *could* have drowned, but there's the rope." He picked up its frayed end. "Where did you say the other end was?"

"Directly out." Suranto pointed. "Where that reef is."

"We'll have to send out some divers," the sergeant said, straightening up. "You didn't move the block?"

"Not an inch."

"All right, give me a hand. We'll take her back for refrigeration. It might be a few days before the doctor gets here to examine her."

With Pak Suranto's help, Sergeant Atmosaputro lifted the corpse and put it in the body bag. It was grisly work. The dead woman's missing eyes and mutilated labia were grotesque. They hauled the bag to the Nissan's trunk, locked it, and quickly drove away with windows open, thankful to have a fresh breeze swirling about their bodies.

Although he couldn't be sure how the woman died, Atmosaputro was certain of one thing: she'd been the victim of a crime. She could very well have been murdered, but even if she died of natural causes, it was highly unusual, not to mention illegal, to discard a dead body in the sea. And why weigh it down? The obvious answer was to keep the cadaver from being found.

This was very bad business indeed. He had a feeling this was going to be a long investigation. Unless the divers turned up something, he was starting the investigation with no leads whatsoever.

A little more than an hour later, Steve found Ted's new residence on Dune Road. Over the years, Steve had looked at various pieces of beachfront property and considered them way out of his league. This house had been recently remodeled. It was now an enormous, ultramodern split-level home of glass and chrome, with wraparound views, vaulted ceilings, a pool, and a tennis court. Steve parked his Saab, rang the doorbell, and was escorted inside by a uniformed butler, who indicated that Mr. DiGiorgio was already on the beach. Would the doctor care to change? An assortment of bathing suits, towels, and toiletries was available.

"Steve!" DiGiorgio called from his beach chair. "Saved you a seat." He tossed a bottle of suntan lotion to his friend. "Take your robe off and put some of that on."

It was a magnificent pre-summer day, with an occasional fair-weather cloud and a gentle wind. Steve remained standing while he covered himself with lotion, casually looking to the right and left. The shoreline was uncluttered, and there were only a few beachgoers, an uncrowded condition not to be seen again for the next few months.

"When did you get here?" Steve asked.

"Last night. I'm going to try to come out as often as possible. What do you think of the house?"

"Impressive, even for this area. How many bedrooms?"

"Five," Ted said, "and six baths. Cost me a small fortune."

Steve sank into the empty chair. "The Herbalist pleading poverty? This is a little steep for your budget?"

Ted laughed, averting his eyes to stare at two bikini-clad women strolling at water's edge. "Jeez, getta load of that."

"Which one?"

"Both of 'em. Those are two hot-looking babes."

Steve slowly shook his head. "Is this the same Ted DiGiorgio who's supposed to have gotten that out of his system?"

Ted lowered his sunglasses to mid-nose and looked askance at his friend. "Excuse me? I may be in my forties," he said, taking a sip of Corona, "but I'm not dead. How'd the shoot go?"

"Pretty good. If I ever get bored with medicine, I suppose there's always commercials."

"I told you, Steve, you're a natural. If you hadn't been so fuckin' dedicated, you could have been an actor."

"In my business, sometimes I am. Have you had any complaints from the director?"

"What're you sayin'?" asked Ted. "Is there something going on I should know about?"

"Not really," Steve replied, leaning back in his chair, tilting his face toward the sun. "I just don't want to come across as insincere."

"With the products I make, that's impossible. Don't tell me you're having second thoughts again."

"I never really got over my first thoughts," said Steve. "It'd be a lot easier if I was as convinced about nutritional supplements as I am about most drugs."

"Jesus, I hope you're not humming that old tune again. What does it take to convince you?"

"Something called hard, old-fashioned data. Look, I'm not knocking your products. Compared with the other crap that's out there, the Ecolabs line is pure gold. You're ecologically honest and have great quality control. It's just that this isn't why I became a doctor."

"Ah, here comes the Mother Teresa bit."

"I'll tell you something, Ted. The first time they gave me a stethoscope in med school, I wanted to hear what

disease sounded like. 1 wanted to hear the raspy sounds of
pneumonia, or a heart murmur. I wasn't that interested in
normal breath sounds or blood pressures. But I listened to
a lot of normal stuff because that's what it took to go into
family practice."

"That's wonderful, Steve, but what—"

"What I'm saying is," he continued, "people make com-
promises in life. Ten years ago, you wouldn't have even
seen me looking at herbal remedies. Now, they're everywhere you turn. My patients want them. Even my daughter's interested in them, though at her age there's really no
need to take them. The bottom line is, I've had to change
my mind."

" 'You've got to change your evil ways'," said Ted,
crooning the Santana tune. "So when it came to Steve
McLaren, if he couldn't beat 'em, he joined 'em, huh? And
I'm supposed to be thrilled about this?"

Steve laughed. "I wasn't talking about thrilled. It's like
I told you before: maybe the stuff works, maybe it doesn't.
But I *am* convinced that it probably doesn't do any harm.
So if I'm going to recommend something, it may as well
be the best. And that means my old pal Ted's stuff."

Ted applauded softly. "Thank you, Doctor, for that moving testimonial. Now that confession's over, do you feel
better?"

"Yes, thank you, Father. Loads. Very cathartic."

"That's wonderful." Ted waited a beat. "You want hard
data? I think we can give you some soon with Restore-
Tabs. Have you looked through the product literature yet?"

"Come on, Ted. Don't rush me. The stuff's only been
out, what? Four weeks?"

"Three months."

"Really? That long? Don't hate me for being a slow
reader."

"*You?* That'll be the day. But I'm telling you, this product really works. It's so damn good, it's going to put everything else we make to shame. You must've seen the
commercials."

"You can't exactly miss 'em. Every time I turn on the
tube, there's the little brown miracle tablet. I know this is

a little out of my area of expertise, but don't you think there's a risk of overkill?"

"What'd I just say?" asked Ted. "This stuff is unbelievable! It does everything it claims."

Baked by the late spring sun, Steve was fully relaxed. "You know what they say about sounding too good to be true."

Ted sat up, suddenly animated. "Steve, I really need you in my corner on this one. Don't go all moralistic on me. Restore-Tabs is going to be the greatest herbal moneymaker of the decade."

"The decade's just started."

"I'm serious. Public response has already been incredible, and why not? It does everything it claims, and then some."

"Everything, huh? It increases bra size a cup or two and helps older women look younger? It's some kind of female Viagra that turns frigid women into nymphomaniacs?"

"Please," replied Ted, "we never said anything about nymphomaniacs. Although I wouldn't mind. We implied it might improve women's sex lives. You don't think that's possible?"

"I'm saying it sounds too good to be true, that's all."

"That's because it is. Look," he said, "I know your logical mind wants scientific proof. I realize you need a rationale for how it works, and I want you to have it. Just be patient, okay? In the meantime, all I'm asking is for you to keep an open mind, okay?"

"Sure, Ted. Don't I always?"

Several hours later, rested and revitalized, Steve returned home to get ready for the evening. He'd been invited to a gala fund-raiser in Easthampton, where the wealthy and well-heeled rubbed elbows with the less fortunate for the benefit of the cause du jour. The number of such events peaked in August, lasted until Thanksgiving, and resumed the following Easter. During the past year, he'd been a guest at fund-raisers for haul-seine fishermen, for the whales, for Sag Harbor deer, for breast cancer, and for the Shinnecock Indians. Tonight's gala was for the benefit of migrant workers.

Ever since he'd been doing Ecolabs commercials, Steve had become something of a celebrity. It wasn't something he sought out, and he didn't want to be considered a salesman. Although he'd been a guest at charitable events for years, he was never so highly in demand as he was now. Fashionable guest lists invariably included his name. His increased notoriety was good news to Ted DiGiorgio, who encouraged his friend to turn social events into Ecolabs promotions.

But Steve could not. It wasn't that he was a snob; he just had little in common with the high-profile guests, many of them performers, who reveled in the glitz and glamour of the occasion. A lot of the attendees came not to further the cause, but to be seen—to make a fashion statement, to pose for the paparazzi, to rub elbows with aspiring politicians. Steve considered such pompous attention-getters airheads.

What's more, he was tired. Solo practice was an anachronism, and being overly busy was a recipe for burnout. When he first went into practice almost fourteen years ago, he was an idealist who aspired to make a difference in people's lives, hoping to cure the ills of rich and poor alike. When, after several years in the competitive arenas of both managed care and physician advertising, he discovered that he couldn't achieve what he'd hoped, he became disillusioned and jaded. But eventually, he came to view medicine as a business. A very special business, but a business nonetheless.

He arrived in Easthampton at eight P.M. The benefit was held in an old, twenty-one-room, three-story wood-frame house off Lily Pond Lane. Residential privacy was assured by a phalanx of tall, stately maples, and the property was bordered by thick hedges that shielded the occupants from curious passersby. A town policeman directed Steve into the driveway, where a parking valet took his car. As the attendant drove away, Steve noticed that his Saab seemed out of place among the Cadillacs, Mercedes, and the occasional Rolls Royce.

Although he was on time, the floodlit grounds were already crowded. The house had a wide veranda, and guests spilled down the front porch onto a perfectly manicured lawn, wearing tailored Armani suits or Versace tops. Servers glided through the crowd, bearing glasses of Long Island wine and hors d'oeuvres prepared from local seafood. Steve cajoled one into bringing him an iced tea. Soon, carrying his frosty glass, he strolled through the crowd, greeting people he knew, half expecting to spot a banner proclaiming the plight of local migrant workers.

The hostess, a stout, matronly woman of sixty, wife of the owner of a fishing fleet, was a descendant of generations of Hamptonites. She regally worked the crowd with practiced grace. "Dr. McLaren," she said, taking Steve by the elbow. "So good of you to come."

"Pleasure to be here, Mrs. Laird. This is quite the turn-out."

"Isn't it? And for such a worthy cause. I really can't wait to introduce our guest speaker, Mr. Lopez. He's a very intriguing man, and he's going to address the squalid conditions these poor people have to endure."

"And then ask us to part with our money," Steve said, only partly in jest.

Mrs. Laird smiled. "As generously as possible." Then she drifted away.

Lopez was due to speak at nine. Steve restlessly bided his time, trying to hide his impatience. As a minor celebrity and respected member of the community, he was doing what was expected of him—mingling, making small talk, flirting with attractive women. Before long he had to relieve himself. He was directed indoors, past a sitting room and through an enormous paneled library, where a half-dozen people chatted together before a fireplace. A built-in wide-screen TV was on across the room.

As he walked by, a middle-aged woman caught Steve's eye. She was thin and blond, wearing a white pantsuit. Her deep blue eyes were a stark contrast to her deep tan, and the fine lines at the corners of her eyes were a testimonial to decades in the sun. She glanced at Steve, then at the TV, before finally lifting her glass his way.

"You make a catchy commercial, Doctor."

Turning toward the screen, Steve caught the tail end of

a recent Ecolabs pitch. "Lord, look at that grin. It's no wonder they never wanted to show it to me."

"False modesty, I suspect," she said with a smile. "I've never met an attractive man who didn't know it."

There was something vaguely familiar about the woman. "Steve McLaren," he said, walking over and extending his hand.

Her return handshake was soft and warm. "Phoebe Atkinson. Tell me, Steve. Do you believe in what you're selling?"

"The products sell themselves, Ms. Atkinson. I'm just giving my professional opinion."

"How wonderfully evasive," she said. "Seeing how you're a doctor, I'd hoped for a more honest answer."

The barb in her tone was thinly veiled, and he had to hide his annoyance. "Well, Phoebe, don't we all? But I *was* being honest. As far as I'm concerned, they're the best damn nutritional supplements money can buy."

"I'm sure you're being well paid to say that."

"Whether I'm being paid or not is my business. But why are you so hostile?"

"Don't confuse my desire for a straight answer with anger."

"Have you got a problem with supplements?"

"I have a problem with anything not based in fact, and with spokesmen who act like charlatans."

"You sound like some doctors I know," he said. "Are you in the health field?"

"I'm just a concerned citizen, Dr. McLaren. But you haven't answered my question. Do you believe they work, or not?"

"Your fellow citizens believe they work. Sixty percent of Americans use some form of alternative medicine."

"I can't believe how hard it is for you to look me in the eye and tell me what you really think."

He started to squirm, eager to get away. Yet he sensed she'd follow him. "All right," he began. "Here's your honest answer. I *do* think they work, but maybe not the way manufacturers claim. Look at some of the herbal diet products out there—not necessarily Ecolabs'. Diet pills, for example. Most of them contain something like ephedrine or caffeine. They're stimulants, but they also increase metabolism a little, so there's a direct effect. But beyond that, there's a secondary effect. People on diet pills usually eat healthier foods and exercise more. It all adds up."

"I'm sure diet pills are only a small part of the market."

"Yes, but it's the same analogy. Sometimes things work because people want them to work. Call it the power of positive thinking, or the placebo effect. A positive attitude can have a tremendous effect on your immune system, or your sex life." He paused. "That answer your question?"

"Yes and no," she said. A frown suddenly crossed her face, and she appeared to wince.

"You okay, Phoebe?"

She nodded unconvincingly. "Just a cramp. I guess what I'm really asking is, are they safe?"

"That I can answer with more conviction. In medicine there's this old Latin saying, *Primum non nocere*. It translates as, 'Above all, do no harm.' And I can categorically say, when used as directed, supplements are absolutely safe. At least Ecolabs products are." He watched her frown return. "You sure you're all right?"

She handed him her glass. "Excuse me," she said, heading for the ladies' room.

What was that all about? he wondered, watching her slink away. It was almost as if she had a grudge. He put the glass down and went in search of another rest room. He found it and was soon outdoors again, struggling to endure the remainder of the evening. Seconds later, one of the servers came out of the house calling McLaren's name.

"I'm Dr. McLaren."

"Somebody passed out inside," said the worried server. "Mrs. Laird wants to know if you could take a look."

"Lead the way."

He followed her through the library and into a hallway beyond. At the end of the corridor was a brightly lit powder room. Someone lay unconscious on the floor. As Steve drew closer, he saw that it was Phoebe. Her beautiful white pantsuit was reddened at the groin by an angry splash of blood.

He quickly knelt and felt for her pulse. The beat was full and slow, a good sign. She'd probably just fainted. Her ashen complexion almost matched her outfit. He recalled her obvious discomfort minutes before, and she was now bleeding copiously. It wasn't unusual for women with heavy vaginal bleeding to get lightheaded and even lose consciousness. But as he watched, the liquid stain slowly widened. Could she be pregnant? This was not the place to determine that, and her bleeding was substantial.

"Call an ambulance," Steve said. "Tell them there's an unconscious patient here who's hemorrhaging."

He propped up Phoebe's feet on cushions to allow more blood to reach her brain. He again checked her pulse and then her pupils, which reacted normally to light. Not having a stethoscope, he bent over and placed his ear to her chest, listening to the heart sounds. The rhythm was regular, and there were no detectable murmurs. What most likely happened was a vasovagal reaction, a temporary episode of profoundly low blood pressure related to the cervix being dilated by blood clots. If other causes were ruled out in the ER, there was little to do except wait it out.

Fifteen minutes later, the EMTs lifted their patient into the van. Phoebe was now awake, and she was mortified. As the ambulance pulled away, Mrs. Laird was similarly apologetic. But, she said, like on Broadway, the show must go on. As soon as everyone had another drink, she'd introduce the guest speaker.

The commotion provided a good opportunity to slip away. The day had been long, full, and tiring, and the last thing Steve needed was a prolonged gabfest with people more interested in self-promotion than social issues. He managed to call for his car, tip the valet, and make his escape before Mrs. Laird noticed.

The night air was pleasant, and as he lowered the Saab's windows, he could smell the fragrant spring air, redolent of the sea. An unusual day, he thought. Here he'd attended to two patients at opposite ends of the reproductive spectrum who had almost identical problems. He'd never been a strong believer in coincidence, and he wondered if the two events were in some way related.

Absolutely not, he quickly concluded. There was nothing remotely similar about Alyssa and Phoebe. If they were in some way linked, it had to be by an act of God.

He'd put money on it.

3

The night was uncomfortably sticky. A southerly breeze blew across Shinnecock Bay, carrying rich sea smells of salt and nearby marsh through the boardinghouse's open windows. The young man rolled off his fiancée and reached for his cigarettes. A match flared, illuminating the couple's nakedness.

"There's somethin' the matter with you," he said.

She covered herself with the thin sheet, afraid to say anything. They had been down this road before.

"It's not normal," he continued. "All you ever do is lie there like a freakin' dead fish."

Her chin quivered. "I'm sorry, Martin."

"Cut it out, Lisa. I'm not interested in your bein' sorry."

"I . . . I'll do anything. I just don't know what you want."

"What I want," he said, exhaling a plume of smoke, "is for you to *feel* somethin'! I'm so sick of your damn pretending. You don't think I can tell?"

At first, she hadn't thought he could. In the nine months they'd been sleeping together, she thought she'd been doing it right. She'd watched the movies, seen the videos. She imitated the actresses, doing what they did—writhing, moaning, pretending to enjoy his furious thrusts. The problem was, she didn't enjoy them at all. It wasn't that she disliked having sex; rather, she just didn't feel a thing. And so, after a while, she stopped pretending.

In the beginning of their relationship, he had seemed satisfied and content. They usually had intercourse two or three times a night. Martin was always rushed and impatient. Lisa, not being very experienced at the age of twenty, thought this behavior normal. When, after several months, regular sex was no longer sufficient for him, Lisa agreed to perform oral sex. Although she found the act repellent, she was eager to please him, and she kept her feelings to herself.

"I'm trying, Marty," she pleaded.

"That's not the point, Lisa! I don't want you to try all sorts of shit just to stay on my good side!"

"What *do* you want me to do?"

"How many times do I have to tell you, I want you to like it! You don't have to love it; I don't want some kinda nympho. Just *enjoy* it a little, for Chrissake. Jeez, I've never been with a girl like you! I'm not sayin' you have to get off all the time, but I don't like doin' it with a robot, either. If this is the way it's always gonna be, you can forget about getting married! What goes through that head of yours, anyway?"

She hadn't told him about her recurring dream, and she knew she never would. He wouldn't understand. In her dream, she was lying on her back in her own bed, having sex. In the beginning, everything seemed to be going all right, and she was even getting excited. And then she slowly looked around. The wall of her room unexpectedly turned to glass, and through the window she suddenly saw the faces of her parents and two brothers, staring at her in silent disapproval.

How could she ever tell Martin about that? How could she confide that she saw their faces each and every time he slammed into her? She'd been raised in a strict, observant Catholic family, a family who never missed Sunday mass, who made novenas, who demonstrated against abortion. It was a family so suffocatingly protective that she couldn't wait for someone like Martin to come along and take her away.

Fighting back tears, Lisa nervously twisted the ring on her finger. "I love you, Martin. I want to spend my life with you. *Please* don't say we're not getting married."

"That's completely up to you. Maybe we will, maybe we won't. I'm doin' everything I can, Lisa. I don't know how to make you feel somethin' you don't."

"But I don't know what to do!"

"Shit, that's not my problem," he said, stubbing out his cigarette. "Maybe you need to get your head shrunk."

Lisa suddenly had a premonition he was going to leave her. Frightened and panicky, she quickly rolled onto her side and reached for his groin, desperately wanting to please him, hoping her intensity would seep into him and make him hard again.

Martin pushed her roughly away. "Jesus, Lisa, stop acting like a fuckin' whore! I don't want you suckin' my dick unless you really mean it!"

She watched him swing his legs onto the floor, and she felt weak. "Where're you goin', Marty?"

"I need some air."

"Don't go, Marty, please!"

But he was already pulling on his pants. "Oh Christ, don't get all teary on me. You know I can't put up with that kinda bullshit."

Moments later, he was gone. Hurt and alone, Lisa sat up in bed, sniffling and wiping her eyes. There had to be *something* she could do to get him back, but she didn't know what. But for all her insecurities, Lisa Wells was not a stupid young woman. She knew she could find a solution, if she put her mind to it.

Clearly, feigning interest in sex wasn't going to cut it. Martin could see right through that trick. There was only one solution: somehow learning to like it, to really feel horny. But how? Could one cultivate lust, growing and nurturing it as one did a seedling?

Maybe there was another way, a new pill or drug she could get from her doctor, a kind of aphrodisiac. She'd heard there were such things for men. But did it have to be a prescription drug? What about that new herbal thing that was always on TV? She couldn't recall its name, but it was a hot topic among her friends. The all-natural supplement was a kind of miracle herb that was supposed to make women look younger, help round out sagging figures, and—most importantly—improve their sex lives.

For someone who had nothing to lose, it was certainly worth a try.

Steve McLaren awoke the following morning refreshed after a full night's sleep, the first uninterrupted slumber he'd enjoyed in nearly two weeks. As he stretched in bed and let his eyes adjust to the daylight, he thanked whatever gods there be for letting him wake up without the kind of hangover he used to have when he drank. Until a year and a half ago, with the demise of his marriage, the demands of his practice, and his mounting social obligations, he'd been drinking heavily. Lorraine knew it, and even worse, Andie had seen him drunk, too. He was very worried about the impact his behavior would have on her. On occasion, he'd drunk to the point of blackout, when he couldn't recall the events of the night before. Worse, he sometimes drank when he was still on call. He didn't think he was an alcoholic. But, as he'd often told his patients, if you ever wonder about it, you probably are.

Once he stopped drinking, he had the good sense to sign out to another doctor whenever he had a social obligation. This was hard for a workaholic like him to do, yet he realized that his peace of mind and mental health depended on it. Before he got out of bed, he called his service and checked for messages.

It was a lazy Sunday morning, and after the chaos of Saturday hours, the rest of the weekend was blissfully slow. There were no urgent callbacks, and the covering doctor hadn't admitted any of his patients to the hospital. His ex-wife, however, left word that he could see Andie that night, to make up for Saturday's cancellation.

Steve then called the wards for an update on his two most recent hospitalizations. According to the ICU nurses, Karl Müller continued his remarkable improvement and was being prepared for an angiogram. On pediatrics, Alyssa remained reasonably stable. He'd see both of them when he made rounds.

Steve had two passions, horticulture and scuba diving. As he did first thing every morning, he checked on his plants. In the divorce settlement, Lorraine was awarded the house, which she subsequently sold. Steve had moved into a modest rental not far from the office. When he was younger, he had developed an interest in plants when he helped his mother tend their garden. During his summer college recesses, he worked in several nurseries. After the divorce, although his funds were limited, he wasn't a pauper. One extravagance he allowed himself was to attach a greenhouse to his new residence.

With the landlord's permission, he altered the screened porch, adding glass, skylights, ventilation, and plumbing.

The new greenhouse, accessible right off the den, was ten feet wide and twenty feet long. He installed twin room-length planting tables separated by a central walkway. The greenhouse faced due east, a perfect exposure for his tropical plants. He specialized in ones with fragrance.

He tried to have something in bloom throughout the year, which was not always easy. Late fall and early winter were the most difficult times, because many of the plants naturally flowered in the spring and summer. Yet rarely did a day go by when he couldn't savor the perfume of gardenia or jasmine, the delicate bouquet of camellia or oleander, or the more exotic aromas of stephanotis or frangipani. An escape from the high-stress world of sickness and death, his home was an oasis of sweet, intoxicating scents.

Clad in his boxers, Steve prepared a mug of coffee and sipped it as he strolled through the greenhouse, casually inspecting his floral charges. He gently shook their stems, checked the soil moisture, and misted leaves where necessary. During the night, one of his budded gardenias had bloomed, and its perfume filled the air. He sat on a stool next to the window, savoring the scent, the coffee, and the warmth of the rising sun.

By eight-thirty, he was on the road. The short drive to the hospital took twenty minutes. Parking in the doctor's lot, he proceeded to the CCU, where he got an update from the nurses. He pulled Müller's chart from the rack and leafed through it. All the lab tests corroborated his diagnosis of a massive myocardial infarction. A signed consent form for coronary angiography was on the front of the chart, which he carried to the bedside.

Wires led from the patient to nearby monitors, which beeped reassuringly. Müller's eyes were closed. Steve studied his patient, watching the steady rise and fall of the pulse in his neck. From the sound of his breathing, Müller had been sedated. Satisfied, Steve turned and began walking away.

"What's the rush, Doc?" came Müller's voice.

Steve turned around. "I'm sorry, I didn't mean to wake you."

"Just restin'," said Müller. "You can't get any real sleep in this place."

"How're you feeling?"

"Like my chest got whacked with a sledgehammer. I guess I got you to thank for that. The nurses told me what you did yesterday. Said you broke a couple of my ribs."

"Sorry, Karl. It was unavoidable."

Müller nodded his understanding. "Good thing you did, or I wouldn't be here today. Got you to thank for that, Doc. I'm just sorry the boy had to see it."

"Your grandson's pretty tough. He was scared, but he's going to be okay."

"You fish, Doc?"

"Some," Steve said. "I'm usually too busy."

"Set aside a day for me, all right? Come the end of the summer, I'll take you for the fastest tuna action in this part of the Atlantic. Deal?"

"You got it," Steve said with a smile. "But you better be in shape, or I'll hook the bigger fish."

Leaving the unit, Steve headed for pediatrics. He found Julia in Alyssa's room. Both were reading the Sunday paper. A unit of blood slowly dripped into Alyssa's arm. The color had returned to her face. Her eyes had regained their sparkle, and she smiled when Steve entered the room.

"Good morning, Alyssa. You look a lot better than yesterday."

"I guess it's the blood. It always perks me up."

"Is that her second unit?" he asked Julia.

"Yes. Dr. Richards said she might need a third."

He flipped open the chart to the gynecologist's notes. "What time did he see her?"

"Around two." She paused. "He wants to do a D and C, Steve. He told me yesterday that if her bleeding didn't slow down, he'd have no choice."

"It hasn't let up?" he asked Alyssa.

"Not even a little. It's disgusting. There are these big clots."

"He examined you?"

Alyssa made a face. "That was disgusting, too."

Steve glanced briefly at the chart, then at Julia. "Do you mind stepping outside a minute? Alyssa and I need some quality doctor—patient time."

"No problem." Julia gathered up the papers and went into the hall.

Once she'd left, Steve pulled over a chair and sat down with the chart on his knee. "Did you know Dr. Richards did a pregnancy test?"

"What for?"

"Come on, Alyssa. Don't act dumb. You know what for."

"That's not what I mean. What I mean is, I can't be. I've never even done it." She waited a beat. "It didn't come back positive, did it?"

"No, it didn't. Would you be surprised if it did?"

"*Real* surprised," she said. "I don't think I'm ever going to get pregnant."

"You never know. I'm planning on you being around a long time."

"That's not very likely. But even if I was, who'd look at me? The boys I know aren't interested. They call me Olive Oyl."

"Now who's kidding who? You're one of the prettiest patients I have."

"Yeah, right. Boys don't care about pretty." She tugged at the thin cloth on her chest. "What they want is this."

"Your hospital gown?"

That made her laugh. "No, silly, what's *under* the gown. Or not under it, I guess."

"I see. Do you mind if I asked you who helped you arrive at that incredible insight?"

She rolled her eyes. "It's all they talk about, big boobs. In case you haven't noticed, I don't have any."

He thought about Andie and the similar self-consciousness she'd had less than two years ago. Steve considered asking Alyssa if her breast development mattered, but thought better of it. Quite obviously, it did. For a moment he considered giving her some avuncular advice about growing up too fast. About love, morality, and respect. About patience, and about letting things occur naturally, with time. Yet Alyssa was a bright girl, and they both knew time was one thing she didn't have.

"Have you ever been with a boy, Alyssa?"

"Aren't you listening? I already told you—"

"I'm not talking about sex," he said. "Did anyone ever kiss you?"

"You mean, like on the lips?"

He nodded, saying nothing.

"Well, sort of. Once."

"How was it?"

"It was okay. I mean, I didn't see fireworks or anything like that. Why?"

He shrugged. "Just wondering. I'm trying to remember back that far."

"Maybe kissing was a big deal when you were growing up, but I know some kids that just do it. No holding hands, no Frenching, just . . . you know. You think boys care about kissing? Ever listen to Howard Stern? All they talk about is breasts." She turned away, and her pale eyes had a faraway look. "Breasts that I don't have."

"You'd like to get them?"

"Yep," she nodded.

"What would you do to get them?"

"That's a funny question, coming from you."

His eyes narrowed. "I'm sorry?"

"Hel-*lo?* You make those Ecolabs commercials. Restore-Tabs?"

"That's not one of my commercials."

"Well, same company," she said. "I started it right when it came out. You asked what I'd do, and that's what I did."

He was astonished. "Does your mom know about this? That product's not intended for anyone under eighteen."

"Of course not. She'd freak."

"Let me get this straight. You've been taking Restore-Tabs every day, for the better part of three months?"

She averted her eyes, biting her lip. "Sort of."

"What does that mean?" He studied her evasive expression. "Are you saying you took more than one? You took two?"

She nervously chewed on a nail. "Three."

Steve took a deep breath, frowning. If it was like everything else in the company line, it had been thoroughly tested at various dosage levels. To the best of his knowledge, there hadn't been any reports of side effects from overdosage. What's more, it was an all-natural herb, not a potentially toxic drug. Still, with the number of herbal products on the market skyrocketing, there had been the occasional report of other companies' problems with improper dosage. It was something he'd definitely have to look into. He briefly wondered if Andie might do something like that. God, he hoped not.

"I'm not going to lecture you, Alyssa. You're a big girl, and you realize what you did wasn't very smart. Knowing these things like I do, I'm pretty sure you didn't do any harm. But until you feel better, I want you to promise me you'll stay off the stuff, okay?"

She nodded. "Don't tell my mom."

"Don't worry, I won't. At some point, you're going to have to do that yourself."

A gurney wheeled up to the room, pushed by a young man with Hispanic features. Steve recognized him as one of the OR orderlies. He waved to Steve and walked into the room, asking for the chart.

"You Miss Hagen?" he asked.

Alyssa nodded.

"Time to rock 'n' roll, *mi hija.* I'm taking you to the OR. Can I see your wristband?"

The orderly matched the chart to the plastic ID bracelet just as Julia returned to the room. Once the gurney was in place beside the bed, Alyssa slid atop it, covering herself with the starched cotton sheet. Then the orderly gave her a disposable paper head cover, which Alyssa donned like a shower cap. If she was frightened, she didn't show it; but then, she was an old hand at diagnostic and surgical procedures.

"Can I go part of the way?" Julia asked.

"Yes, ma'am, you can go as far as the OR entrance," the orderly said, wheeling the gurney into the hall. "Then you can go to the waiting room or come back here. All set?" he asked Alyssa.

"Yes."

"What're you having done today, Alyssa?"

"Something called a D and C."

"Oh, the old dusting and cleaning," he said with a smile. "I seen a lotta girls get that done before the summer."

"Really?"

"I think he's kidding you, Alyssa," her mother said.

"You never know with Ricardo," offered Steve. "He's got his finger on the pulse of the OR."

"You got that right, Doc."

They made lighthearted chitchat as they wound through the corridors. Julia softly sang "You Are My Sunshine" to her daughter, a tune she'd sung since Alyssa was a baby, and one she often resorted to in difficult times. Her gaze alternated between her daughter and Steve. He'd been the only doctor Julia had known for a long time, and he'd been there for her through thick and thin—mainly thin. She first became his patient right after he opened his office. When, as an eighteen-year-old, she needed his advice on contraception. But she hadn't followed his suggestions, and she was pregnant and married within a year.

Dr. McLaren was present for the birth of her daughter, and he was always available through the difficult times following her husband's death. And then Alyssa got sick. Although her daughter had been a blessing, Julia often felt as if she were moving from one tragedy to the next.

Throughout, Steve had been a source of strength for her, the constant that held everything together. He had showed no sign of being aware of the crush Julia had developed on him right after her first visit. Her teenage impression was that he was incredibly good-looking, and over the years, little about him changed to alter her opinion.

His eyes were the color of slate, but there was nothing hard about them. His sandy hair, which she guessed had once been blond, now had flecks of gray about the ears, a touch she thought made him look even more attractive. Yet more important than his looks was the fact that he was her doctor, a steadfast, reliable presence, a physician who genuinely cared.

When they reached the OR, Ricardo stopped in front of the swinging doors. "Train stops here, Mom."

Julia finished her song, leaned over, and kissed her daughter on the cheek. Although Alyssa seemed calm, Julia was a wreck. She nervously gripped Steve's arm. "Do you think you could go in with her?"

"In fact," he said, "that's just what I had in mind. Why

don't you go back to the room and wait? It shouldn't take long."

An OR nurse appeared. After introducing herself to Alyssa, she and Ricardo went over the formalities of patient transfer. Soon, with the gurney disappearing down the OR corridor, Steve went to the doctors' dressing room to change. Inside, he ran into Alyssa's surgeon, gynecologist Stanley Richards.

" 'Morning, Stan. I appreciate your seeing the kid."

"I don't suppose it could have waited until Monday?"

"Are you joking?" asked Steve. "Did you see her blood work?"

"Hey, relax, I'm kidding. I'm sure I'll be out of here and on the tee by ten."

Richards had a reputation for sarcasm, and Steve couldn't tell if the man was kidding. The sixty-year-old physician was chief of OB/GYN, and he was reputed to be a good practitioner. Smooth-tongued and silver-haired, he was also part of the Hamptons upper crust, and his priorities were different from his younger colleague's.

"Mind if I scrub in?"

"For a D and C? This is a one-man show. You can't bill for assisting."

"I wasn't planning to," said Steve, reaching for a pair of scrubs. "I've known this patient since she was a baby, and she's had more than her share of problems. Least I can do is a little hand-holding."

"Up to you," Richards said. "I don't think we'll be in the room more than five minutes."

"How come you decided on a D and C? Don't you sometimes try medications first?"

"You wouldn't be trying to tell me how to do my job, would you?"

"Perish the thought."

Richards couldn't tell whether Steve was trying to match his cynicism. "Well, her uterus is a little enlarged. I did a sonogram last night, and there's a lot of tissue in there. For a while I thought she'd turn out to be pregnant, but you saw the pregnancy test. It'd take days for progestins to work, and you don't want her to keep bleeding, do you? A chance to cut," he said smoothly, "is a chance to cure."

"You don't think this could be related to her cancer, do you?"

"Until yesterday, I'd never even *seen* anyone with a thymoma," he said. "Last night I checked the literature, and I didn't find a connection."

In the OR, an anesthesiologist adjusted the flow on the IV. Alyssa lay on the OR table, covered with a green drape. Electrodes were pasted to her chest beneath her gown, and their wires attached to a nearby Siemens monitor. Alyssa looked serene, her lids heavy. Steve walked over and took her hand.

"Hey, princess. How're you feeling?"

"Great," she said, slurring her words.

"You give her anything yet?" he asked the anesthesiologist.

"Two milligrams of Versed. She's pretty mellow."

"I haven't got all day," barked Richards. "What say we get started?"

"Whenever you're ready," said the anesthesiologist.

Richards turned to the nurse, a pleasant Philippine woman named Wanda. Among the OR staff, it was a standing joke that whenever Wanda wanted a physician to fuck off, she said, "Yes, Doctor." She was nearly finished setting up the D&C instruments when Richards nudged her.

"You're ready, aren't you?"

"Yes, Doctor."

"All yours," Richards directed to the anesthesiologist.

Taking a pre-filled syringe of Diprivan, the anesthesiologist stuck the needle into a rubber hub on the IV tubing and began to inject. The milky white fluid snaked slowly into the patient's vein. "You're going to get drowsy now, Alyssa. In a few minutes you'll wake up in the recovery room, and it'll be all over, okay?"

Her lids were now closed, and she didn't answer. Soon her jaw went slack, and she breathed heavily. Steve gently released her hand. At the other end of the table, Wanda placed Alyssa's legs in stirrups. Richards threw on a surgical gown and donned a pair of gloves. Few physicians did a formal scrub for D&Cs anymore. He turned his back to the nurse.

"How about tying me?"

"Yes, Doctor."

Richards reached for the disposable drapes. "You want to bring that instrument table a little closer?" he asked the nurse. Then, to Steve, "Would you mind getting out of the way?"

Steve backed off. Richards picked up what was known as a heavy weighted speculum, an instrument normally used for women who had borne children, and began to separate Alyssa's labia.

"Are you going to use *that* thing?" Steve asked. "It'll tear her apart."

"Don't tell me how to practice medicine," Richards shot. "Last time I looked, it was *my* name on the consent form! You have a problem with what I'm doing, take it up with the medical board."

"Come on, Stan," Steve said, waxing diplomatic. "I'm not trying to tell you what to do, but she's only a kid. I'm sure a guy with your skills could throw in a narrow Graves speculum."

"It'll make it harder to expose her cervix."

"For me, maybe, but not for someone with your experience."

Richards hesitated, then put the weighted speculum down. "See if you can locate one of the smaller speculums," he said to Wanda. "And hook up the suction."

"Yes, Doctor."

She returned shortly with a compact package covered with blue autoclave paper. Unwrapping it, she dropped the sterile instrument onto the table. The slender duck-billed speculum was a fraction of the size of its predecessor and considerably less likely to cause trauma. Richards picked it up and again parted the labia, sliding it slowly into the vagina. He screwed the blades open for exposure and adjusted the overhead spotlight, peering along the instrument's length. The vagina was filled with prune-size gelatinous clots that Richards removed with the suction.

After squirting in antiseptic, the gynecologist grasped the cervix with a tenaculum. He slowly widened the cervix with stainless dilators and called for a plastic aspiration tip.

"No sharp curettage?" Steve asked.

"Too dangerous. The uterus is very soft, and she's got

a lot of tissue in there. Suction's much less traumatic."

Once the suction cannula was in place, Richards attached wide-bore tubing and had Wanda turn on the aspirator. A soft mechanical hum filled the room. Soon, an abundant amount of semi-solid, burgundy-colored material filled the tubing and made its way into a glass collection bottle. Before the flow stopped, Richards had aspirated approximately one hundred cubic centimeters of blood and tissue. The procedure took all of thirty seconds.

With the machine turned off, Richards went to the aspirator. Removing the stopperlike black rubber lid, he detached the inner collection bag, a thin cloth sac that trapped the tissue while allowing blood to seep through. The mushy, purplish bag dripped a trail of crimson as he carried it to the instrument table. With Steve looking over his shoulder, the gynecologist inspected the contents.

The tissue within looked like a mixture of raw ground beef and small, spongy currants. Richards ran a finger through it, checking its consistency.

"Awful lot of tissue," he said. "I doubt it's a problem, but I should have asked for a frozen section."

"Does it look suspicious?"

"Hard to say without a microscope, but it's a possibility. Wanda, call the lab and see if the pathologist's in. If not, have them call him at home and tell him we need him for a frozen."

"Yes, Doctor."

Richards announced that he was done, stripped off his gown and gloves, and left them in a heap on the floor.

Steve waited until Alyssa woke up. After helping slide her off the OR table, he accompanied the stretcher to the recovery room. He knew it would take at least fifteen minutes to get the frozen-section diagnosis, if the pathologist was available; if not, it would take at least an hour. He decided to wait with Julia.

THE SOUTH PACIFIC

Far from Long Island, in a remote corner of the world, the first pink fingers of dawn reached across the purple sky. The early morning breeze shifted from south to west, carrying the smells of river and mangrove toward the ocean. It was already eighty degrees, and the day promised to be murderously hot and humid. In the river's estuary, the night creatures settled in for the long day, while sun-loving fauna began to stir. Embracing the dawn, a stately great-billed heron began stalking the shoreline for prey, while pairs of mudskippers glided just below the water's surface, at eye level.

There was a fluttering overhead, and great clouds of bats temporarily blackened the brightening sky. The jungle beneath their wings was draped with exotic fruits, tangles of lianas, and long, gnarled roots that snaked along the ground. Beyond the shoreline, the dense jungle slowly rose toward volcanic hills, whose verdant canopies, seen from the air, were a uniform green carpet. A widening dirt road crept through the undergrowth, leading to a clearing hacked out of the foliage.

A long, low wooden structure stood in the center of the clearing, a *Bugis* house built on stilts to keep slithering creatures at bay. The house had a thick thatched roof, and the windowless apertures in the sides were covered with mesh screens that didn't keep the mosquitoes out. A single light illuminated the gloomy interior. The front door opened, and a woman emerged, yawning. She wore a rumpled nurse's uniform, and she carried an enamel basin. Walking to the building's front steps, she tossed the dirty contents into the scrub growth nearby.

Low, plaintive sounds came from within the building. The nurse named Claudia shook her head, accustomed to the noises, although at the end of a long night, her patience was wearing thin. Two hours remained in her shift before she was relieved. With a sigh, she turned and reentered the building, heading toward the moans. The sounds came from her charges, nine critically ill women in various stages of pre-terminal distress. The situation was hopelessly depressing. Although the nurse's heart went out to the women, there was little she could do except make them comfortable.

Inside, the heat was already stifling, and the nurse turned on a ceiling fan. She was under strict instructions to conserve electricity, but to withhold relief would be inhumane. The *Bugis* house was a single long room. It had no toilet facilities and only one cold-water sink. The patients lay on mildewed cots arranged in parallel rows. They all wore similar threadbare gowns, a concession to modesty.

Claudia refilled her basin with water. With the coming of dawn, those patients who soiled themselves during the night had to be cleaned, and they all deserved to be bathed. Although the water was tepid, to someone who had endured a damp night of endless perspiring, it was immensely soothing. There were no urinary catheters to ease their suffering, and no IVs.

Many of the patients were severely dehydrated. The only concession to improving patient welfare was large doses of the local brand of Demerol, which the nurse liberally dispensed. As soon as she finished bathing her charges, those who needed medication would get it. It mattered little that she was only allowed to use one hypodermic syringe per day. Her patients were so ill that the idea of contracting an infectious disease was an irrelevant afterthought.

The nurse put a dry rag in the basin and moved to the first cot, reflecting on what seemed like such a cruel predicament. She'd been working there for many months, twelve-hour shifts five days a week. The routine varied little, save when one of the patients died and another took her place.

Claudia had a good idea of what afflicted her patients, but she discussed it with no one. Thus far, there had been dozens of deaths. She had no idea what the men did with the bodies. As she approached the bedside, she noted that the patient's vaginal bleeding had returned. For some reason many of the patients bled, frequently and profusely. It was the leading cause of death, for there were no transfusions.

The patient in bed one was young, perhaps thirty. She looked up at Claudia and smiled, her pupils dilated and narcotized. They both understood they were fighting a losing battle, and what they were doing now was merely a holding action. As she wiped the patient's brow, the nurse doubted the woman had a week to live. Yet the patient continued to smile, with a level of acceptance unusual for her age. Perhaps she realized this was because her family would be well provided for.

For she, like the nurse, was being extremely well paid for what transpired in that remote longhouse.

The split-level house Lorraine shared with her daughter was in a modest area of Bay Shore. It was closer to Manhattan than the home she'd shared with Steve, which was to her liking. Steve's rental was due east, a forty-five-minute drive, barring summer traffic.

Steve arrived precisely at eight P.M and had three hours to spend with his daughter before Lorraine returned.

Andie answered the front door right after he rang the bell. She was a slightly overweight fifteen-year-old with short dirty-blond hair and her father's slate-colored eyes. She smiled broadly. "Hi, Daddy."

"Hello, sweetie," he said, hugging her tight. "You look great. How's school?"

"Great. But I have to tell you ahead of time that I'm getting one B this semester."

"A lowly B? What subject is that?"

"Social studies. I hate it."

"Maybe you need someone to quiz you," he suggested. "Before the final, why don't we get together and go over it for a few hours?"

"Sure."

Like some other teens, his daughter had recently struggled with her weight. Lorraine, who was very image-conscious, made more of an issue of it than he did; he thought it counterproductive to focus on appearance for its own sake. Rather, he stressed his daughter's good qualities, such as her work habits and selflessness. Still, Andie was a teenager at a time when teenagers struggled with peer attitudes and body consciousness. She often asked Steve's advice on diet and nutrition. At five-feet-five, and generally weighing in the upper one-forties, she appeared to have gained a few pounds since he'd last seen her. "So," he said. "You looking forward to the school year being over?"

"I can't wait. The kids in tenth grade say it's pretty, well, hectic."

"Hectic?"

"You know, better."

"Yeah, I know," he said with a smile. "What about camp? Do you start the week after school?"

"Yes," she said, nodding, "but I've got to lose some weight first. Mom says I look terrible in a bathing suit. Do you think I'm fat, Dad?"

"No, Andie, I don't. We've been through this already. To me, fat means being at least thirty percent over what you should weigh. I'm not saying you shouldn't lose weight. Just do it sensibly."

"What weight do you think is good for me?"

"What're you now, around one-fifty?"

She nodded sheepishly.

"For someone your age and height, I'd say one-thirty. Just keep away from fads, quick fixes. If you lose a pound a week, you'll be where you want by Christmas. How about exercise? You getting any?"

"Of course!" she said brightly. Then she paused, hesitating. "Dad, is it okay if we don't go to the movies tonight?"

"Hey, this is our time to do what we want. Would you rather go out for something to eat? Something healthy?"

"Well, not really. What I'd rather do is listen to some music."

"No problem," he said. "I love music."

"With Jeffrey."

"Who's Jeffrey?"

"You know, Jeffrey Hirsch. You met him at my birthday party, don't you remember?"

"Well, now that you mention it, maybe I do," he said, not remembering at all.

"Have you heard of Renata?"

"She's another friend of yours?"

"No, Dad, they're a group!" she chuckled. "Jeffrey bought their album today, and he's bringing it over. That's okay, isn't it?"

"To tell you the truth, precious, I'm a little hurt. I was hoping we could spend some time together."

"Come on, Dad, this is my only chance to listen to it! Mom doesn't like their music."

"She never had much taste in that area," he said. "All right, Jeffrey can come over. But only if you've done your social studies. And he's got to leave by ten."

Soon, with the music blaring from Andie's room, McLaren settled in to watch a Mets game. So much for quality time together. Jeffrey seemed harmless enough, but then, so did he at that age. Finally, the CD ended, and the two teenagers came downstairs to reheat pizza. They seemed to be having such a good time that McLaren thought it pointless to feel hurt. When the ball game ended, he strolled casually through the house, waiting for Jeffrey to call his parents.

Lorraine had an eye for decorating, and she'd done a good job fixing the place up. He was glad her tastes weren't that expensive. He'd never been to the house when his ex wasn't there, and when he finished on the ground floor, he took a look upstairs. The second floor had two bedrooms, two baths, and an ample guestroom, all comfortably decorated. Andie's room, in particular, with its built-ins and study nooks, was a tribute to young adult practicality.

He used his daughter's bathroom. When he was finished, washing his hands in front of the mirrored medicine cabinet, he idly opened its door. The usual bottles of Pamprin and Motrin were on the shelves, along with Q-Tips, various colors of nail polish, and a large container of chewable vitamins. Immediately next to it was a bottle of Restore-Tabs.

For several seconds, he stared at it, feeling his blood run cold. Then he took the bottle out and scrutinized it, turning it over in his hand, as if it were something alien. In his mirrored reflection, his face was turning beet red. His lips pressed into a thin line, and the pulse in his temple was pounding. The fury arising in him was thinly restrained. It suddenly occurred to him that his daughter was physically quite similar to Alyssa Hagen.

"Andie!" he thundered from the second-floor landing. "Young lady, get up here this instant!"

4

"Coffee? All you're having is *coffee*?"

"You got it," Karen said.

Karen Trent smiled primly at her friend as the waitress took their menus away. Her friend Annie, a two-hundred-pound African American with a pungent sense of humor, had ordered cheesecake to Karen's decaf cappuccino. It had been two weeks since Karen tasted her last slice of Sara Lee, and she didn't miss it. If she couldn't have her husband, at least she could have herself: that was a cardinal tenet of what she learned in Overeaters Anonymous. She'd also been taught that she had choices. She'd discovered that one's primary responsibility was to oneself.

In the two months since she'd been attending OA—her presence preceding Jared's departure by several weeks—she and Annie routinely went to the nearby Chuck Wagon Diner after the meeting was over. At first, they both had small portions of cake or pastry. But more recently, especially since Karen began to see the effects of Restore-Tabs on her face and figure, she started seriously watching her weight. It wasn't so much willpower as it was positive reinforcement for responsible behavior.

"Can't say as I blame you," Annie said with a sigh. "You've been so good lately, I absolutely hate you. You know what? It shows. I can tell. And so can everybody else."

"Really? Who?"

"Oh, a few folks at the meeting. But believe me, honey, you're getting noticed."

Karen's face reddened. "Thanks, Annie. I haven't heard anything like that for a long time. Jared was never one for compliments."

"Well, you deserve it. And trust me, girl, you're better off without that loser."

Their orders arrived. As Karen sipped her coffee, she wondered if what Annie said was true. Regarding Jared, she had no doubt; he was truly a miserable sort, with a negative attitude and generally sour disposition. She was indeed better off without him, but old feelings died hard. His behavior still didn't stop her from wanting him back.

As for herself, with her improving physical image and increased sense of self-worth, it was an entirely different matter. Annie was right. She *did* deserve to feel good about what she'd accomplished. What she was doing wasn't easy. Pulling oneself out of the physical and emotional doldrums was one of the hardest things she'd ever done. Perhaps Jared didn't notice, but at least others did.

"It could be that the program's finally sinking in," Karen said. "Maybe after four decades I'm finally learning how to take care of myself."

"How 'bout rubbing some of that off on me? Every time I break one-ninety, I have a Häagen-Dazs relapse."

When they both shared a laugh, Karen was pleased. In the two months she'd been attending meetings, she'd seen numerous people fail. By entrusting the end results of their efforts to an elusive Higher Power, they'd evaded responsibility for themselves. Karen was determined to succeed where they'd failed. With determination, a new sense of direction, and by putting in the footwork, she was already seeing results.

Of course, a healthy dose of Restore-Tabs didn't hurt, either.

With a mounting sense of annoyance, Steve drove away from Lorraine's house. Andie, initially apologetic, had grown argumentative as he cautioned her about the dangers of Restore-Tabs. Why was he lecturing her? she asked. Wasn't he always on TV raving about the Ecolabs stuff? Besides, a lot of her friends were taking the product, and he wasn't making such a big deal about them.

Steve was astonished. He lectured Andie about growing up and responsible medication-taking. Thinking of Alyssa, he had to struggle to keep from shouting. Andie was far too young to use something intended for adults, he said. Yet as he talked, he felt like the cannabis-smoking parent who warned his children about the dangers of drug abuse. He knew Andie was thinking that, too.

It bothered him that the pills were so freely available.

Andie said she'd bought a bottle in the nutrition shop in the mall, but mostly, she used her mother's. Steve was astounded, then infuriated. How irresponsible was that? Lorraine was an intelligent woman; hadn't she ever heard of ephedra, and the problems it could cause for adults and children alike? Wasn't she aware of the potential dangers many over-the-counter products posed to minors? And why wasn't she keeping track of what Andie was taking?

Andie revealed she'd been taking Restore-Tabs for over a month, but he was relieved that she'd had no heavy periods. Then again, his daughter had always had irregular menses. Maybe it was too early to tell. She said she'd call him if she did. Although she promised not to take any more pills, he couldn't be sure she'd keep her word. Where it came to body image and one's sense of self, teenagers were often less than truthful.

He wasn't really all that angry with her. In truth, he was scared—scared that his only child, the precious daughter he loved so much, might develop physical problems from a supposedly safe over-the-counter medication, like the ones he so publicly praised. He wanted only the best for his child, and that would only be possible if the child were safe. He clearly saw that; why didn't Lorraine? Perhaps it was because Lorraine now rarely listened to anything he had to say.

His own teen years had been just as difficult as Andie's, maybe more. It was a supremely perplexing time, seven confusing, uncertain years filled with second-guessing and rash decisions, many of which reflected poor judgment. He'd heard it said that good judgment came from experience, and most experience came from bad judgment. If that was true, by the time he was twenty, his judgment should have been phenomenal. But it wasn't.

He thought he'd finally grown up in the past two years. Before then, other than for his job performance, he'd been a prisoner, an emotional captive to his own bad judgment. And prior to that long thirty-year stretch, he'd last been truly free when he was a child. His family had lived across from a large parcel of undeveloped real estate filled with hills and trees and wide-open spaces. It was probably no more than ten acres, but in his child's eye, it seemed to stretch forever. He'd been a cowboy then, and sometimes a wild Indian. Riding his pretend horse, he'd gallop across the prairie for hours at a time, without a care in the world.

Steve began to wonder exactly how many young teens were doing precisely what Andie claimed. He doubted that taking a Restore-Tab here or there could do much harm, but in large quantities, who knew? There was probably no research in that area. What's more, the warning on the label about the product's use by adults was insufficient. There damn well ought to be an unequivocal warning about it not being used by anyone under eighteen.

Nagged by a sense of guilt, Steve's greatest fear was that his daughter might have already done some harm to herself. As soon as possible, he was going to call her pediatrician and suggest some tests.

SOUTH PACIFIC

As strong men went, he was not especially tall at five-nine; nor, at one hundred and sixty pounds, was he particularly powerfully built. What made him a dangerous man were his phenomenal physical condition and his quick reflexes. At forty-five, Jack Buhlman had a work ethic that kept him in amazing shape. He ran six miles a day, rain or shine. He swam thrice weekly, biked with the same frequency, and worked out with medium weights as often as possible. The result was a middle-aged man with five-percent body fat, a washboard abdomen that would be the envy of eighteen-year-olds, and well-defined, taut musculature that was the repository of his strength.

Jack had been to the area several times during the past year, scouting locations, overseeing the building's construction, and directing the project. The trip from New York took twenty-eight hours, during which he changed planes twice and rented a car for the final trip to the remote location. As he turned off the dirt road and entered the hacked-out clearing, the Philippine-trained nurse came out of the building to greet him.

He turned off the Toyota's air, opened the car windows, got out, and stretched. The sun was blinding, and he had to squint. The elevated heat and humidity were oppressive for Westerners, even for one in good physical condition.

As he slowly ambled toward the *Bugis* house, he once again admired the builder's adherence to tradition.

"Hello, Claudia."

"Good afternoon, Meester Buhlman," she said. "How was your trip?"

"Long, but uneventful. How are things going?"

"About the same. Many women are dying, but I make them comfortable. I don't think there is much suffering."

"Good," said Buhlman. "That's about all you can do. You dispose of the bodies in the usual way?"

"Suroto and his men bring supplies, and they take the dead women away. And when the other women become ill, the doctor sends them here."

"Great. You have your report?"

"Here, sir." She handed him a sealed manila envelope containing three months of vital statistics.

"Thanks." In return, he handed her an envelope with three thousand American dollars in new hundreds.

Claudia inclined her head in thanks. She was never sure what to say to this man. Although he moved slowly, his steps were deliberate and powerful. He always struck her as being ready to spring, like a coiled snake. Polite though he was, he frightened her, and consequently she said little.

Buhlman turned and took several steps, gazing through an opening in the encircling trees. The clearing was high in the hills, and from his vantage point, he watched the tranquil turquoise sea unfold toward the horizon. Despite the stifling conditions, he considered this land of thirteen thousand islands to be astonishingly beautiful.

"Would you like to come inside for a cool drink, Mr. Buhlman?"

"I don't think so, Claudia. You're probably used to it, but I find this place depressing. I'm going to head back." He turned to look at her. "You've done a great job here. Fact is, we have almost all the information we need. We'll probably shut the operation down in a month or so."

"As you wish, Mr. Buhlman."

He nodded, then started walking toward his car. "Have a nice day, Claudia." After several steps, he turned and asked, "You haven't had any trouble with relatives or unwanted visitors, have you?"

"No, sir. Nobody even knows we're here."

"Good. If anyone comes snooping around, you know where to reach me."

On Monday, Steve called Andie's pediatrician, a man he'd known and respected for years. As nonchalantly as possible, Steve brought up his daughter's use of Restore-Tabs. He downplayed the sense of urgency he actually felt and claimed he just wanted to bring the pediatrician up to speed. He did, however, mention another young patient who'd bled on large doses of the supplement. The pediatrician promised to keep his eye out.

Late Monday afternoon, Steve got a call from the hospital pathologist. The preliminary results on Alyssa's frozen section hadn't been good. At first glance, the endometrial curettings looked malignant, although a precise diagnosis would have to await the permanent slides. These were now ready, and the diagnosis was confirmed. Alyssa had endometrial cancer.

Although Julia was prepared for the worst, Steve knew he'd have to give her the bad news. Alyssa would also have to be told. She'd been down this road before, and if her reaction was anything like it had been previously, she'd accept the news with steely aplomb.

Equally disturbing to Steve was *why* this was happening.

"Have you ever seen a case like this in someone this young?" he asked.

"Not quite," said the pathologist. "I've seen one or two in older teenagers—the sort of moderately obese patient who goes months without menstruating, who has a lot of unopposed estrogen on board. Not at all like your patient."

"That's what I thought," Steve agreed. "I just have no idea where this poor kid's getting all that estrogen from. You don't think it's related to the thymoma, do you?"

"Not very likely. I've never even seen it reported. I have a call in to Stan Richards, but I haven't spoken to him yet. Any idea what he plans to do?"

"He thought that if the permanent sections came back frankly malignant, he'd have to do full surgical staging."

"A hysterectomy on a thirteen-year-old?"

"I don't want to put words into his mouth, but that was my impression."

"Talk about ball busters," said the pathologist. "I usually get accused of not giving a damn about the patients, but I feel really bad about this one."

After ringing off, Steve had the unpleasant task of notifying Julia. She reacted as he expected, initially appearing to take the news in stride, but then breaking down. Fate, she finally said, had never looked kindly on her daughter.

The plan was to send Alyssa home to await the earliest possible vacancy in the OR bookings. But before she was discharged, there came word of a last-minute cancellation for early Wednesday morning. Steve had Becky reschedule his patients so he could assist at the seven-thirty A.M. slot. Although Richards preferred to have another gynecologist assist him, he reluctantly agreed to Steve's request, knowing that hospital protocol called for referring family practitioners to be afforded the opportunity to scrub.

Much of late Monday afternoon and Tuesday were devoted to preop testing. Steve considered much of this unnecessary, because Alyssa's recurrent thymoma would kill her far sooner than the endometrial lesion. Nonetheless, Alyssa received another unit of blood and had extensive blood tests, a chest X-ray, an intravenous pyelogram, and an exhausting barium enema. All tests were negative except the chest film. On the X-ray, the malignant thymoma was rampant, the signs of its spread showing as moth-eaten white blotches against the normally dark background. Whatever Richards planned to do would be merely a holding action.

Julia was exhausted. She'd been up most of the night, dozing in her daughter's room. Steve got to the hospital at seven-fifteen, just as Alyssa was being wheeled to the OR. He had a few words with Julia and then went down to change.

Richards had a reputation for punctuality, and he was right on time. His surliness was immediately apparent. Steve kept his distance, remaining with Alyssa while the surgeon scrubbed. Once Alyssa was asleep and Richards entered the room, Steve changed places, lathering up while the sterile drapes were being applied. Then it was time to cut.

Traditional surgical staging of endometrial cancer called for a generous vertical incision. But here Richards departed from tradition, performing the procedure through a modest, four-inch bikini cut. What might challenge lesser surgeons, he opined, was routine for him. The gynecologist had to do some gymnastics, but he managed to perform pelvic washings, diaphragmatic swabs, lymph-node sampling, an appendectomy, a hysterectomy, an omentectomy, and removal of the tubes and ovaries in less than ninety minutes. Richards's self-congratulatory attitude aside, Steve was impressed.

For all his gruff talk, coarse personality, and mercurial temperament, the man was a consummate surgeon. When Richards was finished, all that showed was a clean, dry incision with eight small stainless-steel staples. The patient would be home in two days. He took off his gloves and left.

Steve remained in the OR until Alyssa was awake. Once her eyes opened and she could squeeze his hand, he went to the dressing room, where he changed and cried.

As the school year was drawing to a close, most high-school sophomores were eagerly looking forward to the summer. Andie was ambivalent. She'd loved the warm weather and the outdoors until last year, when her weight gain became obvious. As a result, she grew self-conscious and spent less time than ever before at the beach or by the pool. This year was even worse. After gaining another ten pounds, she looked and felt like a blimp.

She knew what the problem was: food. She'd simply become unable to control her appetite. Not that she hadn't tried; but ever since her parents' divorce, food had become a nurturing, surrogate mother, soothing and consoling her as her own mom became increasingly critical. Still, she couldn't keep blaming Lorraine for her weight.

Until she was thirteen, however, Andie's weight was normal, and sometimes she was even lean. She'd regularly played soccer between the ages of four and thirteen, when she became noticeably fat—too fat, she thought, to prance around in a skimpy uniform. It didn't matter that she had a pretty face and a good personality, despite what older people said. Being sweet in life got you a C+ at best.

As Andie lay there in bed that night, knowing what she had to do, she slowly explored the hills and dells of her softly rounded body. In her thoughts, she was no stranger to sex. It was all around her—in music, in print, on TV, and on the Web. She dreamed and fantasized about it. For over a year, she'd understood and liked what those powerful thoughts did to her body. Now, as she closed her eyes and surrendered to her imagination, she had a mental image of a smiling young mystery man approaching her at a time she was slim, carefree, and voluptuous.

What made Jack Buhlman especially dangerous was his utter lack of morality. Ethics meant little when one's motivation was absolute goal-directedness. To Jack, what mattered was getting from point A to point B with speed, efficiency, and determination. If something blocked that path, whether human or inanimate, it would be either circumvented or eliminated, whichever was more expedient. Strategic retreat was rarely an option.

Buhlman had thought this way his entire life. He'd been raised in New Mexico in a hard-working family that regularly attended church. He wasn't much of a theist, however; his God, if any, was something akin to the universal spirit at the heart of American Indian spirituality. He was most at home outdoors anywhere in the great Southwest, from the lower Rockies to the Sangre de Cristo Mountains. He learned to run on ochre steppes, to swim in glacial lakes, and to hunt on windswept plains. It was an area of phenomenal beauty and deep serenity. When he was eighteen, he left to join the Marine Corps.

It was 1973, and the last American troops were leaving Vietnam. Jack's father had been a marine who'd seen combat on Okinawa, and Vietnam was to have been Jack's war. Yet by the time he finished basic training, going to war wasn't possible. He soon found himself stationed at Twenty-nine Palms in the California desert, serving in the quartermaster corps.

Jack enjoyed his tour in the marines. His body hardened,

and his mind was honed to a fine edge. It was there that he commenced his habit of daily running, jogging early in the morning when the desert was cool but spectacularly beautiful. Similarly, his work ethic crystallized there and, with it, his determination. He quickly understood that a marine division functioned smoothly only when properly supplied. Jack saw to its provisioning with ruthless efficiency, letting nothing stand in his way.

His commanding officer wanted Jack to become a lifer, but when his tour was nearly up, Jack decided it was time to move on. He knew he could become an officer, and he enjoyed military perks. But he was in his early twenties, and his whole life was ahead of him. Besides, he wanted to see the world.

Jack's quartermastering efficiency did not escape the scrutiny of the federal government. His personnel file could be inspected by various government agencies, and those who did so liked what they saw: a young, healthy, overachiever. The organization most intrigued was the Department of State, and its representative made his interest known when he approached Jack one night in the enlisted men's bar.

"Buy you a beer, corporal?"

Jack recognized the face of his father's old friend. "Hey, Mr. O'Rourke! It's been a long time. What're you doing here?"

"I came to talk to you, Jack. Man, you look great. I haven't seen you in, what—five, six years?"

"About that. My dad told you I was in the marines?"

O'Rourke and the elder Buhlman had served in the military together, after which O'Rourke went into government service. "Yeah, we still talk once or twice a year. I've been meaning to get back there for a while now. Anyhow, he told me you were finishing up your tour, so I thought I'd pay you a visit."

"You still work for State, Mr. O'Rourke?"

"No, forty years was long enough. It's freelance consulting now."

"Is that why you're here?"

O'Rourke laughed. "You always were sharp, Jack. You have a top-notch service record. I've seen your file, and

I've spoken with your CO. But when I talked with your dad, he mentioned you had a little wanderlust. I think I might be able to help you there. What do you know about the State Department?"

"Other than that you worked there? Not much."

"Fair enough. Usually, people who work for State are interested in foreign service. Embassies, missions, get to know the natives, that sort of thing. But State has thousands of other employees with special skills, people who don't necessarily want to become ambassadors."

"I don't have many special skills, Mr. O'Rourke."

"Oh, but you do. You remember those embassy bombings a few years ago? There was a pretty big shake-up after that, and not just in security. The boys at the top reevaluated all aspects of foreign-service life, especially what you might call their quartermastering. The undersecretary for administration in Washington decided they didn't have enough skilled personnel. You're one helluva supply person."

"You want me to supply the State Department?"

O'Rourke laughed. "Not the whole damn thing, my friend! I'm not just talking about pens and paper clips. Foreign missions have tremendous material needs, and you already know the business. You can travel to your heart's content and become involved in things most Americans never dreamed of. It's a great opportunity, Jack. Think about it."

Buhlman did think about it. When he was discharged from the marines, he went to work for State, supplying everything for U.S. embassies worldwide, from California wines to computers to condoms. In the first few years, however, he didn't get to travel as much as he'd hoped.

The undersecretary told him that his skills were superior, but in order to advance in the job, a college diploma was mandatory. Jack didn't have to think twice when they offered to pay his tuition at Georgetown. After six years, he received his bachelor's degree and even passed the Foreign Service Examination.

At State, Jack performed his work with the same single-minded efficiency he'd displayed in the marines. He let nothing stand in his way. Soon he was posted abroad. There he learned that, when one didn't speak the native tongue (and sometimes when one did), it was occasionally necessary to use quasi-legal means in pursuit of one's goal. Who one knew was as important as what one knew. If a bottle of Napoleon-era brandy was needed, it could be obtained through the right contacts.

Occasionally, when dealing with less than reputable intermediaries, things got rough. Jack had excelled at judo in the marines, but one night when he found himself in a back alley, he proved no match for multiple opponents. After suffering several black eyes and broken ribs, he decided to improve his self-defense skills. When his job took him to the Far East, he studied martial arts with local masters.

Jack was a street fighter. He quickly became proficient with defensive tools other than firearms. By the time he was thirty, he was an expert in his own brand of fighting, particularly with a knife. As a man who lacked morals and whose only ethic was work-related, he had no second thoughts when it came to doing what had to be done.

Jack enjoyed his career in government service. During his two decades at State, he accumulated substantial savings. He had few expenses, a high pay grade, and abundant "favors" from his extralegal associates. What he treasured most were the contacts he'd made on the job, whether from the upper or lower classes, or the underworld. As long as they helped him get the job done, what his contacts did with their lives was their own business. Unfortunately, word of Jack's questionable relationships and methods reached ambassadors' ears. Although most of them preferred to look the other way, this was becoming increasingly hard to do, particularly when some unfortunate soul died with a knife in his ribs.

Jack knew the time had come to get out. At the age of forty-two, he submitted his resignation. He had no intention of retiring, however. He still wanted to work, and there were just too many areas of opportunity for someone with his skills and contacts. He soon became an independent consultant for companies with international interests. If someone wanted the best price for a dozen surplus tanks, advice on trade and tariffs, or suggestions on how to get the local government to look the other way, they came to Mr. Buhlman.

You da man, Jack.

By the third week in June, summer in the Hamptons was in full swing. Steve's normally busy practice became even busier with the influx of seasonal vacationers, especially on weekends, when city dwellers mobbed the area. He was happy to be busy, but he felt an obligation to his regular patients, who often had to wait hours to see him.

Perhaps in the fall, he thought, finances permitting, he could renovate the office and maybe even look for an associate. Finished with one patient, he moved down the hall to the next exam room. He removed the chart from its wall rack on the door and saw that it was Karen Trent. He knocked and entered.

" 'Morning, Karen," he said with a smile. His practiced gaze quickly took in her appearance, evaluating her coloring, expression, and body contour. "Lost weight, haven't you?"

"Around ten pounds."

"Intentionally?"

"Yes and no," she said softly. Her suddenly averted eyes and trembling chin suggested something amiss, and the tears filling her eyes confirmed it.

"Talk to me, Karen. Is this about Jared?"

"Yeah," she nodded. "You said you thought he'd come back by now, but I guess he still needs his fucking space."

"How long has it been?"

"Nearly four months," she said, wiping away a tear. "The antidepressants work, but I keep wishing he'd come back already. There's just no way I can compete with some thirty-year-old bimbo with a huge chest."

Steve shook his head. "Jared just doesn't seem the type."

"What type? Maybe if I knew there was a type, I'd have been more careful. Does every man who leaves his wife have a type? Did you?"

The interchange suddenly became too personal, too painful. He opened her chart. "So what brings you here today? Skipped any more periods?"

"No, just the opposite. I've been bleeding pretty heavy

for over three weeks. I didn't think menopause was supposed to go like this."

"It's not," he said, for the first time noticing her slightly pale complexion, annoyed he hadn't seen it before. "Just how heavy is it?"

"I have to wear pads. I'm going through a box every other day."

"That's heavy, all right. Is it painful?"

"Some cramps, no big deal. I take a few Tylenol."

"No aspirin, large doses of Motrin? A lot of vitamin E, or female hormones?"

She shook her head. "I don't take that stuff. Well, an occasional multivitamin. That shouldn't matter, should it?"

"Not at all. What about other medications? You still on the Lipitor?"

"Yes," she nodded. "Sometimes I take a diuretic, maybe once or twice a week."

"What about over-the-counter products? The chart says you picked up a couple bottles of Restore-Tabs."

"Is there something wrong with that?" she said defensively.

He noted her change in tone and the sudden folding of arms across her chest. "Not at all," he said, thinking of Alyssa and Andie. "Not if you're taking the recommended dose. You're not taking more than one a day, are you?"

Her face took on a wounded look, and she couldn't return his gaze.

"Karen . . . have you been doubling up? According to the dates you picked them up, you don't have enough for more than two a day, right?"

Her voice was modulated. "Four a day."

"*Four?* Where'd you get enough for four?"

"Your office isn't the only place that sells it."

Steve's mind was racing. From a psychological perspective, he understood why Karen was taking such large doses of Restore-Tabs. She was hurt, vulnerable, and probably a little desperate. The advertising could be very persuasive. Yet here, two of his patients had taken intentional overdoses of one of the herbal products he stocked, and both developed excessive vaginal bleeding in a relatively short period. He prayed his daughter wouldn't be a third.

He was sure it was just a coincidence. At least, he hoped so. After all, according to company projections, by now hundreds of thousands of women were taking the supplement, and he hadn't heard of any adverse effects. Still, he'd have to check with Ecolabs to make sure they weren't dealing with the tip of an iceberg.

"Tell you what, Karen. I'll do a blood test to see if you've become anemic from the blood loss. But regardless of what it shows, I want you to see your gynecologist as soon as possible. And until this is straightened out, lay off the Restore-Tabs."

Steve saw to it that Becky set up an emergency gyn appointment for Karen before he let her leave the office. He seriously doubted her problem was related to the Restore-Tabs, but he couldn't be certain. The problem was that he didn't really know what the product's active ingredient was. Even the most innocuous substances, used to excess, could prove harmful. He decided to call Ted DiGiorgio and inquire.

What about his other patients who were using the supplement? As a distributor, he kept a running tally of all Ecolabs products sold. He picked up the log, thumbed through the pages, and did a rough computation. It appeared that he'd thus far sold two hundred units of Restore-Tabs to about ninety patients. Alyssa was not one of the purchasers. Like Karen, she must have gotten her supply elsewhere.

Of his eighty known female patients on Restore-Tabs, only two, to his knowledge, had hemorrhaged. That amounted to two-and-a-half percent, hardly a large number; but in the world of medical statistics, it was a significant complication rate. Moreover, if his sample were representative of the population as a whole—where, according to most authorities, up to a quarter of all patients took medications improperly—that small sample translated into several thousand patients nationwide. Patients who were just now showing up in emergency rooms, or coming to doctors' offices. No, he concluded, he should have heard of something like that by now.

"Becky," he said, "in the last month or so, do you remember any patients besides Karen and Alyssa Hagen who had heavy vaginal bleeding? Or maybe who called for an appointment, but since it sounded like a gyn complaint, you told them to see their gynecologist?"

"Not off the top of my head. Why?"

"Just curious." He slowly walked away, frowning, nagged by uncertainty. For some reason, he recalled the woman at the East Hampton gala who'd passed out, Phoebe something . . . *Atkinson,* he recalled. She'd described herself as a concerned citizen. He had no reason to suspect she was taking Restore-Tabs, yet she'd badgered him about the safety of Ecolabs products. And then she'd bled profusely and lost consciousness. On a whim, he went to his consultation room and picked up the phone, dialing the hospital switchboard.

Moments later, he was connected with the medical records department. Although patient information was confidential, medical records staffers routinely divulged it to physicians on staff, even if they weren't the attending of record. After a short search, the records tech located the chart. Atkinson was a patient of Dr. Richards, who'd performed a D&C. The pathology report revealed atypical endometrial hyperplasia, a pre-cancerous lesion. Steve frowned and requested the patient's phone number. He thanked the tech, rang off, and dialed the number without hesitation.

He recognized her voice the instant she said hello. Once he identified himself, her speech took on an acerbic quality.

"I was just wondering how you're doing, Miss Atkinson. I'm afraid I didn't get a chance to follow up after you went to the hospital."

"How did you get my number? It's not listed."

"Oh, I'm sorry," he lied. "My receptionist got it for me."

"You have a habit of stepping in where you're not wanted, Dr. McLaren. You really ought to mind your own business."

Unprepared for her hostility, he grew defensive. "I was only trying to help out, Miss Atkinson."

"Maybe you should have tried harder. The staff in the emergency room said you did more harm than good."

"Come off it. I know everyone there, and I know they'd never make a comment like that."

"Then I'm sure you won't mind taking it up with my attorney."

His jaw dropped. "You can't be serious! Haven't you ever heard of Good Samaritan laws?"

"I see no reason to continue this discussion, Doctor," she said frostily. "And if you ever call my home again—"

"Just one question, Phoebe. You seemed determined to knock Ecolabs products. You weren't by any chance taking Restore-Tabs, were you?"

There was a momentary hesitation. "Whether I was or not is none of your damn business." With that, she slammed down the phone.

Disconcerted, Steve found that the remainder of his morning was difficult. He couldn't concentrate on his patients, and he kept mentally replaying Phoebe's threat. Initially indignant, his anger soon turned to fear, and his ingrained self-doubt resurfaced. Why does this woman hate me so much? he wondered. She just met me. All I really did was prop her legs up and check her vital signs.

Should he have acted differently? Maybe he should have accompanied her to the hospital. Was there anything else he could have done? Worst of all, did she have a case? A little voice in the back of his head kept repeating, *What's wrong with you? Can't you do anything right?* It was the voice of his father, a voice from which he could never, ever, completely escape.

Shoulda-woulda-coulda, he thought. It was his hindsight game, a self-destructive way of thinking that emerged in times of stress and led nowhere. He'd promised himself time and time again not to play that game. He knew he'd have to notify his malpractice carrier about the conversation, and maybe his personal attorney. They wanted to be kept abreast of potential litigation. Christ, he thought, how did I get into this mess?

When office hours were finished, he called Ted. When DiGiorgio came to the phone, he sounded half-asleep.

"Hey, get with the program," Steve said. "You can sleep during the week."

"But the problem is, I never do. What gives?"

"I hate to bring this up on a weekend, but I was wondering about something. Have you had any problems with Restore-Tabs?"

"What kind of problems? You talking about price, availability?"

"No, I mean side effects."

"Like what?" Ted said.

"That's what I'm asking. *Any* side effects. You keep track of these things, don't you?"

"Of course. Not me personally, but my people are on top of that. Come on, Steve, spit it out. Have you heard about any problems?"

"I'm not sure yet." He briefly related what happened to Karen and Alyssa but decided not to mention Andie. He also touched on Phoebe Atkinson, who he suspected was also taking the product.

"Jesus, this is a nightmare," said Ted. "You think the little girl's uterine cancer comes from the Restore-Tabs?"

"There's an old medical saying—one case doesn't make a series. I'm neither an epidemiologist or a statistician, and I have no way of knowing. I just think someone ought to check it out."

"But it wasn't just one case; it was three," said DiGiorgio, sounding worried.

"*Maybe* three," Steve corrected. "So, I gather the answer to my question is, this is the first you've heard of it?"

"Damn right. Christ, can you imagine what this could do to our sales? If word of this gets around, the product'll be dead in the water! Or maybe our whole line, who knows? Man, I'm going to have to touch base with our legal department right away. I sure hope you haven't mentioned this to anyone yet." He paused. "Have you?"

"Only a reporter from the *New York Times*."

"*What?*"

"Lighten up, Ted," McLaren said with a smile. "Of course I haven't said anything. There's nothing to say. As far as I'm concerned, the whole thing is just a coincidence. But tell me something. Your research guys study the product at different dosage levels, don't they? Just like prescription drugs?"

"Of course they do. And like I said, there haven't been any adverse reports. But tell you what, did you ever meet

Bob Whitt? Bob's our research coordinator, a very bright guy. I'll have him give you a call Monday. In the meantime, try to resist the temptation to tell the whole world about this, okay?"

5

Sunday dawned gray and overcast, and the entire East End was shrouded in thick fog and drizzle. Nonetheless, the Hamptons social scene functioned independently of the weather, and in midafternoon, Steve attended yet another fund-raiser. Throughout the afternoon, he kept one eye on the door, half-expecting Phoebe Atkinson to walk in. He couldn't get her threat of litigation out of his mind.

That night, he slept fitfully. He had a frightening dream about his daughter hemorrhaging, lying helplessly in her bedroom while he couldn't get the door open. His subsequent dreams were filled with the specter of a lawsuit. He woke in a cold sweat. He'd seen how malpractice suits could chop down the most powerful physicians, and he never wanted to experience one.

The next morning, before hours began, Becky interrupted his backlog of paperwork.

"Do you know a Dr. Robert Whitt?" she asked.

"Who?"

"He says Mr. DiGiorgio asked him to call."

When Steve picked up, Whitt introduced himself as a research chemist who'd been in Ecolabs R&D for five years. "I was told you had some questions about product testing, Dr. McLaren."

"Not all the products. I'm only interested in Restore-Tabs. Can you tell me a little about the clinical trials?"

Dr. Whitt reviewed the mechanics of their clinical research. Their methods were modeled after the FDA-approved clinical trials used by prescription drug manufacturers, although firms like Ecolabs had more latitude. And yes, they did study various dosage levels, sometimes up to ten times the recommended daily dose.

"And you didn't run into any problems, even with the higher doses?"

"None whatsoever. Oh, there were occasional side effects some women considered annoying, like a little nausea, increased vaginal lubrication, and mild breast tenderness.

But these usually disappeared over time. There was certainly none of the vaginal bleeding you mentioned to Mr. DiGiorgio."

"Is this stuff a hormone, Dr. Whitt?"

"You're familiar with the package literature, Dr. McLaren?"

Once more, he was overcome with the all-too-familiar feeling of inadequacy. "I know what's on the label, sure, but not the inside information."

"Restore-Tabs' active ingredients are phytoestrogens," Whitt went on. "You're doubtless aware that all phytoestrogens are naturally occurring diphenolic compounds that resemble pharmaceutical estrogens. There are several kinds of phytoestrogens, including isoflavones—the ones found in soybeans—and others called lignins, tripterins, coumestans, and saponins. A lot of these compounds are in ordinary foods like fruits, vegetables, and whole grains."

Steve couldn't believe it. "Natural" or not, Restore-Tabs clearly contained the hormone estrogen. He recalled his conversation with the hospital pathologist about where all the estrogen that stimulated Alyssa's uterus was coming from. His inclination was to think there was a cause-and-effect relationship, but he didn't want to jump to conclusions. And of course, what Whitt was saying about phytoestrogens being contained in ordinary foods was true. God knew there were enough soy supplements on the market. "Are you saying Restore-Tabs' active ingredient comes from ordinary grains?"

"No, I'm saying there's always new research being done in the area. And we're the only company to discover a whole new source of phytoestrogens, namely, undersea sources."

"They come from fish?"

"No, from marine plants."

"Like kelp and seaweed?" Steve asked.

"I'm afraid I'm not at liberty to say. Mr. DiGiorgio's orders. Proprietary concerns, I'm sure you understand."

"Of course," Steve said, not really understanding at all. "But I'll take your word for it. It's not exactly my area of expertise. I presume this is all FDA-approved?"

"It doesn't have to be. Restore-Tabs is a dietary supplement, not a drug. If you recall the ninety-four Dietary Supplement Health and Education Act, the FDA has no authority over our products so long as we don't claim they effect or cure disease, which we don't."

"So the bottom line is, you haven't seen any reports of the kinds of problems I mentioned?"

"Absolutely not. This product is completely safe. But I don't want you to take just my word for it. Have you ever met Francesca Taylor?"

In fact, he had. And she was unforgettable. He'd met her six months before at the Ecolabs Christmas party at company headquarters in Westchester. Francesca was one of the most beautiful women he'd ever met. With dark hair and a full figure, she had a sultry look. But what would otherwise have been an exquisite face was marred by one feature: a noticeable, horizontal inch-long scar above her right eyebrow. He wondered why she'd never had it surgically revised. Yet despite this imperfection, she was still very attractive.

Unlike most truly beautiful women he'd encountered, Francesca was completely approachable. Maybe her personality had been altered for the better by her scar. Watching her, he could see that she drew people to her, rather than scaring them away. And it was a quality that unnerved Steve. Oddly enough, perhaps sensing he had nothing to lose, he usually felt more comfortable when attractive women were distant and aloof.

But he found Francesca strangely intimidating. After they'd been introduced, he self-consciously retreated, nursing his iced tea, refusing to make prolonged eye contact with her, but sneaking the occasional glance. He rationalized his behavior by deciding that someone so appealing had to be incredibly stupid. Yet despite this rationalization, Francesca had slipped in and out of his thoughts for days afterward.

"At the Christmas party," he said. "Just briefly."

"I'm sure she'll want to talk with you. Call me back if you have more questions."

Learning to enjoy sex seemed like an impossible task to Lisa Wells. Was it something that could be learned at all, like riding a horse or playing cards? She wondered if it was in her. She always thought the girls she knew who claimed to like sex were different from her. Maybe it was their personalities, as outgoing and bouncy as cheerleaders. Perhaps it was their go-getter attitudes. Or maybe it was their figures, roundly provocative. In contrast, Lisa considered herself shy, passive, and thin.

Yet Lisa was bright enough to realize that a large part of her outlook lay in her upbringing. Her parents were strict religious conservatives who railed about immorality. They never talked about sex and frowned on its mention in school. Her mother's simple advice was to keep your skirt down and your pants up. If you didn't, one thing inevitably led to another, and before you knew it you were a tramp. No matter what the form, any kind of premarital sex was a base, unforgivable evil. Lisa entered her senior year in high school keeping boys—like life—at arm's length.

And then she met Martin.

His cheerful, self-assured attitude meant everything to her, and before long, she would do anything for him. Her self-respect was the first casualty of her relationship. If Martin wanted, she would gladly suffer any embarrassment, any humiliation, to keep him happy. But when she did, her mother's words rang painfully in her ears. Deep down, Lisa realized she could never change her past; and if she wanted something more from the future, she had to change herself.

SOUTH PACIFIC

When it came to hustling, thirty-one-year old Tentrem Suroto was a natural. Born into a large family in the slums of Jakarta, Tentrem learned at an early age that the quickest way to succeed was living by one's wits. By the time he was fifteen, he'd conned his way across Java. A glib and crafty young man, he discovered that foreigners in general, and Americans in particular, were easy marks. When more and more tourists headed for the nightspots in Bali, Tentrem made his way there, too.

For ten years he led an easy if precarious life as a petty thief, tour guide, and hustler. When one lived on the edge, the money was good, and life was fast. But the fast lane also carried risks, and one night Tentrem's world came crashing down in a hotel parking lot when he was shot by a smuggler. It was only through luck and a skillful surgeon that he survived. While he recuperated, he resolved to take things a little slower.

He moved north to the island of Sulawesi. He looked for so-called normal jobs, but he couldn't escape his hustler's mentality. Much as he hoped to stay out of trouble, corruption was everywhere. There was simply too much money to be made, and too many people who wanted it. Tentrem decided that if he couldn't live a risk-free existence, he would at least try to minimize the risks. For several years, he skirted the fringes of the law, making enough money to be comfortable.

In the circles he traveled, rumors abounded. Keeping his ears open, Tentrem soon learned that a small mountain clinic needed help in disposing of its dead. One didn't have to be a genius to realize that if the cadavers couldn't simply be buried, something was afoot, and that spelled money. Much of the funds were thought to be American, which meant *big* money. Within a short while, Tentrem and his lackeys were doing numerous profitable jobs for the clinic.

He never dreamt that burials at sea could be so lucrative.

Ted DiGiorgio's office was glassed-in, which made it appear open and spacious. Francesca Taylor paused at the receptionist's desk and was told to go inside. Ted was on the phone but smiled up at her, gesturing that he'd soon be off.

"Francesca," he said, putting down the receiver. "What's up?"

"Sorry to bother you, Ted, but I was just speaking with Bob Whitt. He got a call from Dr. McLaren—"

"Steve? I know you've seen his commercials. You met him at the Christmas party, didn't you?"

"Yes, briefly." Francesca recalled him as a handsome but reserved man, the kind she would have wanted to get to know better, had he seemed more approachable. "Bob asked me to call him."

"About what?"

"Restore-Tabs. Manufacturing and testing, apparently."

"Oh Jesus, not again," Ted said, rolling his eyes. "No matter what we do, there's a guy who'll never be happy unless he's on a crusade. Years ago, when he and Lorraine first moved out here—"

"Lorraine's his wife?"

"Ex-wife. Anyway, the first time I visited them, he was out demonstrating for some endangered bird that no one ever heard of. Been like that ever since I've known him. Loves the goddamn rulebook and hates to cut corners. I tell you, recruiting him for Ecolabs was like pulling teeth. He always wanted to know if this was okay, if that was kosher, you name it. But in spite of it, he's a pretty good guy." He studied Francesca's wide-eyed look of interest. "Don't get all goggle-eyed on me, and keep your perspective about the situation. Go ahead, call him. Kiss his ass, make him happy. Just don't let him get carried away by some crazy crusade."

From his office, Steve dialed Lorraine's number. What Dr. Whitt told him about the phytoestrogens scared the hell out of him, and he was very worried about his daughter. After four rings, the answering machine came on, and Andie's singsong voice gave instructions to callers. Never home, he thought. Here it is, barely middle of the day, and Lorraine's out prancing around somewhere. Or maybe just screening calls. When he heard the beep, he said, "Lorraine, pick up, it's Steve. It's important. Pick up if you're home. It's about Andie's health."

There was a click. "Don't bullshit me, Steve. She's perfectly healthy."

"I'm talking about the Restore-Tabs."

"What about 'em?"

"Remember when I was over there the other day? I found the bottle she hid in her medicine cabinet."

Lorraine's tone grew caustic. "What in the world were you doing in her medicine cabinet?"

"That's not the point—"

"That *is* the point! Doesn't the word *privacy* mean anything to you? How is she ever going to learn responsibility and self-respect if her parents don't respect *her*? My parents used to snoop on me, Steve, and it's something I won't let happen to Andie."

Now there's a switch, he thought. That's precisely what Andie claimed her mother was doing. He briefly wondered if his daughter was manipulative enough to play them off against one another. But the family's internal dynamics were not the issue now. "I'm talking about a possible problem with the pills, Lorraine. Especially with young people. This product might be acting like traditional estrogen, stimulating the uterus. Kids her age shouldn't be taking it, period."

"You don't say? Excuse me for noticing, but aren't you the same guy who stands up on television and tells everyone how wonderful that company's products are? I may not be the great healer you are, but soybeans can act like an estrogen too, right? So far, I haven't heard anything about problems with tofu." Suddenly she calmed down. "Okay, you're the doctor. What problems are you talking about?"

"It's complicated, but I'm starting to suspect that if some people, especially young girls, take too many Restore-Tabs, they could develop serious bleeding problems. I've talked with Ted DiGiorgio about it, but he might not be all that objective. He's got a vested interest in this. I'm worried about Andie, Lorraine. Any idea how many she's taking?"

"I seriously doubt she's taking more than a couple a day. She's certainly not having any period problems. Honestly, I take the stuff, and I think it's done wonders for me."

"A *couple*?" he shouted. "Christ, Lorraine, that's twice the recommended dose! She's a teenager, for God's sake, and if you think she's taking two, it's probably more like three! What the hell is wrong with you?"

"You bastard, with all your problems, you're the last person on earth who should be lecturing me on responsibility! If there really were a problem, I'm sure the FDA would have yanked the stuff off the shelves by now. You know what I think? That you're trying to cover up a problem you're having with Ted. You just can't stand his success, can you? Maybe you should stop complaining about my attitude and look at your own!"

He closed his eyes and shook his head, discouraged. He might as well be talking to a wall. "Okay, fine. Just do me a favor. If you won't tell her to stop, at least make sure she doesn't take more than one a day. Please, Lorraine. I'm begging you."

She paused, exhaling slowly. "I'll think about it." Then she hung up.

*   *   *

The remainder of Steve's workday dragged by. He found it difficult to concentrate on his patients. He told Becky he was expecting a call, and in the middle of the afternoon, she buzzed him.

"A Miss Taylor from Ecolabs for you," she said over the intercom. "Want to take it in your office?"

He did and he didn't. He felt like an adolescent again, with an adolescent's inadequacy. "Sure. I'll pick up in a second."

Moments later, he was sitting in his reclining desk chair, feeling strangely tongue-tied. He picked up the receiver and said hello.

"Dr. McLaren, it's Francesca Taylor," she began, her voice playful. "Remember me? From the Christmas party?"

"I'm not sure."

"Well, I remember you," she continued. "I thought I must have stepped on your toes, the way you ran into a corner and sulked like a little boy."

"Are you certain that was me?"

"Oh, yes," she said, her voice effervescent. "Six feet, around one-eighty. Dark blue suit, paisley tie, the most attractive man there." She paused. "Am I scaring you off again, Steve?"

"No, of course not. You have a remarkable memory."

"Thank you. My father once told me you win or lose in the details. I have an eye for little things, and I love to win. Anyway, Dr. Whitt asked me to give you a call. You had some questions about Restore-Tabs?"

"Right," he said, his confidence building. He briefly outlined his concerns about the product and the patients who hemorrhaged. "I just want to make sure it's safe."

"Of course. That's something we insist on. Restore-Tabs has had a tremendous public reception so far, and they promise to be our biggest moneymaker. We're not going to do anything to jeopardize their success, but obviously we don't want anyone hurt, either. If there are potential problems, we want to nip them in the bud. But I can assure you, the product's been thoroughly tested."

"How can you be so sure of that?"

"Well, under the law, the FDA can restrict or ban a product that's shown to be unsafe. L-tryptophan, for example. We'll never permit something to reach that point. This is a hot market," she explained, "and there are a lot of herbal cowboys in it, selling what we call 'junkie products.' For instance, a lot of the raw materials for supplements are imported from Europe and Asia. Even though they have certificates saying they are what they claim to be, that's not good enough for us. We have much higher standards, higher than the rest of the industry."

"Meaning what, precisely?"

"Meaning that we have the resources to send our own inspectors over there, rather than waiting to inspect materials shipped here," she said. "No other manufacturer does that. Also, in a lot of cases, we're our own inspector. Take Restore-Tabs: we collect, process, and refine the raw materials ourselves, then ship them here. There's no middleman. There's no question about purity."

"That's very commendable," he said. "But what I'm really asking about is their safety, not purity. Dr. Whitt mentioned clinical trials. The problem with the two, and perhaps three, patients I know was short-term overdosage. How many women were involved in your trials? Were any of them given three or four times the recommended dosage?"

"Our trials included over twelve hundred patients, all phases. They were followed over fourteen months. And yes, we used many different doses. And I can assure you, Steve, none of them had the kind of problem you describe. Understand, I'm not trying to pass the buck. If there is a problem, we'll do everything possible to address it. But without more information, what you're describing sounds to me like a sad coincidence."

She sounded so bubbly, so enthusiastic. "You're probably right," he said. "But you can understand my concern. So you think we should just overlook it for now?"

"I think so. Of course, we'll continue to keep our eyes open."

"What about reporting the bleeding to the FDA? They're always interested in adverse reaction reports. It would certainly cover our asses."

"Well, the FDA gets about five thousand reports on herbals a year. They're usually anecdotal, complaints about bad trips from self-medication."

"What I'm referring to is physician-reported, not patient-reported."

She recalled what Ted had said about McLaren's tendency to get carried away. "Sure, we'd consider it, if you really thought it was essential. Just remember that the FDA has this annoying habit of making mountains out of molehills."

"You're worried about sales?"

"Not me. Ted's the worrier. But beyond sales, I'm concerned about outsiders, officious meddlers. Or about competitors who'd take FDA reports and blow them way out of proportion. I'm not saying it shouldn't be done; it's just that we'd have to be cautious about it. Tell you what. I'll send a memo out right away to all our physician distributors, asking them to report *anything* out of the ordinary. If something's going on, we'll be on top of it, okay?"

"Sounds good to me," he said. "You know, I used to do some clinical research when I was in residency. How about if I did a little clinical trial of my own? I'll come up with the patients, and you guys can help with the paperwork. I'd feel better about it, and we can all stay one step ahead of the game."

"I hear you. Taking precautions is a great idea. I just hope I can sell it to Ted."

"You think he'd give you a hard time?"

"Well," she said, stretching the word out, "I'm sure you know Ted better than I do, but he's not always one for sticking to protocol. Tell you what. Let me see which way the wind's blowing around here, and I'll get back to you, okay?"

Steve hung up and sat there for several minutes, smiling contentedly. He wasn't prepared for Francesca's reaction. He presumed she'd be confrontational, wanting to protect the company's reputation at all costs. But as the conversation unfolded, he even began to contemplate the possibility of seeing her again.

By the middle of the week, although work was hectic, Steve hadn't forgotten Francesca Taylor. The conversation left a sweet taste in his mouth. He wondered if she was at all interested, and beyond that, if she were available, and the pleasant speculation reduced his customary feelings of inadequacy. He wondered, though, if he should have mentioned the Food and Drug Administration.

That might have been coming on too strong, and it went beyond what he intended. Still, he couldn't shake his concern for his daughter. What Lorraine, in all her bitterness, had said about going through proper channels was correct. Even if it was impolitic to mention the FDA to Ecolabs, he might consider contacting the FDA directly. Until he did, perhaps he should keep the idea of further research to himself. Still, Francesca sounded so open to suggestion that he doubted he'd created a problem.

It was early evening, and he was repotting orchids in his greenhouse, preparing to put them outdoors for the summer. He was preparing a mixture of bark and osmunda fiber when the phone rang. He wiped his hands and went inside to pick it up.

"Steve, it's Francesca," she began, her playful voice upbeat. "I hope you don't mind my calling you at home. I got your number from Ted."

"Of course not. But I have to admit, I wasn't sure if I was going to hear from you again."

"Well, I hope I'm as good as my word," she laughed. "That's why I'm calling back."

"I'm glad you did."

"I've been thinking about what you said. I have to admit, I was a little worried by what—"

"Really? You certainly didn't sound like it."

"I'm pretty good at hiding my emotions. The fact is, what you said was hitting too close to home. You see, I've been taking Restore-Tabs myself, ever since they first came out."

"You have?" he said, genuinely surprised. "I hope you won't misunderstand when I say that someone with a figure like yours is the *last* person I'd ever think would take them."

"Thank you, Steve, that's very sweet. But I take a lot of our products, and not just for health reasons. From a PR standpoint, I think I'm more credible when I put my money where my mouth is."

And what a lovely mouth it was, he thought. "I presume you don't take more than the recommended dosage."

"Nope, never have." Once more, her intoxicating laugh. "Anyway, I wanted to tell you that I ran your idea about clinical trials by some of our people here, and they think it has merit. None of our research to date has been done in a private-practice setting. The way they see it, we have a lot to gain and nothing to lose."

He didn't want to bring up his reconsideration of going to the FDA. "Did you mention that I'd like to be involved?"

"Absolutely. In fact, you're perfect. You have research experience, you're already familiar to the TV public, and you're believable. So if you're serious about doing it, I'm hoping we can iron out some of the details."

"You bet. Do you want to get together up at Ecolabs?"

"Actually," she slowly articulated, "I was thinking of something more relaxed. I'm going to be in your neck of the woods this weekend. If you're not busy Friday night, could I treat you to dinner?"

"How does she look to you?" Julia Hagen asked.

"Like she's in pain," Steve admitted. "Is she taking her medication?"

"Every four hours. It seems to make her feel better, but I wish it didn't make her so drowsy."

"Can't be helped. At least it looks like she's enjoying herself right now."

Indeed, Alyssa had a big smile on her face as she was whipped from side to side on an amusement park ride called the Snake. She had recovered enough from her surgery to be up and about. It was a spectacular early summer evening at the Suffolk County Airport, with a warm breeze, a rosy sailor's sky, and low humidity. A traveling carnival had set up for a week on the airport's grounds, and Julia had brought her daughter and two of Alyssa's friends to the fair. Steve, who dropped by after his hours were over, ran into Julia at the cotton-candy concession. Soon they were sitting together on a bench, watching Alyssa's delight.

"She doesn't laugh as much as she should," Julia said. "When I was her age, everything seemed wonderful."

"Come on, Alyssa's one of the happiest kids I've ever

seen. She's always got a smile on her face, no matter how she feels. You're so involved that you don't see the bright side."

"What bright side? I'm not an idiot, Steve, and I'm not in denial." Her tone turned glum. "We both know she's dying."

He considered his words carefully. "That may be, but—"

"*May* be? What're you talking about? When we were at her oncologist the other day, he pulled me aside after her chest X-ray. Did you know she has lesions in both lungs?" There were tears in her eyes, and her chin quivered. "I asked him how much longer she has, and he said he didn't think she'd make it through the summer."

"He actually said that?"

"Well . . . that's the impression I got."

His arm went around her shoulder, and he gave her an avuncular hug. "Julia, stop beating yourself up. You can never tell what the future has in store. Tomorrow, or next week, there just might be—"

"Please, don't patronize me with that 'there's always hope' bullshit!"

"You know who you're mad at?"

"I'm not mad."

"You're mad at yourself," he said. "You're pissed off and guilty and furious at yourself for not being able to do more for her." He paused. "That's a dead-end game, one nobody ever wins."

"So what do you suggest? I should just roll over and give up the fight?"

"You remember what Dylan Thomas said about raging 'against the dying of the light'? Perfectly understandable, but it won't get you very far. What I'm saying is, you should never lose hope."

Her anger raged anew. "What hope? Is one of us brain-dead here? Where is this elusive hope you're talking about?"

"Not for Alyssa, maybe," he said softly. "I'm talking about hope for yourself. When you run out of options, it might be time to think about acceptance."

She turned, cocking her head to one side, staring at him oddly. "What is this, twelve-step propaganda?"

He straightened up, wondering if she, or any of his patients for that matter, was aware of his drinking problem. "What do you know about that?"

"Just that it's all my father talked about for the last five years of his life. He was a poster boy for self-righteous AA slogans. By the time he died, I was so full of the word *acceptance* that I thought I was going to puke."

"So now you're feeling sorry for yourself."

"Oh God," she said with an exasperated sigh. "Let's change the subject."

They both fell silent, watching Alyssa exit the ride and get in line for another go-round. A sudden warm gust came up from behind, sending Julia's hair flying. Glancing to his side, Steve watched the fine strands play about her face like gossamer. He'd once considered Julia to be an attractive young adult, and now, despite the worry etched in her face, she was a very attractive woman.

Had she been the type who exploited her looks, she could have gone far. There was a wholesomeness about her. Julia had looks, charm, and intelligence, all without any trace of guile. But she married as a teenager and immediately devoted herself to her husband, motherhood, and domesticity. He doubted she could have done anything differently.

"I've come here every year for as long as I can remember," Julia finally said. "Before Jimmy died, we came two or three nights a week. The vendors change; the rides change. But the fair's a constant."

"I could watch the Ferris wheel for hours."

"Do you still bring your daughter?"

"Not in the last two years."

"How's that going, anyway?" she ventured.

It was his turn to sigh. "Like you said, let's change the subject. What's doing at work?"

She had to laugh at his clumsy segue. Dr. McLaren's marital problems were often discussed by his patients. His unexpectedly single status produced a sudden excess of unsolicited matrimonial suggestions from male and female patients of all ages, suggestions he politely deflected. On occasion, even Julia offered her opinion on ways to improve his social life, though if the truth be known, she occasionally fantasized about herself and the good doctor. Handsome, intelligent, and sympathetic, Steve was considered a catch by everyone.

"Work's fine, thank you."

"Your insurance is still covering all Alyssa's expenses?"

"Yes, thank God."

"How long has it been since Jimmy died? Four years?"

"Five, this September," she said. "Hard to believe how quickly it's gone by."

Indeed it had, thought Steve. He recalled the day well, a day after which everything in Julia's life seemed to go wrong. James and Julia Hagen were a lively, enthusiastic couple. Alyssa was born when they were young and struggling. But after years of hard work, they'd saved enough to buy a home and were considering another child. And then, on the evening of their wedding anniversary, while Jimmy's car was stopped in a traffic jam on the Long Island Expressway, it was rear-ended by a truck. He was killed instantly.

Julia fainted when the police delivered the news. But eight-year-old Alyssa, resourceful even then, had the good sense to call the doctor right away. Steve immediately rushed over. He tended to the family during their grief and helped with funeral arrangements. It was a difficult time for everyone. Fortunately, Jimmy had a small insurance policy that took care of the mortgage and the funeral expenses.

Emotionally, Julia had a hard time coping. She went into a tailspin that ended in a deep depression, alleviated by taking time off from work, doting on her child, and consuming large doses of Prozac. Finally, after two years, she slipped out of her funk and went to work at her current job. Steve thought that she'd done remarkably well. And then Alyssa got sick.

A remarkable woman, Steve thought, just as Alyssa was a remarkable child. Not far away, the Snake slithered to a stop. Alyssa and her coltish friends got off and walked toward the bench, laughing wildly, filling the night air with their burlesque babble.

"I'm so glad she can still laugh," Julia said.

"Given what she's gone through, it's a gift."

"Just remember your promise, Steve McLaren. I don't want her to suffer."

Steve looked away, beyond the burgundy light of dusk, toward the evening's first star. When lives, like days, drew to a close, nothing was as simple as it seemed.

She'd reserved a table at Indochine, a trendy eatery on Dune Road. The establishment had opened to rave reviews the previous fall, and it was always packed. It specialized in a marriage of French and Southeast Asian cuisines: sole poached in a coconut—lemon grass sauce, or spicy medallions of pork marinated with green curry paste and *nam pla*. Although the fare was superb, more guests came for the ambience, to see and be seen, than for the food. It was precisely this kind of pretentious upscale atmosphere that Steve tended to avoid.

The reservation was for seven. At that hour there was already an overflow crowd that spilled out of the atrium and into the perfectly laid-out parking lot. As he approached, whisper had it that there was a two-hour wait. Steve waded through the swell of beautiful people, squeezing past their tight, toned bodies until he reached the reservations desk. Francesca hadn't arrived yet. Steve thought she must have wielded considerable clout, for a table was waiting. He was shown to the outdoor deck, where their table straddled the main dining room and the ocean. He ordered iced tea and gazed out over the watery horizon.

Francesca showed up ten minutes later. Steve was looking back into the main dining room, trying to spot her. He saw a flash of leg and short skirt, and he recognized her before she saw him. The boisterous din around him continued, but concentrating as he was, he no longer heard it. He found himself gawking at the woman who gracefully walked his way.

He hadn't forgotten her looks or her scar, but now that she was dressed up, she seemed lovelier than he remembered. In an establishment filled with young, attractive people, Francesca was an undeniable magnet. He thought the attraction owed more to her figure than her face. She was around five-eight, and her long, shapely legs had a radiant tan. She wore oversize Oscar de la Renta sunglasses. She'd slipped into a black miniskirt, and her ivory-colored, low-cut top accentuated her full breasts. A thin gold chain hung around her neck, and its small, diamond-studded heart fell just short of her cleavage. There was a slight wave to the thick, dark brown hair that tumbled to her shoulders. And for Steve, most important of all, she was smiling at him.

Francesca moved like a dancer. She had an unprepossessing slinky stride, more Margot Fonteyn than Claudia Schiffer. To Steve, she seemed to glide across the deck, long hair luffing in the gentle breeze. As she neared the table, he rose to greet her. Holding his gaze, she removed her glasses and extended her hand, trailing the scent of Joy. As she took her seat, he glanced at the swell of her breasts.

"Hello, Francesca. Do I have to tell you how great you look?"

"Yes, you do," she laughed. "I never get tired of hearing that. Were you waiting long?"

"Just a few minutes. How'd you manage to get a table? Are you a regular?"

"Oh, no. This is my first time here. I guess it helps to know the owner. He's been after me to come by since he opened." A waiter arrived, took her order for Campari and soda, and left menus. "Do you know anything about this place?"

"Just by reputation. To be honest, it's a little too exclusive for my taste. But you seem perfectly at home here."

"When I was younger, I used to hang out in places like these. After a while, you learn to tune out the crowds and the sycophants."

"Was that before you worked for Ted?"

"Way before," she nodded. "Around ten years ago, I did some modeling. That was before this," she said, pointing to her scar. "You can't escape the hangers-on—the photographers, the press, the guests. Cast of thousands."

"Where was this?"

"Mostly overseas. Paris, Milan."

As she looked at the menu, he studied her face. Francesca was a salad of Mediterranean genes, part Italian, part Iberian Peninsula. She had flashing eyes and dimples, bright teeth and full lips, and the beginnings of fine lines around her eyes. He estimated her age at about thirty-five.

"How long have you worked at Ecolabs?" he asked.

"Six years. I didn't go to college until I stopped modeling, and then I worked for an ad agency for a while. Ted's job offer came along at just the right time."

After the waiter brought her drink, they discussed the menu and ordered. Francesca sipped her Campari, leaning forward with elbows on the table, looking at Steve with a disarming smile. Dr. McLaren was most definitely a handsome man. Perhaps owing to his tan, he was more appealing than he'd been at the Christmas party six months before. She sensed that under his shirt, he had a well-muscled chest and plenty of upper-body strength.

"Ted mentioned something about a patient of yours, a little girl with cancer. Was she taking Restore-Tabs?"

"Yes, she was. A huge dose. Alyssa's thirteen—not exactly a little girl, but she weighs all of a hundred pounds. She was taking three tablets a day. For a normal size woman, that's the equivalent of five a day."

"You think that's related to her cancer?"

"No," he said, shaking his head, "I doubt it. I suppose anything's possible, but it appears pretty unlikely."

"What kind of cancer did she have?"

"A few years ago, Alyssa developed what's called a malignant thymoma. A very rare neoplasm, and usually not life-threatening. But in her case, it turned out to be. She's gone through surgery, radiation, chemo, the works. Unfortunately, it looks like her disease is going to get her."

Francesca's smile vanished. The fingers of one hand had risen to her lips, and her face was lined with concern. She slowly shook her head. "God, Steve, that's horrible."

"Yes, it is. She hasn't exactly had what you'd call an easy life. Just before we discovered the thymoma, her father died—"

"Oh, no."

"But despite everything that's happened, she remains this cheerful, upbeat, pleasant kid."

"Does she realize what's happening to her?"

"Yes, she's known from the start. There are several schools of thought on what to tell these kids, but Alyssa's very bright. You can't hide things from her. Anyway, with her outlook as positive as it is, she's tried to lead a normal life, whatever that means for a teenager. She tries not to miss school and she has a lot of friends. She loves music and, now, boys. But within the past year or so, she's become a little fixated with her appearance."

"I see you're frowning," Francesca said. "Does that surprise you? I've never known a thirteen-year-old who wasn't concerned with how she looked."

"Sure, but in Alyssa's case, it went way beyond that. She's thin as a rail, and she developed this obsession about being flat-chested." He paused. "Something tells me that's not exactly a condition you suffered from."

Again, her guileless smile. "Are you kidding? I was a tomboy, as flat as they come. It actually helped my modeling career, in the beginning." Noting his puzzled look, she glanced down at her chest. "These? I had my first boob job when I was twenty-five. Can't you tell?"

"Well, no, actually. You say your *first*?"

"Yeah, I had them redone four years ago. The first ones were saline, and they never really felt natural. Give me your hand." Before he could react, she lifted his palm off the table and pressed his fingers to her upper breast. "Now honestly, Dr. McLaren. Can you tell whether they're real?"

"Seem real to me," he said, feeling his face redden. "Very perky."

"Perky . . . I like that, perky. Thank you."

Sitting there, touching her softly rounded breast, looking into her strange, smoky eyes, he was at a loss for words. He was suddenly aware that the people on either side of them had stopped talking and were watching intently. He quickly withdrew his fingers. Sensing his discomfort, Francesca placed her hand atop his.

"I hope I didn't embarrass you."

He smiled at himself. "I'm not embarrassed," he said in a whisper. "I'm mortified."

Her chuckle was deep, throaty, and completely sensual. "Touché. I didn't mean to interrupt. You were talking about your patient's lack of curves."

"Right," he said, content to let her hand remain where it was. "Neither her mother nor I were aware how desperately Alyssa wanted her breasts to develop. It was a body-image thing, probably related to her surgeries and the loss of her father. She was looking for a magic potion, and she thought she found the answer in Restore-Tabs. You've got to admit, you can read a lot into the advertising."

"It doesn't suggest taking an overdose."

"You can't really blame her, can you? We all did stupid things at that age, remember? Bottom line, she hemorrhaged. She had a D and C, and it turned out to be endometrial cancer. That was a few weeks ago. As of today, she's holding her own. But she no longer has a uterus."

She was shocked. "A hysterectomy? God, how unfair is that?"

"Cancer's never very fair, Francesca."

Sliding her hand away, she slumped back in her chair, saddened. "I want to keep an open mind, Steve. Not to mention that I'm taking the stuff myself. Recommended dosage, of course. Do you honestly think what happened to her is related to the supplement?"

"Like I said, it's possible, but unlikely. Nothing like that showed up in the Ecolabs research?"

She shook her head. "But it wasn't the same population. From what I understand, all the studies were overseas, and there weren't any American-style private patients. That's why we really have to do a clinical trial around here. Do you mind if we go over it?"

To his right, the orange sun was setting. Cast in its fiery light, Francesca's warm brown limbs were softly alluring, compared with her dark-lidded eyes, which were heavy with concern. When he'd first met her at the Christmas party and feigned disinterest, he wanted to believe she was the stereotype of stupidity men often thought beautiful women were. He'd obviously misjudged her completely. Francesca Taylor was an intelligent, stunning woman who seemed to care deeply. As he watched her sip her drink, he discussed what he had in mind.

He was fairly sure Francesca knew most of it anyway, yet he wanted to explain himself. Proper clinical medication trials, he explained, should be blinded. This implied that the patients didn't know whether they were receiving the drug or a placebo. Occasionally, they were double-blinded, meaning that the person dispensing the product was also in the dark. An adequate number of patients were required to make the trial meaningful, and it had to have a minimum duration. Informed consent was not only wise but mandatory. Clinicians had to be available to evaluate outcomes, and statisticians were required to summarize results.

While Steve spoke, Francesca watched him closely. She was growing increasingly interested in this charming, outgoing man. He had an easygoing yet authoritative manner of speaking. He was certainly attractive enough, and his shyness gave him appealing vulnerability. But beyond that, he was different from most physicians she'd known.

In the course of her work, she encountered a lot of medical doctors, and for the most part, they were extraordinary egotists who often lacked Steve's integrity. Few had the selflessness of an Albert Schweitzer or the idealism of a Patch Adams. Many had an exaggerated sense of self-importance. Steve, however, was quite different. He genuinely seemed to care—not only for his patients, but for the medical profession as well. She placed her elbows on the table, put her chin in her palms, and contentedly studied him.

The waiter brought their orders. Throughout dinner, they discussed the parameters of the clinical trial. As Steve moved from one aspect of the project to another, Francesca was impressed with his clever mind and facile manner. Steve was equally taken with her insights and suggestions. They grew comfortable in one another's company. The evening passed quickly. Before they realized it, it was ten P.M., and they were finishing dessert and coffee.

Steve found himself growing captivated with her. It wasn't just her looks and alluring figure. For an appealing woman, Francesca Taylor had the added draw of poise endearing self-deprecation. She was an enthusiastic listener, and her openness tended to draw people closer. What's more, she had the maddeningly provocative habit of absentmindedly stroking the back of his hand while he talked. It was the simplest touch, but one he found very stimulating. When she pushed her coffee cup away and looked at her watch, he found he didn't want the evening to end.

"Time to go?" he asked.

She nodded. "Have to get up early tomorrow. I'm staying

with some friends not far from here, and they want to take me fishing for stripers—"

"You like to fish?"

"Not really. I just like the water."

He stood up, moving to her side of the table. "You parked in the lot?"

"No, I took a cab."

"Perfect. If you'd like, I'll drop you off."

Her smiling eyes met his. "I'd like that very much."

Her friends had a house in Westhampton Beach, a few miles away. When she slid into his front bucket seat, her short skirt rose well above mid-thigh, and he found himself glancing at her legs. She wasn't wearing stockings. Her long slender legs were deeply tanned, the flesh remarkably firm. Both her knees and ankles were perfectly sculpted. For the first time he noticed she was wearing stylish open-toe heels with thin, black leather straps. Her toes were unusually long and delicate, their nails covered with clear gloss.

Soon they reached the address, a frame cedar house painted white. The crushed-gravel driveway, hidden by tall hedges, led to a street-level double-garage. The second-story living area was ultramodern. When Steve opened Francesca's door, she took his arm and let him lead her up the steps. Reaching the door, she turned to face him. Her fingers played about his elbow, and a smile was on her lips.

"Thanks, Steve," she said. "I had a wonderful time. Not to mention that we got a lot done, and the food was great."

"I think I'm the one who should be thanking you. It's not every day that a beautiful woman pays for my dinner."

"My pleasure." For a long moment, her deep hazel eyes fixed on his. He wanted to say something memorable and clever, but nothing came to mind. Yet while he stood there in artless silence, Francesca raised her hand and touched his cheek with her fingertips. Leaning toward him, she closed her eyes and kissed him softly on the lips, mouth lingering. He could feel her body momentarily press against his before gradually pulling away.

He took a deep breath, gazing at her fondly, suddenly liking everything about her, including the scar above her brow. "It's still early," he said, nodding in the direction of the house. "I don't suppose . . ."

"Maybe another time." Her fingers traveled down his arm, and she squeezed his hand, a parting gesture. Then she turned and stepped inside.

For several moments, he stood at the top of the landing, staring at the closed door. He could still feel the warmth of her mouth, still smell the sweet cachet of her perfume, its fragrance more intoxicating than his finest orchids. Before his sense of inadequacy returned, he walked down the stairs to his car.

6

The next morning, with the lemon yellow light streaming about his shoulders, McLaren breezed into the office, whistling a tune. He was an atrocious whistler who couldn't carry a tune, and years ago, the staff had asked him to refrain from trying. Nonetheless, he insisted on attempting "Let the Sun Shine In," irrepressibly off-key. Heads turning, they silently watched him with pained, bewildered expressions. There was a spring in his step, and his self-assured body language was unusually cheerful.

Becky kept her eyes lowered as he walked by. "Sounds like somebody got lucky last night," she mumbled.

"Pardon?"

"Either that," said Donna, "or Lorraine got remarried."

They both looked his way with identical quizzical stares.

"What?" he said. "Why can't I just be in a good mood?"

"It's not your mood we're questioning," Becky said. "You're *usually* in a good mood. What makes us curious is that god-awful whistling."

"Okay, so it's an old tune."

Becky looked at Donna. "Do you get the feeling there's something he doesn't want to tell us?"

"Come on, don't keep us in suspense. How'd it go last night?"

He patronized her with a smile. "It was a very pleasant evening."

Becky gave him a goofy look. " 'It was a very pleasant evening.' Is that all you've got to say? Was she a hot babe, or what?"

"And the meal was fantastic, too."

"Oh, brother." Suddenly Becky turned toward the waiting room. It was still thirty minutes before hours began, and the patients hadn't yet arrived, so she was surprised to see an unfamiliar man striding purposefully to the reception window. He wore an inexpensive business suit. "Can I help you?" she asked.

Steve also turned, gazing at the man with silent curiosity.

"Is Dr. McLaren in?"

"I'm sorry, do you have an appointment?"

"Maybe you could just give him this."

"I'm Dr. McLaren." Steve slowly approached and took the proffered sheets of paper, which were folded in thirds. Seeing the word *Subpoena* written in bold print, he frowned. "What's this?"

"Just doin' my job, Doc." He removed a pen and notepad from his pocket, concentrating on McLaren. "You're around six-one, a hundred-ninety or so? Gray eyes. Could you just give me your date of birth?"

"No, I could not. Do you mind telling me what's going on?"

"Just your ordinary subpoena, Doc. I'm sure you've seen one before." Then he smiled, turned, and walked away.

In fact, Steve hadn't. It suddenly sank in that he was being sued. He knew many physicians who'd been in that predicament, some several times; but in all his years of practice, it had never occurred to him. His fear intensified as he slowly unfolded the papers. Stapled to the first page was a check made out to him from the summons-processing service, in the amount of twenty-five dollars. He thought it peculiar that an anonymous organization was paying him a token fee to commence a malpractice suit. Somehow, he didn't think that was going to cover his expenses.

"What is it, Dr. McLaren?" asked Donna.

"Son of a bitch," he said under his breath. "I think I'm being sued by that whack job Phoebe Atkinson."

"The one who fainted at the fund-raiser?"

He slowly nodded, reading on. In obtuse legalese, the papers commanded him to appear before a judge in the Supreme Court in Riverhead, twenty days hence. The remaining two pages were more specific. *"Ten million dollars?"* he suddenly thundered.

"An awful lot of money for a ruined pantsuit," Becky said.

"What a bitch! I should have let her lie there bleeding!"

"Let me see that," Becky said. She took the subpoena from his hands and scanned it quickly, reading selected phrases aloud. "Failure to meet reasonable and customary standards . . . damages . . . gross and willful negligence . . ." She looked up. "Jesus, boss, what'd you *do* to the poor lady?"

He was furious. "Not a damn thing! God, of all the fucking nerve!"

"You want us to cancel hours, Dr. McLaren?" Becky said lightly. "We can reschedule the patients while you go out and strangle the slut."

"Very funny. I just can't believe it!" he said, pounding his fist on the sign-in desk. "What happened to being a Good Samaritan? Doesn't that count for something?"

"That was last millennium," said Donna.

"How about if I just throw the papers in the trash?" Becky said. "Pretend you were never served, and start the day anew?"

"Give it to me," he snapped, leafing through the pages, exasperated. "Isn't there some number I'm supposed to call?"

"Yeah," Donna replied, "your attorney. Come on. Dr. McLaren, lighten up. This happens all the time."

"Not to me it doesn't. But I think you're right about the attorney thing."

"Of course she's right," Becky said. "I saw it on *Chicago Hope*."

Steve whirled around and stormed into his office, nearly overcome by rage. He couldn't recall ever being this angry. Once again, he racked his brains trying to figure out what he'd done to incur Atkinson's wrath. The nerve of that woman! The wording of the summons made him out to be the contemporary medical equivalent of Genghis Khan. Here, he'd simply been trying to help out another human being, without thought of personal gain, and look what he had to show for it! Where was the justice in *that*? Isn't that how they taught him to respond to crises in medical school? No wonder so many doctors were unwilling to stick their necks out!

Sitting at his desk, he grabbed his phone and pounded his attorney's number, impatiently drumming his fingers as one ring followed another. Finally, a recorded message announced that the office was closed until Monday morning.

Fuming, Steve slammed down the phone, not sure what to do next. He briefly considered the possibility of calling one of his colleagues, someone with experience in these matters. But he dreaded the snide comments.

Then he remembered his insurance policy. He'd always considered malpractice insurance an inconvenience, something doctors grumbled about when paying tens of thousands of dollars a year in premiums. Suddenly, however, it seemed like money well spent. Maybe it was time the system worked in his favor for a change. Steve removed the manila folder labeled Malpractice, thickened by years of premium notices and policy clarifications. He located the Manhattan number and dialed.

Like his personal lawyer, none of the company attorneys were in. But the switchboard operator put him through to one of the more senior clerical staff, who'd obviously fielded such weekend inquiries before. After calming McLaren down, the woman had him read the relevant information from the subpoena. Then she took his name and number, promising that a company attorney would call back Monday.

Knuckles white, he finally replaced the receiver. It was going to be a long weekend.

"Jeff, you promised!" Andie whined. "You said you'd buy it for me!"

"All right, what's your problem? I told you I'd get it. I didn't get a chance yet."

"You better. I gave you enough money for two bottles. I really need it, Jeff!"

"Jesus, gimme a break! You sound like some kinda drug addict. I'll get it today, okay? Why are these pills so important, anyway?"

"I just don't want anybody seeing me buy them, that's all."

Sitting on her bed, holding the phone to her ear, Andie stared across the room. She'd known Jeffrey for twelve years, since they'd first started going to day camp. She really loved him. He was certainly her oldest friend, if not her best. She could tell him everything—except this. Her weight was just too personal a problem, too private. And as much as she wanted to boast and shout about her five-pound weight loss, she just couldn't. Jeff always said whatever she weighed was fine with him, that she shouldn't make such a big deal about it. But it *was* a big deal to her. She wished he'd be as proud of her as she was of herself. At this rate, she'd be down to one-thirty not by Christmas, but by the end of the summer.

Maybe it was a combination of things, like her diet and the little bit of exercise she'd been doing, in addition to the pills. But she was determined, desperate even, to keep making progress. She was afraid that if she deviated from what got her here, she'd blow right up again. She hated having to sneak behind her parents' backs. She knew her father had forbidden her to take them anymore, and her mother's halfhearted suggestion that she stop for a while was about as forceful as her mother got. Yet she simply couldn't. Any concern about side effects was more than offset by what good the Restore-Tabs had done.

"They just are, that's all. I'll get them from you in school tomorrow."

SOUTH PACIFIC

After dropping off Pak Suranto, Sergeant Atmosaputro delivered the body to a temporary refrigeration unit attached to the jail. The unit was little more than an old walk-in refrigerator. It had racks for four bodies, although rarely was there more than one. The refrigerator was a temporary way station. Medical examinations were performed in Manado, seventy miles away, where the sergeant did most of his police work. A government physician came only when needed, and only when he could fit it into his schedule. This was rarely more than twice a month.

The autopsy was performed ten days after the body was shipped to Manado. The physician flew six hundred miles from Ujung Pandang, the island's business and administrative center. The autopsy was more a surgical examination than a postmortem in the Western sense. Dental and whole-body X-rays were rarely taken, and routine toxocological analyses were deemed unnecessary. That was certainly true in this case. A cursory inspection of the victim's outward appearance told the pathologist everything he needed to know.

His suspicions were confirmed by a quick autopsy. When he was done, he had the clerk contact Sergeant Atmosaputro.

"I read your report, Sergeant. Very thorough. I take it you noticed the deceased's genitalia?"

"I did, Doctor. The fish and crabs made a mess of it."

"The reason her labia were devoured was because she'd been bleeding. For marine creatures, blood of any kind makes the flesh around it irresistible."

"Is her bleeding important?" asked Atmosaputro.

"It is in this case. You see, I ran across another case identical to this one two months ago. Right down to the rope around her leg. There was a cement block in your case also, correct?"

"Yes, the divers retrieved it. I can forward it, if you'd like."

"That won't be necessary," said the doctor. "You see, like the other victim, who was found about ten kilometers from yours, this woman was already dead when she was dumped into the ocean. The sea was just a convenient place to get rid of her."

"Do you know what killed her?"

"They both died of natural causes. In this case, advanced uterine cancer."

"Cancer?" asked Atmosaputro. "You know we honor our dead around here, Doctor. Why would the family want to get rid of her?"

"We don't know that she had a family, do we? And if she did, they may not be aware of her death. I can tell you this: both women came from poor backgrounds. Their teeth showed little or no dental care, and their bones showed signs of malnutrition. In these parts, it's not unusual for women from poor families to disappear."

"True, but when that occurs, it's usually due to drugs, prostitution, or both. Was there any indication of either in your examination?"

"No," said the doctor, "there was not. So, if they're estranged from their families, it may be for less common reasons, like romance. Or kidnapping. Or maybe they were paid to do so. But that really begs the question, doesn't it?"

Atmosaputro slowly saw what he was driving at. "You mean, why were women who died of uterine cancer weighted down and thrown overboard?"

"Exactly. And the obvious answer is, to keep them from being found. Whoever did it—and I'm assuming it was the same person or people—wanted to hide their bodies. Why would that be?"

"I don't know. Who found the first victim?"

"She was hauled aboard in a fishing net."

"Hmmm. If these two were found by chance, that suggests there may be more buried at sea."

"Yes, the thought occurred to me," said the pathologist. "Did you notice the tattoos, Sergeant?"

"Around the wrists? Yes, but I didn't pay much attention to them."

"I had a little more time," the doctor said. "They're very intricate, on both forearms and hands. I took photos. I'm sure they're Dayak."

Dayak, a nondescript term similar to *Indian*, was applied to groups of people who originally lived in the interior of nearby Borneo. Genetically Malay, they were former headhunters who often retained tribal customs, one of which was distinctive tattooing.

"I wasn't aware of that," said Atmosaputro. "And the other woman?"

"No tattoos, but she has the same Malay features. I wouldn't be surprised if they're both from coastal Kalimantan."

"Do you have pictures of these women's faces, Doctor?"

"Yes, and I'm having an artist make a facial sketch of the recent one. I'll send you copies of everything."

"That would be very helpful."

At this point, Atmosaputro thought, *anything* would be helpful. The idea of God-knew-how-many cancer-ridden women dumped overboard was repugnant. Once the pictures arrived, he'd definitely have to speak with the captain. There weren't many clues, but at least he now had something to go on.

Steve found the remainder of the morning difficult. Try though he might, he couldn't get the impending lawsuit out of his mind. He felt violated, justifiably indignant. His emotions wreaked havoc with his bedside manner. His usual cheerfulness vanished. He was brusque and curt with the patients. A few of them were bold enough to ask what was wrong.

Steve usually spent a lot of time listening to his patients' concerns. But given his curtness, morning office hours ended earlier than usual. When he was done, he realized that a couple of double scotches would feel good, and he immediately hated himself for even contemplating it. The problem was, he now had an entire weekend on his hands with virtually nothing to do but think of the damn subpoena.

At least, he thought, he could muse about Francesca. After the bitterness of his divorce, he truly wondered if he could ever fully trust someone again. But the evening he'd spent with Francesca suggested that he could. It was one of the more enjoyable nights he'd had in a long time. Beyond her looks, he liked everything about the woman: her openness, her warmth, her endearing self-effacement, even the little scar on her face. Despite it, she was undeniably attractive, with a body to die for. As he changed out of his lab coat, he wondered if she was still sleeping, or if she was on the beach working on her tan.

Becky buzzed him. "Julia Hagen called while you were with the last patient. She wonders if you could call her at home."

He knew Julia's number by heart and quickly dialed it from his desk. Julia answered after the first ring.

"Thanks for calling, Steve. I'm worried about her."

"How's her pain?"

"Worse than ever," Julia said. "She's trying to tough it out, but I can hear her moaning. The medication barely touches her."

"You sure she's taking it?"

"Absolutely. I gave her the pills myself. And this morning, she developed a fever, almost a hundred and three. Tylenol doesn't touch it."

"I'll be right over."

Steve rarely made house calls, but the Hagens were an exception. Alyssa's illness had progressed to the point where he now visited her at least once a week. Ten minutes later, his Saab pulled into the driveway of the Hagens' modest frame home. Dressed in her robe, Julia immediately let him in. Worry lines deeply creased her forehead.

"Alyssa's still in bed," she said. "Says her chest hurts."

"Is she coughing?"

"A little, but nothing's coming up."

He followed her to Alyssa's second-floor room. The bedroom door was open, and Alyssa lay under a quilt, watching TV. She appeared listless. Her normally pale complexion now had a slightly olive hue, and her face had the faint sheen of drying perspiration. Despite her condition, she looked up and smiled when the doctor entered the room.

"Hi, Steve."

"Hello, gorgeous. Anything good on the tube?"

"Just MTV. Reruns."

He sat beside her on the mattress and briefly looked at the antique grandfather clock against the wall. Sometimes its steady ticking was the only sound in the room. "Your mom tells me you don't feel so hot."

"It's okay," she said with a sigh.

"Come on, you can't con a con man. You look about as energetic as something on a bagel."

"Huh?"

"That's what I thought," he said. "When did you get the cough?"

"I had a little yesterday, when I woke up. It was worse this morning. And it hurts when I breathe."

"You're taking the Percocet like I told you?"

"Yeah, but it makes me want to throw up."

"Can't be helped. Let's go, sit up," he said, taking her by the hand and pulling. "I want to listen to your chest."

She was wearing white panties and a loose T-shirt. She'd recovered astonishingly well from her recent surgery. As Steve donned his stethoscope, Alyssa exposed her back with practiced ease. Steve leaned forward and listened to her lungs, periodically telling her to cough. Then he straightened up and removed the stethoscope from his ears.

"Sounds like you've got some congestion in there. I'm going to start you on antibiotics," he said, opening his doctor's bag.

"Do I have to?"

"No, silly goose, we could just let you lie here and toast like a marshmallow." He removed several syringes, a vial of powdered antibiotic, and a bottle of sterile water. "I know you hate injections, but it goes with the territory."

"I have to get a *shot*?"

"Just one," he said, dissolving the drug. "I want to get a head start on this bug of yours, and then we'll switch to capsules. Okay, I'm ready. Now roll onto your belly, because this is a butt shot."

"Oh, great."

The injection given, he put away the syringe. Then he took out a small rectangular envelope, peeled it open, and removed a skin patch. Alyssa watched, frowning.

"What's that?"

"A fentanyl patch," he said, applying its adhesive side to her shoulder. "A little stronger than the Percocet. It'll help with your pain."

"Will it make me puke?"

"Maybe, but you're going to feel so relaxed, it won't matter." He turned to Julia, who was standing behind him with arms folded across her chest. "I'll give you a prescription for prochlorperazine suppositories—"

"Jeez," Alyssa whined, "another butt job."

"Alyssa!" Julia said.

"It's okay," Steve said, getting up. "She's entitled. I'll give you the rest of the scripts downstairs. Call you later, Alyssa."

"Later," she said brightly.

On the stairs, he turned to her mother and shook his head. "Most kids in her predicament wouldn't be able to stop feeling sorry for themselves. But your daughter, well . . . She's got such tremendous heart. She might be turning into a little wiseass, but what an incredible attitude."

"You can't buy time with attitude."

"Don't be so sure. You've heard of the power of positive thinking? That area's just starting to be scientifically studied."

In the living room, he slowly wrote out four prescriptions— three for the drugs, and one for an X-ray. He went over the directions as he wrote. Julia studied his face, thinking how fortunate she'd been to find a doctor who genuinely cared. And she cared, as well, for the caregiver. Not that she could ever share her feelings with him; she had him on too high a pedestal. She was worried that if he somehow discovered her thoughts, she'd scare him away, and he'd be out of her life forever.

"Have you ever considered a hospice, Julia? There are some excellent new places out here. A few of them cater to kids."

"Actually, I have. I looked into it a few months ago. They all have Web sites. But I honestly don't think they're for Alyssa."

"They're as much for the parents as they are for the child," he explained. "Maybe more."

"I realize that. But no matter how comfortable the surroundings, they can't prolong the inevitable, can they?"

"No, they can't."

She walked very close to him, inches from his face, gazing into his eyes. "I just don't want her to suffer, Steve."

"I realize that."

"She's very comfortable here. This is the home she grew up in. I'm going to hold you to your promise, Steve McLaren. When the time comes, I know you'll be there for us. I know you'll do what's right."

"And I will."

She lifted her lips to his face, kissing him softly on the cheek. "Thanks for coming."

He simply smiled and waved farewell. Stepping out into the bright early afternoon glare, he was halfway down the walk when a thought struck him, and he stopped short. All along, he'd presumed that by "being there for them," Julia meant keeping Alyssa comfortable and pain-free. But now he wondered if she was talking about something else entirely.

Was it possible that she was referring to euthanasia?

7

The vast complex of outlet stores was located at the end of the Long Island Expressway, just north of the Hamptons. The mall attracted shoppers from all over the island. Steve needed a new pair of dress loafers. After he left the Hagens', he drove to the outlet complex and parked near the front. The weather was fair that weekend, and the outlets were crowded. But he was in no hurry. He began leisurely strolling across the parking lot.

"Steve?" a man's voice called. "You out spending your patients' money?"

He turned and spotted Norman Rothstein, an internist from Southampton. He'd known Norman for years and had served on several hospital committees with him. "Buying some shoes, Norm. What about you? You off this weekend?"

"My partner's on call. But after I'm done here, I have to run back and see a patient I admitted last night. Then maybe I can squeeze in some golf."

"I thought you were off."

"Yeah, well, I've known this patient Lisa Wells for years. She's a sweet kid with this jerk for a boyfriend," he said. "She developed very heavy vaginal bleeding yesterday, out of the blue. She doesn't have a regular GYN, so I admitted her, got her transfused, and called someone in to see her. It's the weirdest thing."

"What?"

"She doesn't have any of the usual causes of bleeding," Rothstein said. "I can't figure it out."

"Not your field," Steve said. "She's not pregnant, is she? I got burned like that once."

"No, that's the first thing I checked. The only thing unusual in that area is some sexual dysfunction. And she's gone herbal and eats all kind of organic foods." He paused. "In fact, she's on one of your products."

Steve suddenly felt chilled. "Which one?"

"The one that's supposed to increase sex drive. 'Restore' something. It can't really do that, can it?"

"I'm honestly not sure. You don't know how much she was taking, do you? And for how long?"

"Not really. Is there something I should know about it?"

"I don't think so," Steve said with a smile. "Just out of curiosity, do you know if any of your other patients take Restore-Tabs? And for how long?"

"I'm sure plenty of my patients are taking 'em, but no complaints so far." Rothstein squinted at his colleague. "Why do I get the feeling there's something you're not telling me?"

Steve laughed self-consciously. "I'm just looking out for the best interests of the Ecolabs folks who pay me. What kind of spokesman would I be if I didn't keep my ears open?"

"If you say so," Rothstein said, unconvinced.

Steve slowly returned to his car, no longer in the mood to shop. The number of patients whose hemorrhaging might be related to Restore-Tabs was increasing. It was clear that he'd have to start investigating—calling other colleagues, speaking with nurses and patients, inquiring of health clinics. He couldn't begin the clinical trial soon enough. And he was going to have to find out about Rothstein's Lisa Wells as soon as possible. A quick call to the hospital switchboard, and then to the head nurse on her floor, was all he'd need.

He was beginning to regret his involvement with Ecolabs. He'd been Mr. Good Guy, listening to Ted's pleas and the requests of his patients. If he hadn't been such a people pleaser, he would have listened to his better judgment and never signed on. He now felt like a fool for making those commercials; worse, he was worried about the possible harm Restore-Tabs had done to Andie, Alyssa, and a host of others. He had to seriously rethink what was happening.

He could definitely use some cheering up. His thoughts almost automatically returned to Francesca. She'd been the one bright spot in an otherwise dismal twenty-four hours. On the return drive, he mentally replayed the all-too-brief encounter that was still fresh in his memory: her warm laugh, the touch of her hand, the softness of her lips. He wanted to see her again.

Without thinking, he began heading for the beach house where he'd dropped her off. The logical part of him knew he was behaving like an irrational adolescent, while the emotional part felt an overpowering need. He waged a brief mental skirmish. His decision reflected an alcoholic's thinking, where the desire for gratification was the most important thing in the world. Intellect succumbing to emotion, he continued driving toward the beach.

It wasn't clear to him just what he was looking for. He didn't think it was a relationship; he was still too gun-shy from the trauma of his divorce. And it wasn't merely sex, although the thought of it was enticing. Perhaps, he thought, it was refuge, the tiniest pocket of warmth in his darkest hours.

When he reached Westhampton Beach, it was nearly four. The afternoon was hot, in the low nineties. He crossed the bridge and turned right onto Dune Road. He had no plan. He wasn't sure what he'd do or say if he saw her. The idea of his "just passing by" seemed very contrived. Still, right now that didn't really matter.

He thought it unlikely that he'd see Francesca. Given her tan, she was obviously a sun worshiper, and the best exposure was on the other side of the house, the beach side. He reached the house and slowly drove by. The shades were drawn, and there was no one in sight. The property was a long, rectangular parcel. There were narrow paths on either side of the house, bordered by rose of Sharon, yucca, and black pine hedges. Steve peered down their length.

He drove another hundred yards, hung a U, and pulled to the side of the road, where he waited a few minutes. Then he returned, creeping along the shoulder. Peering down the house's bordering path, he could just see the crest of a dune, beyond which the property sloped toward the beach. The crash of distant breakers rolled inland from the sea. He slumped down in the driver's seat, motor running, gazing out the passenger-side window.

He sat in furtive silence for ten minutes, feeling ridiculous. If any of his patients did this, he'd give them a referral to a psychiatrist. Yet he sat there drumming his fingers on the car seat, feeling childish. And then Francesca came into view, cresting the dune, heading toward the house. At the sight of her, his self-annoyance vanished.

He peered at her a long moment, mesmerized. Her scantily clad figure was as stunning as he'd imagined it. Her long, sculpted legs were lightly muscled, and she walked with a confident stride. She wore a white, midriff-baring tank top above a black bikini bottom. Whoever had done her breasts was a skillful surgeon for, unlike most breast augmentations—which often left the breasts unnaturally widely spaced—Francesca had noticeable cleavage.

She hadn't yet looked his way. Steve suddenly felt an overpowering urge to be by her side. He was about to shout out her name when he saw her stop and turn toward the ocean. Steve hesitated, watching. A man walked over the dune and toward Francesca. Bald and overweight, the man was fiftyish, with a noticeable paunch. When he reached her, the pair exchanged a few words and continued toward the house.

Steve was completely demoralized. In his fantasies, he'd presumed the friends she was staying with were female. It never occurred to him that the friend might be a man. He felt unaccountably jealous. It was an uncomfortable feeling, and its intensity surprised him, although he took some comfort in the fact that the man was both older and heavier than he.

He suddenly felt like a fool. Exactly what had he been expecting? That he'd appear out of nowhere and she'd be thrilled to see him? Get a grip, he told himself. As the pair disappeared into the house, he put the Saab in gear and drove away.

SOUTH PACIFIC

Sergeant Atmosaputro had a problem. It had been weeks since the diver's discovery of the body, and thus far he had no more clues. Both refrigerated victims remained in the morgue in Manado awaiting release to the next of kin. The sergeant desperately wanted to speak with the relatives. However, no one came forward to claim the bodies.

Given what the pathologist said about the tattoos, Atmosaputro thought it might be helpful to advertise. The country had nearly three hundred newspapers, but two of the most widely read were the *Jakarta Pos Kota* and the respected Catholic publication, *Kompas*. He used some of the department's meager funds to take out a personal ad in the eastern Kalimantan and northern Sulawesi editions of both papers.

The ad stated that the police had discovered the bodies of two women in their thirties, possibly from Kalimantan, one of them Dayak. It asked that anyone having information on these or other women who'd disappeared should please contact Sergeant Atmosaputro at the number listed. Thus far, there had been several unrewarding replies. Two callers reported missing women; but from their descriptions, they weren't the women in the morgue. The sergeant took the information nonetheless.

It wasn't until he added the facial sketches to the ad that Atmosaputro got results. A fifty-year-old woman from Sangkulirang in Kalimantan contacted him. Her daughter had disappeared from home nine months earlier. Well, not exactly disappeared, the woman said. Rather, her daughter Aida Suryadi left home voluntarily, for work in Sulawesi. She wasn't sure what kind of work it was, but it paid well. Every three months, the mother received one thousand U.S. dollars by messenger, ostensibly on behalf of her daughter.

Of course, the woman continued in a quivering voice, she was very worried. She hadn't heard from Aida in six months. A thousand dollars quarterly was a fabulous sum, and she feared her daughter was doing something dangerous, perhaps illegal. Aida was a good girl, the woman claimed, not likely to be involved in drugs or prostitution. But now, her worst fears were confirmed.

Atmosaputro asked what impelled the daughter to leave home. The woman claimed Aida had responded to an ad in the *Samarinda Times*, the largest newspaper in the region. The sergeant kicked himself for not having thought of that earlier. He quickly thanked Aida's mother and told her how to claim her daughter's body.

The next step was to see the ad in the *Samarinda Times*. Area newspapers weren't sophisticated enough to be stored on microfilm, so he'd have to review the pages personally. Unfortunately, local libraries kept, at best, a week's worth of the most popular papers. That meant Atmosaputro would have to make a trip to the paper himself.

Such a trip wouldn't be that simple. The flight from Manado to Balikpapan was six hundred miles, and the drive from there to Samarinda was another seventy-five. For a trip of that magnitude, he needed authorization and expense money. Finally, several days later, he had both.

Reluctantly, he said good-bye to his wife, bought a round-trip ticket, and headed for the airport. His wife was a gentle woman dedicated to raising their two small children. After a decade of living in downtown Manado, the family had moved to a remote, sparsely populated suburb. It was a desolate area, and Atmosaputro didn't like to leave his wife alone for extended periods. But it couldn't be helped.

The Garuda Air flight left at ten and reached Balikpapan after noon. Atmosaputro rented a car and drove north, arriving in Samarinda at two-fifteen. He'd called ahead the day before, spoken with the newspaper publisher, and gotten directions. When he reached the editorial offices, he showed his police ID and was directed inside. The publisher greeted him and escorted him to the room containing the back editions.

Atmosaputro took off his jacket and settled in to work. He began with newspapers from the previous September and worked forward. He wasn't sure what he was looking for, but he hoped he'd recognize it if it were there. Painstakingly, he turned each page, inspected every column, and examined the fine print. He came across nothing. But then, in the September twenty-ninth issue, something stood out.

The instant he saw it, he knew this was what he'd been searching for. An organization known as Medical Specialists was recruiting women aged twenty to fifty for unspecified pharmaceutical research in the town of Garontalo. Garontalo, on northern Sulawesi's southern coast, was fifty miles southwest of where Aida's body had been found. "A five-hundred-dollar recruiting fee will be paid to accepted applicants," the ad specified, "followed by substantial additional payments. Selected participants may be employed for up to a year. All replies will be kept confidential. Those interested should reply to Box 102, Central Post Office, Garontalo."

Atmosaputro quickly leafed through subsequent editions of the paper and found that the same ad ran daily for a month, after which it abruptly stopped. He took the paper to one of the secretaries, who directed him to the classifieds editor. The editor examined the ad and nodded. He remembered it, but only vaguely. He did, however, have a listing of advertisers on computer. He called up the file, made a hard copy, and handed the printed page to Atmosaputro.

"Do you have any idea who ran this ad?" he asked, looking at the page.

"I think I do," the editor slowly said. "It was unusual. We simply received a short, typewritten note with the ad copy and instructions that it run for a month."

"What about payment?"

"Right here," indicated the editor. "A money order for the entire amount. No checks, no signatures."

"What about a return address?"

"Just the same Garontalo post office box."

"Strange. I wonder why." The sergeant frowned while he studied the document, then briefly explained the situation.

"Well, I don't know much about medical research," said the editor. "I suppose your woman could have died of medical experiments, but why throw the body into the sea? That would be illegal, wouldn't it?"

"Not to mention unethical. Do you get a lot of advertising from anonymous sources?"

"All the time."

"I don't suppose you have the original request on file?"

The editor did, and he gave the original to the officer. Atmosaputro thanked him and left for the airport. If he was lucky, he could make the seven P.M. return flight to Manado.

He'd need much more luck in Garontalo, where he'd try to locate often-elusive post office boxes from the preceding year.

First thing Monday morning, Steve spoke with his insurance company's attorney. Unfortunately, because there were no office records, there was little the man could offer except a promise to contact the doctor as soon as he received the written complaint. He did say that such cases were very unusual, and it would be extremely difficult for the plaintiff to prove negligence. To Steve, this was little consolation. He went to the hospital to make rounds.

While there, he casually sounded out several colleagues. He was still worried about his Saturday conversation with Dr. Rothstein. After he'd returned home, he'd called the hospital to inquire about Lisa Wells. Questioning the head nurse, he learned that Wells had indeed been taking three Restore-Tabs per day for at least a month. After asking the nurse to keep him posted of any patients with similar problems, Steve hung up.

With the other doctors, he was careful not to directly implicate Restore-Tabs. Rather, he broached the subject in a roundabout manner, feigning nonchalance when he raised the topic of nutritional supplements. Given his position with Ecolabs and his prominence as a spokesperson, most physicians wound up asking *him* about Restore-Tabs. None of his colleagues was aware of any serious problems with supplements, though one did recall a recent patient with heavy vaginal bleeding. He promised to look into it and let Steve know. But what Steve found most interesting was one's suggestion that he try the Internet.

Steve kicked himself, annoyed that he hadn't thought of that himself. The minute he got to the office, he went online. There were over fifteen thousand health-related Web sites, many physician-dedicated. In addition to Medscapes and Emscopes, there were sites for various governmental agencies, including state health departments and the Centers for Disease Control. He checked out several of them, selecting the general category of complementary and alternative medicine. Then, using the keywords *adverse reactions,* he began a search. There were no reports of problems with Restore-Tabs.

He thought it might be a little premature, since adverse-reaction reports took a while to generate and the product hadn't been around that long. And not just anyone off the street could make an unsubstantiated claim against a product. It was more likely that such allegations would take the form of anecdotes found in chat rooms or posted to Internet bulletin boards. Yet when he checked, these areas were similarly empty, except for one brief entry. A Massachusetts physician reported treating a patient with uterine hemorrhage who'd been taking Restore-Tabs. He asked if any other health-care providers had encountered that problem.

Steve quickly emailed a reply. He revealed his own experience, outlined his suspicions, and asked for more information in return. That done, he now knew he needed help more than ever. It was time to get the government involved—slowly, diplomatically, and hopefully without a backlash on Ecolabs. He returned to the Web and found the FDA Web site. Next, he located directions for logging onto a site called MedWatch, a program designed for reporting by health-care professionals.

He found what he was looking for in MedWatch Form 3500, a five-part form that could be submitted online. He carefully typed in the sections for patient information, using Alyssa, then adverse reaction or product problem, suspect medication, and reporter. He described Alyssa's bleeding as a *possible* problem. Finally, confirming his submission, he was done.

Steve wondered how long it would take to get a reply, if he got one at all. This was, after all, the federal government, an agency not known for its speed. From the way the form had been worded, he wasn't even sure he would *get* a reply. That wouldn't be acceptable. If and when the time came, he'd follow up with phone calls, even if he had to call the commissioner.

Karen Trent's gynecologist was Stanley Richards. She'd last seen him a year before, when she'd first started skipping periods. He diagnosed her as peri-menopausal, meaning she was near the time of menopause. Otherwise, except for being slightly overweight, she was in good health. Now, when she returned bleeding, he immediately performed an endometrial biopsy in the office, suctioning off some uterine cells and sending them for pathologic exam.

The results revealed a condition called atypical endometrial hyperplasia. Dr. Richards said it was considered pre-malignant, and if the heavy bleeding recurred, he'd have to recommend a hysterectomy. At that point, Karen inquired about Restore-Tabs. It wasn't that she distrusted Dr. McLaren's judgment; she just wanted another opinion.

Dr. Richards told her, in no uncertain terms, that he thought his younger colleague was way off base. Richards had personally checked the literature and found nothing to implicate Restore-Tabs as the cause of Karen's problem. Besides, he said, Steve McLaren was being overly cautious. He had a proprietary interest in the company that sponsored him. That was good enough for Karen.

She'd stopped taking the product right after she visited McLaren. But given what Dr. Richards said, and now that she had a clean bill of health, she thought it safe to resume taking the supplement. Besides, she'd lost fourteen pounds. Her breasts were full again, her figure softly rounded.

Yet what really tipped the scales was the call from Jared. Apparently, he no longer needed his space, and he wanted to get together to talk. He implied that his thirty-year-old paramour was having second thoughts about a man his age. For a while, Karen mulled it over. She wanted to make him suffer, to hurt him the way he'd wounded her. After all, she'd given her best years and the better part of her life to the man. But at the same time, she desperately wanted him back.

She finally said yes to a meeting—and the instant she did, she resumed taking large doses of Restore-Tabs. She realized that Dr. Richards's opinion was no doubt based on following the package directions, but in her heart, Karen doubted a few more would hurt. And if four a day helped her lose weight and become more curvaceous, five would be even better. After all, she wanted to be in the best shape possible for her reunion with Jared.

That had been weeks ago. Unfortunately, the meeting with her husband didn't turn out as she'd hoped. Despite his words to the contrary, Jared remained uncommitted, saying he needed more time. Karen glumly acceded to his wishes. One had to crawl before learning to walk. At least Jared seemed to have an open mind. Best of all, she thought he was impressed with her weight and figure. Encouraged, Karen continued taking the supplement.

And then, quite unexpectedly, her bleeding resumed. At

first it was only a trickle, without the relentless cramps she'd experienced before. But as the day wore on, it got heavier. She debated whether to call Dr. Richards. She remembered what he'd said about a hysterectomy, and she was frightened. She decided to wait. That night, as she lay in bed, wrestling with her concerns, she lightly explored her entire body with her fingertips, as if testing the integrity of her flesh. It was then that Karen discovered the breast lump.

Jack Buhlman knew a tremendous amount about computers. No geek or weekend hacker, he had supplied them for State Department ventures worldwide. He was more familiar with prices, shipping dates, and means of volume transport than with the internal workings of a mother board or computer syntax. But in the last two years of his government employment, when he began to realize that his career at State might be in jeopardy, he learned as much as he could about the fine points of computer manipulation. And he learned from experts, not only at the State Department, but also in sister agencies. Before he left, he knew a great deal about master systems, encryption, computer surveillance, and security.

After he went into business for himself, he continued to learn. Before he could ship twenty thousand IBM clones, peripherals, and accessories to a developing nation, he had to know precisely what he was selling, which meant that he had to be intimately familiar with computer capabilities and applications. A Third World nation might want to know the best way to keep tabs on troublemakers, or how to most efficiently supply its army, something Jack could write volumes about. Most of the time that meant helping install expert systems for intercomputer communication. By the time he began consulting for Ecolabs, he was a master at tweaking the Internet, and he used his former federal contacts to help him gain access to government agencies and their computers.

At the beginning of the year, he got a copy of the experimental software program called Minuteman from a technogeek who owed him a favor. Originally designed for the National Security Agency, Minuteman let its user discover who on the outside was trying to request often-classified information from mainframes on the inside. Like its Revolutionary War counterparts, Minuteman was an early-alert tool, and like the missile, it could be put into action at a moment's notice. Minuteman was Jack's radar, and he used it as an early-warning system. By entering the keyword "Ecolabs" or one of its products—with an emphasis on Restore-Tabs—he could discover when someone was seeking or transmitting information about the company or any of its supplements.

Minuteman surveillance had been scoring hits for over six months. Jack was primarily interested in communications with the FDA, although he ran across other messages sent to various cabinet departments and executive agencies. Since the entire context of the message or request showed up on his monitor, he was able to learn exactly who was trying to find out what. By intercepting these messages and their replies, he could often redirect the messages to other areas, or send additional replies in official-sounding but meaningless governmentspeak. Most inquiries were of the meddlesome or nuisance variety and didn't concern him much.

But then came a communication from Dr. Steven McLaren, something that upset Jack a great deal.

The shipment from Ecolabs was delivered to Steve's office by UPS that afternoon. Steve was a little surprised that the shipment actually arrived, but Francesca was as good as her word. Becky and Donna helped him unload the boxes. There were hundreds of unidentified, hundred-tablet bottles labeled Clinical Trial—Not Intended for Sale. Each bottle bore a different identifying number, and Steve understood that some were Restore-Tabs, while others were placebos. There were also reams of professionally printed documents shrouded in legalese, and several posters for the waiting-room wall.

Steve slowly read the form entitled Investigational Informed Consent. The document outlined the expectations of both provider and trial patient, revealed certain possible mild side effects, explained the study's purpose, underscored that a patient might receive either product or placebo, and most important, emphasized certain risks and complications. It explained that Restore-Tabs was a new natural source of estrogen, and that although none of traditional estrogen's disadvantages had been documented, that remained a remote possibility. While this last section was largely boilerplate gibberish, Steve was gratified to see that it included, in bold type, the statement that "one physician reported cases of heavy vaginal bleeding in patients taking the supplement in much larger doses than recommended."

In addition to the lengthy consent form, there was also an enrollment form. Besides requesting patient demographic information, it explained that the intended study length was three months. There was also a page entitled Patient Expectations and a separate hold-harmless document: in return for enrolling the patient in the free clinical trial, the form indemnified both Ecolabs and Dr. Steven McLaren from any future litigation.

"They certainly did their homework," he said, putting the documents down. Describing what their roles would be in the trial, he explained to Becky and Donna the purpose of the double-blind technique.

"So we don't know who's getting what?" asked Donna.

"You don't know, and neither do they," he replied. "That's why it's called double-blind. After three months, we ship everything back to Ecolabs. They collate all the data: which patient got what, patient satisfaction or lack thereof, perceived results, objective results, and any side effects. Then they break the codes and let us know how everyone did."

"How many patients are they looking for?"

"The more the better, but at least a hundred," he said. "At the rate this stuff is selling, we should have no problem giving it away for free."

When they were done, Steve was doubly satisfied. Although the Restore-Tabs patients who bled were never far from his mind, he felt he hadn't compromised his intellectual integrity. He truly believed he was doing everything possible for the patients' benefit, and he was satisfied that his conscience was clear.

At least for now.

*   *   *

He was in a good mood when he woke up Tuesday morning. The previous night had been cool, and Steve had left the window open, knowing he always slept better when there was a chill in the air. He got out of bed, walked across the room, and looked outside, resting his fingers on a sill wet with glistening dew. A trio of nervous sparrows fluttered away to a nearby tree. The air was celery crisp, its freshness calling to him. It was a morning for outdoor puttering. Since a full hour remained before he had to leave for the office, he put on his robe and went downstairs.

Outside, he picked the newspaper off the stoop and stretched, feeling alive. The morning air was rich with scents of pine and humus. The edge of his property by the road was sparsely planted, with large gaps between the oaks. The previous fall he'd ordered specialty lilacs and honeysuckle from an exclusive mail-order firm and planted them before the frost. Now they were in full bloom, and their fragrance swept over the front yard in waves of perfume. He slowly walked toward the street, savoring the slowly warming morning sun.

He was training the honeysuckle to grow over a trellis. The variety had unusual orange-red blossoms and was a vigorous grower. Several curling vine tendrils reached skyward, looking for a place to attach themselves, hovering tentatively like mantises. Standing on the blacktop in his slippers, Steve pushed the wayward tender shoots back toward the house, wrapping their spiraling tips around the trellis. He was almost finished when he heard the loud roar off to his right.

Turning in the direction of the sound, Steve looked in paralyzed disbelief. Not more than fifty feet away, a vehicle was bearing down on him. It seemed to have come out of nowhere, and as he stared at it, frozen in shock, he watched it swerve off the road and tear up the grass until it headed right for him. In an instant of icy clarity, he noticed that it was a Mercedes SUV, its three-pronged logo dazzling on the hood. Gathering his wits only seconds before the car hit him, Steve hurled himself toward the trellis.

The vehicle roared past in a wave of exhaust, fumes,

and pebbles. As Steve hurtled through the latticework, the hem of his robe got caught in the bumper of the Mercedes, and the robe was ripped from his body. Spun by the torque, his torso crashed heavily through the trellis, turning it into splinters. His body did a three-sixty before plopping heavily onto the earth.

Wincing from the impact, more stunned than hurt, he opened his eyes and stared at the departing SUV. The vehicle was accelerating away from him, and he couldn't make out the license plate. A dull, jarring ache ran through his body but slowly lessened. He rolled onto his back, breathing heavily as he stared up into the placid sky.

All he could do was wonder why. He had the impression the driver was a man, although the vehicle's tinted glass obscured the face. As he lay there amidst dirt and splinters, stripped of his robe and vulnerable in his boxers, he felt shaken to the core, and more frightened than he'd ever been in his life.

8

Steve told no one about the attempted hit-and-run.

It had all happened so fast. One minute he'd been relishing the fresh summer morning, and the next he lay bruised and filthy in a pile of splinters. He supposed it was possible that an out-of-control driver had simply lost control of the SUV, although he doubted it. He'd been lucky: physically, his only injuries were bumps and stiffness; emotionally, he was stupefied, in a kind of posttraumatic shock.

It occurred to him that he should report the incident to the police, but that seemed pointless. He'd been eyeball-to-eyeball with death, yet he'd seen virtually nothing. He had absolutely no idea who'd tried to run him down, or why. Although Phoebe Atkinson came to mind, the idea that she'd do something so ruthless seemed preposterous. Moreover, he had no desire to have the cops publicly examine his recent life for people who might have motives.

As for telling his friends what happened, that would simply make them worry at a time he was doing enough worrying for everyone. The bottom line was that he was going to have to live his life very cautiously, more carefully than ever before. If someone had a grudge to settle, Steve would find out soon enough. And so he got up, brushed himself off, straightened up the mess, and went into the house.

By the end of the week, there had been no suggestion of further trouble, and Steve began to relax. Maybe it had just been a freak accident. He still hadn't heard from the FDA, but the clinical trial was fully under way. Most of his patients were aware of Dr. McLaren's involvement with nutritional supplements, from seeing either his TV commercials or the posters in his office. The new poster mentioned Restore-Tabs and had the word *free* printed in large block letters. By Thursday afternoon, more than sixty patients had signed up.

The call from Francesca was as unexpected as it was welcome.

"I just called to see how things were going," she began. "The shipment arrived okay?"

"Yeah, a few days ago. How's everything with you?"

"Good, thanks. Did you have a chance to look over the materials?"

In his mind's eye, he imagined her in her bikini. She stimulated thoughts and feelings that were light-years away from Restore-Tabs. Right now, the last thing he wanted to discuss was the clinical trial. "I did. Very professionally done."

"Great. It all seemed pretty straightforward to me, but I wanted to make sure everything was understandable. Do you or any of your staff have any questions about it?"

"No," he said, "we got the hang of it."

"Did any patients sign up yet?"

"The word *free* always brings 'em running."

"What about the patients? Is there any confusion, especially about the consent form?"

"Not exactly confusion," he said. "More like complaining. Some of them want to know if there's any way they can be sure they won't get the placebo."

"What does your staff tell them?"

Steve could almost picture the playful smile on her face. "They give them a version of the 'there's no free lunch' routine: If you want something for nothing, you've got to take a risk. Everyone who signs up has an equal chance of getting Restore-Tabs."

"That's perfect, Steve. I'm happy it's going so smoothly. I guess there's nothing to do now but wait."

He closed his eyes, inhaling deeply. He could picture her face with hallucinatory clarity. The idea of waiting was totally unacceptable to him. His eagerness to see her bordered on desperation, and he *had* to find out who the older man was. "Tell you what, Francesca. I know how important this study is to both of us. Instead of waiting three months, why don't I fill you in on a regular basis? We can get together, have a cup of coffee, and I'll bring you up to date."

She wanted to see him too, but she didn't want her interest to be too obvious. "Great idea. Is once a month too often?"

"Come on, I really need your input. I was thinking of once a week. In fact, what are you doing this weekend?"

"No study goes *that* fast," she said with a laugh. "Seriously, is that the only reason you want to get together?"

"Okay. I really enjoyed having dinner with you last week. You're a terrific conversationalist, and I was more relaxed than I've been in a long time. I was hoping we could do it again."

There was a lengthy pause. "We will do it again, I promise. It's just that . . . you're right, this study *is* important. I hope it'll lead to the conclusion I want, but more than anything, the answer you come up with has got to be an honest one. Nothing should sidetrack you from that goal. What I'm saying is, I don't think it's a good idea to mix business with pleasure."

"All I'm talking about is a latte at Starbucks, not a long-term relationship."

"I know, Steve. But not right now. I want to feel comfortable about this, and now's not a good time for me."

He hung up, demoralized. As often as he'd been shot down when he was younger, it had never felt so painful. As his old feeling of inadequacy returned, he wondered if Francesca was beyond his reach.

Maybe he just wasn't her type.

SULAWESI, INDONESIA

Sergeant Atmosaputro turned off his computer and got up, shaking his head. Computer literacy was little more than a humorous buzzword in his country. Most people were too impoverished to buy computers. The majority of the populace still lived in rural areas on one of the country's thirteen thousand islands, and computerization was a big-city phenomenon. Metropolitan areas like Jakarta, which teemed with students, were hubs of silicon interaction.

Of course, smaller cities like Manado were increasingly computerized, mainly in the private sector and, to a lesser extent, in government. The slow pace of computerization in the public service sector was a disappointment. With President Suharto's resignation, reformers had called for westernizing technology. Technological advances were supposed to occur once the new leadership was elected in

1999, but so far, little had changed. Atmosaputro had hoped to communicate with the postal service via his email, but that proved impossible.

Alas, he'd have to track down what he wanted the old way, in person. The drive from Manado to Gorontalo took five hours. He left early and arrived at noon, impressed, as always, by the town's appearance. Gorontalo was a pleasant Muslim city, its center a set piece of whitewashed, verandahed, and wooden-shuttered Dutch bungalows. The town retained much of its colonial charm, and many downtown residents spoke both Dutch and English.

He'd never met the head of the local post office. He decided to come without calling ahead.

Pak Warno Soetrisno, regional postmaster for twenty years, was a short, wizened man in his fifties. He was about to break for lunch when the sergeant knocked on the door and presented his ID.

"Sorry to disturb you, Pak Warno," Atmosaputro began. "I am investigating the disappearance and deaths of several women found in the ocean north of here."

"I am always happy to assist the police. But I know nothing of such deaths."

"No, of course. I was hoping you could shed some light on this."

Soetrisno examined the newspaper ad. "Yes, this box is here, all right. When did this run?"

"In September of last year."

Pak Warno arose from his desk. "Let me see what I can find."

He left and went down the hall. Atmosaputro looked around the room, the cramped work area of a tidy bureaucrat. The floors and walls were covered with neatly stacked files, and the office smelled of yellowing paper and *sambal*, a spicy sauce. Moments later, Soetrisno returned.

"I remember this, now," he said. "We rarely get requests from anyone in the health field."

"Is the postal box still rented?"

"I'm afraid not," said Soetrisno. "The rental was for only two months."

"Do you know this organization, Medical Specialists?"

"No, but I know the gentleman who rented the box. I

didn't take the order myself, but I saw who did the paperwork with the clerk. It was Dr. Sayed."

Sayed, Atmosaputro thought. He was familiar with the name. Although the physician had a modest practice, he was well known to the authorities in northern Sulawesi for botched abortions. "That's very helpful, Pak Warno. I would appreciate your making a copy of the paperwork. By any chance, do you happen to have Dr. Sayed's address?"

The sergeant called his office in Manado for an update on Sayed. Half an hour later, he pulled up at the doctor's office, a neat white bungalow like the others on the block. He showed the startled receptionist his credentials and was immediately escorted to an empty consultation room.

The doctor was not happy to see him. Mohammed Sayed was a man in his late forties. His sudden frown enhanced his distinguished appearance, as he was well-dressed in the latest Western style.

"I'm rather busy today, Sergeant. I hope you'll make this brief."

"I'll come right to the point, Doctor." He showed him the ad and the postal paperwork. "I wonder if you could tell me about this."

Sayed managed to glance at the documents without twitching. He was either ignorant of their significance or a very skillful liar. "I've never heard of Medical Specialists."

"And the postal box?"

The doctor's voice betrayed no emotion. "I can't help you with that. All my mail comes here."

"I see." From his jacket pocket, Atmosaputro removed the notes of his conversation with his office. "Are you familiar with a missionary named Birgit Von Riel?"

Sayed stared at him. He kept quiet, but the jaws in his muscles began to work.

"Sister Birgit was a problem for the Catholic mission in Parepare. It seems the sister was not as chaste as the church would have liked. Apparently, she'd had an illegitimate child sometime in the past, and to the best of our information, she recently got pregnant again."

"I had nothing to do with the birth."

"Of course not." Atmosaputro spoke in a calm monotone. "As a medical professional, I'm sure you'll be distressed to learn that Sister Birgit died in May at a hospital in Ujung Pandang. Complications from an illegal abortion."

A twitch began in Sayed's eye, but he remained silent.

"Although the church mourns her loss, I am told they are not displeased with the outcome. They wish no major investigation and its attendant publicity. The police, however, look at it differently. You see, wherever there are patterns . . ."

Beads of sweat broke out on the doctor's forehead. "I don't know what you're talking about."

Atmosaputro approached in slow, deliberate steps. "Let me come right to the point, Doctor. Much as you may wish it, we are not a Western democracy. With one call, I could have you arrested in minutes. Led through your waiting room in handcuffs, disgraced. Yes, you might eventually be released, but not before your office was thoroughly searched. I'm sure we could convince your staff to cooperate in searching for certain records. Do you want me to go on?"

Sayed removed a silk handkerchief, wiped his brow, and slumped into a chair behind his desk. "And if I tell you what you want?"

"Like I said, the church considers this matter a disgrace. If you cooperate, we could probably let the matter slide. Assuming there was no repetition." He paused. "How much did they pay you to place the ad?"

Sayed had to think for only a moment. "Five thousand U.S. dollars. My involvement was minimal," he went on, appearing relieved. "All I did was screen some women. I sent them a medical questionnaire, and when they replied, I selected the fittest. I directed the ones selected to an address up north. When I was told they arrived, I authorized payment to them, or their families."

"How many women were there?" the sergeant asked.

"There were many replies, but I chose about fifty."

"Chose for what?"

"That, I don't know."

"Medical research?"

"I suppose that's possible," Sayed said, "but I never learned. I had no contact with them once they went away."

"Was it something that might have gotten them killed?"

"I can't say."

"Where did you send them?"

"You know Inobonto?"

Inobonto was a town in the northern hills overlooking the Celebes Sea. It was close to the spot where Pak Suranto found the body. "Of course."

"I am told there is a clinic in the hills east of town. The women took public transit, and when they got off the bus, they were taken to the clinic."

"This clinic is run by Medical Specialists?"

"I don't know."

"They're the ones who paid you, weren't they?"

"No," the doctor replied. "I was paid by a company called Ecolabs."

"Did you hear from that son of a bitch yet?"

"Not yet, Miss Atkinson. But it's only been a week. Normally, he'll contact his malpractice carrier and let them carry the ball. They still have two weeks to respond."

"Do they respond to you or to the court?"

"What usually happens," her attorney explained, "is that the lawyer for the malpractice company contacts the plaintiff's attorney to let him know he's on the case. Then the plaintiff's attorney withdraws the subpoena."

The indignation in her voice was apparent. "Suppose he never notified them? You don't know the man! He's one of those arrogant doctors who'd just throw the damn thing in the trash!"

"I suppose that could happen," her attorney replied. "Maybe you can explain something to me. One thing I'm not clear about is why you're going after this man. If I'm going to represent you, I'd like to have the complete picture."

"That doesn't concern you. I'm certainly paying you enough."

"Actually, Miss Atkinson, everything about this case concerns me. The last thing any lawyer wants to do is to go into court blind. Is this some kind of vendetta? Is there something personal between you and the doctor?"

Phoebe fell silent. She had no desire to discuss her motives with the hired help. Anyway, it was a long time ago.

Ten years, in fact. Ten years since a young Dr. McLaren
let her best friend die of breast cancer.

Just thinking about it made her shiver. Her friend had
gone to the bright, new doctor on the block because she'd
been frightened about a breast lump. Maybe he was incom-
petent because he was so recently out of training, but
McLaren made light of it. He patronized Phoebe's friend
and said he didn't believe the lump was anything serious.
That was a laugh. Within eighteen months of the misdi-
agnosis, her friend was dead. The family didn't pursue it,
and McLaren had gotten off without so much as a wrist
slap.

Over the years, Phoebe had fumed when people raved
about the doctor, and she was infuriated when she saw his
face on TV, touting a supplement she'd just begun taking
herself.

And then there he was at the fund-raiser, smugly saying
he *believed* nutritional supplements were safe. She wanted
to doubt him; but the problem was, she liked the product.
Okay, so she'd taken a larger than recommended dose of
Restore-Tabs. It certainly seemed to work for her, making
the fine lines near her eyes much less noticeable. But then,
coincidentally, she hemorrhaged. Her doctor placed her on
a medication that seemed to help. Yet McLaren was a char-
latan, and she dearly wanted to nail him—especially after
she received that incriminating letter about him.

"Of course there's nothing personal," she said. "I was
never a patient of his, and I'd just met the man. I just think
the way he bungled my case was criminal. Don't you think
the public should be protected from incompetents like
him?"

"All right, Miss Atkinson, I'll keep on it. There are only
a few malpractice carriers in this region. I'm sure I can find
out who insures him and if he has notified them. If so, I'll
try to speed things up."

Before he left the office on Friday afternoon, Steve tried to
follow up his online adverse-reaction submission with the
FDA. He was annoyed that he hadn't been called or been
emailed a reply all week. How could they be so sloppy, so
inconsiderate? They were dealing with the lives of young

women here, including his daughter! They could at least have had the courtesy to get back to him.

He got the number of the regional FDA office from information and phoned them. Since he didn't have a particular name, he was connected with the complaint coordinator. The woman explained that not all form 3500s were replied to, and those that were usually took several weeks. She sounded tired, bored, and a little annoyed, but she wasn't nearly as annoyed as Steve. He threatened and cajoled until he was finally given a number to call in Washington.

It was a little after four when he reached CFSAN, the FDA's Center for Food Safety and Applied Nutrition. The switchboard operator told him that most people were gone for the weekend but did put him through to the office of the director, Joseph Hubbard, Ph.D. Considering the time, Dr. Hubbard's executive assistant was reasonably sympathetic, but there was little she could do except take a message. Steve tried to sound civil when he was given the director's voice mail.

"This is Dr. Steven McLaren," he began, after leaving the time and date of the call, his office number, and his address. "I'm a family practitioner in eastern Long Island. Last Monday, I forwarded a form 3500 online, and so far I haven't heard a thing. I was reporting a possible problem with Restore-Tabs, a supplement made by Ecolabs in Westchester. Let me make it plain up front that I have no ax to grind with Ecolabs. From what I can tell, they're a very reputable herbal product manufacturer. In fact, I work as a paid spokesperson for their general product line." He considered adding that the director may have seen him on TV but thought better of it.

"The reason I'm going about this through the back door, so to speak, is because I'm not sure some of the company's higher-ups want to go the voluntary route. But to make a long story short, I'm starting to wonder, though I have no real proof of this, whether very large doses of Restore-Tabs might be related to some patients' developing heavy vaginal bleeding. I'm a little worried, and also concerned that no one's gotten back to me. I'm trying to be open-minded and not overreact. I hope that if there is a problem, and I'm not certain there is, we can touch base on this and see where to go, or just drop it. So please, *please* get back to me as soon as possible." Then he hung up, not sure he'd accomplished anything at all.

In days gone by, Steve had not been a great lover of orchids, whose requirements seemed too fastidious for him. Their need for a certain temperature range, an unusual growing medium, steady humidity, and summering outdoors was too demanding. But that was before he'd built his greenhouse. As the room grew more lush, the dappled light within became more junglelike, and by keeping the root bark damp, the greenhouse grew acceptably humid. Orchids thrived in those conditions.

Unfortunately, only a small number of orchids had a fragrance. But the ones that did were delightful. Some had a citrussy aroma; others smelled like vanilla. Better growers were able to supply him with unusually fragrant varieties. Angraecum was delightful, as was *Cattleya lawrenceana*. His favorite, however, was an oncidium whose dainty, lavender fleur-de-lis blossoms had an indescribable cinnamon scent that turned his greenhouse into a spice factory. He was repotting it early in the evening when the phone rang.

"Steve, did I get you at a bad time?" Francesca asked.

"It's never a bad time to hear from you. You always seem to get me in my greenhouse."

"I'm developing this bad habit of calling you at home."

He laughed. "Well . . . I think I can be persuaded not to call Bell Atlantic security. Go on, persuade me."

"That's why I called. I've been having second thoughts about mixing business with pleasure. I didn't mean to come across like an old-fashioned prude."

"There was nothing remotely old-fashioned about that outfit you wore for dinner."

"Thank you. You know, I just finished up a business meeting not far from you, and I'm going to take a long weekend. Are you still up for that cup of coffee?"

Jeff's mother picked Andie up at seven-twenty for the movie due to start half an hour later. Jeff sat in front, Kevin and Matt were already in the backseat, and Andie squeezed in beside them. It wasn't unusual for the four of them to go out together. They'd been in the same class since the sixth grade and were extremely comfortable in one another's company. Andie never thought of it as dating, not in the same way her mother dated a generation before. Rather, she and her friends just hung out together, often joined by even more kids. Although she didn't have a formal curfew, it was understood that she'd be home by midnight at the latest, and usually by eleven P.M. Andie never tested those limits.

That night, however, she didn't feel well. While the guys joked and kibitzed, she said little and didn't join in. When the boys tried to draw her out and asked her what was wrong, she said, "Nothing," a generational reply meaning 'don't bother me,' or 'I don't want to talk about it.' She didn't share any of their nachos or down her customary two slices of pizza. The fact was, she was a little nauseated, and her stomach was bothering her. She couldn't wait to go home.

The movie was pretty good, but all she could think of was when it would end. It was a little after nine when she felt the wetness. It wasn't much; it didn't drip or seep through her clothing. It was just there. She didn't have to touch herself to know it was blood. That figures, she thought. The icing on the cake. She didn't have any cramps yet, but she knew they would come. The worst thing about an irregular cycle was that her period could come any time it wanted. She wasn't wearing a tampon, but she always carried a small napkin in her purse. She got up and headed for the ladies' room.

As she walked up the aisle and through the doorway, Andie couldn't help feeling a little guilty. She was also getting worried. She hadn't been honest with her father, and she'd lied to her mother when she said she wasn't taking any more Restore-Tabs. But she'd lost seven pounds, and . . . She *was* going to stop taking them. That much she promised herself.

Soon.

They got together at an out-of-the-way coffee shop in Hampton Bays, where they had cheeseburgers and decaf. Steve asked about her day. Francesca was the only person

at Ecolabs who did public relations—preparing press re-
leases, writing copy, fielding inquiries, working with ad
agencies, and coordinating print, radio, and TV slots. She
described her job with enthusiasm, and Steve could tell that
she loved it.

When she inquired about what he'd been doing, he told
her about his passion for fragrant tropical plants. At first,
she thought it odd that an eligible man should be so interested in plants. Something about the concept struck her as
effeminate. Yet there was nothing remotely feminine about
Steve McLaren. He had a ruggedly masculine appearance,
and if this was a hobby he enjoyed, so be it. He described
the greenhouse he'd installed. Steve had an animated way
of speaking about things he liked, and Francesca loved
watching his expression while he spoke. In truth, she'd
thought about him a great deal since they'd had dinner. She
remembered every one of his mannerisms, and although she
didn't want to appear too aggressive, she wanted to see him
again.

"There's something very therapeutic, even spiritual,
about working with plants," he explained. "And they have
fewer demands than pets."

"You never have to take them for a walk?"

"You got it," he said, nodding with a smile. "But they
still need food and water."

"What makes you so passionate about plants?"

He looked away, thinking. "I suppose it's because raising plants like these gives me a different perspective on
life. I'm always wondering about my place in the universe,
the cosmos."

"What it all means?"

"Something like that," he said. "I'm not a religious person, but I've wrestled with who I am and where I'm going
for a long time. I can't say that I believe in an afterlife.
But with gardening, I feel 'part of.' This might sound
weird, but I feel a kinship with growing things, like we're
all part of some big cosmic continuum. In a way, I think
that we never really die, because all our molecules and
atoms ultimately become another form of energy. And that
energy leads to more energy . . . Does any of this make
sense to you?"

"All that really matters," she said, "is whether it makes sense to you."

"Yes, I suppose," he said with a nod. He looked into her eyes. "I'd like you to see the greenhouse sometime."

She pushed her coffee cup away. "What about now?"

Fifteen minutes later, he pulled into his driveway. Francesca followed in her rental car. He unlocked the front door and let her in.

"This looks like a very comfortable place," she said, looking around.

"Good choice of adjective," he said. "Comfort is about all I can afford right now. I guess you heard that I'm divorced."

"Ted mentioned it. He also said you had a daughter."

"Fifteen," he said, "going on twenty. Anyway, the settlement's costing me an arm and a leg. Come on, I'll show you the plants."

It was an old house, lived-in but tidy. Steve led Francesca toward the east-facing greenhouse. The aroma was immediately noticeable, a pleasantly overpowering perfume. Francesca stopped, breathing deeply.

"My God, what's that fantastic smell?"

"Jasmine and gardenia. Some people think it's a little over-the-top, but I never get tired of it."

"I can understand why. It's like being at the florist's, only more intense. Richer, deeper."

"That's from the humidity," he explained. "It enhances the fragrance. The nice thing is that the aroma's always changing, depending on what's in bloom. Sometimes it's spicy, sometimes a little pungent, or even fruity." He paused and looked around. "There's something very earthy about this room. Peaceful, you might say. To me, it's a jungle paradise."

She approached a small shrub with glossy green leaves and creamy white flowers the size of boutonnieres. "Which one is this?"

"Gardenia jasmenoides, an ever-blooming variety. I have two of them. One blossom follows the next." He took scissors and snipped off a fresh flower. He skewered its stem with a safety pin and carefully attached it to Francesca's blouse. "There you go. Ready for the prom."

She inclined her head and inhaled its bouquet. "Hmmm, intoxicating. Thank you," she said, kissing him lightly on the cheek. "I could stay in this room all night. Have you ever slept in here?"

"Now there's a thought," he said, feeling slightly unnerved. "Maybe someday I will. Can I get you something to drink?"

"You're beet red," she said with a smile, touching his arm, liking what her presence was doing to him. "Did I say something that embarrassed you?"

"This is the first time I've been kissed in a greenhouse."

"I see," she said, gazing at him intently. Then she looked around the room. "Why don't you show me what else is here?"

He did so, feeling relieved. Her light touch continued, as if she were holding his arm for balance. He distracted himself by explaining his collection. Never letting go of his arm, Francesca asked about plant care and propagation. A quarter hour later, he picked up both gardenia pots and headed outside.

"Can you grab that door for me? It's time to put these guys outdoors for the summer."

She followed him down two concrete steps to a patio, where he placed the potted shrubs under a cutleaf Japanese maple. A full moon shone overhead. He led her to a bench swing, left behind by the original owners. Rocking gently, they leaned against the soft seat backs, gazing up at the moon. Moments later, she got up and stretched out on the grass.

"I remember nights like this when I was growing up," she said. "I used to lie on my back in the grass, looking up at the moon, and try to mentally transport myself to the Sea of Tranquility."

"How was the trip?"

She laughed. "The only trips I made were with funny little cigarettes."

"Where'd you grow up?"

"A little town in Ohio."

"Why don't we try some telepathy together?" he suggested. "Sort of harness the force. Let me get something to lie on, and I'll join you."

She watched him go inside. She found him a very likable man: well-built, athletic, and entering middle life gracefully. The way he blushed was touching. Obviously intelligent, he still had a young man's vulnerability. There was something appealing about his sensitive side, and she felt drawn to him.

Returning, he spread the blanket on the cool, slightly damp grass. Francesca rolled onto it, and he joined her. Soon they lay side by side, arms touching.

"Ready?" she asked, seeing him nod. "Okay, go."

For several moments, they concentrated intently on the starlit sky. Steve glanced at her out of the corner of his eye.

"You there yet?" he asked, trying to restrain a laugh. "I'm afraid it's not working for me."

"Me neither," she said with an exaggerated sigh. "Thwarted again."

"You know, Francesca, I'm glad you had second thoughts about mixing business with pleasure."

"So am I," she said, touching the back of his hand.

Her nearness emboldened him. He wanted to know with whom she'd stayed. "I'm glad you could make it out here. But to tell you the truth, you're the *last* person I thought would have a weekend free. No main man in your life?"

"Not right now. Oh, I see one or two people, but nothing serious."

"That's a relief."

Francesca unexpectedly sat up. Her fingers flew to her face, and McLaren looked at her, concerned.

"What's wrong?"

"Something in my eye," she said apprehensively, tugging at her lid. "I think it's a bug."

"Don't rub it," he said. "Just keep blinking until your tears wash it out."

Head inclined forward, her lids fluttered rapidly. In the moonlight, he could see her eyes reflexively fill with tears. At length, her blinking slowed. He could just make out a dark speck in the corner of her eye. He wiped it away with his thumb and then used a corner of the blanket to dry her tears. With her moist cheeks and crooked little scar, she looked so vulnerable to him, like an injured child.

"How's that?" he asked, gently kneading the back of her neck with his fingertips.

"Much better," she said, nodding. Their faces were nearly touching, and she gazed into his eyes. "I left my insurance card at home."

"I'm sure we can arrange another form of payment."

He slowly drew her face nearer, and her mouth parted just before their lips met. He gently stroked her mouth with his, a satiny caress. Compared to the night's cool breeze, her lips were dry and feverish. Then he kissed her still-damp eyes, tasting the salt of her tears. He folded her face into the hollow of his neck and put his arms around her.

She felt wonderfully soft. The night air was scented with honeysuckle and early-blooming tuberoses. As he pressed her body to his, he inhaled deeply, savoring the hint of Joy on her neck and shoulders. The breeze lifted her dark tresses. Her blown hair was sweet on his face.

He felt her lips start to explore his neck, and he closed his eyes contentedly. Her slender fingers, tingly on his arms, gently stroked his shoulders. Her warm breath rolled across his skin. He held her, his face lying tangled in her dancing hair. His hands fell to her lower back, thin yet supple beneath her top. Her back arched, and her rising bosom pressed into his chest.

"Kiss me," she whispered.

His mouth found her soft, pliant lips, lips touched by fire. Then her lips parted, and her tongue slid past his, testing, probing, seeking. His throat felt impossibly dry. All at once he hungered for her. His encircling arms squeezed her tight, and his open mouth crushed hers. The way she returned his kiss was stimulating, and her lips seemed to suck forth his soul.

Francesca grew increasingly aroused. She knew that sometimes she came on too strong, but now she wanted him.

The bright, filtered moonlight bathed them in marbled, chiaroscuro shadows. Their faces parted, and he gazed intently into her dark, smoky eyes. Her chest was heaving. He leaned forward to kiss her neck. Her hands went to the back of his head, and she drew his face to her bosom. He slowly rolled his head from side to side, caressing the swell of her covered breasts with his cheeks.

She was delighted by his nearness, but she wanted his skin to touch hers. She undid the buttons on his shirt and slipped the soft cotton off his shoulders. His arms were muscled and strong. She massaged his shoulders, moved to his collarbones, and then slid the flat of her palms to the pectoral muscles of his chest.

He tugged the bottom of her knit jersey. Francesca lifted her arms above her head and allowed him to remove her top. He pulled it aside and gazed at her sculpted breasts, her tan line visible in the moonlight. He slid the straps from her shoulders.

The tan line ended just above her areolae. In the cool breeze, her nipples grew erect. The skin around them was white as milk, soft as smoke. When he touched her, Francesca reached for his neck, more urgently this time. She lay back, pulling him down on top of her. His face quickly found the notch in her neck, and his kisses worked downward.

"Don't be so gentle," she urged.

He wasn't. When she couldn't stand it anymore, she pushed him down, kissing him roughly while undoing his belt. When they were both naked, she raked his abdomen provocatively with her nails. His arousal was complete, and his voice grew husky.

"This isn't the best moment to talk about contraception," he managed, "but—"

Her finger silenced his lips. "I have an IUD."

Before he could reply she slipped a leg over his torso and straddled him. Steve watched her breasts swaying before his face. Then he and Francesca came together as naturally as a couple who'd spent years together. Francesca made a deep, throaty moan, and her hip movements grew frenzied. His ardor likewise increased. He found himself thrusting rapidly, barely able to contain himself. Francesca seized his wrists and pinned them to the blanket, wanting nothing to interfere with what she was feeling.

Steve couldn't hold back. He quickly neared the brink and exploded over it. Francesca held his wrists tight. A hoarse groan began in her throat, and then her body convulsed in a series of spasms until her movements finally slowed, and she collapsed against him.

As they lay there, a gentle night breeze swept over them.

"Comfortable?" he asked, after a moment.

"Very." His hands played softly on her back, and she was struck with what a paradox he was, possessed of such obvious strength, yet capable of such tenderness.

"You said you sometimes come on a little strong," he said, "but I think we have a role reversal here. It's considered unprofessional to take advantage of people who get something in their eye."

"That's sweet. But if you're trying to apologize, forget it." She raised her head and softly kissed his eyes, his nose, his lips. "I loved every minute of it."

They gazed fondly at one another. Francesca slowly ran her finger against his face, tracing his profile. Warmed by the afterglow of their lovemaking, Steve experienced a conflicting rush of emotions, from contentment to longing to a peculiar guilt. In the hollows and dells of his memory, he couldn't recall feeling this way about a woman before. Not that he remotely understood his feelings; it was all too new, too fresh, and much too exciting.

But as he lay there savoring the sweet scents of sex and flowers, the one thing that was perfectly clear was that he wouldn't allow it to end now.

9

Downtown Larchmont was a working community in lower Westchester County, just north of New York City. Ted DiGiorgio had purchased an old factory building on Palmer Avenue, renovated it, and converted it for Ecolabs' use. The four-story building housed corporate offices, an administrative section, and the production facilities. The blending, compounding, and packaging of all nutritional products took place on the middle two floors. The plant was efficient but crowded. After four years, DiGiorgio was already looking for a larger facility.

Chemist Robert Whitt's office was on the top floor. Although much of his work dealt with quality control, he was also in charge of mixing the initial batches of raw materials. Moreover, he was responsible for his primary interest, research. Always on the lookout for both new products and new applications of existing products, he was the ideal man for the job.

After receiving his doctorate at Stanford, Whitt immediately went to work in the pharmaceutical industry. Over the years he worked for Sandoz, Roche, and Pfizer. Although he had some experience with antihistamines and sedatives, his main area of expertise was vitamins. Whitt was a lifelong vegetarian, and when the first "natural" supplements appeared on the scene, he lobbied hard for their inclusion into traditional pharmaceutical offerings. But his efforts fell on deaf ears. Mainstream companies simply weren't interested in upstart, unproven ventures that had little appeal to the medical community.

One December, at a pharmaceutical convention in Sarasota, Whitt met Ted DiGiorgio during the cocktail hour. The entrepreneur engaged the chemist, drawing him out on various topics. During their conversation, Whitt's disenchantment with his work became apparent. Before the hour ended, Ted offered him a job. Dr. Whitt accepted and never looked back.

Ecolabs was the perfect environment for him. The atmosphere was fresh and exciting, and every day there was talk of new ventures, new directions. Whitt plunged into his work with enthusiasm. It became a passion for him, a calling. He enjoyed what he did, and he was very good at it.

Within a year of his arrival, he was instrumental in setting the direction for almost all Ecolabs products. After studying preliminary European reports on phytoestrogens, Whitt saw the tremendous potential of such products in the United States. Ted gave him carte blanche. But it took him several more years to study the field exhaustively and do his own research, followed by still more time devoted to the company's own basic clinical trials. But because Restore-Tabs had such enormous financial potential, he knew it was time well spent.

The processing area of the plant employed standards every bit as stringent as those in major pharmaceutical companies. The interior air was filtered and regularly vented. Workers—required to wear gloves, surgical caps, and booties—were dressed in white, disposable coveralls that they changed daily. Whitt donned his own garments in a sterile changing room before entering the processing area.

It was noon. He made rounds on the unit three times a day—at eight A.M., midday, and four P.M. He strolled through the processing area, observing, checking dials and meters, and chatting with the workers. Most worked in assembly-line fashion, although certain employees had their own cubicles. He approached one such space and peered around the divider. The woman inside was speaking into a mobile phone.

"Gladys," he said, "you know that's not permitted."

"I'm sorry, Dr. Whitt, but my daughter, she—"

"Take the call outside, please. Make sure you change before you come back."

She returned within minutes, contrite. "I apologize, Dr. Whitt. There was an emergency in my daughter's school, and she was getting hysterical. They asked the teacher to contact me."

"Don't worry about it, Gladys. Is everything all right?"

"It is now. She should be fine."

"Very handy, those phones. It's hard to be without one these days."

"Especially for a single parent," she said. "I encourage my daughter to call me, but sometimes she phones me at the craziest times."

"Kids are like that." He paused. "I have no problem with people calling you here, especially when there's a problem. But the reason we like to keep phones out of the processing area is that people tend to remove their masks, like you did."

She reddened. "It won't happen again, sir."

"You see, when you remove your mask, you also disrupt your head cover. I'm sure we can handle a few extra germs and an occasional stray hair, but why should we, when it's not necessary? I really want you to be there for your family, Gladys. But I also insist on utmost purity for our products, and for our consumers. You understand that, don't you?"

Gladys nodded. "Yes, I do. And I appreciate your consideration, Dr. Whitt. It won't happen again."

"Well, if it does," he said with a smile, "just take it outside, okay?"

As he walked away, Gladys gave her head a satisfied shake. Everyone at Ecolabs was very considerate, and Dr. Whitt was the most understanding boss she'd ever worked for.

SULAWESI, INDONESIA

It took several hours to drive to Inobonto and a while longer for Sergeant Atmosaputro to find the clinic. Dr. Sayed didn't know the address. Indeed, there *was* no address for a hewn-out mountainside clearing. In Inobonto, the sergeant talked to local townsfolk, using either charm or threat, where appropriate. Bit by bit, one villager led him to another to yet another.

Eventually, he found a laborer who'd helped clear the forest ten kilometers away, about a year ago. The man couldn't be certain, but rumor had it that the building they erected was intended for some sort of medical facility. He gave the sergeant directions.

The road that wound into the mountains was rough and dusty. The first time he passed it, Atmosaputro missed the intersecting trail, for in the space of a year, the trail had been narrowed by vines and jungle overgrowth. But soon he found the clearing. In its center was a recently constructed but traditional *Bugis* house.

He pulled to a stop in front of the building. When he parked, a white-uniformed woman came out. From experience, he could tell she was foreign—Filipino, to be exact. She eyed him warily.

"This is a private facility," she said.

"Oh? And who might you be?"

"I'm not at liberty to answer your questions. Please leave."

Atmosaputro showed her his identification. "Maybe this will increase your liberty."

Startled, her eyes widened. "My name is Claudia, sir. I'm the nurse in charge here."

"Really? What kind of place is this?"

"It's a hospice. I take care of very sick women."

"You look nervous, Claudia. Why is that?"

"I . . . I'm not nervous. It's just that we rarely see strangers here, certainly not the police."

"You wouldn't have something to hide, would you?"

"Of course not."

"Then you wouldn't mind my looking inside?"

She hugged herself nervously. "As you wish."

He followed her up the wooden steps. Ascending, he was struck by the mounting odor, the faint but indelible smell that human waste left in a building's walls. Walking through the entrance, he was thankful there was a fan. A breeze ruffled the cheap curtains. Despite the room's relative darkness, he could see a row of beds on either side of the room. A woman was on each bed, and some of them lethargically looked his way. Others lay in unmoving silence.

"What's wrong with these people?" he asked.

"I'm not sure. Something has made them very ill. I suspect they have cancer."

He recalled what the pathologist said. "Uterine cancer?"

"That's possible. Many of them bleed."

"Why do they look that way?"

"Because they are drugged, Sergeant. I'm under orders to keep them comfortable, and I do so with narcotics."

"Orders from Dr. Sayed?" He took in her suddenly

averted eyes. "Look, I already spoke with that quack. You don't have to protect him. I just want to know what's going on."

"All right," she said, nodding. She began to wring her hands, clearly disturbed. "He sends drugs along with the new patients."

"How often do you speak with him?"

"Not often. The last time was months ago. He doesn't like to be disturbed. Dr. Sayed is a very unpleasant man."

"So I noticed. Look, why don't you tell me everything? I'll do my best to keep you out of it. I already know about the newspaper ads and Sayed's involvement. Just tell me what goes on here and what you do with the dead."

With that, Claudia broke down. She hurried onto the veranda, softly sobbing. It took a while for her to stop crying and wipe her eyes. "I needed the money," she began, her voice tremulous. "Everyone here needs the money. I know God will punish me for what I've done, but that's the truth."

"Go on."

"Most of these patients come from Kalimantan," she continued. "Sayed didn't tell me much, but the women talk to me. As I understand it, they reply to an advertisement and eventually make their way to Dr. Sayed. He gives them some sort of drug or herb in return for more money than they've ever known."

"Is he doing research?"

"Apparently. There are many women—"

"More than fifty?" he interrupted, recalling what the doctor had told him.

"Many, many more. He puts them up in cheap housing, and they visit him every two weeks. Although they were told to keep silent, the women talked with one another. Not everyone received the same quantity of the drug. Some more, some less. Sayed followed all of them for three months. Those that remained healthy went home. Those that were ill, well . . ." Her hand unfolded toward the building.

"Do you know what was in the drug?"

"No, but there was talk of something from the sea."

"Does everyone who is sent here eventually die?"

"Most of them," Claudia said, hanging her head. "Forty-five patients have come here since last winter. Six got better and left. Of the others, there is about one death per week."

"Not very good statistics. What do you do with the bodies?"

"I have a phone here for emergencies. I call the number and leave a message. Mr. Suroto, the same man who brings the patients, takes away the dead. I think he works for Sayed."

"I see," said Atmosaputro. "Do you know what he does with them?"

"I suppose he buries them somewhere. What else would he do?"

You don't want to know, thought the sergeant. "Do you mind if I talk with the women?"

She shook her head no. While she remained outside, Atmosaputro returned into the building, notepad in hand. When he came out fifteen minutes later, he looked grim. Before he left, he admonished her to say nothing to anyone.

The instant his car disappeared, Claudia went indoors to the phone. It wasn't Dr. Sayed she called, but rather New York, and a man named Jack.

Steve turned on his computer. "I think you ought to see this," he said to Francesca as the computer booted up. "I left messages on a lot of bulletin boards asking other doctors to let me know if they came across anything. I downloaded their emails. Does Ecolabs sell products in England?"

"As of the first of the year. Why?"

He worked the mouse until the computer opened the file. "Because this first reply came from a family doctor in Newcastle. He didn't say precisely how many tablets his patient was taking, only that she exceeded the recommended dose 'for several months.' The patient bled and had endometrial hyperplasia. This second one," he continued, "is from a gynecologist in Milwaukee. His thirty-four-year-old patient hemorrhaged and had a D and C, which showed endometrial cancer." He looked up at her. "They're all variations on a theme."

Francesca studied the monitor, concerned. "How many responses in all?"

"Five. To me what's most important is that they all came this week." He explained to her what he now considered to be a growing epidemic, one that involved patients taking overdoses of the product for at least several months. They then developed a highly stimulated endometrium that eventually bled.

"Is it possible this is some terrible coincidence?" she asked. "This is frightening, but could there be other factors, like diet or lifestyle?"

"Of course there could. I'm not saying anyone should panic over this, but I do think it has to be looked into as soon as possible. Together, these cases are a red flag."

Francesca looked pale. "Do you think we should halt distribution?"

"I suppose that's up to Ted. If it were up to me, as Andie's father and Alyssa's doctor—"

"Andie's your teenage daughter?"

"That's right. As I was saying, I'd take everything out of distribution immediately. But most investigators would consider that a little extreme. They'd probably prefer to notify physicians—gyns, family doctors, and internists. And maybe a disclaimer on the TV slots, or a more explicit package warning about not exceeding the recommended dose."

From behind, Francesca bent over and put her arms around his neck. She kissed him on the temple and nuzzled his ear. "You really are a concerned, wonderful doctor. I may even become a patient of yours myself."

"I'm afraid that would be considered unethical."

"Oh?"

"Sleeping with one's patient is frowned upon these days."

"Too bad," she sighed. "Either I'll have to let my lecherous old gyno keep examining my breasts, or—"

"Don't even think about it."

She laughed, kissed him on the neck, and straightened up. "I'll call Ted first thing on Monday. I'll pass along what you said, and I'm sure he'll know what to do. It might also be a good idea for you to email him that file so he can contact those doctors personally."

She turned to a nearby table and picked up a copy of *Scuba Times*. "Do you dive?"

Logging off, he turned to see what she was talking about. "Yeah, I love it. But I haven't gone in about a year."

"I just learned to dive last summer."

"Are you certified?"

"I'm an open-water diver, my dear," she said proudly.

"That's fantastic. Where'd you learn? Ever dive around here?"

"I took a resort course in the Bahamas. Someone told me Long Island diving is the pits."

"Oh, it's not that bad. The visibility's nothing like the Caribbean, but I'll tell you one thing: learn to dive around here, and believe me, you can dive anywhere."

"Why don't we go diving sometime?" she suggested.

"I'd love to. But like I said, you can't see that much. And the water's pretty cold."

"I'm not talking about here, silly. I can get a couple of days off if you can. Why don't we go someplace really warm? My treat."

SULAWESI, INDONESIA

As a supply person at State, Jack Buhlman was only peripherally involved with treaties. Still, he appreciated their importance to both the American and foreign signatories, including Indonesia. He had studied their intricacies while still in government employ, and he quickly learned that international trade was an area ripe for graft and corruption, for Americans and Indonesians alike wanted new markets for their products. Exploiting Indonesia's untapped natural resources was of particular interest to American firms.

The primary commercial agreement from which later ones were derived was the 1980 bilateral memorandum on trade and commerce. This was followed by a 1992 U.S.—Indonesian agreement concerning trade in textiles. Despite this modest success, attempts to broaden agreements between the two nations were hampered by self-interest and deep-seated distrust. In many areas, the countries didn't see eye-to-eye.

For example, the United States was involved in formulating protocols for the protection of natural resources and the prevention of pollution in the South Pacific region, but Indonesia, fearing interference with its fledgling industries, wouldn't sign. Furthermore, through the State Department and the NOAA, the United States was a signatory to coral-reef protection agreements, while Indonesia was not.

Such disagreements were very profitable for Jack, who sold his services to Americans and Indonesians alike. He was particularly effective in the maritime area. A number of firms desirous of extracting the wealth from Indonesia's rich waters sought his counsel. Not the least of them was Ecolabs. Jack made sure they received the required permits for coral mining.

Jack almost always flew Singapore Airlines, because no major carriers flew nonstop from the eastern United States to Indonesia. From Singapore, he took connecting flights to the Manado or Gorontalo areas. Now, as he arrived in the latter, he paused to soak in the magnificent sunshine. Having anticipated this unfortunate turn of events with Dr. Sayed the last time he'd been in town, he knew he still had a little time. It would be several hours before he would have to deal with Sayed.

On his previous trip, he'd carefully studied the doctor's comings and goings. Sayed always finished evening hours precisely at seven. He kept his vehicle in a small parking lot behind the office. The fact that the space was hidden from the street discouraged passing thieves from being tempted by his Acura. Unfortunately, its sheltered location was also an inducement for others with less than honorable intentions.

When Sayed entered the parking lot, he unlocked the car and took off his suit jacket. Jack moved quickly, stepping noiselessly out of the shadows. He pressed the stun gun to the doctor's neck and fired. Startled, Sayed began to turn but instantly crumpled, sagging into Jack's waiting arms. Jack deposited the physician in the front seat, closed the door, and entered on the passenger side.

"Sorry about that, Doc. But things just aren't going to work out when you rat on me. Anyway, we're closing down the operation, and that includes you."

Sayed stared motionlessly through the front window, his breathing slow but regular. After leaving the airport, Jack had purchased a cheap but untraceable Balisong knife, which he now drew from his pocket. He reached over, grasped Sayed's left arm, and unbuttoned the shirtsleeve, carefully rolling it up to the elbow.

"Funny thing about suicides," Jack said. "A lot of 'em hate to make a mess. A guy'll blow the back of his head off, but he doesn't want to get his clothes dirty." Holding firmly to the doctor's left wrist, he made a few shallow, seemingly haphazard lacerations. "They call these farty little cuts 'suicidal gestures,' and . . . Jeez, will you listen to me? You're a doctor, I'm sure you know all this. But *this* big guy," he said, slicing deeply through the radial artery, "is the real thing."

He immediately turned the wrist downward to avoid the suddenly spurting arterial blood. The vessel sprayed the door's side panel, which drained to the floor. "Now, it'll take a few minutes for you to bleed out. Mind if I keep you company?" He watched the physician closely. There was a faint twitch in the man's neck muscles. "Starting to get some movement back? Sorry, pal. Can't allow that." He used the stun gun on Sayed again, and the man's neck and shoulders relaxed.

The interior of the Acura was quiet except for the unmistakably liquid sound of a briskly squirting artery. After the fatal cut, the artery initially spurted every three-quarters of a second. But as Sayed's blood volume depleted, his heart began beating faster, and the vessel now pulsed every half second. The car was growing uncomfortably warm, and Jack rolled down the window.

"Eyes getting heavy, Doc? They say you start feeling light-headed when you're about two pints down." He eyed the pool on the floor. "You should be about there now. Man, there's no mistaking the smell of freshly shed blood, is there? Let's check the old pulse."

Jack lifted the doctor's other arm, found the pulse, and clocked it with his watch. "One-ten and rising, atta boy. Shame on you, Doc. You're starting to steam up the windows on your side. I don't suppose you feel like writing a suicide note, do you? I'd help you out if I could, but I don't know the lingo. No problem. We'll just put the knife where it belongs."

With his handkerchief, he carefully wiped down the knife and then wrapped the handle in the physician's palm. "Shouldn't be much longer now. After around three pints, an out-of-shape guy like you loses consciousness. And then, my friend, that's it."

The seconds passed. Jack carefully scanned the secluded parking area. They were alone. Sayed's lids were now half-closed, and his eyes were glazed. The car's metallic, butcher-shop stench was overpowering. The spurting sound was very rapid now, but also very faint. Jack knew he wouldn't have to stun the doctor again. Under his fingertips, the man's pulse was nearly undetectable. Half a minute later, as the heart began fibrillating, it made a birdlike flutter, then stopped entirely.

Jack carefully looked around. Then he quickly closed the window, got out of the car, and locked the door before shutting it. Keeping his head down, he strode purposefully away.

It was time to pay a visit to the sergeant.

During Monday afternoon office hours, Steve got a call from the Center for Food Safety and Applied Nutrition director Joseph Hubbard.

"I listened to your message today, Dr. McLaren," said the director. "Normally, executive assistants follow up on physician reports. But I sensed the urgency and decided to call myself."

"I appreciate that, Dr. Hubbard. Maybe you can suggest how we can go about this diplomatically."

"I'll be happy to, as soon as I get a copy of the report. You said you'd submitted a form 3500 online, but it's not in our computers. If we fax you another form, if you fill it out and fax it back, I'll get on it right away."

"You never received it?" Steve said, incredulous. "How is that possible? My email prompts indicated it'd been sent."

"Unfortunately, I have to admit this isn't the first time that's occurred. Computer glitches, human error, whatever."

"Can't you just act on a verbal report? Believe me, I

wouldn't be calling you if I didn't think it was important."

"I could, if you were a government agency that suggested there was an immediate threat to public welfare. But the rules on this are strict, Dr. McLaren. I need either a hard copy or something on my monitor. Sorry for the delay, but if I put my secretary on, do you think you can give her your email address and fax number?"

Steve sighed in exasperation. "I suppose, if that's the only way. But I want your word that when I send it, your people will get right on it."

"You've got it."

Steve and Francesca decided to spend the long, upcoming weekend together. He refused to let her pay for everything but did agree to share the cost. Four days after Francesca had suggested it, Steve booked the trip online and managed to reschedule most of his patients to allow for a four-day trip to points south.

Late Tuesday afternoon, Steve still hadn't heard from Director Hubbard. He realized it had only been twenty-four hours since they'd spoken, but every time he thought about Andie, he got worried. He was torn: he didn't want to make waves for Ted and Ecolabs, but he was very concerned for his daughter and his patients. He called Hubbard's Washington number and reached his secretary. She assured him that they'd gotten his report and were working on it. However, owing to the nature of bureaucracy, he shouldn't expect to hear from them for at least another week.

Before he left the office, Steve made two more calls. The first was to Julia Hagen to check on Alyssa. He promised to stop by again on Thursday. Next he called Lorraine, explaining that he'd be away for the weekend and asking if he could drop by Wednesday evening to spend some time with Andie. Maybe he was overdoing it, he said, but he'd been worried about her ever since she admitted to taking Restore-Tabs. Reluctantly, Lorraine agreed.

Wednesday night, he was on the road by eight, heading for his short visit with Andie. It was a forty-five-minute drive from his house, and he'd told Lorraine he'd be there by nine. He wasn't planning to stay long. All he wanted to do before he left town was to share a Coke with his daughter, talk a little, and see how she was doing. He'd be out of there by ten and home in time to watch a little Leno.

He reached Lorraine's house just before nine and pulled into the driveway. These were the longest days of the year, and it still wasn't completely dark. More often than not, Andie was waiting for him on the stoop, a smile on her face. That evening, there was no one in sight.

He got out of the car, went to the front door, and rang the bell. He heard indistinct voices inside. At length the door opened and there stood Andie, sans her customary smile.

"Hi, honey," he said cheerily. "What gives?"

Her chin betrayed the slightest quiver, and she took a step backward. Mystified, Steve stepped inside. He saw uncertainty in his daughter's eyes, uncertainty tinged with fear. "Andie, what's wrong? Why the long face?"

Her voice was tremulous. "Daddy . . ."

There was a shadow in the far corner of the room, and he turned his head. It was Lorraine, glaring at him. His ex-wife looked good: her blue eyes were sharp and focused, and her cheeks were red. Then he recalled she always looked loveliest when she was angry.

"You bastard," she slowly said.

"Excuse me?"

Her hands were balled into fists, and one of them was clutching some papers. She took swift, menacing steps toward him. "Your own daughter, you miserable son of a bitch!"

Completely befuddled, he looked at his daughter, then back at his ex. "What in the world are you talking about?"

"As if you didn't know." She crushed one of the papers and threw it at him. "I'm talking about this, you sick fuck!"

The crumpled wad struck him in the chest and fell to the floor. He picked it up and slowly unfolded it. It resembled a hard copy printed off a computer screen.

"North American Father—Daughter Love Association," it was titled. "Bringing fathers and daughters together in physical bliss." Beneath the caption was a half-page photo of a man's bare midsection. A nubile, pigtailed young adolescent was performing fellatio on the man's huge erection.

"What the hell is this?" he said with a frown.

"You bastard! I've already called my attorney. How *dare* you email this to your own daughter!"

Steve shook his head; then he looked back at the paper and read the message at the bottom of the page.

"Andie, princess," it continued. "You are my precious, sweet child. You know how well we get along and how much I adore you. People who love each other can show it in many special ways. Soon, I'll teach you these ways. Love, Dad."

Sickened, he raised both palms in a placatory gesture. "Lorraine, believe me, I didn't—"

"Believe *you*? Are you out of your tiny mind? I stopped believing you years ago! But *this* . . . How could I be so blind? This explains a lot, oh, yes."

He stuffed the paper into his pocket. "Lorraine, please. I'm not capable of something like this. You must know me well enough to realize that! This is somebody playing an incredibly sick joke . . . And what in the world does it explain?"

"Get a life!" she shouted. "All those tender young teens you helped over the years, and how you once told me the ideal female body should be slender and cellulite-free!"

"Come on, I was talking in abstractions."

"Oh no, I know now what you were hinting at! Jesus, how could I have been so blind?"

He turned to Andie. "Where'd you get this?"

"It was there when I logged on this morning," she timidly said.

"No *way* I did this," he said, turning back to Lorraine. "In fact, I haven't used my home computer since last weekend!"

"I had enough of your goddamn denials when you were still drinking!" she spat, slowly continuing toward him. "You practice denial like it's an Olympic event! It's a very, very sick man who can't take responsibility for his own perverted actions!"

"Lorraine, please—"

"Get out."

"Andie," he pleaded, "tell your mother I've never—"

There was a broom propped up against the wall, and Lorraine grabbed it in both hands. Her face contorted with rage. She lifted the broom over her head and charged him, shrieking, "How dare you? Our own daughter!"

She rained blows about his shoulders, swinging as hard as she could. Andie screamed. Steve lifted his arms to deflect the strikes. Stepping inside Lorraine's reach, he seized the broom and threw it down. Then he grabbed her by the shoulders and shook hard.

"Stop it, dammit! I'm telling you I didn't do this!"

Lorraine stared at him defiantly, eyes flashing. Suddenly her expression softened. Her lips slowly curled downward, and her eyes filled with tears. Her entire body began trembling. When she finally broke down, her heart-rending sobs were like those of a wounded animal.

Steve drew her toward him and put his arms around her. Lorraine's face sank to his chest, and her tears dampened his shirt. He held her until her body stopped shaking, and then patted her on the back. "I'll get to the bottom of this if it's the last thing I do."

"Just get out."

He realized it was pointless to argue. He pulled away and, on the way to the door, stopped and kissed Andie's pale cheek, whispering, "I love you."

As he started for his car, his own anger began to rise. He was furious that Andie had received the email to begin with. Whoever had sent it obviously knew her email address, which suggested a friend, associate, or relative. Could it be Lorraine? Had she grown to despise him so much that she'd stoop to something like this to discredit him? He sincerely doubted it. But then, who?

Pulling onto the highway, he was unexpectedly racked by a wave of nausea, and he had to grit his teeth to keep from retching. Suddenly a horrible thought occurred to him, and he had to grip the wheel tight. The idea was so sickening that he had to pull to the side of the road, where he managed to open the door before the bile and vomit came up.

Confused, demoralized, and full of questions, he went to bed late and slept little. He couldn't wait to get away with Francesca. But before their trip, he had one more day of office hours and his promised visit to Alyssa. Unable to get the image of the repulsive email out of his thoughts, he somehow managed to get through most of Thursday in a sullen mood that made Becky and Donna shake their heads.

Alyssa was growing progressively weaker, and now required constant care. Julia took a leave of absence from her job to be available for her daughter full-time. Despite her continued antibiotics, a low-grade fever continually flushed Alyssa's cheeks. Pain was an unwanted, ever-present companion. Somehow, Alyssa managed to smile through it all. That night, Julia met him at the front door.

"Hi, Jules. How's she doing?"

"About the same," she said. "The best I can say is she's holding her own."

He spotted Alyssa sitting on the living-room couch, reading a book to the blaring of a background TV. "What's up, Alyssa?"

"Hi, Steve," she said, waving a greeting without looking up from her book.

He looked at Julia. "How's her pain?"

"That patch helps a lot. She always looks a little glassy-eyed, like when we used to smoke dope."

"God almighty, what makes you think I smoked dope?"

She gave him a long look. "Right. You were probably the beer type."

He felt uncomfortable, wondering if she knew about his drinking or was guessing. "What about her appetite?"

"That's where I've got my work cut out. Between all the drugs and her disease, she hardly eats a thing."

"I suppose I don't have to ask if she's getting the three main food groups?"

"Are you kidding? On a good day, she might have some French fries and a Coke."

"Sounds like a normal teenager to me."

Alyssa wore a rose-colored terry robe and fluffy pink slippers, and her feet were propped up on a coffee table. She looked considerably thinner and was developing the wasted appearance that was the hallmark of end-stage cancer patients.

"Hey, Twiggy," he said, "you dieting or what?"

"Who's Twiggy?"

"Before your time. Looks like you've lost some weight there."

The book fell to her lap. "I'm just not hungry, Steve."

He looked at her gaunt face. "I hear you. But as a doctor, I sometimes have to give real skinny people their vitamins through an IV."

"I take my vitamins."

"You know what I mean."

"Okay already. I'll try harder."

"That's my girl. What're you reading?" he asked.

To Kill a Mockingbird. It's on the eighth-grade reading list."

"Great book." He sat beside her, tenderly brushing wisps of hair off her febrile brow. "Look, kiddo. I'm going away for a few days, but someone's covering for me. I told him about you."

"Where're you going?"

"Puerto Rico. I'm going to do a little diving."

"Scuba diving?" she said, brightening. "Can you teach me?"

"Absolutely," he said, getting up. "Gain five pounds, and it's a deal."

In the other room, Julia frowned as she let him out. "I hope you weren't serious about the IV."

"Yes and no. Some patients can literally starve to death."

"You know how I feel about prolonging the inevitable," she said. "What kind of life is there when there's no quality to life?"

He evaded the question. "Since you brought dope up, have you ever considered marijuana?"

"For me, or for her?" She waited a beat. "No, I haven't," she replied. "You think it'll help her appetite?"

"It might. Might help with the pain, too." He gave her a farewell hug. "Think it over. I'll call you when I get back."

"Have a wonderful trip," she said, fighting the tears in her eyes.

SULAWESI, INDONESIA

For close-quarters work, Jack Buhlman preferred custom fighting knives. While the latest rage in the admittedly limited field was for gadgets with hook blades and extreme concealability, Jack relied on fine knives with extreme hardness, utter reliability, and custom craftsmanship. Such items often went for a thousand dollars and up. His current carry weapons were a one-of-a-kind combat folder from Elishewitz and a stainless, fixed-blade, custom fighter from Steve Johnson. The first was for pocket carry, the second for the sleeve or the boot.

His plan was to simply track Atmosaputro to his home, force his car over on a remote stretch of road, and kill him. He had nothing against the sergeant, personally; the man simply knew too much, and as such was dangerous. Jack wanted the encounter to be quick, deadly, and witness-free. He already had a close-up photo. When Claudia called him, Jack's first instruction was to get a photo of his quarry. Unfortunately, the photographer—a low-level con man—was arrested on different charges shortly after taking the picture and couldn't provide any other information.

Finding Atmosaputro proved more difficult than locating Dr. Sayed. Although Jack had contacts in the local police department, he couldn't very well ask them where the sergeant lived. Rather, he spoke with a man he knew in the construction trades, careful not to inquire only about Atmosaputro. Ultimately, he learned that the officer lived near the town of Airmadidi, just outside of Manado.

Photo in hand, Jack parked down the block from the police station. He spotted Atmosaputro the instant he exited the building. The sergeant got in a beat-up Nissan and began the long trip home, a twelve-mile journey beyond the mountains that were Manado's backdrop. Jack followed at a safe distance. The road wasn't crowded, and he was able to remain a quarter-mile away.

Jack loved the island nation's natural splendor. As his car wound its way upward through the highlands, the distant clouds piled up like bales of fleece. Airmadidi was a mile-high town on the way to Mount Kalabat, a six-thousand-foot-high volcano that was popular with climbers. When the vehicle was three-quarters of the way up the mountain, Jack was shrouded in a mist that immediately gave way to a dazzling rainbow. Soon, with the emerald jungle always crowding the road, the road leveled off. Unfamiliar with the highway's twists and turns, he began to lose sight of the vehicle in front of him. As the sergeant neared his destination, Jack's car fell further and further back, unable to keep up.

Yet, when the winding road straightened out, Jack caught sight of the Nissan once again and accelerated, closing the gap. Finally, the sergeant's car turned onto a small side street hewn out of the mountain greenery. The car threw up considerable dust, and Jack only knew where he was going by following the cloudy trail. At length, the cloud ended at a small bungalow with a traditional thatched roof. It was the only house for several hundred yards.

So much for the best-laid plans, Jack thought.

He parked his car at a distance and waited. Plan B also called for a direct assault, but first he wanted to draw Atmosaputro outdoors. Jack believed that killing should be straightforward, and there was no point doing it in front of a man's family. His plan was a simple ruse to entice the sergeant outside, ostensibly for assistance with his car. Almost all the Indonesians he met were friendly and eager to extend help.

The side entrance had a two-step wooden stoop. As Jack mounted the first step, he felt cold metal press into his neck, and he heard the snick of a hammer being cocked. He slowly raised his hands over his head.

"American or Australian?" a man's voice asked.

"Have a heart, mate," Jack calmly replied. "I just want bloody directions."

"That's the worst damn Aussie accent I ever heard," said Atmosaputro, patting Jack down with his left hand. Then he shouted something in rapid-fire Bahasa Indonesian.

Jack looked up and saw a woman carrying a small child retreat into the house.

"Keep your head down and your back to me," Atmosaputro sternly warned. "And tell me why you've been following me since I left the station."

"I don't know what you're talking about. I've been trying to find the road to Gorontalo and I got lost, okay? I saw your car up ahead, and I've been trying to catch up. No harm in that, is there? Can I put my hands down now?"

"Shut up." Satisfied that the American wasn't wearing a

firearm, Atmosaputro removed Jack's wallet and flipped it open, eyeing the Washington, D.C., driver's license. "I'll ask you again, Mr. Buhlman. Why were you following me?"

"While you're looking through my wallet, check all the documents in there. You'll see that I'm retired State Department. I'm here consulting on a trade mission."

True enough, the stranger did appear to be a former employee of the American government. That didn't mean he was law-abiding, but it did buy him a little respect. Atmosaputro took a step backward. "Lower your arms and turn around. *Slowly.*"

They always think gun, Jack reflected. I could be a world-class swordsman, and they'd still frisk me for a Glock. Knives were so much less suspect, not to mention more lethal for close-quarters work. It was why he always wore long-sleeved shirts. As he nonchalantly put his arms down, he subtly twitched his right forearm. The Johnson fighter slipped from its strap-on scabbard and fell, blade-first, to his hand. Jack held the heavy point between thumb and forefinger, with its ivory handle still up his sleeve.

"Thank you," he said, slowly beginning to turn. As his eyes rotated, they took in the sergeant's Beretta 92FS, pointed directly at his head. Not smart, Jack thought. Stupid cop should have lowered it to my central body mass. With an imperceptible shake of his fingers, the knife slid into Jack's waiting palm. As he completed his turn, his knife arm slashed upward.

The Johnson's ten-inch blade smashed into the sergeant's ulna, knocking Atmosaputro's arm upward. The gun fired harmlessly over Jack's head, but not before the knife slashed through skin, muscle, and major arteries. Blood spurted everywhere. The officer could no longer hold the gun because his flexor tendons were severed. The Beretta slipped from his grasp. Jack lowered his arm and unleashed a vicious strike, hoping to catch the sergeant in mid-abdomen with a thrust that would carry upward into the heart.

But Jack was a stealth knifesman, not a street-fighter. He relied on one or two lethal blows to achieve the desired result. As he had no idea that Atmosaputro was a martial-arts expert, he was unprepared for the lightning speed of the sergeant's parry. The officer quickly locked his arms in a downward X, catching Jack's strike in the crotch of his forearms. Despite his useless right hand, Atmosaputro somehow managed to seize Jack's knife hand and twist hard. Jack screamed in pain, and the big knife somersaulted away.

Before he could react, the officer lashed out at Jack's nose with a left-handed heel thrust. But the pain threw off his aim, and the base of his palm crashed instead into Jack's cheek. Jack saw stars. Before he knew it, he was on the ground. The wiry sergeant expertly wrestled Jack onto his abdomen and was quickly around the American's neck, grasping his useless arm viselike with his good one.

Blood from the severed arteries sprayed Jack's face and mouth, tasting of metal and salt. The extreme pressure around his windpipe was relentless, and his lips bared in a grimace. As he lay there choking, it occurred to him that Atmosaputro might eventually bleed out, but not before Jack died of suffocation. With his retina twinkling from oxygen deprivation as the life was being squeezed out of him, Jack fumbled under his belt buckle. His numb fingers located the folder and flicked it open. He realized that in the few seconds remaining before he passed out, everything depended on one last, desperate thrust.

He slashed behind him with all his might. The blade of the Elishewitz found the officer's ribs, and the sergeant grunted as the four-inch blade slid in up to the hilt. As his strength slipped away, Atmosaputro rolled off, weakened by extreme blood loss and a punctured lung. Choking for air, Jack scrambled to his knees. He spotted the Johnson, grabbed it, and made a forceful backhand thrust toward the sergeant's body. Atmosaputro tried to block it, but he was far too weak and much too late. The heavy knife stabbed through the diaphragm and penetrated his chest.

The sergeant rolled onto his side, feeling the pain tear through his lungs. His vision narrowed to tiny pinpoints of light, and he feebly looked up, toward the house. His eyes locked on those of his wife, who appeared to be saying something. But he could no longer hear it, and he couldn't breathe. A moist and sticky froth rose to his lips. He felt everything slip away, and then it was gone entirely. He slumped onto the hot earth.

Jack momentarily relaxed, sucking in deep breaths. Muffled screams reached him, and he turned, startled. Just beyond the screen door, the woman stood in wide-eyed terror, hands at her lips. Jack couldn't afford the luxury of waiting to recover fully. Sweating and blood-streaked, he sprang to his feet and sprinted for the car, slashing the exterior telephone wires as he ran. He leaped into the driver's seat, started the motor, and floored the accelerator, leaving a thick cloud of dust in his wake.

Still hungry for air, Jack rolled down the windows and breathed in deeply. By the time the Atmosaputro woman gathered her wits and got to the nearest house to make a call, he'd be long gone.

The first order of business was to clean himself up and change his appearance. The countryside was filled with fresh mountain streams in which to work his magic. It would soon be sundown, and the darkness would make his job easier. He always carried personal repair necessities in his toiletries kit: hair dye, contact lenses, even a fake mustache. If he drove all night after his physical metamorphosis, he'd be in Palu before morning, and then on to Jakarta and home, where other responsibilities awaited him. Should he be stopped by the authorities en route, his new passport would reveal a blond-haired, blue-eyed Jack Buhlman, a recent retiree from U.S. government service.

10

The plan was for Steve to meet Francesca at the American terminal at JFK Airport. Their ultimate destination was Rincon, a beach town on Puerto Rico's western shore that, until recently, catered more to surfers and honeymooners than to divers. To get there, they had to fly to San Juan and connect with a turboprop flight for Mayagüez, a fifteen-minute taxi drive from their destination. It would be a tiring trip, one that began with a midafternoon flight and didn't end until midnight.

Steve reached the airport at one-thirty but couldn't find her. According to airline regulations, if they didn't check in an hour before their three-thirty departure, they wouldn't be allowed to board. He was traveling light, with one suitcase and a carry-on. He bought a paperback novel but was too edgy to concentrate on it. Pacing nervously, he kept looking at his watch.

Francesca finally arrived at two-twenty, waving as she ran toward him. A porter wheeled her bags to the counter. They briefly hugged and kissed before entering the roped-off waiting line.

"Traffic was horrendous," she explained. "Were you waiting long?"

"Not really," he said with feigned nonchalance. "I'm just glad you got here in one piece. Before we go any further, is your dive computer in your carry-on?"

"Actually, all I brought are my mask and fins. I can rent the other stuff there, right?"

"Absolutely. Worst-case scenario," he said with an easy smile, "we'll buy new gear."

She took his hand and leaned her head on his shoulder. "I'm really excited, Steve. We're going to have a fantastic time, aren't we?"

"That we are, my love. That we are." He bent over and kissed her on the scar over her eye. "How did this adorable little blemish get on your face?"

"It happened a few years ago and wasn't fixed right. Think it could use some plastic surgery?"

"Adds character, I think."

Try though he did to be relaxed and worry-free, Steve couldn't get Wednesday's confrontation with Lorraine out of his mind. He'd brought the email printout with him. He wanted Francesca's opinion, but he didn't want to spoil her obviously upbeat mood. Perhaps he'd show it to her during the flight.

Over the years, he'd accumulated enough frequent-flyer miles to upgrade both of their seats to business class. Francesca had brought several magazines with her—not fashion periodicals, but *Forbes* and *Smart Money*. The onboard air was cool. When the meal ended and the cabin lights dimmed for the in-flight movie, Francesca snuggled closer to Steve. She leaned her head on his shoulder and caressed his forearm.

"Have you been to Puerto Rico before?" she asked.

"Christmas week, four years ago."

"You were married then?"

It was one of the things Ted had told her about him. "Yes, I was. Twelve years, at that point. Our marriage was going downhill fast, and I suppose that trip was the mandatory attempt at reconciliation. Obviously, it didn't work out."

"Selfish person that I am, I'm kind of glad," she said. "Are you comfortable talking about what went wrong?"

"A little bit of everything. I'm not sure we were ever right for each other. We probably got married too young. But most of all, I guess the marriage was a victim of prosperity. I'd become very busy in solo practice. Still am. I made good money. She spent it; I spent it. 'Things' became more important to us than we did to each other." He paused, exhaling slowly. "Just another thing I failed at."

She silently looked at him, waiting for him to continue.

"Sometimes I feel like my life's been one failure after another."

She looked at him oddly. "What on earth are you talking about?"

"It's a long story," he continued. "Goes back to my

childhood. To begin with, I always felt a little distant from my father—"

"Is this one of those I-hate-my-father things?" she interrupted.

"Not at all. I loved him. He was a kind and gentle guy, but the problem was, he was hardly ever home. I never really thought he was there for me. But man, he had these tremendous expectations! Most of all, he wanted me to do well academically, and I did. But no matter what kind of grades I got, it never seemed good enough."

"Is he still alive?"

"No, he died ten years ago. Anyway, that's how I lived my young adult life, wanting to please my dad, wanting him to be proud of me. Now, I realize that what I was really after was his love and approval, but back then, it seemed like this endless quest. And even though I always did well in school, deep down, I was terrified of failure. This shrink once told me I feared my father's scorn and rejection. The things I *did* fail at, like my marriage, just wound up worsening my self-esteem. It's like, all my life, I've been waiting for the next thing I could screw up at."

"And here I thought it was all due to a drinking problem."

Startled, he looked at her askance. "Meaning what?"

"Ted mentioned you had some difficulties there."

"Good Lord, looks like he gave you my whole life history."

"I told him I was curious, that's all."

Sighing, he leaned back into his seat. "Jesus, I didn't always have a problem. As far as alcohol goes, let's just say that, a few years ago, I started burning the candle at both ends. The harder I worked, the more I would socialize. Alone, a lot of times. Lorraine wasn't interested in that sort of life." His voice softened, and his expression grew distant. "Between the partying and the long hours, with not much to look forward to at home, I was a setup for some hard drinking. It was a self-fulfilling prophecy. Before long it was all I looked forward to. I think that's all behind me now. At least, I hope it is."

She slowly nodded. "Did you originally come from this area, Steve?"

"No, I grew up in Columbia, Maryland. A suburb of Washington. I went all over for school. Gettysburg College, where I met Ted. Med school at NYU, where I met Lorraine. And residency at Long Island Jewish."

"How'd you wind up where you are now?"

"I fell in love with the Hamptons," he said. "Used to go out there on weekends, had a share in a house, like everybody else. Along the way, I decided it's where I wanted to work. That was another problem. Lorraine was a city girl. She didn't mind spending summers out here, but she hated the idea of living in the sticks year-round."

"How were things between you sexually?"

Again, his squinty look. "What're you, a lay shrink?"

"Call it a psych major's curiosity."

"Well, Miss Curious, there are some things a gentleman doesn't talk about."

"Was she sexually inhibited, Mr. Gentleman?"

"You don't give up, do you?"

Her hand slid under the blanket to his thigh. "Are *you* inhibited, Steve?"

He closed his eyes and leaned back into the headrest. "God, I love this airline."

SULAWESI, INDONESIA

In 1976, the government of Indonesia purchased several squadrons of Vietnam-era, surplus UH-1D Huey helicopters from the U.S. Army. The Huey was a practical workhorse with a proven track record, and the Indonesians put it to work in transport, military/police, and medical roles. It was often used for medical evacuation and triage of casualties. That evening, Sergeant Atmosaputro clung to life as he was helicoptered from Airmadidi to Manado.

A country scattered among thousands of islands had an uneven system of health care. Although care was centralized, much of the actual hands-on treatment was administered in thousands of local community health centers or, in more rural areas, by traditional healers known as *dukun*. Better-equipped urban hospitals tended to have more physicians and higher health-care spending than did rural hospitals. As a city of two hundred and fifty thousand people, Manado had superior hospitals.

It was barely a five-minute flight from Airmadidi to Manado. The helicopter gently but quickly descended to sea level from five thousand feet. With the mountains disappearing in the background, Atmosaputro emerged from unconsciousness and opened his eyes. The first thing he was aware of was the searing pain in his chest. He breathed with difficulty, and each fiery inhalation made him wince. He weakly looked around, aware of the deafening *thwap-thwap* of rotor blades above him. He felt a jab in his forearm, and out of the corner of his eye he saw a medical attendant taping something in place.

"That's an IV, Sergeant. Try not to move. We'll be there soon."

His voice was hoarse and weak. "Where . . . ?"

"The hospital, in Manado. You have been seriously injured. They are waiting for you in emergency."

For a few seconds, Atmosaputro thought about his wife, his family, and the stranger who'd stabbed him. Then his lids closed, and he again slipped into unconsciousness. Soon the Huey set down near a waiting ambulance. Atmosaputro's stretcher was quickly offloaded to the ambulance, and the vehicle sped several blocks to the hospital, sirens blaring.

The hospital didn't have a CAT scanner or MRI equipment, but the emergency physician on duty didn't need one. When he removed the saturated pads applied by the corpsman, his unconscious patient's injuries were readily apparent. There were two significant punctures on the right side of the torso—one between the sixth and seventh ribs, and a larger one beneath it in the area of the liver. In addition, there was a hastily-applied but effective tourniquet midway down the right forearm, where an extensive laceration penetrated to the bone.

The injuries were scarcely bleeding. When a nurse took vital signs, the reason was clear: the patient was in profound hypovolemic shock, with barely detectable blood pressure and an extremely rapid pulse. They had to get fluids into him soon, preferably blood. He ordered an emergency crossmatch and squeezed in the bag of IV fluid by hand, as quickly as possible. As the nurse immediately hung another, the doctor listened to the victim's chest. On the right, the breath sounds were very diminished, and the patient had a collapsed lung. No doubt the lung was punctured and the liver lacerated as well. The only possible way to save the man was by performing emergency surgery. It was time to call the Chinaman.

Born near Manado, the ethnic Chinese physician was trained in surgery at Jakarta's University of Indonesia. His specialty was thoracic surgery, and he had both a professorship and a large private practice. Nearing retirement, he returned to Manado and cut down his hours. Nonetheless, he was the man to call in dire surgical emergencies.

Twenty-five minutes later, the sergeant was on the operating table. The Chinaman had hastily examined him in the corridor outside the OR. He knew an extensive thoracotomy was the only way to save the man's life, and even that was doubtful, given his patient's precarious condition. Transfusable blood was not yet available. However, replacing fluid was mandatory, and as soon as the patient was on the table, the surgeon inserted a subclavian line and quickly started a second IV. Then, when intubation was complete, he began to cut.

He made a midline sternal split and carried the incision down to the upper abdomen. As he expected, the incision was nearly bloodless, as much of the patient's blood had already been shed. Before proceeding with his repair, the surgeon inspected everything closely. The larger knife wound had lacerated the dome of the liver but had not transected any of the vessels.

The wound was directed upward, through the diaphragm, past the base of the right lung, and into the middle lobe. But fortunately, it didn't reach the major arteries at the lung's hilum. The arm, however, was a different matter. In major medical centers in Western countries, they might have attempted to microsurgically repair the damaged arteries and ligaments, but not a hospital in Indonesia, no matter how large. The lower arm would have to go.

All in all, the physician thought, the man had been incredibly lucky. The weapon had to have been quite sharp, for all the lacerations were clean and smooth. And although there was blood in the chest cavity and somewhat more in the abdomen, the organs could be saved with simple suturing.

He was a skillful, speedy surgeon. Soon the lung, diaphragmatic, and liver lacerations had been oversewn, and the lung reexpanded. While his assistant closed the chest, the physician concentrated on the arm. He quickly performed a below-the-elbow amputation with a saw, but he took care to create a clean stump. Fifty-five minutes later, the repairs were complete and the dressings applied. The first unit of blood was being transfused. Although the patient remained critical, his vital signs were slowly but perceptibly improving.

With a great deal of luck, and with considerable help from the Buddha, the man might survive.

The Horned Dorset Primavera was one of the few four-star hotels in Puerto Rico. The Spanish colonial—style resort was tucked away amidst lush landscaping overlooking the sea. When the courtesy van dropped off Steve and Francesca, they were serenaded by the crash of the distant surf and the lilting trill of night creatures. At that hour, the lobby was subdued, but an enormous parrot squawked a greeting.

They were lodged in Casa Escondida, an eight-room villa designed as a turn-of-the-century Puerto Rican hacienda. They both thought the resort had charm and class. Their room had all-wood floors, a terrace, black marble bath, and an antique four-poster bed. Very quiet, very romantic, very luxe. They were both tired. After briefly taking in the view from their room, they unpacked and collapsed on the bed, where they made slow, gentle love before falling asleep in each other's arms.

Rincon was located on the Mona Passage, the watery strait between Puerto Rico and the island of Hispaniola. They were diving with an outfit called Mona Divers. Since they had at most three days of diving, Steve researched the dives before they left. The highlight of their underwater adventure would be a full-day trip to Desecho Island, an arid, nineteen-acre parcel of rock and scrub fifteen miles out to sea. If conditions were suboptimal, Desecho could prove a difficult dive. Steve therefore decided their first day would be spent exploring the less challenging, double-reef system near the shore.

They awoke early and had a light breakfast of coffee and *pan dulce*. Feeling more relaxed than he had in a long time, Steve put the printout in one of the terry pockets of his hotel robe. As they started on the pastries, he took it out and handed it to Francesca.

Francesca gazed at him uncertainly. Then she closely examined the crumpled printout. "This is disgusting," she soon said. "Where'd you get it?"

"It showed up in Andie's email two days ago. She's my fifteen-year-old daughter, remember? She lives with her mom, and when I went to say good-bye to Andie Wednesday night, Lorraine accused me of sending it to Andie. Lorraine was furious, can't blame her for that. I was absolutely stunned. But there's nothing I could do, since I don't know who emailed it."

"I can't believe *any* father—much less you—could actually send this filth to his daughter. Does this Father—Daughter organization really exist?"

"How would I know?" he snapped. But he quickly mellowed. "Sorry. This whole thing has really messed me up."

"I can understand why. You don't deserve this, Steve. And you have no idea at all who might have sent it?"

"No. But the worst thing," he said, exhaling slowly, "is that I wonder if it might actually be me."

She stared at him oddly, slowly shaking her head. "That's ridiculous," she said. "We both know you're not that kind of person."

"Yeah, well, until Wednesday night I didn't think I was that kind of person, either."

"You're kidding, right?"

"Just remember what I said on the plane about how heavy my drinking got. You've heard of 'blackouts,' where the drinker can't remember what happened? Toward the end of my drinking," he said, "I used to get them all the time. There's a theory some shrinks subscribe to, though it's not widely accepted, that a problem drinker can continue to have blackout behavior even after he stops drinking. That he can do bizarre things while he's dreaming, kind of like sleepwalkers."

"Is that true?"

"I don't know, it's a theory. But suppose it *is* true? What's to say I didn't log onto my computer after I fell asleep? Surfed through some nifty porn sites and cozied up to this Father—Daughter Love thing?"

"That's insane," she said.

"So is sending incestuous email."

She thought about it. "You could find out, you know."

"How?"

"The phone company, for starters. I'm sure they have records of outgoing phone calls. If you used your modem Tuesday night, they'd be able to tell."

"They could only tell if I logged onto America Online."

"Hmmm . . . There's a guy at work, a real computer whiz. When we get back, I'm sure he could find out who used which Web site during a certain time frame."

"It's worth a try," he said.

"And if that doesn't help, you could check your credit card charges. Most porn sites require them."

"Oh, you know about things like that?"

She smiled at him. "Trust me on this."

"Fine. Let's say we find out I did it. What then? Shrinksville?"

"Steve, you're way ahead of yourself. One thing at a time. I'm sure nothing's going to turn up."

"I hope to hell you're right."

"What about the police?" she asked. "Do you think they should get involved?"

"Lorraine might have already called them. She said she'd called her attorney."

"And lawyers usually don't call the cops. They prefer to screw you financially."

Gradually, he felt his fury lessen. He put down his coffee, got up from the breakfast table, and started pacing, head lowered. The warm tropical air was freshened by a breeze. "I'm really glad I showed that to you," he told her. "I didn't feel like keeping it all to myself."

She looked at him fondly. "That's what I'm here for, my love."

"After this, I don't trust myself anymore. I think I better get some help for this. I might even try AA again."

"You've gone before?"

"In fact, I did. But I was terrified I might run into some-one I knew. I wound up going to meetings thirty, forty miles from home."

"Why did you stop going?"

He shook his head. "I couldn't get into it. They claimed it was supposed to be a spiritual program, but I found it much too religious. All this Higher Power and confession stuff."

"I see." She eyed him quizzically. "So you're going it alone."

"Not exactly. I have you."

She nodded. "Maybe we can solve this thing together."

"More than anything, Francesca, I have to know where that email came from. If it turns out I'm not to blame, you better believe I'm going to find out who is."

After breakfast, they packed their gear and went to the dive shop, where they showed their certification cards and rented more gear. Francesca wore a waist-tied floral sarong over a pair of white shorts, which she removed just before taking a seat on the dive boat. She looked stunning, and her fellow female divers looked her closely up and down.

The sea was calm, but they both wore scopolamine patches. On the short trip to the dive site, Steve reviewed diving etiquette and procedures. Finally, the boat clipped onto the mooring buoy, and they were ready. The dive-master announced a pre-dive briefing, and several passen-gers came aft from below deck. Steve thought he recognized a man accompanying a teenage boy.

"Rick?" he called. "Rick Haas?"

The man removed his sunglasses for a closer look. His eyes widened. "God Almighty, is that Steve McLaren?" He walked closer and extended his hand. "How the hell are you?"

"Great, thanks. How long's it been—fifteen years?"

"About that. You never made it back to the ten-year reunion, huh?"

"No, I'm afraid not. Were a lot of guys there?"

"Maybe fifty percent," said Haas, turning to his side. "This is my son, Tom. Tom, Dr. McLaren's a med-school classmate of mine." He looked at Steve's companion. "I'm sorry, but I've forgotten your name."

"That's because you never knew her name," Steve quickly interjected. "This is my friend Francesca Taylor."

Rick took her hand, bent over with a flourish, and kissed it. "*Enchanté.*"

Tom rolled his eyes and mouthed the word *dork*.

In the rear of the boat, the divemaster instructed everyone to gather around. Haas grabbed Steve's elbow and leaned closer. "I take it this is not the woman you married in school?"

"You take it right. I was divorced two years ago."

Haas stole another glance at Francesca. "If you got her from the Victoria's Secret catalog, I want the order number."

Steve smiled to himself. Their American divemaster gave the briefing, and the divers donned their gear. Steve and Rick decided to link up as a foursome of two buddy pairs. Moments later, after Haas and his son were in the water, Steve watched Francesca do a perfect, giant-stride entry, followed by a thumb-and-forefinger okay signal. For a novice, she certainly looked comfortable in the water. Then four of them buddied-up and descended feet-first to the bottom.

They reached the sand at a shallow forty-two feet. The visibility was good, and the water temperature was a balmy eighty-three degrees. According to the divemaster, most of the reefs were novice-to-intermediate skill level. Because Steve had the most experience, he was the agreed-upon leader, whose job it was to be point man while overseeing his charges. He needn't have worried. The Haases' skills were more than adequate, and for someone who'd hardly dived at all, Francesca was very much at ease. As Steve watched her closely, she showed no signs of panic or exhaustion. She acknowledged each of his hand-signal inquiries with an encouraging okay signal.

They explored the reefs, grottoes, and swim-throughs at a leisurely pace, enjoying the different types of coral and brightly colored marine fish. Steve had a waterproof card that illustrated prominent underwater flora and fauna, and he pointed out brain coral, barrel sponges, sea fans, and various species of fish.

After forty minutes of diving, it was time to surface. They all had ample air, but two-thirds of an hour underwater was more than enough for their first dive. Steve led them back to the ascent line. They slowly kicked toward the surface, briefly hovering at the fifteen-foot safety stop before coming up near the stern ladder.

Steve lowered his mask around his neck. "You looked pretty relaxed down there," he said to Francesca.

"That was wonderful! I wasn't nervous for a second!"

"Dad," Tom called, "did you see that barracuda?"

"Sure did. Three feet, at least."

"*Three?*" Tom exclaimed. "It was at least four!"

"Looked like six to me," Francesca chimed in light-heartedly.

Steve laughed. "What about that enormous lobster?"

"Had to be at least ten pounds," said Rick.

"That thing was huge!" Tom exclaimed.

"Ten? I'd say twenty pounds, minimum!" Francesca added.

Their shared laughter was raucous.

To some, diving was considered a form of underwater excursion. And as with other types of travelers, it engendered a unique camaraderie born of shared sights and experiences. Once on board, the foursome switched tanks and waited out the surface interval, a period during which accumulated nitrogen in their blood was reduced. They swapped underwater observations in a heady, buoyant manner. Soon it was time for their second dive. They entered the water excitedly and didn't want to surface when the dive ended.

Over the din of the diesels on the trip back, Steve reminisced with Rick, while Francesca chatted with Tom. They were discussing the next day's dives, when the divemaster approached.

"I was watching you guys underwater," he said. "You've got your shit together. I'd say you're ready for Desecho. Want to give it a shot tomorrow?"

They agreed with alacrity.

"Great. I'm doing that dive. Boat leaves at eight o'clock sharp. And unless you want to chum the water, no big breakfasts, okay?"

Back at the dive shop, Steve and Rick parted company. Haas and his son were making a turnaround afternoon trip to see the sights of La Pargeura, a short drive south. They were staying at a small Rincon parador, and they promised to link up with Steve and Francesca early the next morning.

The latter had no plans. The day remained sunny, and Francesca wanted to work on her tan. That was fine with Steve. He had his book to read, and nothing seemed more idyllic than lazing at poolside, reading a novel, and enjoying the warm salt breeze in the company of a woman he adored.

He finally admitted to himself that he was falling in love. It was an emotion he hadn't experienced in thirty years. Whatever he'd felt for Lorraine, it hadn't been romantic love. Rather, in the beginning, it was a relationship based on mutual neediness, one in which affection vanished as the years went by. But Francesca . . .

As far back as the Christmas party, she'd stimulated his senses. Now she stimulated his mind and his feelings as well. To Steve, this seemed the closest he was going to come to mature love. He had no idea where their relationship was going. Satisfied with the general direction things were heading, he was content to take it one day at a time.

By late in the afternoon, they were both exhausted from the sun, wind, and water. Before dinner, they took a nap. When they awoke, it was eight P.M., and the sun was setting. Francesca put on a black slip-dress. With a fresh pink hibiscus in her hair, she looked elegantly Spanish. Hand in hand, they walked to the dining room. The romantic hotel-restaurant had reserved European service, and the couple ate by flickering candlelight.

"Let's take a walk," Francesca said when they finished.

"Sure. Where to?"

"Along the beach. Let's bring a blanket."

On Saturday night, most of the social activities were in town. The beach was largely deserted. Francesca took off her shoes and slowly walked through the sand, still warm from the day's sunshine. A three-quarter moon shone overhead, and fair-weather clouds danced in and out of its light. They strolled together in contented silence.

The waves pounded the shore just beyond them. In the inconstant moonlight, beads of breaking surf glittered like blue pearls. They came to a secluded cove. Steve spread out the blanket and sat down. Placing her shoes on the blanket's corner, Francesca sank to her knees. He motioned for her to sit beside him, but instead, she crossed her arms, took her dress by the fringed hem and pulled it over her head. Save for a pair of black bikini underpants, she was naked.

Backlit by the moon, Francesca was an alluring siren. Steve looked around.

"Aren't you worried someone might come by?" he asked.

"No," she calmly replied. "Should I be?"

Before he could answer, she leaned forward and silenced him with a firm kiss on the lips. Then she drew his face to her breasts, grazing his mouth with her stiffening nipples. His hands rose to cup her breasts. She thumbed down her briefs and kicked them aside. Then she pulled his face away and looked into his eyes.

She was an enchanted temptress, he the willing victim. She eagerly pulled off his shirt and slowly reclined. He knelt and kissed the warm brown skin of her navel. Her tan line was very low, and the contrasting skin beneath it appeared opalescent.

Despite the cooling sea breeze that crept along the sand, Francesca's warm skin was dewy with perspiration. Steve's kisses now wandered upward, past her abdomen and heaving breasts to the soft hollow of her neck, where he felt the beating of her heart. Ever so slowly, her breathing increased in tempo. He rolled onto his back beside her, and for a while they both stared up at the ivory moon, wondering about the promise of their future together.

11

Anticipating the dive at Desecho Island, they awoke early the next morning. Steve got out of bed and looked at the sky through the villa window. Outside, the sky was partly cloudy, but there was a steady breeze, and the sea had a light chop. Crossing the Mona Passage would be an adventure. He was glad they both still wore their scope patches. Mindful of the divemaster's admonition, all they had for breakfast was a demitasse of espresso.

Francesca dressed in yet another beautiful outfit, knotting a decorative wrap around her waist. Sitting at the edge of the bed, Steve watched her get ready. He was trying to remain objective about Francesca, for he knew that when courting, both partners were on their best behavior. Yet everyone had both secrets and a dark side. If the relationship was to last, everything about her would eventually surface. But as he sat there, he could find absolutely nothing to spoil the image. At the very least, he was infatuated with her; at most, he was falling deeply in love.

He gathered his gear. "All set?" he asked.

"I think so. Can you think of anything I forgot?"

"Nope. Is your patch on? Sometimes they slide off."

She felt behind her ear. "Still there."

Slinging her dive bag over one shoulder, he got up and took her hand. "Then off we go."

They reached the shop at seven-forty-five. Most of their fellow divers had already signed in. The Haases were the last ones to show up.

"Cutting it a little close, don't you think?" Steve asked.

"Yeah, but we're here. I was having trouble getting my camera together."

"What kind is it?"

"A Nikonos," said Rick. "Wanna see it?"

"Sure."

Rick opened the case and removed an orange-bodied camera. It sported an expensive wide-angle lens and a strobe. In a corner of the valise-size case was a compact, black-leather doctor's bag.

"Nice camera, but what about . . ." Steve asked, nodding at the bag.

"Force of habit," Rick sheepishly admitted. "Call me compulsive, but I take my bag wherever I go."

The onshore breeze freshened, and Francesca pulled back her hair. "Steve, did you take my hairbrush?"

"No, did you leave it in the room?"

"I bet I did." She eyed the dockside clock. "There's still time. I'll be right back." Wrap flying in the breeze, she quickly ran toward the hotel. The men watched her departure.

"That is one seriously hot-looking woman," Rick observed. "Please don't tell me this is just a weekend fling."

"Actually, we met last Christmas. Believe me, she's more than just another pretty woman. I'd say she's the whole package."

"You're breakin' my heart, my friend."

The divemaster shouted good morning and waved everyone together for a pre-boarding briefing. Steve asked him to wait a few minutes, and soon Francesca came running up, apologizing. After some lighthearted comments from fellow divers, the briefing wound up, and everyone boarded. The divers prepared their tanks and regulators and bungied their setups to their seat-backs.

As expected, the trip across the Mona Passage was anything but pleasant. There were two- to three-foot seas, and the boat rocked dizzyingly up and down between the swells. Within fifteen minutes, several pasty-faced divers got up and leaned over the leeward rail, Rick Haas among them. Returning unsteadily to his seat, Rick wiped his pale and sweaty brow as his breathing returned to normal.

"Damn chorizos," he managed to say. "What do you call someone who wolfs down sausages before a dive?"

"Complete idiot, in my book."

Throughout the choppy trip, Francesca remained serene and unperturbed, bothered only by the occasional smell of diesel exhaust. She took Steve's hand and held tight. Soon the island enlarged on the horizon. Eventually, the boat slowed and tied up to a buoy. The divemaster put on a mask and jumped overboard to check the underwater conditions. When he climbed back on deck, he called everyone together.

"First of all," he said, "if anyone still feels sick, do *not* make this first dive. This isn't the time to practice your underwater barfing skills. Just stay on board or snorkel around, and you should be okay for the second dive.

"There are seventeen sites around Desecho," he continued. "The reefs are some of the healthiest in the Caribbean. The whole area was suggested for national park status by the Department of Natural Resources. I know we all had a rough ride, but the payoff is usually one-hundred-foot-plus visibility. Today we had a little surface chop that stirred up the bottom and lowered the viz to seventy or so, which is fine for us.

"We're on the southwest side of the island," he said, "and most sites range from twenty to ninety-five feet. The site we're on now is called Candyland, and it's a ninety-five-footer. This is a very pretty reef. There are lots of brain and star corals topped with really big sea fans. The tables give us a bottom time of twenty minutes, but you're all using computers. Just remember to dive conservatively and don't push the limits. Start at depth and wander around, working your way shallow back to the ascent line. I want tight buddy pairs on this dive. When you're ready, suit up and hit the water."

Rick felt well enough to dive, and he and his son wanted to practice their underwater photography. This left Steve and Francesca to themselves. They each checked the other's air one final time and reviewed emergency hand signals. Once they'd donned their tanks, they entered the water one at a time. Pairing up on the surface, Steve awaited Francesca's thumb-and-forefinger okay before giving the thumb-down descent signal. Deflating their buoyancy compensator vests, they began a slow descent.

Steve watched as Francesca periodically stopped to equalize the pressure in her ears. Each time she did, he checked their depth: twenty-five feet, then forty-five, then seventy. As the bottom rose up to them, he kept watching Francesca, whose long dark hair floated weightlessly around her, and whose nipples were provocatively erect.

He suddenly wanted her and briefly fantasized about doing it underwater.

When they reached the sandy bottom, Steve checked out the area and took a compass reading on the dive boat, now dim overhead. Francesca sank to her knees in the sand, awaiting instructions. Looking around, he spotted several large barrel sponges rimmed by orange fire coral. He gave the follow-me signal, received her okay, and slowly finned toward the sponges.

The reef was spectacular. Although not pristine, it was one of the healthiest he'd ever seen, with relatively few bleached-out, white coral skeletons. The deeper they descended, the more the normal surface colors were lost. But even at ninety feet, the multilayered reef was capable of turning into a spectacular prism, with breathtaking purples, oranges, and reds. When he directed his light on them, the undersea flora shined like jeweled shields.

It was a lazy, unhurried dive. The reef had numerous swim channels that began at the periphery and slowly worked upward toward the centrally located ascent line. When he found something interesting, Steve pointed it out on his reef identification card. Francesca nodded enthusiastically, her pleasure apparent. Twelve minutes into the dive, they'd risen to seventy feet, then sixty. Steve checked their air; they both had plenty remaining.

He turned into a different rising channel and looked over his shoulder. From just behind and above him, Francesca circled thumb and forefinger. Steve felt more relaxed than he'd ever felt in his life. It was turning out to be a splendid dive, and he was in the company of the woman he loved.

Just overhead, a school of blue chromis moved together in an indigo wave. As he swam past a sand-level cave, he spotted the head and eyes of a large spotted moray eel. Jaws slightly open, with rows of razor-sharp teeth visible, the huge snakelike creature looked particularly vicious. Maintaining a safe distance, Steve inched slightly closer.

And then it happened.

The sudden stinging around his neck was excruciatingly painful. He winced, nearly blacking out from the pain and biting partway through his mouthpiece. His neck was ablaze, and it felt as if he were being stabbed by a thousand tiny daggers. Fighting a sudden, nauseating wave of vertigo, he figured he'd been attacked by a second moray. But when he reached behind him, he saw a veil of long, translucent tentacles. He immediately realized that he'd been stung by a jellyfish.

He'd been stung several times before, by hyoids, Portuguese man-of-wars, and countless fire corals. But as he frantically reached behind him to swat the damn thing away, this time seemed different. The pain was intense and unrelenting. Thinking a tentacle with its poisonous nematocysts might still be on his skin, he brushed at his neck, fanning salt water over the area. Nothing seemed to help. Might he have swum into a whole school of the damn things?

He remembered Francesca and quickly turned around. She was ten feet away, slowly moving backward in the water, the eyes behind her mask wide with terror. Trembling, she pointed at the jellyfish, and he nodded. With a huge honeycomb of bubbles rising from her regulator, he could see that she was hyperventilating, and he signaled for her to calm down. But in truth, he was the one who needed calming. The agonizing pain wouldn't quit, and he felt his head start to pound.

When she finally saw the jellyfish drift off, Francesca swam closer. She pointed to him and made the okay sign in inquiry, and he shook his head emphatically no. Beyond the pain, his heart seemed to be beating unusually rapidly. His vision was constricting into pinpoints, and his breathing became labored, as if he were low on air. He immediately checked his console and was relieved to find fourteen hundred psi. He quickly looked around, as did Francesca. There were no other divers in sight. Francesca gestured upward with her thumb, asking if he wanted to ascend. Steve lethargically nodded yes.

Suddenly, he felt terribly weak. He didn't know if he had the strength remaining to swim to the ascent line. His muscles turned heavy, and his breathing became more and more difficult. Even worse, he felt the icy touch of panic. His spinning mind frantically tried to recall the various forms of emergency ascents. The *last* thing he wanted to perform was an emergency buoyant ascent, the so-called blow-and-go in which he inflated his buoyancy compensator and floated rapidly to the surface. But although it was very dangerous, he thought he could do it if he had to.

His lips were becoming numb. Motioning Francesca closer, he pointed to his BC inflator button and wagged his finger no. Then he placed her hand on top of one of his shoulder straps while taking hold of her strap, bringing them face-to-face. With his free hand, he scissored his first two fingers back and forth and pointed at her, indicating that she should make a swimming ascent for both of them. Francesca nodded and pushed off the bottom.

The fiery pain was maddening. His heavy limbs felt leaden, and his strength was fast disappearing. He had a clear, sickening awareness that he was developing a toxic paralysis. As his strength deserted him, Steve hung limply in his harness. He prayed that he'd retain the ability to breathe and that Francesca could do what had to be done. Virtually unable to move, he closed his eyes and concentrated on willing his lungs to expand.

He knew he was on the verge of unconsciousness. There was an awful ringing in his ears, and he sensed a peculiar merry-go-round lightheadedness. Although his eyes were closed, everything seemed to spin. Yet on some primitive level, he was aware of the ascent, for the water pressure was lessening. Finally, they broke the surface. He felt the vest tighten as someone inflated his vest, and he heard someone shouting his name. As if emerging from a deep slumber, his lids fractionally parted, and there was Francesca, beautiful Francesca. He felt arms, lots of arms. And then, as he bobbed on the surface, everything went dark.

"Tommy, keep his head out of the water!" Rick shouted. To Francesca, "What the hell happened?"

"Thank God you're here!" she cried. "I think something stung him, or bit him!"

"Is he breathing?"

Her terrified voice warbled. "I don't know!"

"We've got to get him on the boat. Tom, keep his mask and second stage in place, and inflate your sausage!"

The sausage was a six-foot-long, bright red, inflatable vinyl tube used for signaling. The boat was fifty yards away, and between shouts, hand signals, and the waving sausage, they quickly attracted the attention of the crew. As they began towing Steve to the boat, one of the crew members threw a rescue board over the side and quickly followed it into the water. He met the struggling divers halfway and carefully rolled McLaren onto the long board. Haas ripped out Steve's mouthpiece, took off the mask, and hurriedly checked for respirations.

"He's breathing, barely," said Rick. "And those marks on his neck are jellyfish stings, all right. Come on, move it!"

They had him on board in less than two minutes, and everyone helped remove his gear. After Rick identified himself as a doctor and explained the emergency, the captain radioed for help. As Rick knelt and placed his ear to his friend's chest, he told Tom to get his doctor's kit.

"The heartbeat's erratic. Tommy, get me my bag."

When his son brought it over, Haas quickly found the drugs he wanted. Isolating a vein, he deftly threw in a butterfly needle and injected twenty-five milligrams of Benadryl, followed by one hundred milligrams of the steroid Solu-Cortef. Then, using a TB syringe, he injected four-tenths of a milligram of epinephrine under the skin.

"That'll help with the inflammation and allergic reaction," he said. "Is help on the way?" he yelled to the captain.

"The Coast Guard'll let us know soon."

"What'd you do with the camera, Tom?"

"I put it under my seat."

"Bring it over here. I want to get a picture of . . . Oh Jesus, he stopped breathing!"

Haas jumped up, grabbed his bag, and quickly placed it beside Steve's increasingly gray face. In a non-breathing emergency, the patient needed to be intubated fast. Fortunately, as an allergist, he was proficient at the skill. First, he opened an orange endotracheal tube and readied it. Then he removed his laryngoscope and lay it prone on deck just behind Steve's head. Flicking the lighted instrument open in his left hand, he used his right to tilt his friend's head back and pry open his jaws. Quickly, carefully, he used the scope to expose the vocal cords. Then he slid the tube into Steve's trachea.

"Okay," he said, inflating the tube's cuff and taping the whole thing in place. "Now comes the hard part."

"The Coast Guard's sending a helicopter!" shouted the captain.

"Since I don't have an ambu bag," Rick quickly explained, "we're going to have to breathe for him. If there's any oxygen on board, bring it over here fast! And someone check his pulse!"

Rick showed two crew members how to perform oral inflations directly into the tube. He sealed his lips around the end and exhaled hard enough to make the chest rise, about once every seven seconds. The captain wheeled over a green oxygen tank and cranked it open. Twice a minute, Rick filled his own lungs with oxygen, which he breathed directly into the tube. Soon, Steve's frightening cyanosis lessened, the skin turning a healthier pink. When he tired, Rick let one of the crew members take over, under his watchful eye.

As the artificial respiration assumed a smooth pace, Steve's erratic heartbeat returned to normal. He was as stable as conditions would permit. But he remained unconscious, and he was going to need a higher level of care: respirator, IV fluids, and comprehensive medical evaluation.

Twelve minutes later, they heard the helicopter approach. It hovered overhead as a rescue corpsman lowered himself to the boat deck, ambu bag in hand. He quickly hooked an oxygen cannula to the bag's port and connected everything to the tube. A minute later, a stretcher was lowered by cable, and Steve was carefully winched up to the hovering aircraft.

After a hurried discussion, Rick was allowed to come along. The helicopter's destination was Centro Medico, the largest hospital in Mayagüez. As it whirled away over the horizon, a tearful Francesca followed it from the starboard railing, knuckles white, chin quivering.

She didn't know if she was ever going to see Steve alive again.

12

The boat captain decided it was best to forgo the second dive and return to shore. Nobody was in the mood to dive. The voyage back was glum. Heartsick, Francesca sat next to Tom. Most people said little, suffering the swells in silence. They docked at noon.

"I got the hospital's number," the skipper told Francesca. "But I couldn't get any information."

She took the scribbled note, nodded her thanks, and disembarked with her gear. "Come on, Tommy, let's make a call."

In the hotel lobby, she explained the problem to the concierge, who immediately dialed the hospital's number. After long delays interrupted by rapid-fire Spanish, he handed her the phone. She said a cautious hello.

"Francesca, it's Rick. I'm in the ICU with Steve. It's a little too early to tell, but I got the impression he's going to make it."

Her eyes brimmed with tears. "Thank God, Rick. Thank God."

"Don't count your blessings just yet. He's in for a rocky twenty-four hours. All in all, I think we were very lucky."

"The luckiest part was that you were there when it mattered."

"Well, I took my cue from you. When I saw you coming off the coral head, swimming up with him looking like deadweight, I figured you had a problem. Are you coming over?"

"As soon as I get changed," she said. "I'll bring Tom along. Want to speak with him?"

An hour later, Rick met them outside the ICU. Francesca's smudged eyes were red, and she hugged her new friend long and hard before pulling away. "Is there any change?"

"He's not any worse, that's for sure. The head of the ER was trained in Miami, and he told me Steve's problem is like a severe toxic reaction. What they mainly have to do is flood him with IV fluids until the toxin washes out. But he also said he's never seen a jellyfish sting this severe, with paralysis. He suspects it was an unusual type, or maybe not a jellyfish at all."

"I'm pretty sure it was a jellyfish," Francesca said. "A huge blob with a mop of pale vermicelli."

"That works for me," Rick said, then gestured toward the ICU's swinging door. "Want to go in?"

Worry lines etched deep into her forehead, she simply nodded.

The unit was relatively modern. The big, open room was intimidating, with the incessant beeping of audio monitors and the muted hiss of respirators. Half the patients were unconscious, or nearly so. Francesca entered with trepidation and followed Rick to a cubicle at the far side of the unit.

Steve lay on his back under a thin cotton sheet, eyes closed. The endotracheal tube in his throat was attached to a respirator. Every so often, the machine would cycle, and Steve's lungs would expand. His face was very puffy, and his eyes were swollen to slits. Francesca was shaken by the sight.

"Is he in a coma?" she softly asked.

"Not really. Whatever stung him packed a wallop, but the paralysis didn't last very long. He started coming out of it while he was in the ER, where they tried to extubate him. But it was still so hard for him to breathe that they decided to keep the tube in for a while."

"That must really be uncomfortable." She leaned over and kissed his cheek. "I love you, Steve. Can he hear me?"

"Probably not, but you never know," Rick said. "He's sedated, so he won't struggle. I doubt he's uncomfortable at all. They said they might try to wean him off the tube this evening."

"And then?"

"Then we wait for him to get his strength back. Once he wakes up, I really don't expect him to be here more than a few days. Take a look at this," he said, pointing to Steve's neck.

Francesca bent over the metal side rails and looked closely. There were numerous thin red streaks on the back and sides of Steve's neck, haphazardly arrayed, like the strands of a mop. "Jesus, are those from the stings?"

"Yes, the tentacle marks. Look real close. See the tiny crosshatches in the tentacle marks?"

She nodded. "What do they indicate?"

"They're not sure. All they said was, it's not your typical jellyfish sting. I took some pictures of it with a close-up lens, and I'll run them over to a one-hour photo place. If I can find a scanner, I'll email them to a friend of mine. The guy's an expert. I'm sure he'll be able to identify it."

"Will they leave scars?" she asked.

"Hell if I know. But somehow, if he comes out of it okay, I don't think he's gonna worry about little scars."

She took a deep breath and straightened up, shaking her head and feeling useless. "Isn't there anything I can do, Rick?"

"I'm afraid not. Right now, it's all up to IV fluids and Mother Nature."

"But I'm so damn helpless!"

"I know what. If you want to do something, be here when he wakes up. I have a feeling he'd want that."

He was dreaming about Andie. He and his daughter were drifting along in a peaceful stream when the water suddenly churned and turned to blood. Andie choked and started to go under. She looked at him helplessly. He shouted to her, but no words came out. He tried to grab her, but he couldn't lift his arms. Then the dream receded, and he was floating.

His body felt leaden. It was a peaceful heaviness, the pleasant inertia of one just awakening, but not quite ready to get up. If he could, he'd remain like that forever. But then he sensed something in his throat, and he wanted to cough but couldn't. He felt as if he were choking and then gagging. He tried to lift his arms, but they didn't want to move. Finally, mercifully, the sensation passed, and he wanted to drift off again.

"Dr. McLaren?" a woman's voice called. "Wake up, Dr. McLaren!"

It was a distant, quivering sound that seemed to echo, as if through a tunnel. Whoever was speaking did so with an accent, pronouncing his name "meek-LAH-ren."

Strange, he thought. But it was a conundrum too difficult to solve. And then he felt a spanking on his cheeks, followed by "meek-LAH-ren" over and over, impossible to ignore. Reluctantly, he opened his eyes.

A woman dressed in white swam into view. As his weary eyes focused, he saw short dark hair and dark features, but her black eyes smiled at him. There was something familiar about her appearance. It finally dawned on him that she was a nurse, and he struggled unsuccessfully to recognize her. But she was squeezing his hand—rather tenderly, he thought in his confusion.

All of a sudden a familiar face hovered over his, and everything started to come back to him. It was the face of an angel, one with long hair that grazed his face. *She* was holding his hand, not the nurse. As she gazed at him with concern, she softly called his first name.

His throat was dry. "Francesca," he rasped.

Her face broke into a smile, and she began kissing his cheeks, his nose, his mouth. "Welcome back, my love," she whispered.

How wonderful, he thought. Was it simply a term of endearment, or did she actually mean it? "Where am I—"

"I'll explain everything," she said, silencing him with a finger on the lips. Then she told him that he was in the ICU of Centro Medico in Mayagüez and that he'd been on a respirator.

"That's why your throat hurts, buddy," came a voice. From the opposite side of the bed, another familiar face appeared.

"Hey," was all Steve could manage.

"We owe everything to Rick," Francesca said. "Do you remember getting stung by the jellyfish?"

He hadn't known it was a jellyfish, but he remembered all right. He silently nodded.

"I don't think I could have gotten you to the surface by myself, but Rick was there when I needed him. He did almost everything."

"She's got that right," Rick said with a smile. "You owe me big time."

"Once they got you back on board, you stopped breathing and scared me to death. And then your addled heart couldn't decide if it wanted to work or not, but Rick handled that, too."

"CPR?" Steve asked hoarsely.

"Not precisely," Rick replied. "Your heart was fine. All you needed was that ET tube I had in the bag you made fun of."

Filled with gratitude, Steve found his friend's hand. His voice quivered with emotion. "I owe you one."

"Just concentrate on getting better, buddy," Rick said. "That's payment enough for me."

"How long have I got to stay here?"

"Whoa, slow down, okay?" Rick said. "You look like an Eskimo on steroids, and the IVs still have to flush the venom out of your kidneys. And then you've got to get some calories and horsepower into that decrepit body of yours. I'd say thirty-six hours, minimum."

"What time's it now?"

"Almost seven. At night."

"So," Steve said brightly, "if everything goes all right, I should be out of here by seven A.M. Monday?"

Rick looked at Francesca. "Does he do everything this fast?"

"Not at all. With me he does things nice and slow."

For more than twenty-four hours after she discovered the breast lump, Karen Trent lived in abject terror. If she'd been worried about the resumption of vaginal bleeding before, she was now positively terrified. She suddenly recalled that Restore-Tabs contained estrogen, and she'd heard of estrogen's possible detrimental effect on breast tissue. She assumed the worst.

She was so convinced she had widespread breast cancer that she considered it pointless to call the doctor. As scared as she was about the possibility of harboring a fatal malignancy, the thought of disfiguring surgery, radiation, and chemotherapy was even more frightening. And so she did nothing for days except think herself into a deep depression. In her morbid state of mind, she even began to dwell on funeral arrangements.

She remained in a funk, not going to work and speaking with no one. Nothing could persuade her that she wouldn't die at any moment. Terrified though she was, she felt compelled to continually touch the lump. And the instant she did, she quickly jerked her fingers away, as if she'd touched a hot coal. It had gotten bigger. She felt her heart start to race, and it became difficult to breathe. She was in an all-consuming panic that only slowly subsided.

It had been a long time since she'd picked up her phone or returned her messages. Yet as miserable as she felt, she knew she'd always been a social creature who needed human contact. So that night, when she heard Annie's voice on her machine, she picked up the phone with a mixture of guilt and reluctance.

"Love of God, where you been, girl? It was getting to the point I was fixing to come over there myself. You okay?"

"I'm . . . it's a long story, Annie."

"And you're not goin' to meetings, either. What, you becomin' a chubbette again? Afraid to tell me you're putting on a few pounds?"

Despite Annie's lighthearted tone, Karen knew her friend was concerned. She'd called a dozen times and variously threatened or cajoled on the answering machine. As she thought of what to say, Karen broke down. In a trembling voice, she told Annie what had happened.

"You outa your mind, woman? You better get yourself to a doctor as soon as possible. Now listen: soon as I hang up, I want to hear you dialing the numbers from my house!"

"But what's the point? It's hopeless. I'm just going to die anyway."

"Nonsense, you don't know any such thing!" Annie persisted. "Your know-it-all self already has you in a pine box, when that lump's probably . . . What's the word? . . . *Benign.*"

"You're wrong. Don't ask me how, but I know it's not!"

"Lord, you're stubborn." Annie hesitated. "If you won't listen to me, give me the number of that no-good bastard you were married to. Maybe he can talk some sense into you."

When Jared finally called back, he seemed concerned, and Karen was grateful for small favors. He reminded her that she'd had cystic breast disease before, and it turned out to be nothing. This was probably just another episode. But still, he agreed with Annie: his wife should see a doctor. This was precisely the prodding Karen needed. As soon as he hung up, she called Dr. Richards.

The receptionist informed Karen that Richards was on vacation. Listening to Karen's complaint, she referred her to one of Dr. Richards's colleagues, a general surgeon named Destefano. Early the following morning, Karen called for the soonest possible appointment. Unfortunately, the surgeon couldn't see her until the end of the week. This was actually beneficial, the nurse explained: it would give Karen an opportunity to get the required mammogram.

Fingers trembling, Karen called the radiology office.

Monday afternoon, they flew back to New York. Most of Steve's strength returned, although he was somewhat unsteady on his feet. He remained shaken. His facial swelling diminished somewhat, although the unusual stings on his neck were red and angry-looking. The flight attendants were very helpful, but his fellow passengers eyed him with curiosity. The stings were still painful. A thin film of Neosporin and steroid cream was applied to the injured area, which was covered with a clear, plastic-wrap, occlusive dressing. His most significant wounds, however, were emotional. They would take longer to heal than the physical ones.

He loved diving. He liked the taste, smell, sight, and texture of all creatures above and beneath the sea, from the smooth velvety undersides of stingrays to a lobster's speckled shell. Diving was a feast for all the senses, an effortlessly pleasurable experience. Yet now, the thought of ever returning underwater left him trembling. Every time he closed his eyes, he pictured the translucent creature lurking behind him. Intellectually, he realized that what happened was a freakish, once-in-a-lifetime occurrence. But on a visceral level, the horrible experience remained too real, too recent, and much too terrifying.

They finally reached his home at nine P.M. He was exhausted from the trip and the lingering effects of his injury. Francesca wanted to stay the night with him. She helped him undress and changed his dressing. Then, with her in his arms, he fell into bed. Sleep came swiftly. Unlike his fitful rest in the hospital, it was a deep, dreamless slumber, and he slept uninterrupted until morning. When he awoke, Francesca was gone. She'd left a note on the night table.

Dearest Steve,
You looked so peaceful lying there in the altogether, I didn't want to wake you. Took an early limo home. After I unpack, I'll check things out at work. Call me later.

I love you, F.

And I love you too, F., he thought. God, what a source of strength she'd been—helping with his rescue, taking care of the hotel room, remaining with him in the hospital, notifying the insurance company, nursing him back to health. He put the note down and smiled. He was starting to believe she was everything he wanted in a woman. His divorce now behind him, perhaps the time had come to seriously consider a long-term relationship.

His thoughts shifted to Andie. It had been nearly a week since his confrontation with Lorraine, yet he clearly recalled the anguished look on his daughter's face. In his hospital bed, he had thought about Andie a lot. He wouldn't allow anything to hurt her. He'd call Lorraine back and try to smooth things over, and he also wanted to touch base with Andie again, make sure she was okay. The hell with it; no sense procrastinating. He dialed Lorraine's number, but it was midmorning, and both she and Andie were out. He left a message on the machine, without mentioning his ordeal.

Steve got out of bed and stretched. Although his neck still hurt, he felt fresh and relaxed. He inspected the tentacle marks in the bathroom mirror. They couldn't be missed. Now brownish in color, no longer acutely inflamed, they appeared to be healing. When he looked closely, each mark had fine, fernlike cross-hatchings. He'd never seen anything like it.

His objective side knew he needed to rest. He was scheduled to see patients Wednesday, though the sensible part of him suggested he take the rest of the week off. He doubted his covering doctor would object. His compulsive side, however, wouldn't permit it. So he put on shorts and flip-flops and went outside. The air was still, and the day was already sweltering. Going back indoors, he uncapped an Arizona Iced Tea, found the novel he hadn't finished reading, and returned outside to the welcome shade of a stately maple.

He'd never mastered the fine art of relaxation. An obsessive person ever since he'd been in high school, he'd always been anally punctual, arriving early for all his classes. He felt that if he arrived late, something drastic would befall him. It was a behavior that dogged him in college, med school, and later in practice. He drove himself relentlessly.

It took him decades to appreciate that this neurotic compulsion was really an attempt to instill order into a disorderly, chaotic world. And while this often succeeded, the practice eventually took its toll. His need to punctiliously structure his life left him so hands-on that he could rarely step back and simply let events unfold. A prisoner to self-imposed orderliness, relaxation was an elusive confection Steve could rarely savor.

As he lay back on a chaise trying to get into the book, it occurred to him that a cold beer would taste damn good in the heat. But he knew where that would take him. Once he started, one would never be enough. He was shirtless, and as the heat baked his skin, he began reading in earnest. And despite his lifelong inability to let go, as he slowly turned the pages, languor overtook him. He began to feel a heavy-lidded drowsiness. So he put the book down and leaned back on the chaise, taking a deep breath. Closing his eyes, sleep came swiftly.

The hot sun creeping over his face awakened him. He sat up and checked his watch: two P.M. His first thought was of what Francesca might be doing. He went inside, picked up the phone, and dialed the Ecolabs switchboard. The operator put him through immediately.

"Steve!" she said delightedly. "I'm so glad you called! I was starting to get worried."

"I woke up kind of late and then took another nap, believe it or not. It takes a while for all those medications to wear off. But my neck's healing well. All in all, I feel pretty good."

"I hope you didn't mind my sneaking off like that. I couldn't bring myself to wake you."

"That's fine," he said. "I probably needed the downtime. What's going on up there?"

"Just catching up on the messages that came in while I was gone. They didn't expect me back until tomorrow. I told Ted what happened. He couldn't believe it. But . . . anyway, he sends his regards."

"But what?"

"I don't know. I'm sure it's nothing, but he sounded more, well, annoyed than concerned." She paused. "It's probably just me."

"Probably. That's not the Ted I know. Say hello to him for me. So," he said, "when am I going to see you again?"

"The sooner the better. I have some uncancellable commitments tomorrow and Thursday, but I can be out there Friday night. Think you can stand another weekend with me?"

"I think I can handle it."

After he hung up, he made a mental note to cancel hours Saturday morning so he could spend more time with Francesca. He was also going to call Lorraine back and check on how Andie was doing. Then he ventured outside again, but it remained uncomfortably hot. Returning indoors, he sat down to his novel but quickly tired of it. Much as he liked to read, neither his head nor his heart was in it. He kept thinking about his practice. Just as he had an alcohol problem, he was a committed workaholic. After a brief mental debate, he put the book down and dialed his office.

"Dr. McLaren!" Donna exclaimed. "Enjoying yourself? How's the weather down there?"

"Same heat you've got. I'm home. We came back early."

"Oh?" she said, waiting for him to elaborate.

"It's a long and complicated story. I'll tell you when I see you. What's up in the office?"

"Well, you didn't get anything from the FDA yet. You told us to keep our eyes open, but nothing's come in." She waited a beat. "And we had a little excitement around here. Hold on, I'll get Becky."

Rebecca immediately picked up. "Didn't expect you back so soon, boss. How'd everything go?"

"Becky, what kind of excitement is Donna talking about?"

"Nothing that bad. We had a break-in the night before last—"

"What?"

"The cops were here, and they checked the office out. It doesn't look like anything was taken."

"Stay there, I'll be right over."

He threw some clothes on and rushed to the office. When he dashed inside, Donna and Becky were sitting calmly at the reception desk. They took one look at his harried expression and gestured for him to calm down.

"Take it easy. I told you, nothing was taken," Becky said, immediately eyeing his injuries. "Jeez, what the hell happened to your neck?"

"Look, just tell me what—"

"No way," she said, defiantly crossing her arms in front of her chest. "Not until you talk."

He rolled his eyes and sighed; then he launched into a terse account of what happened in Puerto Rico. When he was done, both women exchanged looks of worry and confusion.

"Man, you're lucky to be alive, Dr. McLaren," said Donna.

"I don't know whether to laugh or light a candle," Becky said. "That's the weirdest thing I ever heard. You're telling me those scratches on your neck came from a poisonous jellyfish?"

"What's wrong, don't you believe me?"

"If you said your girlfriend got carried away with her nails, *that* I could believe."

He laughed. "Actually, it was *me* who got carried away. Underwater, by Francesca and by Rick Haas. Now tell me what happened here."

"Well, when we came in yesterday, the front door was unlocked. Not wide open, just a little ajar. Somehow they bypassed the alarm. For all we know, they could have been here for hours. But we checked the place from top to bottom, and as far as we can tell, everything's still here."

"Did you look in the safe?"

"Of course," Becky said. "What're we, idiots? The narcotics are still there, and so is the petty cash."

"The computers, electronic equipment, EKG?"

"Not moved an inch," said Donna.

"So what were they after?"

"Who knows?" Donna said with a shrug. "Maybe they just wanted to chill."

"Yeah, right. Let's see if I can find anything missing."

For the next twenty minutes, he slowly strolled through the office, checking everything thoroughly. His first thought was that drug addicts had broken in. But the drugs and supplies were there, as well as the needles, tourniquets, and syringes. No one seemed to have touched the personal items on his desk. He inspected the exam rooms, checking the cabinets and tables. Nothing. Finally, he went into the waiting room, looking at the pictures, plants, and the table display of Ecolabs products. A thought occurred to him.

"Are any patient charts missing?"

"Not that we can tell," said Donna. "We looked."

"What about the charts on the Restore-Tabs patients?"

Becky got up and walked to a nearby cabinet. Opening its third drawer, she sifted through its contents, then quickly checked the other drawers. She slowly turned back to him, slightly pale.

"That's funny," she said. "They're gone."

Jack Buhlman could not believe his eyes when McLaren and the woman boarded the plane for the return trip to New York. From his vantage point inside the terminal, he watched the pair walk across the tarmac. The doctor was bandaged and moved with some difficulty, but he was nonetheless very much alive. This was not the way it was supposed to happen. When his Indonesian contacts outlined the plan, the method seemed virtually foolproof. Yet clearly, it didn't live up to its advance billing.

At first, he hadn't wanted to kill him. Jack was initially content to let McLaren stumble around behind the scenes with half-truths and vague suspicions. Yet the doctor proved more resourceful than Jack predicted. He was getting too close, becoming too dangerous. That made him an intolerable liability. And his involving the damn FDA was more than could be allowed. The attempted hit-and-run was a haphazard, last-minute decision, poorly planned. That was not like him. The next step would have to be carefully planned.

Jack had never considered himself a killer. The truth was that he had little patience for the slow-witted thugs who did contract assassinations. Rather, he was a man of expedience. He did what had to be done to accomplish his goal—and right now, Steven McLaren was standing directly in his way.

Karen hated mammograms. Not only was the procedure painful, but the surly old crone who'd performed her last one eighteen months ago never smiled or had a kind word. Nonetheless, Karen called the radiologist's office right away and, after explaining the problem, was given an immediate appointment. En route, she prayed the old woman had been replaced.

But it was not to be. The aging radiology tech was the same one who'd taken her films before. Karen thought the woman took pleasure in inflicting pain. This time, the X-ray cassettes seemed especially cold, and the technician squeezed Karen's breasts particularly hard between the plates. But eventually, mercifully, the procedure was over. Karen waited in the small dressing cubicle while the films were being developed. Soon the tech told her she could go. When Karen nervously asked how the films looked, all she got was a terse "You'll have to take that up with your doctor."

Which she did when, after forty-eight unbearable hours, she saw Dr. Destefano, the surgeon.

"The radiologist sent your films right over," he said, lifting a large manila folder. "I haven't had a chance to review them yet, and I thought we might do that together, okay?"

Sitting on the exam table, clad in a gown, Karen nodded numbly.

The doctor illuminated an X-ray view box. Taking an X-ray from the folder, he slid the film into place. "This is your right breast," he said, peering closer. "The lump is on the left?"

"Yes," she managed.

"Okay. From what I see here, everything looks normal. No densities, calcifications, shadows, or anything suspicious. Now let's look at the other side."

He put up the other film and studied both the anterior—posterior and lateral views. Then he used his pen as a pointer. "This round area is the lump, about two centimeters wide. It looks a little cystic to me. You've had fibrocystic disease before, right?"

"Yes, but usually before my period. This isn't like that."

"Did they do a sonogram?"

"No," Karen said. "Should they have?"

"No matter. I'll put a needle in it and take the fluid right out. First, lie back and let me examine you."

Karen reclined, feeling the slightest hope. Destefano's hands were soon on her breasts, first the right, then the left. He seemed to spend considerable time examining the mass, and then he checked her armpits for lymph nodes.

Terrified, her voice strained, Karen couldn't wait any longer. "Is it cancer?"

"Oh, I don't think so. It feels like a cyst to me. Just stay down, put your left hand over your head, and I'll drain it."

With the nurse's assistance, Karen positioned herself on the table. As the doctor donned latex gloves, the nurse swabbed the area with iodine and covered it with a sterile plastic drape, which had a large hole in the center.

"We call this fine-needle aspiration," he explained. "First I'll numb it up with a little local."

Karen closed her eyes. She felt a tiny pinprick, followed by a burning sensation that made her wince.

"Sorry about that," the surgeon said. "That's the worst part. You probably won't feel the rest of the procedure."

She tentatively opened her lids. Out of the corner of her eye, she saw one of the doctor's hands steadying her breast. The other lowered an empty plastic syringe with a needle attached. Karen looked away, concentrating on the surgeon's face. She then felt pressure on her breast, but no great pain. Destefano concentrated, eyes fixed on his work. She watched him position the syringe, pull up on the needle's plunger, then change position and do it over. A frown slowly crossed his face.

"Is something wrong?" she asked.

He removed the needle, held the syringe up to the light, and checked the contents. "No fluid."

"Oh my God."

"Take it easy, Karen. It's not a cyst, but I have some cells here. I'll send them for examination."

The nurse applied a Band-Aid, and Karen apprehensively sat up. "But if it's not a cyst, then . . ."

"Don't jump to conclusions. Just because it's solid doesn't mean it's malignant," the doctor reassured. "Everything about it seems benign. Now get dressed, come outside, and we'll talk."

Karen nodded in silence, unable to keep her mouth from quivering or her eyes from tearing.

As he closed the exam-room door and stepped into the hall, Destefano motioned the nurse closer. "Send this right over to the hospital, and have the pathologist put a rush on it," he whispered. "I don't like the looks of it, and I want the results as soon as possible."

For the next hour, McLaren and his assistants ransacked the office in search of the clinical trial files. No one wanted to believe that someone had broken in for the sole purpose of pilfering the study patients' data. It made no sense whatsoever. The logical conclusion was that they'd misplaced them. All three of them were over forty, their memories weren't what they were at twenty, and one of them had doubtless moved the folders somewhere and simply didn't remember. Unfortunately, that possibility didn't solve the riddle of the break-in.

But if the charts had indeed been stolen, the larger question was, why? Who could possibly want them? The study was still in its preliminary stages, with no discernible results. The data were inconclusive, and it was far too early to venture any conclusions about side effects.

"Maybe it's some sicko trying to score with older women who want to make their chests bigger," said Becky.

"Or it might be one of those stalkers like they show on *Cops*," Donna suggested.

"Oh, please," said McLaren. "I've heard of grasping at straws, but that's completely out of the question. If it really was a theft, it's got to be something a wee bit more plausible."

They tossed it back and forth for a few minutes but came up with nothing. McLaren retreated to the privacy of his consultation room and called Francesca.

"You're not going to believe this," he said, "but there was a break-in at my office. The only thing that's missing are the Restore-Tabs charts."

"You've got to be kidding. When was this?"

"The night before we flew back."

"That's weird," she said. "Maybe the women in your office were tidying up while you were gone and refiled them somewhere."

"I thought of that, and we looked everywhere. No dice. Unless one of us took them home and doesn't remember."

"But why would anyone be interested in a clinical trial?"

"That's the reason I'm calling you," he said. "Any suggestions?"

"Let me think," she said slowly. "Well, the only thing I can think of was that something valuable was on one of the charts. Information of some kind."

"There isn't. At this point, it's raw, meaningless data."

"I don't necessarily mean data. What about the identities of the patients themselves?"

"What do you mean?"

"Maybe one of the patients was afraid of being identified. Maybe he or she thought of that after signing on. I know the study's supposed to be anonymous, but isn't it possible one of the participants had second thoughts?"

"Why not just ask to be excluded from the study?" Steve said.

"That would be the logical thing, but I don't have to tell you that people don't always act logically."

"I suppose. But why take *all* the charts? There were over a hundred of them."

"True," she agreed. "Maybe it was another company, one of our competitors. Nutritionals are a very hot business. You might find this hard to believe, but the other guys have spies. And so do we."

"Ah—James Greenpeace Bond does his thing for Her Majesty's Nutritional Products? I don't think so."

"Well, okay. It was a thought. After that, I don't know. But I'll tell Ted about it. If he comes up with another angle, I'm sure he'll let you know."

As McLaren returned to the main office, Becky handed him a pink slip of paper. "This guy says he's your malpractice attorney. He called yesterday and wants you to get back to him. I suppose it could wait, but he says he has good news."

"That'll be a switch."

Steve went back and made the call. He dialed the insurance company and, after several minutes, was put through. After he and the lawyer exchanged pleasantries, they got down to business.

"Normally, Doctor," the attorney said, "when we open a file, there's a built-in time delay. We have to get all the records, answer the complaint, and send out an investigator. He makes a report, and then an in-house medical expert reviews the case."

"What kind of delay?"

"The initial phase normally takes a minimum of eighteen months."

"You're joking."

"I said normally," the lawyer went on. "When this case first landed on my desk, it seemed so outlandish that I did some checking on my own, even before the investigator was assigned. When I contacted the attorneys for the hospital—the hospital was named too, because the plaintiff was in their ER—they were a little surprised. It turns out that the plaintiff's lawyer hadn't even requested the hospital record."

"Is that unusual?"

"You bet it is. On the face of it, if we're only considering your involvement at the fund-raiser, this is a bullshit case. What'd you do, take her pulse and elevate her legs? At first I thought there might've been some serious omission on your part that came to light in the ER—"

"Like what?" Steve interrupted.

"That's what I'm getting at. According to the hospital's lawyers, not only did nothing turn up in the ER, but Atkinson's attorney hadn't taken the trouble to check. Which makes the whole thing smell fishy. So I made a few calls,

dug a little deeper. In New York, a licensed physician has
to sign off on a case, attesting to its legitimacy."

"Who signed off on it?"

"That's privileged, and I can't tell you. But it doesn't
matter. You see, he claims the plaintiff's attorney never
even *spoke* to him about the case. Once I heard that, we
petitioned the court. This morning, they threw the case out.
And Atkinson's attorney might get fined."

Steve's shoulders sagged, and he exhaled with relief.
"So it's over? Just like that, this whole thing's just a bad
dream?"

"That's right. I'm sorry you had to go through it. I suppose the only remaining question is, why? This is only my
opinion, Doctor, and I may be going out on a limb. But in
my experience, an accusation this groundless usually turns
out to be personal. Have you ever thought about why?"

"I've thought about it a lot, and I can't come up with a
thing. I could swear I never even met the lady before."

"You might want to go over it again," said the attorney.
"Unless I miss my guess, Miss Atkinson knows you, Doctor. This has all the earmarks of a grudge match."

13

"What a difference a week makes," Julia Hagen said to Steve. "Before you left, you looked great. Fit, excited. Now you're sort of pale, knocked-out, and your neck looks like you tried to shave it with a lawnmower. What's going on?"

"God, I'm so tired of explaining this to everybody."

Julia looked hurt. "I didn't think I was just anybody."

His voice was a soft apology. "No, you're not. Poor choice of words. These are jellyfish stings, and I'm still suffering some aftereffects."

"Good Lord, what kind of jellyfish was it? I didn't know they could sting like that."

"That's the same thing they said in the ER in Puerto Rico, but obviously some of them do. Anyway, what gives with Alyssa?"

They were walking down the lane by Julia's house. It was midday Thursday, and when he called to check on his patient, Julia had informed him her daughter wasn't eating well. Alyssa was frequently nauseated, and she had almost no appetite. McLaren decided to drop by.

"Has she lost weight?" he asked.

"I think so. I haven't weighed her, but she looks thinner."

"Do you think she—"

"Not so fast," Julia interrupted. "You're changing the subject. We have loads of time to discuss Alyssa. First, tell me about your vacation."

"Julia, why this interest in my personal life? Usually, doctors and patients' families exchange pleasantries and then get down to medical business."

"As if you didn't know, you're not 'most' doctors. You're the only doctor I've had since I left my pediatrician. I guess I worry about you."

"That's very considerate, but—"

"I'm not just being courteous," she said. "I really mean it, and I think you know it. I'm concerned about you, Steve. I know you've been through a lot, and I want the best for you." She hesitated. Then, "So what was she like?"

"Who?"

"Francesca Taylor, silly."

"You know about Francesca?"

"It's a small town, my dear," she said. "When it comes to eligible bachelors, *everyone* knows. Besides, her picture was in one of the local papers last week. Some sort of business dinner she went to."

His eyebrows raised. "And?"

"She's gorgeous. Her boobs aren't real, though. But I guess you have firsthand knowledge of that."

He made a sound like a cat. "Your claws are showing, Julia."

"I didn't mean it like that, Steve," she lied. "The article was very flattering. And everyone knows you spent time with her down there. So how was it?"

"Honestly?"

She silently nodded, and he looked away in fond memory.

"Everything considered, even the damn jellyfish, it was one of the best times I've had in my life."

"That's great, really. You think there's a future for you two?"

"There would be if it were up to me."

"That's wonderful, Steve," she said, eyes brimming with tears. "I'm so happy for you."

When he got back to the office, Steve called Lorraine's. He wasn't concerned when Andie's recorded voice came on, and trying to sound as chipper as possible, he left a message that he'd call back later. After office hours were over, he tried again around suppertime. Once more, he got the machine. Strange; they were usually home for supper. Perhaps they'd gone out to eat. No problem. He'd try again later that night.

MANADO, SULAWESI, INDONESIA

It had been a week since Sergeant Atmosaputro was operated on. He'd been in the hospital's small ICU for three days. It took thirty hours for him to regain consciousness, and another twelve until he was extubated. A chest tube had been inserted to reexpand his lung, and once it was removed, his recovery was accelerated. He was a strong, healthy man with a powerful will to live.

Throughout the ordeal, one of the things that kept him going was devotion to his family. When he awoke in the ICU, his wife Eva was at his bedside, and she remained nearby throughout his hospitalization. Despite the long hours required by police work, Atmosaputro was a family man. He knew, as a partial amputee, that he could no longer work, but that was fine with him. He had some savings, and a small pension would keep him financially afloat. What's more, he would now have the freedom to spend time with those he held dear.

He was discharged eight days after his surgery. With the help of transfusions, his blood count had returned to normal, and his wounds were healing. Most difficult for him was the loss of his arm, for he'd always prided himself on his ability to take care of himself. Then again, his grandfather had been a double amputee, losing both legs in World War II. Grandfather had not only survived but prospered, and Atmosaputro was determined to do likewise.

Several years ago, he'd purchased a small beach house. The property wasn't that far from Manado; it was only several miles, in fact, from the spot Pak Suranto discovered the woman's body. It was the ideal place in which to recover—serenely tranquil, isolated, and stress-free. After a few days there with his wife and children, and once he was fully on his feet, they'd return home, leaving him free to relax and regain his strength.

He'd also have an opportunity to think about what happened. He remembered Jack Buhlman vividly. In the hospital, he gave a detailed police report, identifying his assailant by description, name, and prior occupation. The police, in turn, contacted the American Embassy in Jakarta. Its staff seemed helpful. With any luck, they'd have more information within a week. Whether the Indonesian government would be able to act upon it was a different matter.

Atmosaputro's plans for his convalescence weren't very complicated. He hoped to sleep late, read a lot, and get his body back in shape. He wanted to concentrate on the future and on raising his children. But despite this, one thing blazed brightly in his mind.

He prayed he'd have an opportunity to meet Mr. Buhlman again.

"Nalgas hermosas," Francesca said.

"Beg your pardon?"

"It means 'nice butt.' Firm. No sag, cottage cheese—free."

They lay naked on the bed, she on her back and Steve on his abdomen, facing her. Francesca's nails lightly raked his gluteal skin. Despite the breeze that blew through the open bedroom window, it was quite warm, and his skin was still damp from their lovemaking.

"Thank you. My butt is in your debt. And your *nalgas* are pretty damn *hermoso* themselves."

She laughed. "Spanish wasn't your best subject, was it?"

"You don't think my accent blew 'em away last week in Rincon?"

"I wouldn't exactly put it that way. But I *did* think they understood you better when you had a tube in your throat."

"Rat."

He rolled onto his side and kissed her on the lips. It had been a week since they left on vacation, and his feelings for her intensified every day. For her part, as Francesca gazed into his bluestone eyes, she considered him to be one of the most thoughtful, gentle men she'd ever known. The sting marks lining his neck were nearly gone, and she touched them with a fingertip.

"Still hurt?"

"Only when I think about it."

"I know exactly what you mean. That was one of the most frightening things I've ever seen."

"Me, or the jellyfish?" he asked.

"Both. By the way, did you ever hear from Rick about the pictures?"

He squinted. "What pictures?"

"Boy, you really *were* out of it. He took some shots of your neck and sent them to some expert, remember?"

He shook his head. "Nope. My recall's not the best."

"What about your daughter? I'm sure you had to be thinking about her in the hospital."

"I called earlier today, in fact. She wasn't home. I'll try again tomorrow."

Francesca finished her bottle of Evian and sat up. "I'm still thirsty. Want anything?"

"I'm fine, thanks."

Watching her arise and stroll from the room, Steve was as captivated as ever by her alluring figure. She had, bar none, the greatest body he'd ever seen. She was one of those rare women who looked better without clothes. Her body was a magnet, and he constantly had to resist the impulse to reach out and touch, stroke, and embrace her.

While Francesca was gone, Steve picked up the bedside phone and called Lorraine's. He didn't want to break the romantic moment, but he couldn't help it. He *had* to say hello to his daughter. As before, the machine came on, and now he was truly worried. Why was his daughter out after ten on a weeknight? Tomorrow morning, if there was still no answer, he was going to drive over there. After he hung up, he concentrated on removing the scowl from his face.

Moments later, Francesca returned with a cold bottle of Beck's.

"Where'd you find that?" he asked.

"In the back of the vegetable crisper, next to some old blue cheese."

"I don't have any blue cheese."

"You do now." She sat beside him and took a sip. "I think it's time you told me a few details about your drinking problem."

"Didn't we go over that on the plane?"

"To a degree. But I feel like we're getting to the point where we shouldn't have any secrets from each other."

Steve rolled onto his back and looked up at the ceiling. "This is painful stuff, Francesca. I've never really gone over it in detail with anyone."

"We don't have to if you don't want to."

"It's not that. It's just . . . guilt, I suppose. And embarrassment. Oh, what the hell. You don't happen to have any cigarettes, do you?"

"Since when do you smoke?"

"I don't. But I figure if there was ever a time, this is it."
Looking over, he saw she was patiently staring at him. He
sat up. "Okay, okay. It's really not all that complicated.
Basically, I liked booze ever since I was a teenager. You
know how some people hate the taste of alcohol and just
drink for the effect?"

"Sure."

"Well, I enjoyed the taste, especially beer. Still, I hardly
ever overdid it then. Of course, I got wasted once or twice,
but it was more a great social lubricant for me. When I got
older, and especially when I went into practice, I always
managed to drink responsibly, and never when I was on
call. I rarely drank by myself and never, ever got drunk.
At least, not until a few years ago."

"What happened?"

"Lorraine happened, for one thing. I'm not going to
blame her for my problem, but you asked. The way things
worked out, I grew to love this community, while she was
never really happy out here. When we started to drift apart,
I felt guilty about that, too. I forgot about free will and
started thinking I'd forced her to come here with me. I
know this sounds like a cop out, like I was just looking for
excuses to drink. And maybe I was. But I also think it was
this lifelong problem resurfacing, a problem about not being able to face my feelings."

"All feelings?" she asked.

He nodded. "Good or bad, it didn't matter. You see, for
a long time I tried to hide my feelings—not so much in
my work, but certainly feelings about my personal life. You
know the saying about when the going gets tough, the
tough get going?"

"Sure."

He shook his head. "Didn't apply to me," he said.
"When the going got tough, all I wanted to do was run
away. To numb out, to hide from the hurt. Hell, booze was
wonderful for that. For a long time, it was perfect. It kept
me from having to feel anything at all."

"But I've heard it said that the desire to get pleasure
from things like alcohol is human nature."

"Depends on the extent. For most people, yes. And for
a long time, I was most people. But then, at some point I

lost control. I started drinking too much. I wanted the pleasure you're talking about much too often. I began drinking the minute I got home, especially during the divorce. It got to the point where I couldn't remember things the next day—"

"The blackouts?" she asked.

"Yeah, like I told you at the hotel. I started to forget things. Worst of all, I started to drink when I was on call. You can lose your license for that. Thank God I never hurt anyone, but I knew it was just a matter of time."

"So what happened?"

"What happened was that I woke up one morning with a gash on my head and a corneal abrasion. I didn't even realize I'd fallen out of bed during the night and injured myself. When I looked in the mirror that morning, the truth stared back at me. I could no longer deny that I had a problem."

"Did you consider yourself an alcoholic?"

He mulled it over. "That depends on how you define alcoholism. I've never been convinced it's a true disease, like cancer. I think it's more like bad choices, or poor impulse control, or irresponsibility. But whatever it is, it sure as hell screwed me up—big time."

"Does it really matter how you define it?"

"No, it doesn't. It's the behavior that counts, not the definition."

She sipped her beer, nodding in agreement. "Okay. So what did you do about it?"

"I stopped. That day, around eighteen months ago, I just stopped."

"Did you go to a rehab?"

"I know, I know," he said defensively. "That's what I recommend to my patients. Somehow, I didn't think it was for me. Don't ask me why, but I guess I figured I wasn't that far gone. I thought that if I grew up a little, developed better coping skills, and acted more responsible, I'd be okay. And so far, it's worked." He watched her sip the Beck's, dewy with condensation. "Like I said, I have no complaints so far."

"So you think you're cured."

"Cured? That's the AA 'disease' concept, which I don't

really buy. All I can say is I'm in recovery. Who knows? I might even have recovered."

"Really? Is that possible? Sounds like risky thinking, if you ask me."

"It most definitely is, for some people. But you have to know yourself, to be really honest with yourself."

"You're saying you are?" she said skeptically.

"I think I am. Everyone has a different path in recovery, Francesca. Right now, I think I understand enough about my own behavior to drink responsibly again, if I wanted to."

"Look, I don't want to sound like I'm giving advice. But it's only eighteen months, right? If I were you, I'd wait a little longer."

"No, I'm serious," he said, eyeing her bottle. "Except for a little problem with a wayward jellyfish, my life's more together now than it's ever been. Here, give me a sip of that."

She shook her head. "Forget it."

He stretched out his arm her way. "Really, it's okay. Trust me."

"Come on, Steve."

"Francesca, I'm sure about this. Now are you going to give me the bottle, or not?"

"Steve . . ." Her lips made a moue, and she held fast.

Feeling only the slightest pang of self-doubt, he took the chilled bottle from her. Soon the beer was in his mouth, tasting icy and familiar when he swallowed. When he finished, he handed her the empty. "See? Nothing to it. I didn't turn into an ogre or a rapist."

She sank beside him, her voice a soft suggestion. "Too bad."

"Come here, you." He pulled her down to him and hugged her. "Did I tell you I love you yet?"

"Yes, but don't let that stop you. I'd like to hear it forever."

"You don't say? Forever's a long time."

"That's fine with me."

As she lay there against him, he stared wide-eyed at the ceiling. Was she saying what he thought she was? The idea of spending the rest of his life with her was very appealing, but it was in the realm of a distant fantasy. All he could manage was, "That's fine with me, too."

He lay on his back, she on her side, as they embraced one another. Her upper leg fell across his hips, and her breath was hot on his neck. Her nearness was intensely provocative, and once more he began to stir. Sensing this, she pushed herself up on her elbows. Her breasts hovered enticingly before his face, and her stiffening nipples softly grazed his lips, a cottony caress. That was all the stimulation he needed. Francesca's head fell forward, and her long hair did a wispy dance across his chest, sliding like gossamer.

Meanwhile, Steve's hands were doing wonderful things to her body. He had strong hands, and the fingers of one massaged the vertical muscles on either side of her spine, kneading away the knots. She held his face in her palms.

"You have no idea what a beautiful man you are."

"And here I thought it was just my *nalgas*," he said in his most satanic voice.

And then her warm mouth closed over his.

They lay side by side in the contented embrace of afterglow. Her arm hung loosely across his chest, and her head lay on his shoulder.

"I don't know if I can stand so much good luck," he said.

"You might have to get used to it. I don't plan on going anywhere for a long time."

"That, my love, is precisely what I'm referring to."

"For a man who claims it's hard for him to feel," Francesca said, "you're a quick study." She kissed him softly and got up. "There's one more beer left. I'll share it with you, if you don't think that's too risky."

"My turn," Steve said, motioning for her to stay put. "Stay here. I've got a better idea."

He soon returned with the beer, a fifth of thirty-year-old Ballantine, and two glasses with ice. He set them on the night table and poured generous measures of scotch for both, handing her a glass.

"What's this for?" she asked.

"I like what you said before about not going anywhere

for a long time. You know I feel the same way about you.
So if we're both serious about it," he said, raising his glass
in a toast, "this is to us."

"That's so sweet, Steve." She eyed his glass warily. "Are
you positive this is okay for you?"

He smiled. "I'm sure." Before she could protest, he took
a sip of his drink, watching until she did, too.

She sighed, moving closer to him. "How did I ever find
someone as special as you?"

"We owe it all to Restore-Tabs."

She laughed and propped herself up on a pillow. Sitting
shoulder to shoulder, knees bent up, they spoke in languid,
unhurried tones. It was lighthearted banter, freely lubricated
with alcohol. Although neither had the courage to directly
broach the subject of long-term commitment, they both realized they were entering the uncharted waters of a serious
relationship. It was an exciting but frightening subject, and
they giddily waltzed around the topic.

The alcohol's familiar fire warmed his gullet. He felt
he'd been visited by an old friend who'd stayed away far
too long. If one treated liquor with respect, he thought, one
would get respect in return. That's all there was to it.
Everything in moderation. He got up to go to the bathroom,
and when he returned, Francesca's eyes were closed. Her
peaceful breathing was slow and deep.

He gently crept in bed beside her and watched her sleep.
So far the night had been perfect, and he wished it could
go on forever. He touched strands of her hair, brushing
them off her forehead. How much I adore you, he thought.
Sitting up against the headboard, he finished his first drink
and poured another.

The aged Ballantine, which sold for over three hundred
dollars a bottle, had been a gift from a grateful patient two
years before. Although Steve had discarded most of his
liquor when he stopped drinking, he hadn't had the heart
to throw away the scotch. Thinking a discriminating guest
might appreciate it, he'd saved the Ballantine for a special
occasion. And if ever an occasion could be considered special, it was tonight. Feeling enchanted, warm, and mellow,
he wanted to savor the moment a while longer.

He swirled the whiskey around in his mouth, letting it

roll over his tongue like sweet springwater. It was a truly remarkable blend. The secret to drinking, he thought, was to master the drink, not let it master you. He would limit himself to two stiff drinks—just enough to relax but not overtake him. Lying down and closing his eyes, he listened to the rich, enchanted sounds of a warm summer's night.

Along the coast of Westhampton Beach, rows of heaped-up granite boulders created beach-sparing breakwaters. At night, the massive boulders were inky spines that stretched into the sea. The rocks were enormous, and the spaces between them created crevices large enough to shelter young lovers.

Lisa Wells and her boyfriend Martin huddled between the boulders, although they needn't have bothered. Late at night, there were virtually no beachgoers. Still, when the tide was right, their hideaway was comfortable and familiar. They used it often of late, particularly after Lisa had been discharged from the hospital.

Her bleeding had been controlled with an injection of Depo-Provera, a synthetic progesterone-like medication used for contraception. Her hospital gynecologist considered Lisa too young for the bleeding to warrant a biopsy. However, he did caution her to stay away from Restore-Tabs, since her bleeding occurred subsequent to using the product. Lisa promised to comply. Yet no sooner did she leave the hospital than she began consuming enormous quantities of the herbal remedy, up to ten tablets a day.

Although she didn't understand the mechanics of her bleeding, what she *did* appreciate was her heightened sexual arousal. Lisa had no way of knowing that this was an indirect result of estrogen overdose. Her breasts were moderately enlarged and had become tender. Her vaginal secretions and lubrication had increased. While most women would consider such symptoms annoying, Lisa thought them downright pleasurable. They were a concrete indication the Tabs were doing what she wanted. The changes in her body were the dramatic proof of femininity she'd always sought. Once she found it, her whole psyche changed.

As her arousal increased, so did Martin's interest. In turn, as the person who could now say when and where,

Lisa developed a not unpleasant feeling of control. Control was a strange and wonderful aphrodisiac. She became skilled at making Martin want her—to lust after her, to beg for her. When she finally agreed to have sex, which she now did only on her own terms, she was both eager participant and superb performer. She'd come full circle, from wallflower to vixen.

Lisa was on her knees, facing him. They were both naked. Martin was semi-reclining, buttocks in the wet sand, back against a boulder. Lisa slowly lifted up, and he slipped out of her. Although he was becoming addicted to her, she was quickly wearing him out. They'd had sex twice in one hour, and she wanted more. Pressing her breasts seductively together, she threw her head back and moaned.

"Enough already," Martin said. "You're killin' me."

She took his flaccid penis in thumb and forefinger, lifted it, and let it drop. "Poor little man," she purred. "A few months ago, the little man complained about not getting enough. Now he complains about getting too much. It must be very, very confusing." She cupped his damp scrotum and leaned forward, making baby talk. "Is the widdle baby confused?"

He gently pushed her away. "I said that's enough, Lisa."

She felt a tickle in her throat but suppressed it. "Oh really? Am I suddenly too much woman for you to handle? You're saying you don't like it?"

"I'm not sayin' that at all. You're definitely hot, Lisa. I mean, it's unbelievable how you've changed. A while back, you were, like . . ."

"Faking it?"

"Right, at least most of the time," he said. "It's like you were goin' through the motions, not really interested, you know? But now, wow."

The pressure grew in her chest, and she had to cough. She sat in his lap. "I love you, Martin. I'll do anything for you. You're right, I wasn't that interested before. But now I'm not pretending. I *have* changed. I just love to have sex." She slowly caressed her breasts again. "And I love my body."

He wouldn't be tempted. Forcing himself upright, he

found their clothes and put on his trousers. "Come on, get your stuff. We gotta go."

"What's your hurry? It's only one o'clock."

"For Chrissake, you know I have to work at eight. Don't give me such a hard time."

Lisa felt her heart do annoying flip-flops, as if there were butterflies under her breastbone. The pressure in her chest was turning into pain. The tickle in her lungs became overpowering, and she coughed.

"Cut it out, Lisa!" he said, certain her cough was faked. When she didn't, he took a pack of Marlboros and tossed it her way. "If you gotta cough, may as well be from these. Meet me back at the car."

Lisa suddenly couldn't move. Her limbs felt leaden, almost paralyzed. Worse, her chest pain was rapidly intensifying. Growing terrified, she thought she might be having a heart attack. Raising a trembling hand toward Martin's retreating figure, she tried to call out. But she could only cough—a harsh and gurgling cough that brought blood to her lips.

The pain in her lungs was now excruciating. Taking in air suddenly required considerable effort. Lisa's skin turned the color of the granite behind her. The best she could manage was a wheeze, which was hardly enough. After an urgent gasp, her eyes rolled backward. She pitched headlong into the sand.

As her eyes grew dull, death quietly approached. Lisa's heart stopped. She would never know that she'd become a long-shot victim of an unusual side effect of large doses of estrogen and progesterone. With the fatal blood clot firmly lodged in her lungs, Lisa Wells quickly succumbed to a massive pulmonary embolism.

A harsh, discordant sound emerged from somewhere distant. Still asleep, Steve grimaced. As he lay there in a foggy limbo, the sound persisted, growing more strident. His nearly unconscious brain finally recognized the noise as the ringing of the bedside telephone. Eyes still closed, he fumbled clumsily for the receiver. Finding it, he drew it to his head and mumbled a hoarse hello.

"Dr. McLaren, this is your service. I know you cancelled

hours this morning, but do you know if Becky or Donna is in? I have a few messages for them."

His brain struggled to make sense of the words. Everything seemed dulled and remote, and he couldn't quite understand what the woman was saying.

"Dr. McLaren?" the voice persisted. "Are you there?"

His throat felt parched, and his mouth was dry. "I'm here," he rasped. "I don't think they're in. What time is it?"

"It's nine-fifteen, Doctor. Sorry to disturb you."

He rolled onto his side, replaced the phone, and opened his eyes. His lids felt like sandy grit. The daylight was painfully bright, and he shut his eyes, falling back heavily on the pillow. There was an all-too-familiar pounding in his brain. Suddenly, he remembered everything. He sat up with difficulty, fighting the pull of vertigo.

Francesca was no longer there. The covers on her side of the bed had been straightened, and a handwritten note lay on the pillow. Squinting dizzily, he reached for it.

Steve darling,
I had to help out at work. Some minor emergency. I know you have work and want to call your daughter, so we'll touch base later. I couldn't wake you this morning. I know you had a rough night, and I hope everything's okay.

Love, F.

Still sitting, he let the note drop and closed his eyes. Oh my fucking head, he thought. The pain was intense, relentless. Yet his thoughts remained indistinct, his recall incomplete. With some difficulty, he swung his legs over his side of the bed.

And then he spotted the bottle.

The bottle of Ballantine lay on its side on the rug, nearly empty. His glass was beside it. Steve was suddenly aware of a wetness beneath his buttocks, and he roughly threw back the covers, exposing a wide, yellow stain. He quickly stood up, aghast. A wave of nausea swept over him with unexpected fierceness. He could barely control the sudden heaving of his stomach, and he dashed to the bathroom.

He vomited explosively into the commode, only partly into the water. His guts continued churning, and the bowl was soon filled with the stench of whiskey and vomit. When he finally caught his breath, rancid brownish splatterings dotted the commode, the tile floor, and a nearby wall. He stood there spent and naked, arms braced against the wall for support, breathing deeply. His whole body was trembling, and his mouth tasted sour.

Eventually, he flushed the toilet and straightened up. He turned to the sink and ran the cold water. Then he splashed his face and studied his reflection in the mirror. His skin was ghostly white, and his eyes were bloodshot. He turned on the shower and shook his head disgustedly. Everything around him stank, but nothing was so foul as his self-loathing.

Stepping into the shower, he adjusted the spray until the cold water's sharp jets stung him into complete wakefulness. Putting his scalp under the spray, he closed his eyes in thought.

You are, an inner voice said sharply, *a complete asshole. She told you not to risk it. Warned you, nearly begged you. But no, you knew better. Big tough guy, absolutely marvelous. What was that bullshit you fed her about honesty and knowing yourself? Yeah, right. Well, you know now. You're nothing but a stupid, common drunk.*

What the hell were you thinking, man? Serve you right if she never came back. Safer for her, too. What's that old slogan, about one being too many, and a thousand not enough? But no, you knew better. Jesus, what an asshole.

He turned off the water, toweled dry, and slugged down some Motrin. Still walking unsteadily, he went back into the bedroom, turned the AC on high, and changed the linen. It was a struggle, for his head and muscles continued to ache. But finally, mercifully, he was done. He collapsed onto the mattress. Slinging an arm over his eyes to shield them from the light, he waited for his breathing to slow.

He thought: *The basic problem is that I've never learned how to properly deal with my feelings. Last night, for instance. Even at this stage of my life, good feelings are as bad or worse than bad feelings. I just can't handle them. So I wind up drinking myself into a stupor. In the process,*

I lose my self-respect and maybe even the woman I love. I am a loner. I am a loser. I am an asshole.

For the better part of two hours, he lay there wallowing in self-pity, in physical and emotional turmoil. He was the downtrodden victim of relentless self-criticism. But finally, he realized the futility of what he was doing. Drinking to excess was bad enough; turning himself into a martyr was worse. It solved nothing at all. The point is, he eventually concluded, what am I going to do about it?

He didn't know. He'd blown his recovery big time on a foolish bout of self-indulgence, yet now he hadn't the faintest idea how to proceed. But as he lay there exhausted and frightened, he did know one thing.

He didn't dare drink ever again.

14

When he pulled himself together, Steve immediately called Francesca at work. She apologized for not staying, but she thought it best if he figured things out for himself. Chalk it up, she suggested, to a painful growth experience.

"You saw the bottle on the floor?" he asked.

"I did. I must've fallen asleep right after you started drinking the scotch. I got up around five to go to the bathroom, and I saw the empty Ballantine on the rug. I thought about taking it away, but I knew it was important for you to figure out what happened."

"It was an eye-opener, all right. I feel terrible about it, Francesca. Even though you were asleep, I'm sure it wasn't a pretty sight."

"It happens, Steve. Don't dwell on it. I'll come over after your office hours, and you can make it up to me tonight."

He felt better after speaking with her and even considered forgiving himself a little. Forgiving, perhaps, but not forgetting. Before he left for work, Steve brewed a cup of green tea and commenced making peace with himself. Sipping it at the kitchen table, he suddenly thought about Andie and went to the kitchen phone. A frown crept across his face when he got another recording. Now he was genuinely concerned. He found his Palm Pilot and located the number of one of Lorraine's neighbors. He quickly dialed and was grateful when the phone was answered.

Steve explained his concern over the fact that no one, apparently, was home. He added that he was very worried. The neighbor immediately told him that Lorraine and Andie had left on an unexpected vacation on Sunday, going up to Provincetown for ten days. Said it was a last-minute decision. In fact, the neighbor continued, he was keeping an eye on the house. Lorraine already called once and said everything on Cape Cod was fine.

Steve thanked the man and hung up, immensely relieved. At least he knew that Andie was all right. He still wanted to speak with his daughter, but he supposed it could wait.

Francesca arrived at his place right after he got home from the office. They spent the remainder of the evening quietly, strolling through the neighborhood, listening to music, and watching a videotape. Then they made slow, unhurried love before falling asleep in one another's embrace. The phone rang at dawn. It was Julia, and she sounded worried.

"I'm really sorry to bother you so early," she said. "But Alyssa was vomiting all night. She's finally asleep, but I'm not sure what to do if it starts up again."

"What about her pain?"

"It's getting worse. I held off on her medication because it seemed to increase her nausea, but before she fell asleep she said her ribs and back were really hurting. When she wakes up, do you think I should try it again?"

"I'm coming over."

He eased out of bed. Francesca had stirred when the phone rang, but now she was asleep again. After scribbling a note, he put on cutoffs, a T-shirt, and Docksiders. En route to the Hagens', he considered what might be happening.

The chest and back pain, he thought, most likely represented metastases to those areas. Bony metastases caused indolent, chronic pain and were a main cause of suffering in terminal cancer patients. On the other hand, nausea could be caused by brain metastases, or by the narcotics. Then again, perhaps the disease had spread to her stomach . . . He knew he wouldn't be able to make an educated guess until he examined her.

Julia was glad to see him. She thought he looked distracted, but this wasn't the time to ask. She poured him a cup of Starbucks coffee and took him to her daughter's room, where Alyssa sat at her desktop, playing a computer game. A faint but distinctly rancid odor hung in the air.

"How're you doin', champ?"

"I'd feel a lot better if I could get this stupid joystick to work." As if to emphasize her point, she tweaked the controller irritably before slumping back disgustedly in her chair.

"Maybe you should stick to solitaire."

"Too easy."

"How about getting into bed so I can examine you?"

Slight of build to begin with, Alyssa appeared to have lost several pounds. Her skin lacked turgor, and it seemed to sag, hanging as loose as clothes on a hanger. Her eyes were sunken from dehydration, and dark olive semicircles were under her lower lids. When she lay back, he lifted her T-shirt and placed his hand on her abdomen. Her lax stomach muscles now had a concavity, the skin on her abdomen dipping hammock-like between her rib cage and her narrow, bony hips.

"Any discomfort here?"

"Not there. But my back hurts a lot."

Despite her sunken abdomen, the edge of her liver had become prominent. In her neck, the external jugular vein was pronounced. He started considering heart failure. "Are you still using those patches?"

"I think they're making me sick."

"Always a possibility," he agreed. He took out his stethoscope and slipped it under her shirt, where he listened intently to her heart. Then he helped her sit up to check her breath sounds. She was staring at him as he put his stethoscope away.

"I'm so tired, Steve," she said with a weary sigh. "It's summer, but all I want to do is sleep."

"Then sleep. Sleep when you can."

"Can you give me something for energy? I want to go outside. I used to love my room, but I feel like I'm trapped in here."

"Sometimes, Alyssa, it's up to you to make the effort. I know you feel weak, but your real strength has always been in here," he said, pointing to her heart. "I'll give your mom a prescription for some strong vitamins. They'll pep you up."

"Should I go back on the patches?"

"No, I'm going to switch to something else. We'll start right now." He took a vial and a syringe from his doctor's bag.

"It's a *shot*?"

"You suddenly got a problem with shots?"

"No," she said without conviction. "I guess it's okay."

After swabbing her shoulder with alcohol, he gave the injection. "All done. Now get dressed and drag your cute little butt outside."

He followed Julia downstairs. Sipping their coffees, they soon became aware of Alyssa heading outdoors, where she sat with a book, taking in the warming rays of the morning sun.

Julia eyed her daughter wistfully. "God, she loves it out there. She was always an outdoorsy kid, but now she sits out there whenever she can. Why is that?"

"Because she's already mourning it. Nature's calling to her, Julia. She's attracted to the sun and sky as if seeing them for the first time. I suppose when you're losing something, you hang onto it as tight as you can."

"She's aware of everything, isn't she? God, who the hell ever said children don't believe they're going to die?"

"The theory is that when you're young, you think you're invincible—and by extension, immortal," he explained. "But whoever made that nonsense up never met Alyssa."

Julia suddenly turned to him, eyes moist with tears, voice trembling. "I hate this, Steve. I absolutely hate it! I want this torture to end, but a part of me wants it to go on forever, so I can keep her around. God almighty, what am I going to do?"

She looked so utterly wounded that he put down his coffee, walked over to her, and rubbed her sagging shoulder. "You're suffering because you love her, Julia. I'm sure you realize she loves you too—very, very much. Love is how you get the strength to go on, and how Alyssa will remain alive in you after she's gone." He briefly looked through the window, then turned back. "Come on, let her play. Let's go in the other room."

He led her into the living room, where they sat on the couch. "On the way over here, I thought from what you said that she might have metastases to her lower abdomen. Sometimes, if they get intestinal obstruction, they can get nauseated. But she's not obstructed."

"Is it the narcotics patch?"

"That's the most likely thing on my list. But it looks like she might be getting a little heart failure."

"Oh, God, no."

"Some patients get nauseated from that alone, I'm afraid," he said. "But to be honest, it's probably a combination of a lot of things."

"There must be *something* you can give her."

He studied her face. Like her daughter, Julia looked tired; yet her beauty remained. She had the serene look of someone who endured stress with strength and dignity. "Look, Jules. The cancer's in her bones, and it's starting to affect her heart. There's no getting around that. You know she doesn't have much time left. Now, there are all kinds of diagnostic and therapeutic hoops we can put her through. But why? Much as we wish things were different, there's no reversing what's going on."

"That's why I need you, Steve. We both need you. In my heart, I know what you're saying is right. But every once in a while, I can't help getting this little glimmer of hope . . ."

"You're her mother, Julia."

As if to spite the deepening lines of worry on her face, she forced a wan smile. "God, how I depend on you to bring me back to earth. Okay. What now?"

He took out the bottle of Demerol, samples of an anti-inflammatory called rofecoxib, and his controlled-drug prescription pad. Julia already knew how to give injections. He went over the dosing.

"You still have those Compazine suppositories for nausea?"

She nodded.

"Use them when she gets sick. But I also want you to give her a high-potency multivitamin every day. Ask the pharmacist what he recommends. Finally, I want you to give her a caffeine pill when she wakes up and at noon."

"No-Doz? Why?"

"As much for the power of suggestion as anything. I usually don't recommend drugs like that, but I told her the vitamin might pep her up. The caffeine will do that for a while. She loves the summer, and I want to keep her out of her bedroom."

She nodded thoughtfully. "How much longer does she have?"

He shrugged. "You know I can't answer that. But I think

it'll be sooner rather than later. Just keep her comfortable with the Demerol, okay?"

"Of course. There's not much else I can do, is there?"

"I'll stay here a few more minutes to make sure she doesn't get nauseated from the Demerol."

"Thanks." She looked at his neck. "Your stings are almost healed."

"Aren't they? What's so incredible is that a week ago, I was nearly dead."

She leaned back into the couch and shifted verbal gears. "So what's going on with you, Steve? When you walked in before, it looked like you had something on your mind."

"In fact, I did."

"The lovely Miss Taylor?"

"No, my ex-wife, Lorraine. I just found out that she took my daughter on an unannounced vacation. It all started when I went over there last week to visit Andie before the trip, and Lorraine accused me of sending incestuous smut to my kid."

"*What?*"

He slowly explained what happened. "So I'm going to call and see if I can get some answers from the phone company and the Web sites."

"That's the most infuriating thing I ever heard. To my simple mind, it sounds like you're being set up."

Julia's mind was hardly simple. When she wasn't taking care of her daughter, she was a chief investigator for Island Diagnostics, an independent chemical-analysis lab. The company performed sophisticated assays on everything from soil to jet fuel to organic toxins. It was Julia's job to evaluate repetitive patterns of results and the reasons behind them.

"Why do you say that?"

"Because in my work, as in my life, it's unusual that a string of horrible events happens at random. Some people might call it bad luck or a rotten coincidence, but when you scientifically analyze what happened, luck doesn't play a role at all. Or at least very little. I suppose there's a one-in-a-million chance of everything, even winning the lottery. But most of the time, there's a reason for everything."

"I don't know, Jules." But then he considered what she'd

said. He'd already told her about most of his recent problems, including his office break-in. "You really think missing charts and jellyfish stings and pornographic email are related? Come on."

"Not on the surface, I admit. But when something links supposedly random events, it's usually deeper, and subtler. That's my job, Steve: find the related patterns. All I'm saying is, don't be so quick to chalk it up to fate."

He hadn't told her about the other things: the lawsuit, the attempted hit-and-run, and his drunkenness. They were all too embarrassing. But that amounted to five of what she referred to as "rotten coincidences," all in a relatively short period of time. Was what Julia suggested remotely possible? At first, he didn't see how. "All right, I'll look closer. What else do you want to know about my life?"

"Nothing," she said brightly. "I just want you to be happy, Steve. You have such a cloud over you lately, and I hate to see you look glum. So the next time you come over, if you're not happy, couldn't you just fake it?"

He laughed. "Sure. I'm pretty good at faking it when I want to."

They were interrupted by Alyssa. Although she moved slowly, her mood seemed more upbeat.

"How're you feeling after that shot?"

"A little out of breath," she said. "I feel like I have a cold."

"Don't push it. Take it easy when you have to. How's your pain?"

"I can hardly feel it. I'm hungry, Mom. Can you make me something?" she asked, disappearing into the kitchen.

Steve got up. "I guess we don't have to worry about nausea."

She walked him to the door. "What can I say, Doctor? You must be tired of my thanking you by now."

"Nope. I always appreciate a sincere thank-you."

She put her arms around him and hugged, laying her head on his shoulder. "Thanks so much, Steve. You have no idea how much I appreciate everything you've done. I'd be lost without you."

He patted her softly on the back. "Least I can do, Jules. I'll be here when you need me."

Julia kissed him tentatively on the neck and then drew away. There was a look of something unsaid in her eyes, and her fingertips lingered on his. When he left, he felt there was much more than thanks in her message.

Steve paid all his bills from his office. It was early Saturday morning, and the patients hadn't yet arrived. The first thing he did was go over his recent credit card statements. Other than the annual America Online user fee he'd paid three months ago, there were no other online charges. But he was three weeks into the current billing period. Following Francesca's suggestion, he called the credit card companies and spoke with a billing supervisor. Again, there were no charges, which meant that someone else had paid for the online smut.

Next, he contacted the phone company. Without going into specifics, he said he wanted to learn what outgoing calls had been made on his phone. Verifying that the number was in his name, the representative promised that he'd be sent a printout within two weeks. The intercom buzzed.

"There's a Dr. Haas on the phone for you, Dr. McLaren. He says he's a friend of yours."

Steve picked up in the consultation room. "Rick? What's up?"

"That's what I should be asking you about. How's the neck?"

"Getting there, thanks. The stings are almost healed."

"Glad to hear it. And Francesca?"

"I'd be lost without her," Steve said. "She's been a fantastic help."

"I could've predicted that. Steve, do you remember my telling you I took pictures of your neck?"

"When did you tell me that?"

"Maybe I told Francesca," Haas replied. "Anyway, I finally got them developed, and I showed them to a friend of mine. He's a dermatologist at the University of Maryland. Believe it or not, he's a world authority on jellyfish stings."

"Small world. What'd he have to say?"

"Remember those little featherlike cross-hatchings in the stings? Did you get a close look in the mirror?"

"Sure. What about 'em?"

"He claims those marks are absolutely pathognomonic of the Australian box jellyfish."

"What the heck is that?" Steve asked.

"It's a notorious jellyfish around the Great Barrier Reef, and it's considered the most poisonous jellyfish in the world. It's deadly," Rick continued. "As in fatal. There are very few people who survive a stinging without a special antivenin. In fact, the lifeguards down there carry it."

"Really? I guess they should start to stock it in the Caribbean."

"That's just it. These jellyfish have never been reported in the Caribbean. Not before, and not now."

"Well, I've got news for him," Steve said.

"I follow you. I just thought you deserved to know about it."

"Thanks, Rick. I appreciate your help." He hung up the phone, perplexed. Julia's warning was fresh in his mind. If there was a reason behind all these happenings, he had to find out what it was as soon as possible.

Next, Steve dialed Ted's number.

"Back to work, Steve?" Ted asked.

"For a while, now. Work is the least of my problems."

"You always were a workaholic, even on weekends. How's the study coming?"

"I've turned it over to the women in the office," he said. "To be honest, it's a low priority right now."

"Why's that?"

Ted sounded annoyed. Steve had hoped Ted could offer some insight into the string of near catastrophes. He didn't expect such an attitude.

"Ted, this might be hard to believe, but I think someone tried to kill me."

"No way."

"I'm serious." He went on to relate what Rick Haas told him. "The odds against finding that jellyfish in the Caribbean are pretty damn high."

"You're claiming someone attacked you with a poison jellyfish? Steve, listen to yourself!"

"How else could you explain it? The damn thing didn't

just float halfway around the world waiting for me to swim by."

"I'm sure there are a dozen more logical explanations," Ted said impatiently. "I'll bet you I could find a marine biologist or two who'd come up with something more plausible."

"I don't get it, Ted. Why do you sound so defensive?"

"Because I think getting stung made you a little wacky. You're blowing things way out of proportion, letting your mind run away with you. I'm not defensive at all."

He sure sounded it, Steve thought. Deep down, he *wanted* there to be another explanation. Although he couldn't see it, he was willing to keep an open mind. "I don't know. Too many peculiar things have been happening lately."

"I don't know what the hell you're talking about."

"Come on, Ted, don't fly off the handle. For God's sake, I need your help on this. All I'm saying is that ever since I started reporting cases of vaginal bleeding in Restore-Tabs patients, I've had nothing but trouble. Some crazy woman is suing me, my office was broken into, I nearly died underwater, and my ex-wife thinks I'm a smut purveyor. I'm wondering what else can go wrong."

There was a long silence before Ted spoke again. His voice was controlled and icy. "Are you implying there's some connection between notifying me about bleeding patients and experiencing all this personal shit?"

"Of course I'm not. All I'm saying is a lot of weird things are going on, and the only common denominator is my notifying Ecolabs."

"This is the most paranoid bullshit I've ever heard! There's something seriously wrong with you, my friend. Know what I think? I think you've been trying to wreck our friendship."

"Why would I want to do that?" Steve asked, trying to remain calm. "We've known each other way too long."

"Because you're jealous, that's why! Your life sucks! Christ, what the hell has happened to you in the last few years? Ever since your divorce, all you do is whine! You hate your practice—"

"That's ridiculous," Steve interrupted.

"—your personal life stinks, you've got a shitload of unpaid bills, one stinking malpractice suit, and some misplaced office files, and you've got the nerve to blame *me* for everything! Man, you are one sick fuck."

"Whoa, who's paranoid here? I'm not blaming you for a thing!"

"I'm going to say this one time, friend. If I so much as hear a single rumor that you've badmouthed Ecolabs again, I'm going to sue you so bad that when I'm done, you won't even own a stethoscope!"

Steve winced when he heard the phone being slammed down. He was both stunned and annoyed. This behavior was *way* out of character for Ted. Ted had been a flake at one time, but ever since he'd become a business success, he'd turned into a paragon of responsibility. There had to be a good reason why he was acting so irrationally. But whatever it was, it was infuriating Steve.

He was starting to sense that Restore-Tabs in particular, and the whole herbal craze in general, had gone way too far. These remedies were getting a free ride from the medical community. It was time, Steve thought, to get his face off the TV commercials. His belief that "natural" remedies were generally harmless was now in doubt. How many people were using some form of alternative medicine and hadn't even told their doctors? They had no idea what a risky practice that was. There were so damn many herbal products on the market that patients didn't understand which ones might be toxic, cause side effects, or even have serious drug interactions.

At least he'd darn well put a stop to *his* part in this. Storming out of his consultation room, he walked past his stunned staff into the empty waiting room. Images of Andie and Alyssa stark in his mind, he angrily ripped down the Restore-Tabs posters and swept all the bottles off the display table into a trash can. Still fuming, he walked past a perplexed Becky with an admonition to throw all the junk out. He wasn't sure how he was going to handle the TV commercials. Closing the door to his office, he quickly called Francesca.

She silently listened to his recitation. When he finished, he heard her sigh. "I was afraid of something like this."

"What's going on, Francesca?"

"Something's happened to Ted. I've never seen him behave like this before. He's been like this for weeks, annoyed and suspicious. He snipes at everyone. When I asked him what was up, he glowered at me."

"He didn't say anything?"

"Not a word," she said. "At least not to me. But other people said he mentioned a few things to them."

"Like what?"

"Your idea to hold clinical trials really annoyed him. Friendship or not, he acts like the whole thing's a plot of yours to undermine the company. 'After all I've done for that guy,' he keeps saying."

"*Excuse me?*" Steve stammered. "He'd never have gotten his first damn job if I hadn't put in a good word for him!"

"He doesn't see it that way. He thinks you're a vindictive prick blinded by resentment and jealousy. The way he talks, he's convinced you're out to get even with him."

"God almighty, that's insane! I've always done everything I can to help him."

"I know that, and you know that, but Ted's behavior is way beyond reason. For example, he knows you and I are seeing each other, and he actually hinted that I put you up to the clinical trials as a way of hurting him."

Steve sat there in openmouthed astonishment, not knowing what to say. He slowly shook his head. "Medically speaking, he's obviously got a problem. As a doctor, I feel sorry for the poor guy. This is pretty damn sad. You think I could convince him to get some help?"

"I don't think there's much likelihood of that."

"I guess you're right." He paused. "But if I can't help him, the least I should do is protect myself. I might have to distance myself from Ted and Ecolabs."

"Meaning what?"

"The TV commercials," he said. "I don't think it's appropriate for me to keep letting them run anymore."

"That's a good idea, Steve, but I'm not sure if you can do that. I've got a lot of experience with publicity, and if an actor doesn't like the way he comes off, that's too damn bad. He can't just walk away."

"But I'm a doctor, not an actor. This isn't about the way my hair looks or my diction. This is about something I never really believed in. It's something that might really hurt people."

"Well, I could talk to somebody here. Do you have a contract?"

"If I do, I never saw it. Ted probably still has it."

"You must have seen it. A contract's not valid unless you sign it."

"I honestly don't remember. But if you can get a copy, I'd love to see it. I'll show it to my attorney and get his opinion. If I can't duck out of this amicably, I'll try to get my lawyer to break the contract. The less I have to see myself promoting something I don't support, the better."

"Be careful, Steve," she cautioned. "This could really piss him off."

"Yeah, well, it works both ways. Let me ask you something. Do you think the way Ted feels could have made him, say, try to get even?"

"With you? I suppose that's possible, but . . . You're talking about what happened in Puerto Rico?"

"Well, I was just wondering," he said. "Maybe that's a little too far-fetched. But what happened with my office charts and with my daughter is not."

"I don't know, Steve. All I can say is that based on the way he's been acting, he's certainly capable of it."

"Jesus," he slowly said. "There's got to be something we can do, for our own protection as well as his."

"I hope so." Then, more brightly, she added, "By the way, did I tell you I love you today?"

"No, my dear, you did not. It's something you couldn't possibly tell me often enough."

"Great. If I finish work early enough tomorrow afternoon, what are you doing tomorrow night?"

15

SULAWESI, INDONESIA

Given the area's serene beauty, the muffled, early morning explosions seemed out of place. Cottony bands of fair-weather clouds skipped across the azure sky, and the tranquil surface of the tropical sea was as glassy as an inland lake. The emerald-green slopes of the distant volcanoes arched sharply skyward, and the summit was obscured in a wreath of cloud and haze. This was the equatorial Western Pacific, where shallow archipelagoes were cradle to the richest coral life on the planet. Beneath the ocean's surface, a complex tapestry of submarine life unfolded in a vast, jeweled brocade.

They worked off to the west of Manado, in the waters north of Inobonto. The men were far from the protected national marine park, well away from curious snorkelers and scuba divers, and far from the prying eyes of government officials. The area was an undersea paradise. The island nations of the Indo-Pacific were considered the epicenter of planetary coral life, and over four hundred species of corals grew in the lush reefs of the warm, shallow oceans banding the Equator. It was an area where volcanoes and corals worked together in geologic harmony, with the submerged slopes of volcanoes providing the watery infrastructure for coral growth. It was also a fertile ground certain men were exploiting.

At first, they fashioned crude but effective homemade bombs from fertilizer and diesel oil. But as the operation expanded, they moved on to more efficient commercial explosives, like dynamite. Divers placed the explosive at critical spots in the coral, wedging the sticks into spots that would wreak maximum destruction. The blasts ripped the massive coral reefs apart, sending enormous geysers of water skyward and littering the seafloor with large hunks of limestone rubble.

In turn, the rocks were dredged or scooped up by large mechanical shovels, then brought up to waiting overhead barges. When the barge was filled to capacity, it was towed ashore. Laborers transferred the boulders by wheelbarrow to large trucks that quickly drove away from the shore, winding onto little-used dirt roads hidden from view. When they reached their mountain destination, a dilapidated factory, the trucks dumped their cargoes onto exposed clearings, where the coral was dried and left to bleach in the sun.

For centuries, various types of corals had been extracted from the sea. Some types were fashioned into jewelry or transformed into works of art. Coral-reef limestone, when cut into masonry, was used for shelter or crushed into cement. More recently, some corals found applications in science and medicine. And for that purpose, none of the world's archipelagoes was richer, more complex, or more promising than were those of the Indo-Pacific.

Initially, coral skeletons found use in orthopedic surgery as substitutes for bone grafts. Inevitably, an increasing number of pharmaceutical companies got into the act, searching for greater applications of coral. Their investigations quickly turned fruitful. It was an area ripe for exploitation. Coral extracts yielded compounds effective against tumors, inflammations, cardiovascular disease, infections, and viruses, including HIV. Undersea substances were transformed into everything from insecticides to a non-addictive substitute for morphine. As research intensified, so did the rewards. All that had to be done was to mine the rich undersea harvest.

But although such mining was common, it was for the most part illegal. Over the years, coral reefs, like rain forests, had become endangered by pollution, overfishing, dense coastal development, and other forces. It was estimated that ten percent of Earth's coral reefs were destroyed, and another third severely degraded. Environmental protection was sorely needed. By the start of the third millennium, several widely acclaimed international maritime treaties were in effect. Wholesale reef mining was banned, and underwater safeguards were passed.

Enacting legislation was one thing; enforcing it was another. In distant reaches of the tropics, where salaries were meager and lives precarious, the risk-benefit ratio often mitigated in favor of illegal activity. Thus the undersea plunder continued unabated. Once the coral was completely dry and bleached, the pieces were loaded onto a conveyor belt leading into the factory. The sound of heavy machinery came from within the dilapidated building. In its scorching interior, the coral fell into the massive jaws of a pulverizer, where it was methodically crushed, over and over, into a fine, nearly white powder.

Few people knew of the factory's existence. The nearby medical clinic might be closing down, but the factory's work would continue. Armed men hired by Tentrem Suroto closely guarded the operation with fully automatic weapons, M-16s smuggled in from the Philippines. They weren't there so much to watch the workers as to guard against intruders, with orders to shoot on sight. For the talcum-fine powdered coral contained a substance the factory's owners considered the equivalent of medicinal gold, and they would do anything to safeguard its secrecy.

Steve finished office hours early. His muscles felt stiff, and his neck ached. In the afternoon, he puttered around the house for an hour. Then, deciding he could use some exercise, he went to the ocean for a swim. The water temperature was brisk but pleasant, and he swam parallel to the shore in an easy freestyle. Wading ashore, he returned to his car, toweled dry, and changed into a pair of khaki shorts.

It was almost suppertime. He wasn't ready to return home, and he was hungry. At this time of year, seafood in the Hamptons was fresh and plentiful, and he looked forward to the rich flavor of striped bass. He headed for Southampton, where several excellent restaurants catered to the casually dressed.

Reaching town, he parked his car and strolled down Hampton Road. The early evening was fair, and there were quite a few strollers, though not nearly as many as on Sundays. Passing a liquor store, long-standing habit made him slow down to gaze at the prices of finer scotches. An unexpected surge of nausea rose in his throat, forcing him to grit his teeth. A woman's shadow flowed outward from the store. When he turned his head, he saw that it was Phoebe

Atkinson, dressed as stylishly as he remembered her. She looked down her nose at him, taking in his attire.

"Slumming, Dr. McLaren? You're certainly dressed for it. Or are you just looking to get drunk?"

"Save it for court, Miss Atkinson. Didn't your lawyer tell you that? Anyhow, you don't know what you're talking about."

"Don't I? You're a walking inebriate, Doctor. Most people already know about it, but if they don't, it'll come out at the trial."

Steve's face reddened. As his fury mounted, he stared at her defiantly. He felt like lashing out at that gaunt, made-up face of hers—but he restrained himself. Was it possible she actually knew something? "For your information, lady, I was drinking iced tea at that party."

"No doubt you were. But not five years before that. Oh, Doctor," she clucked, her mouth broadened by a sardonic grin, "I have it on good authority the state licensing authorities don't take kindly to practicing drunks." She gracefully turned and began walking away.

He quickly caught up with her, barely able to control his rage. "Where the hell do you get off making an accusation like that? If I ever hear you say that to anyone, I'll nail you for slander!"

She calmly turned to confront him. "In case you're not aware, slander is spreading false statements to harm someone's character. You know perfectly well that nothing I've said is false. *Nothing*. If you try to deny it, I have a dozen prominent witnesses who'll be happy to tell the jury you're a liar."

Steve was dumbfounded. "I'm at a loss for words, Miss Atkinson. What in God's name have I done to you, anyway? Why are you making a personal crusade to hurt me? Whether or not I ever drank too much is nobody's business but mine. But beyond that," he said firmly, "you have no damn right!"

Her face tensed as if he'd struck her. The muscles in her jaws began to twitch, and her eyes were infused with hatred. "No right? You dare talk to me about *right*? What right did Laura Christiansen have when you let her die of breast cancer? I'll tell you, you bastard! She had a right to a competent doctor, a right to a physician who'd listen to her and not patronize her! Laura was my best friend," she said caustically, "and you just let her die!"

Riveted by her words, Steve was motionless. He knew all too well who she was referring to. Laura Christiansen was a vibrant young socialite who'd become his patient when he first came to town. She had a history of cystic breast disease, but one day she came to him with a new solid lump. He'd ordered a mammogram, which was equivocal, and he'd immediately referred her to Dr. Richards. At that time, Stan had been pressing him for referrals. After an inordinate delay, Richards eventually recommended that Laura have a biopsy. For some reason, it took a long time to get the surgery scheduled. When the cancer was finally diagnosed, it was too late.

"So that's what this is all about," he slowly said. "Your chance to get even. I liked Laura, Miss Atkinson. I really did. I feel I did everything possible for her, but I can understand how you feel Laura's doctors missed the boat. But I don't see how that's related to the way I took care of you at—"

"Liar!" she shouted. Nearby, several people looked their way. "I'd nearly forgotten about you and Laura until somebody sent me a letter about your drinking history. Oh, yes, how everything fit then!" She wagged a finger in his face. "She'd be alive today if it weren't for your incompetence!"

Good Lord, he thought. How much worse can this get? "Look, Phoebe, that's not the way it happened."

"Save it for the judge, you lush." She took a five-dollar bill from her purse and threw it in his face. "Even better, buy a six-pack and shove it up your drunken ass!"

As she stormed away, he made no attempt to pick up the five. The passersby eyed him with caution, but he was oblivious to their dark stares. All he could think of was who'd sent the letter: Ted or Dr. Richards?

It was time, Jack Buhlman thought, to get rid of Steve McLaren once and for all. The guy was turning out to be a little too lucky for Jack's taste. He respected the role played by luck and believed the best way around it was with thorough planning. This was particularly because, much as Jack would have preferred to dispatch him with a knife, the doctor's death had to appear accidental.

Fire, on the other hand, was a worthy villain. A major cause of accidental fires was electrical. In the quartermaster corps, Jack had had enough experience with electrical supplies to do a commendable job as an arsonist. The moment he saw Steve leave for the beach, he got to work.

He parked out of sight and, keeping to the shadows, crept to the rear entrance of the McLaren home. He was grateful the security alarm hadn't been set. In addition to his tools, he was carrying two five-gallon cans of military-grade napalm, a robust energy source.

He broke into the house without difficulty. He left the cans on the ground floor and went upstairs to check out the bedroom. Finding out what he needed to know, he returned downstairs and located the basement door. He silently went down into the cellar, not wanting to risk turning on the overhead lights. He found the electrical panel using a small flashlight.

He was in luck. The circuit breaker was old enough to be antique, and the buttressing two-by-fours were dry, aged, and brittle. Jack quickly unscrewed the outer metal covering and went to work on the interior wiring. Using a screwdriver, he was able to produce telltale sparks, several of which blackened the upper interior of the box, suggesting a short. He then lit a small jeweler's blowtorch. Directing its flame above the breaker box, he created a V-shaped burn in the wood leading up to the ceiling. Only one thing remained before he could sit down and wait.

He crept outside until he stood below the second-story bedroom. Using hand- and foot-holds, he scaled the exterior siding until he reached McLaren's window. Using a tube of quick-dry epoxy glue, he squeezed out a sticky ribbon where the window's lower edge met the frame. It would keep the window shut until it was too late, when the flames would consume the epoxy.

Returning indoors, he carried the cans of accelerant to the basement. If he poured the liquid too soon, the doctor would smell it. It would be safer to wait until the man was asleep.

*   *   *

After his confrontation with Phoebe Atkinson, Steve quickly lost his appetite. He felt dazed, and he wandered aimlessly down the street, reflecting on what had just occurred. He was torn between confusion and indignation. Most of all, he tried to understand. He didn't want to believe the depths to which hate could drive people, but he had seen it firsthand too many times in his life. He got in his car and drove slowly home.

He doubted this ended the Phoebe problem. The woman's resentment ran too deep. Naturally he'd notify the insurance company's lawyer in the morning and bring him up to date. Once his attorney spoke with Atkinson's, the case would probably wind down—or so he hoped. It was equally possible Phoebe would find other ways to harass him.

Most of all, he felt sorry for her. The desire for revenge no doubt consumed and embittered her. Hate was a heavy burden to sustain.

When Steve finally got home, he was tired from his swim and the verbal confrontation. He puttered around the house, taking a look in the greenhouse, checking out what was on *Larry King*. During the first commercial break, one of Steve's Ecolabs ads was televised. Steve felt a simmering anger. He wondered if Francesca was having any luck finding his contract. With his growing doubts about Restore-Tabs and the harm it might be doing, he didn't want to be an Ecolabs spokesperson one minute longer. He quickly changed the channel.

Nothing interested him. He turned off the TV, went up to his bedroom, and closed the door. Stripping down to his boxers, he got into bed and mechanically turned on the TV again, hoping it would lull him to sleep. But although he was physically wiped out, his mind was still churning with the evening's events.

In days gone by, it would have been the perfect opportunity to take a drink, or two, or four. He switched off the TV and picked up one of his bedside medical journals. Yet that, too, held no interest for him. With a sigh, he got out of bed, went to the medicine cabinet, and took two Tylenol

PM. Then he selected a paperback novel and listlessly turned the pages until he got tired.

In the darkened basement, Buhlman waited patiently. He was used to waiting, first in the army, then in government service. He had the ability to close his eyes and completely relax in a Zenlike state of meditation. Although he remained alert, his body felt weightless. He took a seat on an empty wooden crate, where he'd be able to hear the nocturnal sounds around him.

The minutes passed slowly. Jack suddenly heard the creaking of the stairs, then the upstairs TV. It was ten P.M. He had to wait until McLaren was asleep. Fortunately, he had an ace in the hole: rather than having to creep back and forth to the bedroom door, he used an electronic ally.

Earlier, he'd attached an electronic bug to the underside of the bedroom telephone. Now, he removed an FM receiver from his bag and switched it on. The small device had a flexible earpiece. Pressing it into his left ear, Jack once more closed his eyes and listened.

McLaren was tuned to CNN. After a while, the TV sound disappeared, and Buhlman heard the flush of a toilet. Then came the creaking of mattress springs as the doctor returned to bed. Jack sat there in the darkness, concentrating yet relaxed. Soon there came the click of what he took to be a bedside lamp. At length, he heard rhythmic snoring.

Jack's eyes opened. It was time. Noiselessly he stood up, removed the earpiece, and switched on his flashlight. In his bag was a paintbrush with inch-long bristles. Unscrewing one of the accelerant caps, he dipped the brush into the jellied liquid. A strong odor of kerosene filled the basement. Using the brush, he painted a funnel-shaped pattern on the wood where he'd made the scorch marks. Then he cracked open the basement window, located directly beneath the bedroom two stories above. When he was finished, he packed up his bag, took the cans, and returned upstairs.

Cautiously cracking the basement door ajar, he peered beyond to verify that the ground floor was vacant. McLaren had left a lamp on. Jack silently switched it off. Then, tiptoeing up to the second floor, he uncapped one of the cans and carefully poured the accelerant on the rug beside the bedroom door.

His knife remained within easy reach in case he needed it. The smell of kerosene was so intense that if the doctor were awake, he'd surely get up to investigate. But Jack heard nothing, and the bedroom door remained closed. He slowly spread the jellied liquid on both sides of the door frame, much of the hall rug, and the landing. Walking backward, he cautiously descended the staircase, trailing napalm as he went. When he reached the ground floor, the container was empty.

He descended to the basement and opened the second can. There he brushed accelerant onto the area immediately above the basement circuit breaker. It was imperative the fire investigator conclude that the fire originated downstairs and rose upward. An experienced investigator might see through the ruse, but that was a chance he was willing to take. Next he spread the gel in an upward and outward pattern on the wall, trying to mimic the route taken by an accidental fire. That done, he linked the wall and staircase with a trail of inflammable liquid.

Buhlman stole outside to the back of the house, where he daubed the exterior wood around the partially opened basement window. Then he painted a line of the remaining liquid upward, toward the bedroom window. Returning indoors, he gathered all his supplies by the front door and checked his watch: ten-forty-five. Finally, he went back to the basement, flicked his lighter, and lit the area above the circuit breaker.

A smoky orange flame ignited the kindling-dry planks. The fire quickly rose, licking at the two-by-eights that made up the ceiling. Jack raced up the steps and hurried to the front door. Grabbing his paraphernalia, he hurried outside and began a slow jog toward his car.

A raspy tickle irritated Steve's throat, and he coughed in his sleep. The annoying sensation remained. Rolling over, he unconsciously coughed again, roused from his slumber. The irritation became maddening. He tried swallowing, but it wouldn't go away. And then his brain registered the strong, unmistakable odor of kerosene. His eyes flashed open. He bolted upright, instantly awake.

Despite the darkness, he could tell the bedroom was filling with thick, acrid smoke. Breathing was becoming impossible, and he cupped his hand to his mouth. He risked shallow, tentative breaths, realizing that if he filled his lungs, he might start coughing uncontrollably. Despite the mild sedation from the Tylenol PM, his mind was sharp. What he now had to do was clear: *keep low.*

Head lowered, he got out of bed and headed for the bathroom in a crouch. He quickly knelt on the tile and fumbled for the towel rack. The air by the floor was fresh and cool. Pulling several bath towels from the rack, he doused them in cold water from the tub. When his eyes grew accustomed to the darkness, he could see the smoke hovering at waist level, then thickening as it neared the ceiling.

Okay, he thought, get ahold of yourself. So far you're safe. Breathe through the towels, and stay on your knees. Find a way out. The door . . . ? No, there might be fire in the hall. The window's better. A quick drop to the bushes, you're out of the frying pan and home free.

Towel in hand, he crawled to the door and peered across the room. The bedroom reeked of petrol. The smoke hovered thick and menacing, and the fumes made his eyes sting. Blinking his lids rapidly, he could still make out the bedroom window. To his horror, flames were licking at the glass from the outside.

He stared at the window in shock. The situation was fast becoming a real-life nightmare. His main route of escape seemed blocked, but he had to be certain. Draping the wet towel around his head, he scuttled crablike toward the window. With the thickest smoke still above him, he reached up, undid the latch, and pushed on the wooden crosspiece.

The window wouldn't budge.

He pressed harder, pushing upward with all his might. The sash stuck tight to the frame. The fire must have warped it. He fell back onto the rug, taking rapid, shallow breaths, trying to keep his head clear. He could hear the roar of the flames in the hall beyond. His house was being

consumed by the inferno. All right, he calmly thought. That
didn't work. On to plan B.

The overhead smoke was descending perilously close to
the floor. Steve realized there could be an all-consuming
flashover at any moment. He had to get out—*now*. Creeping like an infantryman, he squirmed on knees and elbows
to the bedroom door. There, he reached out and felt its
wood, which was scorching. There had to be a fire in the
hall and on the staircase. But he had no choice. He grasped
the burning door handle and, despite the pain, twisted it
open.

In the hall, great tongues of flame reached everywhere.
The roar was deafening. The intense, golden fire seemed
impenetrable. He also knew it was impassable, and he
quickly shut the door. Heading onto the landing would be
suicidal. That left the window. If he got past it, he'd be
okay. Frantic, he quickly scurried back to the temporary
safety of the bathroom.

When he first moved into the house, he had kept a base-
ball bat at his bedside for self-defense. After a while he
thought it foolish and exiled the bat to the basement. Now
he wished he'd kept it there, for the only other mass heavy
enough to break the glass was his own body. His heart was
pounding. Soaking the remaining bath towels in the tub, he
draped them around his head and shoulders.

Sinking to a crouch, wreathed in damp towels, he resembled a ghost. He was nearly paralyzed with fear, and he
hesitated. His lungs ached, and the pulse in his neck was
racing. Yet if he stayed in the bathroom, he'd soon be dead
of smoke inhalation. On the other hand, if he used himself
as a battering ram, the fall might kill him. He desperately
wished he had more time.

Suddenly, the issue was decided for him. The bedroom's
heat and volatile fumes reached a flash point, and the ceiling by the door burst into flame. A wave of orange fire
quickly advanced across the ceiling like a hungry tide.
Needing no more prompting, he sprang from his crouch.

Locking his forearms across his brow, he bolted across
the room, charging the window. The flames licked at his
body, singeing the towels. He lowered his head toward the
center of the glass at the last moment, hurling himself like

a football player. Just before impact, he closed his eyes.

Steve heard the crash of breaking glass and momentarily felt the coolness of the night air.

And then he felt nothing.

16

From his vantage point down the block, Jack watched the fire trucks speed by, lights flashing and sirens blaring. They were soon followed by an ambulance. It had been fifteen short minutes since he started the fire. The volunteer fire company's response was unusually swift. Jack got out of his car and walked closer, joining the growing crowd of neighbors.

McLaren's house was completely engulfed by flames. The wood was dry, and the fire was hungry. Shingles and Sheetrock quickly burned away, leaving the interior frame. The stark, skeletonized beams shimmered in the roiling wall of fire, waiting to become weak enough to be claimed by gravity. The firefighters' hoses were useless against the inferno.

A commotion came from the back of the house. One of the firemen appeared and waved his arms, his shouts masked by the roar of the blaze. The EMTs ran toward him. Jack crept closer, presuming they'd discovered McLaren's corpse. Within minutes, the medics ran back toward the street in a crouch, stretcher between them. The doctor was indeed on it, but not nearly as dead as Jack had hoped.

Incensed, Buhlman whirled and headed back to his car. He had no idea how McLaren had escaped, but he was damn sure the doctor had incredible luck. Next time, he'd do it right, and he'd do it in person.

SULAWESI, INDONESIA

Under a glorious full moon, an Atlas moth slowly folded and unfolded its magnificent wings as it perched on a palm branch. The wings' intricate pattern of browns, whites, and golds was a tapestry unfurled. Protuberances on its wingtips resembled snake heads, a subterfuge intended to repel predators. Potential attackers were plentiful that night, from slithering nocturnal reptiles to raucous kingfishers. In the jungle forest behind the moth, the lyrical *ooom ooom ooom*

of the Papuan frogmouth created a musical backdrop for
the creatures of the night.

Even at midnight, the forest remained uncomfortably
warm and close. A steady onshore breeze, rich with smells
of salt and sea, dulled the sharp edges of the heat. Not far
away, a wide and inky river—the same body of water often
seen by Pak Suranto—turned brackish as it neared the
ocean. A mile upstream, two men extinguished a van's
headlights and parked at the water's edge. The riverbank,
normally darkened by silhouettes of wild breadfruits and
bananas, was thick with tangled vines.

Tentrem Suroto and the other man got out and opened
the van's rear door. Their human cargo lay in the back,
loosely wrapped in a muslin shroud. They removed the
dead body and carried it to a hand-hewn dugout canoe concealed nearby. They lay the cadaver in the middle and eased
the canoe into the river. As the wooden craft yielded to the
gentle current, they took up positions in front and in back.
Their paddles bit soundlessly into the moving water. From
either side of the river, they were serenaded by a symphony
of night sounds.

It was a quick passage downriver. As the roar of the surf
grew louder, the river became shallower. Suroto and his
helper hopped out and pushed the dugout a few yards over
rocks until they were caught in the tidal surge. Then they
climbed back in and paddled hard, skillfully weaving a
course through the breakers. Ten minutes later, far offshore,
they put their paddles aside.

They were in a lighthearted mood. Although the mountain factory continued its work, it appeared that this aspect
of the business was drawing to a close. But they'd made
good money. This might be the last body they'd dump.
Under the bright moonlight, they removed the shroud.

The naked woman had unusually large breasts. She had
been young and moderately pretty, leading the men to presume she was a prostitute. While the paddler in front toyed
with the woman's cold nipples, Tentrem tied her ankles
with a thick rope, fixing its free end to a large cement block.
Unceremoniously, they threw both block and cadaver overboard.

The heavy rock plummeted straight down, dragging the

woman behind it. As her body disappeared feet-first under
the surface, the rushing water forced her arms and chin up.
The last glimpse of her revealed her outstretched arms and
upturned face reaching toward the heavens, as if in prayer.

By the time the ambulance reached the ER, Steve had regained consciousness. He was soon in X-ray having multiple films taken. Two hours later, the ER staff was making
jokes at his expense. Fortunately, nothing was broken. His
assorted cuts and scrapes had been bandaged, and a few
minor contusions had been covered with protective dressings. His main complaint was that he felt stiff.

All he recalled was discovering his home ablaze and
making his frantic lunge toward the window. The EMTs
figured that his torso must have done a one-eighty as he
plummeted earthward, for he landed flat on his back. A
hedge had cushioned his fall, but the ground knocked him
unconscious.

He was none the worse for wear. Physically, he was
relatively unscathed, but his house was a total loss. He
spoke with the police and fire chiefs, but they could shed
no light on how or why his home had gone up in flames.
He didn't mention that it was yet another incident of personal bad luck, or that he no longer believed in coincidences.

Forced by hospital policy to remain in the emergency
room for four hours of observation, Steve desperately
missed Francesca's warmth and comfort. He was tempted
to call her, but it was three A.M. He knew she'd insist on
rushing over to give emotional support, but there was nothing, in fact, she could do. It would be better if he called
her once things had calmed down.

The question still remained of where he'd go. His home
was ashes and smoldering debris. What's more, it was strict
hospital policy that an injured patient couldn't be discharged unaccompanied. He toyed with the idea of sleeping
in one of the on-call rooms, but they thought it best if he
went to the home of a friend. Feeling guilty, he called Julia
Hagen.

An hour later, he was sitting in her kitchen, drinking
decaf. Alyssa was asleep upstairs. One of the ER nurses

had given him a pair of scrubs, which was all he had to his name.

"I still can't tell you how sorry I am," Julia said. "I know how much work you put into that greenhouse."

"It's kind of funny, but you know what bothers me most? My plants. I raised these great tropical plants in that greenhouse, and they were thriving. Thank goodness I took some outside for the summer. But the others . . ."

"So you'll start over again," she said. "The good news is that you're young enough to raise generations of other plants. But no more smoking in bed, okay?"

His stare was humorless. "I don't smoke, Jules."

"You know I was only kidding."

His expression softened. "Sorry. I didn't mean to jump at you. But I'm pretty sure that fire was no accident."

"Seriously?"

"*Damn* serious. Someone wants me dead."

She had an incredulous look. "Arson? You're saying someone deliberately set fire to your house while you were in it?"

"More like attempted murder than arson, and that's precisely what I'm saying. And before you accuse me of paranoia, remember the jellyfish incident?"

She nodded.

"Well, I'm starting to think that was no accident either." He went on to relate what Rick Haas had said about the normal habitat of the box jellyfish being the South Pacific: "The chances against that creature floating halfway around the world to the Caribbean are astronomical."

"So someone planted it there? Come on, I'm sure there's a more rational explanation."

"You're just as skeptical as Francesca."

"Now there's an idea," she said. "I mean, she *was* pretty near you underwater, right?"

He looked at her oddly. "Julia, if I didn't know you better, I'd think you were starting to sound an eensie bit jealous."

"*Moi?* Perish the thought."

He went on to tell her about what else had befallen him. Even if he accepted—which he did not—that bad things happened in threes, what was he supposed to make of four or five catastrophes in such a brief period of time?

"I don't suppose you believe in bad luck, huh?" she said.

"Oh, Julia, please. The real world doesn't depend on luck. And if setting my house on fire is the latest fiasco, Christ, what's next?"

"At least you've got life insurance."

"Julia . . ."

"Okay, okay," she said, raising her palms apologetically. "So who's the bad guy? Who stung you with a jellyfish and stole your files and torched your house? You must have some thoughts on that."

"Actually, I do." He mentioned his run-in with Dr. Richards, and she scoffed. Steve wasn't surprised; he couldn't believe it himself. When he brought up Phoebe Atkinson, they both doubted she was capable of murderous revenge. But then he told her about Ted DiGiorgio, and that seemed more plausible.

"Funny way for a friend to act," she said.

"The problem is, he *is* a friend. Or was. Ted and I have been pretty tight since college. I never thought he'd do anything to hurt me."

"You think he personally did everything you say?"

"Not really. Ted might be a gambler when it comes to business, but I don't think he'd take chances like this. It'd be more his style to hire someone to do the dirty work. He's got enough money for it."

Julia sipped her coffee as she mulled it over. "Is this a money thing, then? If the guy's filthy rich, how come he needs more?"

"I wish I knew. But I think it goes deeper than that. For one reason or another, Ted considers me a threat. He actually accused me of trying to ruin him. Yeah, I know, it's ridiculous. But I figure he thinks I'm capable of destroying everything he's created. Desperate men do desperate things, Jules."

"This is insane," she said, shaking her head. "All this over some stupid estrogens. You said Restore-Tabs were estrogen, didn't you?"

"Right. An interesting, unusual estrogen, but estrogen nonetheless. The way Dr. Whitt—"

"Who?"

"Robert Whitt, a chemist who works for Ecolabs. He told me they'd discovered a new source of natural estrogen from under the sea."

"Really? Like fish or seaweed?"

"Trade secret. He wouldn't say. But whatever it is, it's got to be pretty unusual, and pretty potent. Somebody probably harvests it and ships it to Ecolabs for purification. Then they turn it into Restore-Tabs."

"Jesus," Julia said, annoyed. "And then they market this unknown substance to kids like Alyssa. Isn't that illegal?"

"No, it's perfectly legit. Restore-Tabs isn't a drug, it's a food supplement. Anyone with the money can buy it. And unless Ecolabs claims it cures a legitimate disease—and I'm not just talking about making someone look better—the FDA can't touch the company."

"Even if it makes women hemorrhage?"

He nodded. "If a food supplement poses serious health risks, it can damn well be banned. I'm sure that's what frightens Ted. He told me to back off when I mentioned notifying the FDA."

"Did you? It's not like you to keep things hidden."

"Well, I finally did. About a week ago, I notified the FDA's Center for Food Safety and Applied Nutrition. They say they're looking into it, but you know how the government moves. Snail's pace."

"I don't get it. Didn't Ecolabs test this stuff before it went to market?"

"Whitt told me they *did* test it, in up to ten times the recommended dose. He sounded convincing. Either he's a terrific liar, or someone lied to him about his own trials."

"That should be easy enough to check out. Aren't they conducted here?"

"It's not that simple. First of all," Steve continued, "I'm sure Ted has everyone at Ecolabs under instructions not to talk to me. Even so, I doubt the trials were conducted in the good old U. S. of A. Too much lawsuit potential, for one thing. And then there's the press, nosing into everyone's business. Finally, it'd be much less complicated to do the trial where the raw product was harvested."

"You don't think that was around here?"

"Hell no. The American environmental lobby has too

much clout. Just stick a dirty *toe* in the ocean and they scream bloody murder."

"So where were they done?"

He shrugged. "Haven't a clue. It'd be nice to find out, though. I'm sure that if Francesca doesn't know, she can find out."

"Wonderful." She leaned back, folding her arms defiantly. Then her eyes narrowed in thought. "Would it help if you actually knew what this natural estrogen was? Like, if you knew its exact chemical structure, couldn't you work backward from there and find out where it came from?"

"I don't understand what you're saying."

"Well, in my work at Island Diagnostics," she said, "we do that all the time. Let's say the police have a sample of dirt from a suspect's clothing. I'm sure you've seen this on TV, because there are about a thousand documentaries on it. By determining the trace minerals in the clothing, the cops can tell exactly where the dirt came from. I have a feeling you could apply that same technique to Restore-Tabs. By isolating the exact type of estrogen, maybe you could tell what kind of plant it comes from, and where."

For the first time, a smile came over his face. "I always *knew* you weren't just another pretty face. How long would that take?"

"A few days."

"Okay. I'll bring some Restore-Tabs from the office, along with some placebos."

"Great." In his face, she saw genuine worry, mixed with fear. "So, Doctor, what now? Seems to me you need a place to stay."

"I guess I do. I'll call my homeowner's agent first thing in the morning. The house is a total loss, Julia. While they work out a settlement, I'll get a room somewhere. I might be there a while, who knows?"

"Steve, I don't mean to sound presumptuous, but . . . why not stay here a while? It's not the greatest, but it's not the Bates Motel, either. I've got an extra bedroom, and I'm sure Alyssa wouldn't mind."

"That's very generous, Jules. But you forget somebody out there wants to kill me. Staying here could be dangerous for you guys."

"Don't be silly. Nobody knows you're here. What do you say?"

He relented with a smile. "You're too damn gracious for your own good, you know that? All right, lead the way."

She showed him up the stairs to a small guest bedroom that had seen little use of late. Julia set aside a sewing box and a carton of gift wrap. She turned down the bedspread, fluffed the pillow, and smoothed the sheets. "There you are. It might be a little dusty, but it's clean."

He suddenly felt exhausted from his ordeal. He plopped down heavily and rubbed his eyes. "God, I'm tired. Is there a clock in here?"

"How early do you have to get up?"

"Around seven. I have to call the women at the office."

"No clock, but I get up around then," she said. "I'll wake you."

His lids wanted to close, and he let his head sink into the pillow. "I'm on my way out, Jules. Thanks again."

"Sleep tight, Steve."

As the leaden feeling overcame him, he felt her nearness, smelled her scent. Then her warm lips grazed his. They lingered a while, then were gone.

For several seconds, before sleep enveloped him, he wondered what lay behind the softness of her kiss.

With Dr. Richards assisting, Dr. Destefano completed Karen Trent's lumpectomy and dissected out the sentinel node. Earlier in the week, when he learned of Karen's recurrent vaginal bleeding, Destefano insisted on getting a consultation from Dr. Richards before performing the breast surgery. Given that his previous medication had failed, Richards recommended a hysterectomy. He contacted the surgeon and learned they could combine the two procedures. Karen reluctantly agreed, understanding the wisdom of avoiding two anesthesias.

Once the hysterectomy was completed, Richards helped on the lumpectomy. "I notice a lot of you guys are doing these sentinel nodes recently," he said. "What's that all about?"

"The sentinel node, it's the first lymph node where a tumor drains," Destefano explained. "Theoretically, it's the first place where cancer spreads. We do it in patients that are clinically node-negative. Remember when everybody did radical mastectomies with axillary-node dissections? It turned out there were just too many complications, especially with minimal disease. A lot of recent papers suggest that if you excise the sentinel node and it's negative, the remaining nodes are probably negative, too. At least that's the theory. You can get the information you need, and you can stop right there."

"So the dye you injected near the tumor will lead you to the node?"

"Right. Some people use a radioactive tag, but it's too cumbersome. I like to go right to the axilla and take the node or nodes that are stained bluest. Makes my life a lot easier."

It was a remarkably simple procedure. Within fifteen minutes, Destefano isolated three small nodes with the darkest stain. Richards then scrubbed out. The surgeon closed the skin while waiting for the frozen-section diagnosis.

The pathologist called before Destefano left the OR. "Looks good," he began. "First, as you suspected, the tumor looks mucinous, the colloid variety."

"If you've gotta have breast cancer, I guess that's the type to have. And the nodes?"

"Negative on frozen. Nothing's final until the permanent sections, but I'd say you're dealing with one lucky lady."

When Steve opened his eyes, bright sunlight filled the room, streaming past the drawn blinds. For a moment, he didn't know where he was. Then he recognized the small guestroom, and he lay back and stretched. His muscles ached, and he felt incredibly stiff. Since Julia hadn't awakened him, he reckoned it was a little before seven. Remarkably, despite less than four hours of sleep, he felt fresh and rested.

He couldn't wait to shower. Although he'd donated his smoke-scented boxers to the ER, his skin still reeked from the fire. He was still wearing the scrubs, which were similarly rank. Getting out of bed, he went looking for a bathroom.

"Hello?" he called.

"Hi, Steve," said Alyssa.

The door to her bedroom was open. As he walked past, he found her in bed, watching TV. "How're you feeling, princess?"

"I've got a headache, and I'm bored. Want to play Monopoly?"

"Soon. I have a few things to do first. Where's your mom?"

"Out food shopping."

So early? he thought. Continuing down the hall, he found a bathroom. Taped to the medicine-cabinet mirror was a note from Julia. "Steve," it read, "Hope you had a good snooze. When I came in this morning, I didn't have the heart to wake you. I called Becky, and she said she'd take care of everything in the office. Don't worry, be happy!"

"Alyssa!" he shouted, racing down the hall. "What time is it?"

"A little after twelve."

"Christ!" he swore, under his breath. "Where's the phone?"

"In Mom's bedroom."

He quickly reached Julia's night table and called Donna at home.

"Boss!" Donna exclaimed. "We heard about the fire. Are you okay?"

"I'm fine. I just didn't realize what time it was. They told me I should take off a day or two, though. What are we going to do about tomorrow's patients?"

"Take it easy. We already went to the office and rescheduled everything. Dr. Rothstein's covering for a few days. Don't even *think* about going over to the office. The place is a zoo. We had cops come by, fire investigators, you name it. They all want to talk to you."

"They don't know where I am?"

"Nah," Donna replied. "Julia said not to tell a soul."

"Okay. Did—"

"Oh, before I forget," she interrupted, "Francesca Taylor called three times. She sounds uptight and wants you to call her at work."

"Thanks, Donna. I'll call back later about the other stuff."

Moments later, he had Francesca on the phone. "Oh, Steve, I'm so glad you called! Are you all right?"

"My home's a loss, but I'm okay."

"When did this *happen*? Do they know what caused it?"

"Not yet, but I'm pretty sure I smelled gasoline," he said. "All I know is I wasn't the one who spilled it. I went to bed around ten, so it must have been a little after that. Everyone says I'm lucky as hell."

"Thank God you're all right! I can't tell you how frightened I was when your receptionist called me. Look, I'm going to come over. Where are you?"

"At a friend's. I'm okay, really," he insisted. "I want to see you too, but I have a few things to take care of first. Here's what we'll do . . ."

Julia had begun work at Island Diagnostics when Alyssa was a toddler. Initially, she worked as a secretary, but as her abilities were recognized, she was promoted to lab assistant. Although she was on a leave of absence, she occasionally dropped by to say hello. Now, armed with samples of Restore-Tabs and placebos from McLaren's office, she strode purposefully into the lab.

"Julia!" the boss called out when he saw her. "How's Alyssa?"

"Could be better, Gary. It's a holding action right now. Thanks for asking."

"If there's anything I can do . . ."

"I appreciate that," she said. "I wonder if you could help me with something."

"Name it."

"I'd like you to analyze these for me. I'll pay whatever it costs."

"Don't be silly." He took the two proffered pills, which appeared to be identical white caplets, and turned them over in his palm. Then he put each in a plastic vial. "Is this medication?"

"Ever heard of Restore-Tabs? The everything-from-tits-to-crow's-feet pills?"

He nodded.

"That's one of them. The one like it is a placebo."

"Exactly what is it you want me to do?"

"I'm trying to find out what the active ingredient is. It's supposed to be a new herbal estrogen from undersea sources."

"Technically speaking," he explained, "it can't be herbal."

"Why not?"

"To the purist, herbal refers to derivatives of leaves and stems. You don't find much of that underwater. A better term would be *botanical.*"

"But it could be an estrogen, right?"

He shrugged. "I suppose. A very hot area these days. Just because I never heard of it doesn't mean it doesn't exist."

"What makes it so hot?"

"Well, it's on all the commercials, for one thing. Soy this, soy that. I'm sure you've heard of SERMs, selective estrogen receptor modulators. Designer estrogens. It's a big money product, called yuppies turn fifty," he said. "Longevity, quality of life, that kind of crap. SERMs are neat because they behave like estrogens in some tissues, but they block its action in others."

"But they're not botanical, are they?"

"Correct. Most plant estrogens are called phytoestrogens. Phyto, if you recall, means plant. The major chemical players are isoflavones, lignans, and coumestans. In addition to soy, phytoestrogens come from things like alfalfa and seed oils. There are some other less common phytoestrogens, and probably some not yet discovered." He paused, eyeing the vial. "You think this is one of them?"

"I'm not sure, Gary. That's what I was hoping you could tell me. Let me ask you something. Can any of these SERMs or phyto-jobs cause cancer?"

"Not the SERMs. The tissues where they block estrogen are the breast and the uterus. But the plant products, well, a lot of them aren't that well understood, especially the more exotic ones."

Julia thought about her daughter and grew annoyed. "What about in very high doses?"

"All the more likely, I'd think." He put the vial in his

pocket. "Now that I know the general category, it shouldn't take too long to pin this down."

Steve picked up a spare set of car keys at the office. Julia had lent him some of her husband's old clothes, and the faded blue chambray shirt and chinos went well with the moccasins he bought. That night, he met Francesca halfway, in Port Jefferson, on Long Island's north shore. She'd taken the ferry across Long Island Sound from Bridgeport, Connecticut. When she pulled her car off the ferry's ramp, Steve was waiting for her at the end of the exitway. Lofting a welcoming wave, he got in the passenger side.

They embraced needily. Francesca started to cry, and her body quivered in his arms. They only moved when the cars behind them began honking.

At a nearby waterfront restaurant, they parked, and as they walked she leaned into him, clutching one of his arms in both of hers. Inside, Steve reached across the table, taking her hands in his, caressing her fingers with his thumbs.

"I can't tell you how glad I am you're here," he said. "I thought about calling you from the ER, but—"

"You should have. When your office called, I thought I'd go out of my mind! All I could think of was seeing you, holding you . . ." She noticed his taped gauze. "Are those burns?"

"They're superficial, nothing serious," he reassured her. He waited a beat. "He tried to kill me."

"Who?"

"Ted. I honestly think he's gone off the deep end. If he's convinced I'm out to ruin the company, I guess his solution is to get me out of the way. You said so yourself, that this is definitely something he's capable of."

"But it couldn't have been Ted," she said, sounding confused. "Didn't you say the fire started after ten? I know for a fact he was working late in the office when the fire started."

"I don't mean Ted personally. He doesn't have the guts. I'm sure he hired somebody else. But the fire was definitely arson, no question about it. I spent the whole afternoon talking with the cops and firefighters. The lead investigator found what he thinks are traces of accelerant. The final results won't be in for a few days, but he's pretty sure about it."

As she gazed at him, Francesca's eyes glazed with a teary film. "I'm really worried, Steve. I can't stand thinking about this anymore. God, I don't want to lose you! Did you tell the police about Ted?"

He shook his head. "Not yet. If they questioned him now, he'd just deny everything."

"The bastard," she said acerbically. "I've had about enough of his insanity. God, he's screwed the whole damn place up. The tension's thick as hell at work, and everyone's walking on eggshells. In fact, I've been thinking about getting another job."

"Maybe you should." His expression took on a distant look, and he gazed out over the water. "I just wish I had some answers. A little proof. Somehow, I can't help thinking that Ted's paranoia is related to Restore-Tabs. His weird behavior began the day I mentioned the problems I was having, right?"

"Yep."

He was tempted to tell her about Julia and Island Diagnostics, but there was no point getting Julia involved. "It's a shame I don't know more about that product. Like where it's made and what the exact constituents are. If I only had a few clues, I could make a little more sense out of everything."

She thought about it. "I have a feeling I might be able to find out what you want."

"Are you serious? How?"

"All the proprietary stuff's in Ted's office, either in his personal files or on computer. I'm pretty sure I can get in."

"Forget it," he said animatedly, shaking his head. "Much too risky. If you're caught, you'll get fired on the spot—or worse."

"I'm not talking about during work hours. There's a sales conference in Boston this weekend. Ted and most of the other executives will be gone by six o'clock Friday. If you're up to it, why don't we check out his office then?"

17

Andie enjoyed Cape Cod. The beaches weren't as nice as the ones on Long Island, but the weather had been great, with sunny days and a strong breeze. She had now lost about nine pounds. She was exercising more and eating less. Much as she wanted to follow her father's advice, she couldn't stop taking the Restore-Tabs. To her, they were miracle drugs. Once again, she dared to like how she looked and felt.

The one-piece Speedo fit her well. It was a larger size than she ultimately wanted, but her figure wasn't that bad. Her mother called it *zaftig,* whatever that meant, but the way she said it made Andie feel it was something positive. She had reasonably good boobs for someone her age and none of the cellulite Lorraine was always warning her about. When they had gone to the beach, she even permitted herself, for the first time in two years, to make eye contact with the local boys.

The wind-etched sands near Provincetown offered plenty to do. Besides lying on the beach or strolling through the dune grass, Andie and her mom carried specimen nets off the beaten path to marsh, moor, and tidal flat, collecting and studying interesting specimens. They spent one morning visiting a cranberry farm in one of the Cape's sandy bogs and another afternoon going antiquing. Provincetown itself offered artsy attractions galore. Yet she missed her friends and couldn't wait to go home.

Just before supper toward the end of their week there, Lorraine went out for Chinese food, while Andie took a shower, rinsing off a day's accumulation of salt and sand. The water soothed her increasingly tanned skin, and she loved the smell of the mango soap she found in their rented bungalow. She was about to turn off the water when the cramps began. They were intense, worse than any she'd ever experienced, squeezing her lower abdomen, making her groan and doubling her over. Try though she might, she couldn't stand up straight. Leaning her back against the shower's wall, she slowly slid down until she was sitting on the shower floor, her knees drawn up before her. It was then that she noticed the blood.

It seeped out from under her in a crimson stream that swirled toward the drain. Much heavier than her brief bleeding episode at the movies, it was coming out frighteningly fast. She suddenly remembered her father's admonition about hemorrhage, and she grew terrified. Worse, her mother wouldn't return for a little while, and she was all by herself.

Alone, in pain, and terrified, Andie started to cry.

Steve felt as if they were being watched. After they finished dinner, he took Francesca's hand and stole out of the restaurant, looking furtively over his shoulder. He wanted to spend the night with her, finding safety and solace in her arms. The only question was where to go. They cautiously made their way down the block to Danford's Inn and rented a room.

Neither of them slept well, and even sex wasn't a satisfactory stress-reducer. Eventually, Francesca dozed, while Steve tossed and turned. He lay on his back, sifting through his thoughts as he stared at the ceiling, waiting for sleep to come. Francesca lay on her side, her slender, naked thigh draped over his lower abdomen. He idly stroked her soft, warm skin until slumber overtook him.

They got up early. Francesca had to work, and she drove back to her place to shower and change. Steve didn't know where she lived, other than that it was someplace in Westchester. He wondered why she'd never invited him to spend the night. When he obliquely broached the subject, she said the place just wasn't ready. It was rather new, and she was still fixing things up.

Completely recovered from his fall, he returned to work but spent the next few nights at Julia's. He played chess and Monopoly with Alyssa and chatted with her mother. Alyssa was now too weak to get out of bed for extended periods, and her lusterless eyes took on a pre-terminal look. He doubted she'd live much longer. Nonetheless, her buoyant spirits lifted them all.

Julia put Steve's shirt and chinos in the wash, while he

rummaged through Jimmy Hagen's closet for others. Jimmy's garments fit him well. It felt strange wearing his ex-patient's clothes, but since Steve's had gone up in smoke, he didn't have much choice. Besides, Julia had insisted. On Friday evening, he left after dark. Julia asked where he was going, but he wouldn't say. He wanted to keep his rendezvous with Francesca a secret.

It started to rain. Clouds obscured the moon, and the ominous weather darkened his mood. The driving was difficult. Once he reached Larchmont, he glanced at Francesca's written directions in the dim light of his car's interior lamp. Soon he located Palmer Avenue, crossed it, and turned onto Pinebrook Drive. He followed the signs until he reached the side street she'd indicated.

The lights of Francesca's Jeep were visible halfway down the block. He pulled up behind her, got out of the Saab, and sprinted ahead. When he sank into the passenger seat, she leaned over and kissed him, brushing rain droplets from his face.

"You should've worn a hat."

"Yes, mother. But I don't exactly see your chapeau either."

She lifted a black umbrella. "Big enough for both of us. The rain's actually a mixed blessing. We'll get a little wet, but there's less chance of being spotted."

"Is breaking in that risky? You're an employee."

"I wouldn't say it's that risky, but I'd rather not get caught. If we wanted, I suppose we could just go through the front door right past the security desk. But I'm almost never there at night, and if something disappears, it'd be pretty obvious who did it."

He nodded. "How much security is there?"

"Usually just one guard at the entrance."

"Is he armed?"

"I'm not sure. I never paid much attention to things like that." She looked into his eyes and saw the fear. "Don't worry, my love. We won't have any problems."

"Do I look worried?"

"Petrified."

"Let's just say I'm cautious. You think I'm over-reacting?"

She smiled and squeezed his hand. "No, I don't. Come on, let's go get that information."

He went to her side of the car and opened the door. Francesca got out and opened the umbrella, holding it over both their heads. Chin lowered, she led him down the block in the direction of Ecolabs.

It was raining hard, and he had to speak loudly to be heard. "How are we going to get in?"

"Break a window."

"What?"

"Sorry, bad joke. Just follow me. We're going in from a loading dock in the back."

The rain came in torrents, and despite the umbrella, they were getting soaked. Hunched over, Steve followed her lead as they quickly crossed Palmer Avenue and turned into a back street that paralleled the main road. After a few twists and turns, they reached an open gate in the center of a high, wrought-iron fence. Francesca led him into the parking lot, where a half-dozen Ecolabs delivery trucks were parked side by side.

The lot was bathed in the orange glow of halogen lamps. Francesca kept to the shadows along the fence. Working their way toward the building, they finally reached a wide loading dock. He followed her up its concrete steps. The dock had a large steel overhang that shielded them from the elements. Francesca closed her umbrella and approached a heavy metal service door, beside which was a numeric keypad.

"We'll go through here," she said in a whisper. "I think there are only three security cameras—one we just went around, another in front, and the third on the production floor. We shouldn't have a problem with them."

"Where are we going?"

"Ted's office, on the second floor. I've got a passkey. If we can't find what we want in his file cabinet, I think I know his computer password. Okay?"

"Lead on."

Francesca left the umbrella by the door and punched in the number. The door clicked and popped open. When they entered, Steve found himself in a spooky, poorly lit hallway.

"Where's the light coming from?"

"Security lamps. They're on every floor, but that's better for us, because we don't have to turn on the overheads. Come on."

There was a metal staircase at the end of the hall. Steve followed her, worrying that their soft footfalls were making a monstrous clang. When they reached the second-floor landing, Francesca tried the entry door and found it locked. She took out her key ring, located the heavy Sargent key, and slid it into the lock. The fire door opened without a sound.

Steve nervously stepped into a wide, carpeted hallway, as dark as the hallway on the floor below. A suite of offices ringed an open atrium.

"That's where I work," she said quietly, pointing toward a locked wooden door. "Ted's office is this way."

She led him past the elevator to the end of the foyer, where floor-to-ceiling glass opened into the CEO's quarters. The heavy swinging glass doors had a decorative lock that Francesca opened without difficulty. Inside, they skirted a reception desk that faced Ted's inner sanctum, hidden behind ornate mahogany doors. They, too, yielded to her key. She closed the door behind them and turned on the light.

When the room brightened, Steve's fear of discovery began to lessen. He looked around, impressed. The office was spacious, with enormous abstract murals decorating the walls. For a man who had trouble making it through college, Steve thought, Ted had done all right for himself.

Like the doors, the file cabinets were locked. The master cabinet had a four-digit combination on which Francesca quickly went to work.

"You know that one too?" he asked.

"He gave me the combination: six-nine-five-eight."

"I think that's his birthday."

She shrugged. "No one's creative in everything."

As Steve looked over her shoulder, Francesca opened the top drawer, which unlocked those below it. Steve saw that the files were arranged alphabetically, and the drawer labeled R was third from the top. She located the weighty folder and removed it. The file was nearly two inches thick.

"That's heavier than any of the charts in *my* office," he said.

"This is nothing. There are reams of Restore-Tabs documents, enough to fill half this room. They're in storage. I'm assuming this is the sensitive stuff Ted wanted to keep a secret."

Peering over her shoulder, Steve scanned the individual documents. Most dealt with sales and distribution. Others had to do with marketing and frequently bore Francesca's signature.

Toward the bottom of the folder, they came to several sheets of paper, one labeled Biochemistry and the other Raw Materials. These were more what he had in mind. The information was enticing, but it was also sketchy. What he wanted was more complete information than Julia could get from Island Diagnostics. However, each page had a three-digit number in the upper right-hand corner.

"What do those numbers mean?" he asked.

"They're personal codes for Ted's computer."

"Really. I think I'd like to see that. Can you log on?"

"I'll give it a shot."

At the desk, Francesca sat down and powered up Ted's computer. After she entered "Ted DiGiorgio" next to "User ID," the screen asked for a password. She hesitated.

"Christ, I bet the whole damn thing's encrypted," Steve said.

"I doubt it. Ted's creative, but . . . I bet he uses the same name everybody knows him by."

"Which is?"

Francesca typed the word *herbalist* next to the prompt and hit "Enter." Immediately, the Windows logo flickered to life.

Steve shook his head. "I should have known."

Francesca clicked on the "Programs" icon and scanned the list of files. All Ecolabs products were displayed, Restore-Tabs prominent among them. Yet when she clicked on its folder symbol, all that came up was a blank screen and a blinking prompt.

"What was that code number for the chemistry file?" she asked.

He told her. When she typed it in, a long list of chemical

substances appeared on the monitor. They both leaned closer to inspect it.

"And what might this be?" he asked.

"Most of those are inert ingredients, fillers. We use them in most of our products."

"But what's the *active* ingredient?"

She scrolled down. Several pages later, a complex chemical structure appeared. "That's it, the magic in Restore-Tabs. Recognize it?"

"It kind of resembles a steroid, but it's different. I'd have to show it to an expert. I suppose it's an estrogen. They're built around a steroid nucleus. No doubt Dr. Whitt knows."

"Bobby? He's very conservative, a real Boy Scout. I don't think he'd be very helpful. And I'm not sure we can trust him."

"Whatever you say. Can you print it up?"

A laser printer sat next to the keyboard. Francesca turned it on and quickly made a hard copy of the page. Steve folded it and stuffed it into his pocket.

"What about the raw materials file?" He recited the code number.

Francesca entered the code, and a different screen appeared. The newly opened file started with an outlined map, black on white. Neither of them recognized the water-bounded area.

"Manado? Inobonto?" he said. "Where the hell are they?"

"Somewhere in the South Pacific. That much I know."

"There's something here called 'Clinic,' whatever that is," he said. "And this spot marked 'Factory' must be where they put it all together."

"Actually, everything's mixed here. The factory's usually where the raw materials are refined and bagged."

"Okay. What else you got?"

The remainder of the file was neither long nor complex. As she scrolled down the list of primarily Latin names, many looked familiar to Steve from his diving.

"Recognize anything?" she asked.

"I'm pretty sure these are corals. They always said Restore-Tabs came from undersea sources, so I guess these qualify. I just wonder if it's possible, estrogens from coral."

"Some estrogens are made from soy and alfalfa, right?"

He nodded. "Phytoestrogens, from plants. Most corals are actually tiny animals, but there's plenty of microscopic plant life in the coral skeletons of the reefs. No reason some enterprising chemist couldn't extract it. But I doubt that's legal."

"Why not?"

"There are all kinds of treaties that prohibit undersea mining. 'Save the reefs' and all that. The United States is a signatory to most of them, so if someone's mining coral in the South Seas, it's coming into this country illegally."

"God, could I go to jail over this?"

"I doubt it. The U.S. attorney only goes after willing parties. Print that page up, too."

Within seconds, the document was in Steve's pocket. Although they hadn't been there long, it was longer than either of them felt safe with. Francesca turned off the printer and computer, tidied up the desk, and made sure the file cabinet was locked. Then they both headed for the door.

Halfway there, the door unexpectedly opened. Standing directly in front of them was a uniformed security guard. Ted DiGiorgio stood behind him. The guard's gun was leveled at the intruders. As they both halted, Ted stepped forward with theatrical slowness. A peculiar smile curled his lips, and he shook his head.

"Will you look at this? My one-time best friend, now the prince of jealousy. I might not be surprised, but I'm a little disappointed in you, buddy. I would've thought a little therapy might do more good than a jail cell."

"Ted, listen—" Steve tried.

"Shut up! I expected a stunt like this from you, which is one of the reasons this office has a new silent alarm, and why I come back after work, but Francesca . . ."

She smiled nervously. "What happened to the sales conference?"

"Postponed."

"Look, I can explain," she ventured.

"Bullshit. I trusted you, Francesca! For God's sake, you could've had any man you wanted! Why in the world would you pick a loser like this guy?"

"Ted, *please*," she said. "It's not what you think!"

"It never is, is it? But if my eyes don't deceive me, you and Romeo here are in my office illegally. I'm sure the cops will have something to say about this."

Steve was watching the guard. He looked like a rent-a-cop, gray-haired, well past retirement age. His gun was an old revolver with a faded finish, not one of the new high-tech semiautos. That didn't make it any less lethal. But the guard's hand was shaking, and his reflexes had doubtless slowed over the years. In fact, he wasn't watching the intruders at all. He was looking at Ted.

Steve knew the situation could get quickly out of hand. Ted might've already called the police. If so, he and Francesca would soon be behind bars. Although he doubted they'd remain there long, by the time they were bailed out, Ted would have hidden everything. The folders would be gone, the computer files deleted, and the evidence altered. Any hope Steve had of uncovering the truth—and saving the lives of countless Restore-Tabs users—would vanish.

He *had* to do something. As his eyes nervously flitted about, he saw the guard sniffle and, with his free hand, remove a handkerchief from his pocket. Steve felt certain he could overpower the guard once the opportunity presented itself. He waited for an opening.

"You're the one who should worry about doing something illegal," Steve told Ted. "We're not the ones ripping up the Pacific reefs and feeding people unproven hormones."

"Come off it!" Ted shot back. "My consultants say we're not violating a damn thing. And unproven, my ass! We tested the crap out of this stuff overseas. You've been on my case for weeks, friend, but you don't know what the hell you're talking about!"

"You're twisting things around," Francesca chimed in. "If you didn't have something to hide, you would've—"

Just then, the guard sneezed violently. His handkerchief went to his face, his eyes blinked, and his head bobbed. Steve reacted instantly. He leapt forward, going for the guard's gun hand with both of his own.

He grabbed the guard's wrist and tried to wrench the weapon away. But the old man's appearance was deceptive. He was surprisingly strong and reached for Steve's neck with his free hand, resisting the attempt to disarm him. Steve gritted his teeth and tried to pry the revolver free. Out of the corner of his eye, he saw a sudden blur. Something dark—another guard?—streaked through the open doorway toward them. Before he could react, something heavy smashed into his forehead.

Steve's head felt like it exploded. Everything temporarily went black. His grip on the guard weakened, and his legs no longer supported him. He heard a scream. As he tumbled backward, all he could think of was Francesca.

There came a deafening boom, an unmistakable gunshot. He heard a muffled groan and was terrified. Wincing in pain, he struggled to a sitting position and forced his eyes open. The first thing he noticed was two figures tumbling almost simultaneously to the floor. To his surprise, one was Ted, the other the old guard. He briefly spotted Francesca, who'd retreated to a corner, unharmed but cowering. As he started to help her, his attention was diverted.

The second guard was advancing toward him. Steve looked away only momentarily, but he was able to see everything in remarkable detail. Ted was sprawled out on his back, a large crimson splotch spreading across his chest. The old man, still holding his revolver, lay curled up on his side. A widening bloodstain spread below his armpit. A pale and terrified Francesca stood in a corner. But then his gaze flitted back to the guard.

Although everything happened quickly, to Steve the events seemed to unfold with infinite slowness. The second guard was much younger than the first. And he approached with a murderous look in his eye. Although he was several inches shorter than Steve, his uniform fit tightly, and his muscles bulged prominently. And strangest of all, he carried a knife, not a gun.

"Francesca, run!" he shouted.

As she dashed terrified from the office, the guard came nearer and nearer. Standing with his back to Ted's desk, Steve braced himself. He saw the guard lower his knife hand, preparing for an upward thrust. But before he struck, Steve leaned into the desk, raised his leg, and kicked the guard savagely in the chest.

Stunned, the guard took several steps backward. Despite

the danger to himself, all Steve could think of was buying time for Francesca. He raced around the desk, frantically searching for anything with which to defend himself. There were several beer-mug pencil holders on the desk. He quickly picked one up but then lowered it, realizing the futility. Besides, there were injured people who needed help.

"Okay, take it easy," he said, raising his hands. "I'm not going anywhere. Just let me call 911."

"What for?" said the guard, glaring at him. "Who gives a shit about them?"

Steve's heart began to pound. Judging by the look in the man's eyes, it was suddenly clear that the guard meant to kill him. As the man advanced, knife ready to strike, Steve lifted a mug and threw it. Pens and pencils scattered everywhere, and the empty mug hit the guard's shoulder. He quickly shook it off.

"Piss me off, Doc, and I'll hang your guts from the ceiling."

As the guard started around the desk, Steve hurled the other mug. The guard batted it away with his forearm and leapt forward. He slashed ferociously at shoulder level, but Steve's adrenaline-charged reflexes were razor-sharp. As the knife whistled over his scalp, he ducked under the swipe and swept his leg forward. His shoe connected with the guard's ankle. The man screamed and went down.

But the guard was not out of the fray. From hands and knees, the man lashed upward. The backhand thrust sliced through Steve's pants, lacerating his thigh. Steve was desperate. With the guard struggling to get up, Steve grabbed the computer monitor in both hands. With all his strength, he wrenched it free and threw it just as the man came out of his crouch. The hardware struck him on the side of the neck.

When the guard went down again, Steve ran around the desk and quickly dashed from Ted's office. When he reached the hall, he heard obscenities shouted behind him. Desperate to find an exit, he spotted the stairwell door; he yanked it open and took the steps two and three at a time. While he ran, he frantically looked around for Francesca. She was nowhere in sight.

He was certain she was heading back to the car. Even a thirty-second lead should have been enough to ensure her safety. Soon he was outside, where the downpour continued. He quickly scanned the rain-swept parking lot, in vain.

"Francesca!" he shouted. "Francesca!"

The heavy rain drummed like thunder on the overhang of the loading dock. Although it was doubtful she could hear him, what *he* clearly heard was the clatter of the guard's heels in the upper stairwell. Before the man got any closer, Steve ran down the concrete steps, across the well-lit lot, and past the fenced-in enclosure. He only stopped when he reached the street. Stepping behind a sheltering oak, he hazarded a look back toward the building.

Knife in hand, the guard ran out onto the loading dock. Owing to the torrent, visibility was minimal. He slowly peered through the downpour. But after a thirty-second search, he reentered the building and closed the door behind him. Only then did Steve continue his flight.

The rain thoroughly soaked him. He sprinted down the street, desperately searching for Francesca. Splashing through ankle-deep puddles, he checked every alleyway and possible refuge. Francesca was nowhere to be seen.

Crossing Palmer Avenue, Steve quickly reached Pinebrook Drive and dashed ahead. Turning onto the side street, he squinted through the downpour until he spotted her Jeep. Only when he drew abreast of it did his pace lessen. Lungs heaving, face dripping with rain, he rapped on the driver's-side window, calling her name.

No one answered. He tried the door and found it locked. Bending forward, face nearly touching the glass, Steve's eyes darted around the empty interior. There were no keys, no purse, and no Francesca. My God, he suddenly thought, could she possibly have been hurt?

He straightened up and screamed her name over and over into the wind-driven rain. All he heard was the incessant tapping of raindrops on the metal roof. He walked around the Jeep and then jogged the length of the block in both directions.

All along, he'd presumed she'd returned to her car. But might she have run in an entirely different direction, or even returned to her own apartment? Had she called the police? He doubted it, for that would implicate them in the break-in; but *someone* had to summon help for the two critically injured men. At length, exhausted and thoroughly drenched, Steve returned to his Saab.

He couldn't risk using his mobile phone. His call for assistance had to be anonymous and untraceable. He started the engine and drove slowly back down Palmer Avenue until he found a public phone. Placing his call, he wiped down the receiver and headed back to Francesca's deserted Jeep. Five minutes later, he heard the distant wail of sirens.

The next ten minutes passed slowly. Steve hoped to spot her coming up the block at any moment, but the darkened street remained vacant. Unable to wait any longer, he called her home number. All he got was the unruffled monotone on her machine. Had he known her address, he would have driven to her home, but she'd never told him where she lived.

Deep down, he was worried she'd been hurt, perhaps seriously. For a long, icy moment, he thought she might even have remained in the building and been attacked by the guard. Yet he felt sure she'd fled. If she *were* injured, it was easier for him to think she was now in some nearby emergency room. He felt powerless, but there was absolutely nothing he could do. Nonetheless, cold and soaked, he remained in his car another hour, hoping against hope that she'd show up. Then he phoned her one last time, only to get her machine once more. Finally, he dejectedly turned the car around and returned to Long Island.

NEAR INOBONTO, SULAWESI

Suroto learned what really happened to Dr. Sayed not long after it occurred. The police had initially reported it a suicide, but any fool could see otherwise. Sayed was a pig, an informer who got what he deserved. And if nurse Claudia's suspicions were correct, Mr. Buhlman was involved, the same Jack Buhlman whom Suroto had helped to build the clinic and reconvert the old factory.

The American seemed to have endless money, but he was also a very dangerous man. He still had a few more jobs of the closing-down variety for Suroto, and then that was it. He casually suggested Suroto hang around until

18

His car phone rang as he was crossing the bridge to Long Island. Incredibly relieved, his spirits soared, and he quickly pressed the talk button.

"Thank God," he said. "Where the hell are you?"

There was a pause, and tinny static. "It's Lorraine, Steve. Andie and I are on Cape Cod. I've been trying to get you for over an hour. Your machine at home doesn't work, and—"

"It's a long story, Lorraine. What's wrong?"

"Andie's bleeding. Heavily. Much heavier than her period, and I'm worried."

His bloodless fist clenched the phone. "Oh, no. It's gotta be those goddamn Restore-Tabs. When did it start?"

"A few hours ago, around suppertime. When it didn't slow down, I got in touch with one of the local doctors. He said that if it keeps up, I'm going to have to take her to the emergency room. Whatever's happened between us, Steve, I always trusted your medical judgment." She was starting to sound frantic. "I don't know what to do."

"Did the bleeding let up at all?"

"Andie says it's about the same. She's starting to get a little light-headed."

"Then what are you waiting for? Take her to the hospital!"

"You don't think I should wait a—"

"No, I do not! There's nothing to be gained by waiting. In the ER, they'll start an IV, maybe call in a specialist, and check her blood count. Now get going! Just give me the hospital's number, and I'll call in a little while."

He worried for the remainder of his drive, feeling emotionally assaulted from every angle. When he neared Quogue, it was almost midnight. He couldn't get Andie or Francesca out of his thoughts. His mind was active, though his body felt exhausted. He needed rest and dry clothes. Much as he hated imposing on Julia, he had nowhere else to turn. Somewhat guiltily, he called her. She was still up.

something came up, but Suroto had other ideas. With the operation shutting down and money in the bank, there was no point remaining here.

It was a shame, really. This spectacular region was so different from the slums of his birth. As he drove away from the mountain factory, he stopped to take in the view from one of his favorite overlooks. As he stretched, looking out to sea, he was again dazzled by the beauty of this place, this land, this paradise.

Far in the distance, massive green volcanoes reached skyward, with rainforests huddled between their snowy peaks. Beneath him, tumbling forests rolled down the mountain, their emerald canopies encircled by thin, swirling clouds. Even farther below, within a rugged, harsh-hewn lava terrain, a shining sea-green lake was tucked into folds of volcanic escarpment. Finally, the rocky terrain merged with an endless white beach bordered by palms for as far as the eye could see.

The pity of it was that he had grown to love it here. But he was no match for a brutal man with rigid priorities and a sharp knife. What it really came down to was idyllic surroundings versus personal survival. Sometimes foolish, but never a fool, Tentrem Suroto knew he'd soon be returning to Jakarta.

With the rain lashing at the Saab, it was a long and fear-filled journey. Steve couldn't stop thinking about Francesca. Where was she? Was she okay? If he knew her the way he thought he did, she was as frightened for him as he was for her.

He also thought about Ted. The chest wound looked grave. Whatever Ted had done, he didn't deserve this. Moreover, what happened seemed at odds with his words. Ted didn't seem intent on harming him or Francesca. If anything, he wanted them arrested. But what about the guards? It didn't make sense.

In fact, nothing was what it seemed anymore.

In fact, she said, she was a little worried. She had expected him to spend the night there again, and when she hadn't heard from him, she got concerned. He promised to tell her everything when he arrived.

Julia was waiting for him at the front door. When she noticed his wet and bedraggled appearance, she immediately brought him a bath towel.

"Go in the kitchen," she said. "I'll make some tea."

While she brewed it, he went upstairs to the closet and changed into some of Jimmy's clothes. The tea was ready when he returned. Julia took the chair across the table from him. When he said nothing, she grew exasperated. "I hope this isn't a contest of wills," she said. "Am I supposed to wait patiently, or were you planning to say something?"

"Jesus, Julia, I don't know where to start. Remember I told you that Lorraine and Andie went up to Cape Cod? Well, about an hour ago Lorraine called me in the car and said Andie was hemorrhaging."

"Oh, no. Like Alyssa?"

He nodded. "Lorraine was always pretty damn helpless when it came to emergencies. I told her to get Andie to the local ER fast."

Since he'd told Julia about Andie's Restore-Tabs use, she knew exactly what was going through his mind. "You must be worried stiff."

"I am. Thank God Lorraine had the hospital phone number handy. I'll give them another hour or two to sign in and get Andie examined before I call."

"I'm sure she'll be all right, Steve." She paused, studying him. "Something else's on your mind, isn't it? What happened tonight?"

"Christ, what a nightmare. Where do I begin?"

"I suppose this involves Francesca Taylor?"

He hesitated a moment, then took a deep breath and told her everything.

Julia listened patiently, frowning but saying nothing until he was done. "You're worried as much about her as about Andie, aren't you?"

"I just can't get her out of my mind. I keep wondering if she's hurt. Jesus, maybe she got hit by the bullet. Why else wouldn't she have met me at the car?"

"I'm sure she's fine. She was probably just as scared as you were, and if I were in her shoes, I'd have run as far and as fast as possible. Maybe she went the other way."

"I thought of that, but where could she have gone? Wouldn't she go back home?"

Julia shook her head. "A single woman, living alone? After a nightmare like that, I'd go to a friend's house."

"You think?"

"When women are scared, they don't want to be by themselves. They want to talk to somebody."

"Hmmm," he said contemplatively. "The problem is, I don't know any of her friends."

"You're not going to feel better until you find out what happened to her, are you?"

"Would you?"

"Tell you what. There can't be too many hospitals in that area. Let me call Westchester information and get their numbers."

He sipped his tea until she returned several minutes later. "Did you get them?"

"The operator was very helpful when I said a family member had been injured." She handed him the list.

While he walked to the kitchen phone, Julia stood in front of the sink, arms folded, watching him. Dialing the numbers on the list, Steve identified himself as a physician and was connected with the various emergency rooms. Within ten minutes, he was done. No one named Francesca Taylor had been treated in any of them, nor did recent patients match her description. He slowly hung up the phone, looking glum.

"No luck?" Julia asked.

He shook his head. "Where in the hell could she be?"

"I already told you."

"Yeah, but I don't know . . ." He followed her back to the table. "I'll probably be able to find her in the morning. At least I hope so. You know, what's so weird about this was Ted's reaction."

"Wanting to arrest you, not hurt you?"

"Right. He was furious, but he had that look in his eyes. It reminded me of when we were in college. He'd say one thing, but mean something else."

"So now he's one of the good guys, huh?"

"Not at all," he said. "Ted has to take responsibility for what he did. But there was *something* in his expression. The memory of our friendship, maybe. Or guilt. Maybe both."

"Did you see any remorse in the younger guard?"

"No, what I saw in that guy was pretty damn scary. He wasn't like any security guard I've ever seen. I had the feeling he was just plain evil. He seemed more interested in putting a knife in me than in guarding the building, and . . ."

"What?"

"I just remember something he said. He called me 'Doc.' How could he have known I was a doctor?"

"Maybe Ted told him."

"He didn't come in with Ted. And Ted had no way of knowing who was in the office until he walked in on us. The guy *knew* me, Julia. Somehow, he knew me."

"Frightening. Could he have been an old patient?"

"Out of the question," he said. His expression was distant, reflective. "No, there's something else going on here, but I can't figure out what."

"All in all, was it worth it, this little escapade of yours?"

"I hate to think that Ted and the old man might be dead now. God, I never thought it would come to something like this."

"I meant was it worth it for the information you got?"

"I nearly forgot about that. The papers are still in my pocket." He left the kitchen, dashed up the stairs, and quickly returned, unfolding the documents as he sat down. He quickly reread the damp pages and then handed them to her.

Julia scanned them. "Where in the world is Sulawesi?"

"Indonesia."

"Hmmm." She flipped to the next page. "So this is the secret ingredient in the infamous Restore-Tabs. I might've known."

"How?"

"For the same reason that Sulawesi doesn't surprise me." She took some papers from her robe pocket. "Gary Sullivan faxed me these this afternoon. Look familiar?"

He read her fax and compared it to his printout. "Jesus, they're identical. This is your boss, right? How did he find out so fast?"

"I told you, Gary's a genius. He says it's the formula for a very potent estrogen, more potent than anything commercially available. He's not surprised it causes problems."

"Did he say something about Indonesia?"

"Not exactly. Once he learned the chemical structure, he cross-referenced it against known databases. He said he got a hit on an Australia-based online service that lists recently discovered biological compounds, anywhere from Tahiti to the Indian Ocean. According to Gary, there's this kind of shallow algae that grows in the Celebes Sea. That's near Indonesia, right?"

"Just north of Sulawesi."

"Anyway, this algae lives on coral in those reefs," she said, "and it was recently found to produce our friend the estrogen here."

His eyes widened. "Interesting. So if someone mined the local reefs, they could extract the stuff." He looked at his other printout. "According to the map, they'd just have to dredge it up and transport it ashore. I wonder if Ted knew."

"Why wouldn't he? He's the CEO."

"I don't mean the location; I mean the potency. The Ted DiGiorgio I know would never deliberately hurt anyone."

"People change, Steve."

"Sometimes. And sometimes they wind up dead."

Julia was worried about Alyssa. In addition to her worsening pain, she had developed a fever. Before Steve placed his next call, he went upstairs to check on her. Alyssa was asleep in her bed. Steve didn't want to wake her, but he touched her hot, damp brow and checked her pulse. The rest could wait until morning. Then he returned downstairs.

He called Cape Cod from the kitchen phone. After speaking with a hospital clerk, he was put through to the nurse. A gynecologist was on his way in, she said. Andie's vital signs were stable, though her pulse was a little fast. They'd started an IV and had gotten some preliminary lab results. She thought it best if Mrs. McLaren discussed them with him. Perplexed, he waited for Lorraine to come on.

When she picked up, her voice was flat, lusterless.

"They say she'll be okay, Steve. They did a sonogram and . . . well, she's having a miscarriage."

"What?"

"Andie's pregnant, all right? The urine and blood tests were positive, and they showed me the ultrasound. I'm sorry, I had no idea."

"But . . . did you tell them about the Restore-Tabs?"

"Yes," Lorraine said, "and they told me that didn't change anything. And Andie told me, Steve."

"Told you what?"

"She said she had sex with Jeffrey Hirsch. She said it was only once, about a month and a half ago, but who knows? I guess once is all it takes."

Steve was dumbfounded. It never, ever occurred to his trained medical mind that his daughter might be sexually active. He'd been so worried about the Restore-Tabs that he'd overlooked the obvious. "I don't know how to say this, but I'm actually a little relieved. At least this is something they can take care of. Lorraine, listen to me. If the gynecologist wants to do a D and C, say okay. Don't call back; just sign the consent and get it taken care of."

"I will, Steve." In addition to the hospital's number, she gave him the number of her bungalow. "Will you call back in the morning?"

He promised he would. When he rang off, a little grimace turned his lips down. God almighty, he thought, isn't this the first thing they teach to med students? How could I have been so obtuse? Concerned though he still was about Francesca, he was so relieved to learn Andie didn't have cancer that his whole body began to relax. He went upstairs to bed.

Julia spent the remainder of the night in a recliner by her daughter's bed, sleeping poorly. Every hour, she'd awaken to touch Alyssa's forehead. At four, she woke Alyssa up to administer doses of aspirin and Tylenol. Her daughter was listless. The inevitable seemed to be a fast-approaching reality.

Steve, likewise, had a fitful sleep. In his restless slumber, he relived the confrontation countless times. The brief, intense skirmish rumbled through his dreams like a squall.

Toward dawn, both the rain and his sleep came to an end. The first thing he did when he got up was to call Francesca's number. As before, his call went unanswered.

Next, he phoned the hospital number Lorraine had given him. The switchboard operator transferred him to admissions, which subsequently put him through to his daughter's room. Andie answered brightly.

"Hi, Daddy. I'm in the hospital."

"I kind of gathered that. Is your mother with you?"

"No, she went home to get me some clothes. They're letting me out around noon." Like a balloon deflating, her tone quickly lost its effervescence. There came a pause in the conversation, followed by the sound of sniffling. Andie began sobbing, and her speech turned jerky. "I'm sorry, Daddy, I'm so . . . I was too embarrassed to tell anyone. I didn't even know I was—it was just that one time, and . . ."

"Don't worry about it, sweetie, it happens. That's behind you. The important thing is you're all right now. You have two parents who love you very much and will always be there for you. Look, I'm not going to minimize what happened, because it's important for you to admit your responsibility in it. But we'll talk about it when you come home, all right?"

"Okay."

"Are you feeling all right?"

Her sniffling wound down. "I was once they took out the IV. I got out of bed already and had a little breakfast. The food here is terrible. I can't wait to leave."

"Do you know if they had to transfuse you?"

"You mean blood? I don't think so. Why would they do that?"

He allowed himself a deep sigh. "We'll talk about it soon. But once you're discharged, I want you to take it easy. No hanging out at the beach today; just stay in bed and rest, okay?"

"Okay."

"Tell your mother I called, and I'll try to call back later, honey. Bye."

"Later, Dad. And Daddy?"

"What, Andie?"

"I love you."

*   *   *

He checked on Alyssa. Julia was sound asleep in the nearby recliner, but her daughter already had the TV on. The volume was low, and the old grandfather clock ticked in the background.

" 'Morning, kid."

Alyssa's eyes were glazed, her tone subdued. "Hi."

His trained eyes swept over her thin frame, and he squeezed by the recliner to sit on the mattress. He'd brought his medical bag from the car. After taking her pulse, he listened to her heart and lungs. What he heard was worrisome. Just then, the clock struck six, and the local news came on.

"Can you turn it up?" he asked.

As Alyssa adjusted the volume, Julia opened her eyes and sat up. Under the backdrop headline, "Murder in Westchester," the anchor read the details.

"In today's top story, the bodies of Ted DiGiorgio and a security guard were discovered late last night in the Larchmont headquarters of Ecolabs. Ecolabs is a major manufacturer of popular vitamins and nutritional supplements, like the fast-selling Restore-Tabs. According to police, who responded to an anonymous 911 call, DiGiorgio was found in his office, the victim of a gunshot wound to the chest." In the background, there was video of a sheet-covered body being wheeled out of the building on a stretcher. "The guard, whose name is being withheld, was apparently stabbed to death in the office with DiGiorgio. The knife and a gun with one shot fired were found at the scene, and there were signs of an altercation. Police theorize that DiGiorgio and the guard became involved in a dispute that ended fatally for both."

Steve stared at Julia, who looked as astonished as he did. "Can you believe this?"

"Can I switch to another channel?" Alyssa asked.

"Sure, go ahead," he said. Then, to Julia, "Come outside a second."

Once in the hall, he whispered, "They didn't say anything about a second security guard."

"You think they just left him out of the story?"

"Absolutely not. They would've said something like, 'The bodies were discovered by,' and then given the younger guard's name."

"Maybe he wasn't a guard at all."

"That'd be my guess," Steve said. "He didn't even *look* like a guard. He was too young, and he was very quick, in great shape, like an athlete. Julia, the guy came out of nowhere. Now that I think about it, I bet *he* was the one who popped me in the head, not the old guy."

"And the other things that happened?"

"The way I see it, after I was down, the new guy stabbed the guard. Maybe the guard's gun went off, or maybe the young guy took it and shot Ted."

"I see," Julia slowly said, her modulated tones making it clear she didn't see as clearly as Steve. "So what was the other guard doing in the building?"

"That, I don't know."

"Maybe he was just a burglar, and you got in his way."

"Possibly. But remember, we didn't catch *him* in the act. He barged in on us."

"Right." She looked back toward the bedroom and changed gears. "Did you call your ex-wife back?"

"I did. Thank God Andie doesn't have a problem with Restore-Tabs, but you're not going to believe what happened."

Julia listened quietly to the tale of Andie's pregnancy and miscarriage, a shocked expression on her face. When he finished, she slowly shook her head. Then her eyes turned wistful. "I'm glad your daughter's okay. I know you'll work things out with her. But you know what came to my mind? I kept thinking that I'd give anything to have that kind of problem with Alyssa."

There was nothing Steve could say. He silently squeezed her hands until she blinked the tears away.

"What do you think about Alyssa?" she asked.

"It's not looking good, Jules. She's got some fluid in her lungs. It might be pneumonia, but her heart failure could be a little worse. I'm going to treat her for both."

Julia's expression grew pensive, her eyes watery. "Do you still think she'll make it to Labor Day?"

"I don't have a crystal ball, but I've never bullshitted you. My guess is it'll be much sooner than that."

He couldn't get Francesca out of his mind. He phoned her every hour and always got the same recorded message. He considered calling the Westchester police, but what could he tell them? That he and his girlfriend had been at the scene of a murder and fled, but could the department please look for her? He considered filing a missing persons report but knew that was foolish, too.

Every riddle, every unanswered question, led to yet another. The process was exhausting. Steve distracted himself by calling the office. He didn't want to see patients until his scrapes from the fall had healed more, and besides, he was too preoccupied to devote his energies to medical matters. As usual, Donna and Becky had everything under control. By midmorning, the convoluted obsessional thinking had completely worn him down. He knew he had to snap out of it. He headed for Julia's small vegetable garden and busied himself with weeding.

Julia came out with iced tea. "What are your plans for today?"

"I don't know. Just hang out and keep calling, I guess."

"Sorry, laziness isn't permitted in this house. Alyssa wants to go for a ride. Want to come?"

He stood up, brushed the dirt from his hands, and took the drink. "I'm not sure."

"This business has you paralyzed." She stepped up and took his free hand. "Come on, you're going."

Julia drove an old Mustang convertible. The sky was hazy, but the day was warm. Alyssa took up her favorite spot in the back.

"Where are we going?" Steve asked.

"We'll head down to the beach, do some people watching."

First they drove east, past Hampton Bays to Southampton. On the town's main street, traffic was heavy. As the Mustang slowed, Steve gazed at the passing store windows. Behind the glass of an upscale nutrition shop, Restore-Tabs was prominently displayed. Staring at it, he felt his anger mount. He felt like barging in and ripping down the display.

If it were up to him, he'd do everything possible to stop
the ad campaign in its tracks. It was downright irresponsible
to remain a spokesman unless the problem of hemorrhaging
was cleared up. He felt guilty about the part he'd played,
and he was worried, not only about his daughter Andie, but
for others like her who may have taken too much of the
product. It was time to remove himself from the public eye.
He was certain he and Ted had agreed on a verbal contract
for his TV slots, but unfortunately, Francesca hadn't been
able to find a copy of his written contract. But that no
longer mattered. As soon as he knew she was safe, he was
going to his lawyer with everything he had.

Leaving Southampton, Julia headed for the ocean. With
the breeze ruffling his hair, Steve finally began to relax. He
leaned back against the headrest and tried to enjoy the
drive. It wasn't all that difficult. As Julia turned west onto
Meadow Lane, they began a long circle home. The haze
lessened. With the sun's rays softened by the sea air, the
journey grew increasingly pleasant.

Eventually, they came to Dune Road and drove past Indochine. Steve wistfully recalled his dinner with Francesca,
and in no time at all, she again occupied his thoughts. As
they drove on, he grew tense. Soon he began craning his
neck as they drove past the stylish beach houses. Julia
watched him out of the corner of her eye.

"Are you looking for something?" she said over the
rushing wind.

"Could you go back for a second?"

"What do you—"

"Please," he insisted.

She slowed, made a U-turn, and headed back the way
they came. As they neared a familiar house, Steve motioned
for her to slow down. He stared fixedly at the dwelling.

"Stop!" he shouted abruptly. "It's her!"

"Who?" Alyssa asked.

But he was already standing up, cupping his hands to
his mouth. "Francesca!" he screamed.

Julia stared seaward, down the narrow side yard that
bordered the property. In the distance, a bikini-clad woman
slowly descended a dune toward the surf. She was two hundred yards away, her back to the street. Between the wind

and the crashing waves, she couldn't possibly have heard anyone calling her. Steve seemed to realize that. He quickly sat down and grabbed the door handle. But Julia forcibly restrained him by seizing his shirt.

"Steve, don't!"

He shoved the door open. "I'm telling you, it's her!"

"Listen to me!" she commanded. "Just listen!"

He silently glared at her.

"Let's say you're right, and it is her," she argued. "Think for a minute! What does that tell you?"

"You don't understand, I've got to—"

"Goddammit, use your head! She's not going anywhere!"

Still in her grasp, he relaxed, turning back toward the ocean. "Okay, I'm thinking."

"To begin with, she's obviously not hurt, or she wouldn't be prancing around out there."

"You don't know that. She might be in shock. Maybe she can't remember what happened."

"Jesus Christ, you're saying she has amnesia?"

His voice was subdued. "It's possible. Stranger things have happened."

"Come on, please stop and think! If she can't remember, what's she doing out there?"

"Well . . ."

"Does she live here?"

He shook his head. "She said this place belongs to a friend."

"How convenient. You said you left my number on her machine, right? Here you are, around the proverbial corner, but did she call?" She paused long enough for her words to sink in. "Answer me!"

"What's your point, Julia?"

"Steve, look. I'm not trying to get into an argument with you. But you have to face facts, be realistic."

"I am realistic."

"No, you're not. If she were as concerned as you are, she would've gotten in touch with you, not worked on her tan! Come on, put it all together."

Just then, he spotted someone else. "Christ, *him* again!"

Julia turned around. In the distance, a middle-aged man

approached Francesca and joined her by the surf. Over-weight, slightly balding, he spoke to her animatedly. "Who's that?" Julia asked.

"I don't know, but I've seen him before. I wish I knew what they were saying."

"Well, you can forget about walking over there to find out. I know you think she loves you, but trust me. I don't think she'd give you the time of day."

"You're dead wrong, Julia."

"Can we go home?" Alyssa piped up. "I don't feel so good."

"Okay, honey," said her mother. To Steve, "Like I said before, it doesn't look like she's going anywhere. You want to find out what they're saying? I've got a better idea."

"Go on."

Julia turned the car around, heading for home. "This might sound a little bizarre, but I don't think you have anything to lose. The other night, Alyssa and I watched a show on one of the cable channels about spy gadgets."

"Now we're becoming spies?"

"It was very interesting, especially the parts about electronic eavesdropping," she said. "Apparently, the government is a little annoyed that so many high-tech devices are available to the public, but there's not much they can do about it. One of Alyssa's friends told her there's a spy shop in Easthampton. Want to take a look?"

He wasn't sure what they were getting into, but . . . "Let's go."

The Hamptons in the summer: never-ending traffic jams; dazzling white beaches and offshore breezes; an eclectic mixture of old and new. Antique shops next to glitzy computer outlets. Staid country clubs beside tawdry strip joints. It was a transgenerational culture in which everything could be found, especially if it catered to the chic, moneyed crowd. As Steve and Julia walked down the street, they watched the stream of summer visitors. Occasionally, there was a familiar face. Steve smiled broadly when he spotted Karl Müller.

To Steve's surprise, the older man quickly averted his eyes and looked straight ahead, stone-faced. As the two men passed one another, Steve turned around, thinking Müller hadn't recognized him.

"Karl! Karl Müller!" Steve called from behind. "How're you doing?"

Müller stopped and slowly turned. His blank expression revealed little. "Not bad, Dr. McLaren."

"That's great. I tell you, I always get a little concerned when one of my patients doesn't recognize me. I haven't seen you in a while."

"That's because you're not my doctor anymore."

Steve felt as if he'd been slapped. "I . . . What's going on, Karl?"

"I just go to the cardiologist now, and he says that's all I need."

"What about your regular care?"

Müller looked overhead, scratching his chin. "I'll be seeing somebody else for my follow-up care."

Steve felt a range of emotions, from anger to betrayal. "We've been through a lot together, Karl. I'm a little confused. Naturally, you can go to anyone you want, but help me out here. What am I missing?"

"Nothin' personal, Doc. It's just the rumors, you know?"

"No, I don't know. What rumors?"

Müller looked him in the eye. "The drinking rumors. I've had a lot of that in my family, and I know what it can do to the person, and to the people around him. Not to mention the effect it has on performing your job."

It had to be Phoebe Atkinson. "Where did you hear these rumors?" Steve asked.

"That don't matter. Like I said, it's nothin' personal, but I just feel more comfortable seeing another doctor. One thing I can't deal with is drunkenness."

"But—"

"Good day, Doc."

As Müller walked away, Julia took Steve's arm. "Am I missing something? I've certainly never seen you drunk. What was he talking about?"

"Jesus, it's a long and complicated story. One day, I'll fill you in on the details. Come on, let's get what we came for."

Easthampton's upscale Espion-Age was packed day and

night. The trendy boutique had opened seven years before as a purveyor of cell phones. But competition was keen, and it was hard to make ends meet. Responding to customer requests, the store began offering a line of miniature surveillance equipment like telephone bugs and tiny video receivers. The items were popular and sold well. It changed its name, and Espion-Age was born.

"I hope you know what you're looking for," Steve said. "I'm lost in this place."

"I figure we'll know it when we see it. If you want to hear your girlfriend and the other guy, this stuff should do it."

They cruised the aisles, picking up objects at random. Most were made of plastic, wire, and silicon.

"These look like toys," he said.

"If they do what you want, what difference does it make *what* they look like?"

"I don't quite have your confidence."

"What do you think of these?" she asked of an item she picked up.

He examined the small rectangle. The black device was the size of a matchbox, and it had a one-centimeter lens on the end. "This is supposed to be a camera? It must take the world's smallest video cartridge. Where does it plug in?"

"It doesn't. It uses lithium batteries, and it's not a camera. It's a video transmitter."

"I give up. How does it work?"

She read the informational brochure. "According to this, it transmits a video signal to a nearby receiver."

"One's useless without the other, huh? What does the whole package go for?"

"It's on sale for nine hundred dollars."

"A regular drop in the financial bucket. But all I want is the audio. Let's see what else they've got."

Half an hour later, they left the store with what they thought they'd need. One box contained a directional boom mike similar to that used on football sidelines. Ultra-compact, it had a saucer-size, handheld dish antenna that could pick up voices at two hundred yards. It was a basic amplifier, and all the listener had to do was to plug headphones into its base.

The other item was a miniature FM audio transmitter. Designed to be attached to a window, it transmitted the audio signal to a receiver a short distance away. All of the equipment set him back six hundred dollars.

Their simple plan was that Steve would camp out by the beach house, electronically eavesdropping while Julia took care of her daughter. After dark, when Alyssa was asleep, Julia would join him. She hated leaving her daughter alone; but in an emergency, Alyssa would call on Julia's cell phone. Then they'd plant the window bugs under cover of darkness. The plan didn't guarantee success, but it was the best they could come up with on short notice.

He couldn't simply sit in the convertible aiming his mike seaward. Not only would he be too easily spotted, but passing patrol officers would doubtless take a dim view of his activities. What he needed was cover. After giving it some thought, he had an idea.

"Doesn't the place you work have trucks?"

"They own a couple of vans," she said.

"A van would be perfect. Not even the cops get suspicious of a commercial vehicle parked by the curb. I could sit in one for hours, and no one would be the wiser. Can you get hold of one?"

She mulled it over. "They don't use them on weekends. Let me make a call."

They returned home. After a call to her employer, Gary Sullivan, Julia got the van with no questions asked. Minutes later, she and Steve were again on the road, taking their purchases and a pair of binoculars.

Steve remained convinced there was a less-than-devious motive behind Francesca's actions. Trying not to be confrontational, Julia patiently restated what she thought was incontrovertible fact. Although she pleaded for objectivity, he insisted on proof, not conjecture. But he did promise to go through with their plan. Julia proposed a few tactics.

Reaching Island Diagnostics, they parked in the lot. Julia went inside for the keys, returning moments later and motioning him toward the van. It was the newer of two Ford Econolines. It sported wide, side-entry doors and had tinted glass. Julia suggested that once he was parked, Steve install the mike just behind the van's partially opened doors to keep it hidden. That way he could remain inside, out of sight. It seemed like a decent proposal to Steve. The longer his surveillance lasted, the more time he'd have to think about what had occurred. Steve transferred their equipment, took the keys, and started the engine. As Julia approached, he lowered the window.

"I know you want to talk to her," she said, "but promise you won't do anything stupid."

"Stupid? Not in my vocabulary." He started the engine and drove away.

When he reached Westhampton Beach at suppertime, Francesca and the man were no longer in sight. Steve thought they were probably indoors eating, or perhaps they'd gone out to dine. He didn't have the luxury of finding out. The plan said to stay put, and he was sticking by the plan.

He parked opposite the house, on the far side of the street. Entering the van's cargo area, he opened the side doors slightly. The gap allowed an unrestricted view of the side yard and the beach beyond. Using screw-on clamps, he mounted the mike ten inches behind the doors, aiming it beachward. When and if Francesca came outside, he'd be able to hear her.

But she did not and, try though he might, he couldn't keep from fantasizing about her lying in one of the bedrooms, having sex with the overweight stranger. He thought of the man as Mr. Paunch. It was a ludicrous fantasy in which he imagined her performing unrestrained libidinous acts. It was hard for him to get rid of the intrusive thoughts. He'd do just about anything to hear her deny what was increasingly becoming obvious as the truth.

He sat on the floor of the van, back against the wall, gazing through the opening. The interior was stuffy, and from time to time he started the engine to run the air-conditioning. Alone with his thoughts, he fidgeted and worried. Then, around seven-thirty, he saw her.

His pulse quickened. Crouching, he crept toward the doors and picked up the binoculars. He switched on the dish antenna and put on the headphones. The first thing he heard was the pounding of the surf, as clear as if he were sitting at water's edge. Francesca had changed into one of her sarongs, and its windblown top was caught by the breeze. She was carrying a canvas-backed beach chair, which she opened. Sitting down, she relaxed and stared at the horizon.

Steve wondered what she was thinking. Did he occupy anyplace at all in her thoughts? After the tender moments they'd shared, it was hard for him to accept that he might be nothing more than an afterthought. He stared at her motionless back through the binoculars. The soothing ocean sounds were a soft echo in his ears. After a few minutes, Mr. Paunch showed up with a chair of his own. Steve turned up the volume.

"Magnificent sunset," said Paunch.

"It certainly is. Reminds me of Puerto Rico."

The snap of an opening pop-top sounded crisply in Steve's headphones. Paunch offered Francesca a beer.

"Want one?"

"No, you can have 'em both."

"So when are you leaving?" asked Paunch.

"Two nights from now. We have a nine-fifteen flight out of JFK."

We? thought Steve. Who the hell is *we*?

"It's a long flight, isn't it?"

"That's what I've been told. It stops in Frankfurt and then goes to Singapore. There are connecting flights into Indonesia."

"You'll be dead tired."

"There's plenty of time to rest," Francesca said. "We'll be there about a week."

"It takes that long to close things down and get rid of the evidence?"

"Probably not, but we may as well enjoy ourselves. You should come with us, Bob."

"I've got plenty to keep me busy around here. Now that Ted's gone, I've got a lot of things to straighten out."

The pair fell silent. While Bob sipped his beer, Francesca watched the reddening horizon. As Steve listened closely, staring through the binoculars, he grew aware of the muscles working in his clenched jaws. His face felt hot. He didn't like what he was seeing, and he couldn't *believe* what he was hearing.

So there it is, he thought. The facts were exposed, his naiveté clear. A simmering anger began to grow, much of it self-directed. He'd completely trusted her, and now . . . He'd been thoroughly used, but for the love of God, why?

What was she really after? Francesca was obviously an actress, a damn good one. He was deeply humiliated by the realization that there was a hidden purpose behind her pretense of love. Yet some facts were inescapable, and that knowledge left him chilled: Bob's identity, for one. His voice had sounded familiar, and as Steve thought about it, he had the sickening realization about where he'd heard it before. It had been in a call from Westchester, a call initiated at Ted's urging.

The voice belonged to Ecolabs chemist Robert Whitt.

Steve banged his fist on the van's metal floor. Blinded by infatuation, his jealous resentment had been misplaced. Whitt wasn't a lover; he was a conspirator! Whitt, Francesca, and someone yet unnamed were collaborators in a scheme involving Restore-Tabs. Initially, Steve thought the third party had been Ted. Ted had been a fool; but the more Steve mulled things over, the more he was convinced that Ted was as much a pawn as he had been.

Far too many mysteries, he thought. Layer upon layer, like the skin of an onion. Rather than try to unravel everything, it would be more productive to stick to what he absolutely knew. And right now, the most incontrovertible fact was that Francesca and some as-yet-unnamed individual were going to Indonesia. Their final destination was reasonably obvious. He felt certain it was the area circled in the crumpled map he'd shown Julia.

Much as he hated to admit it, Julia had been right. The more patient he was, the more he'd learn. Confronting Francesca would now be pointless. There was no *way* she'd say, Sorry about that, here's what's going on. Steve was simply going to have to endure the wait.

In the idyllic sunset, the distant pair lazily watched the orange sun sink under the horizon. Whitt silently finished both beers and got up.

"I'm heading in," he said. "When did Jack say he'd call?"

"Around ten. He's pretty punctual."

"You going back to your place?"

"Not if I don't have to," she replied. "I can't risk running into McLaren. He probably calls every hour as it is."

The binoculars suddenly felt leaden in Steve's hands. Crestfallen, he lowered them. It was one thing to feel like a fool, but something else entirely to be confronted with the embarrassing proof. He felt like hiding in the van and going out to wring Francesca's neck at the same time. He slid away from the door. For the first time in months, he didn't want to look at her. The pain of humiliation was too great.

Finally, Francesca disappeared indoors. There was nothing for Steve to do until Julia arrived at nine. As soon as it was dark, he got up and stretched. He worried that Francesca might spot him, but he needed fresh air. He stepped out of the van and walked a short distance down the road to get some circulation back into his legs. When he turned back, the headlights of a slowing vehicle came up behind the van. Julia got out carrying the additional equipment and followed Steve back into the Econoline.

"How'd it go?" she said. "Learn anything?"

"Yes, but not what I wanted to hear."

He told her what had happened. It was a painful admission, and Julia saw the deep hurt in his expression.

"I know how much you cared for her," she said.

"I did, Jules. I really did. But more than that, I felt I knew her. The worst part comes when you feel you really know someone, a day, a week, a month, and you discover it's only an illusion."

"You were foolish, so what? Put it behind you."

"I know, I'm an idiot," he continued, embarrassed. "Just please don't say I told you so."

"Why should I? You feel bad enough as it is. Any idea who Jack is?"

"Not a clue. But he's got to be part of it. Whitt knows him, and Francesca's comfortable enough to travel halfway around the world with him. Jesus, if anybody else's in on this thing, we'll need a scorecard. It'll be hard enough to keep track of the three of them."

"Is that what you want to do, watch them?"

"No, that'd take forever," he said. "I'd like to find out

what's going on in Indonesia. I think that's where the answers are. If I can't learn anything else here, I'll head to Sulawesi."

"It's going to be risky to follow them."

"That's not what I had in mind. Come on, let's set that equipment up."

Steve and Julia got out and stayed in the van's shadows as they studied the house from across the street. The house was big, and they only had two transmitters. They briefly debated where to put them. The living room seemed a likely spot, as did one of the bedrooms. Using window spacing as a guide, they decided to bug what they thought was the master bedroom. The battery-operated audio transmitters were the size of playing cards and had peel-off adhesive surfaces.

The house's curtains were now drawn, something that would help conceal the novice eavesdroppers. Steve switched on the transmitters and gave one to Julia. They waited until all traffic had passed. Then, keeping to a crouch, they sprinted toward the house and squeezed through the bushes. Attaching the transmitters was simple. They returned to the van without being spotted.

"What time is it now?" Julia asked.

"Nine-forty. I can't wait till this guy calls. Did you bring the tape recorder?"

She handed it to him.

"Thanks." The portable machine's input port connected to the receiver with a jack. Steve switched on the tape and gave her a pair of headphones.

Julia hunkered down on the floor, holding the phones to her ears. Steve knelt, staring at the metal floor in concentration. The mélange of soft sounds they heard had a high-pitched familiarity. The voices of actors in a TV movie provided a backdrop. The house was otherwise quiet, save for a footstep or an occasionally turned page. At last the phone rang.

"I've got it," they heard Whitt say. "Hi, Jack. How're things? . . . Good. Hold on. Francesca, pick up."

"Jack, I was worried," she said on the extension. "Where are you? . . . I know. So do I . . . No, I'm trying not to. I'm sure he's called. I'm going to stay here until our trip Monday night."

"You got enough money?" Whitt asked. "At least another ten grand. I think it'll take more like thirty to pay everyone off. We don't need any questions or someone bitching. . . . I'm sure you can, but try not to call attention to yourself."

"Don't worry, Bob. I'll keep an eye on him," said Francesca. "You're going back Monday morning, right, Bob?"

"Yeah, I can't stay away forever. I'll go in and play the distraught researcher. Real crocodile tears . . . No, no regrets. He had it coming, if you ask me. He could be a real prick to work for. . . . Yeah, you too. Soon as you go back, we'll go to the bank and throw ourselves a little party."

After a pause, Francesca said, "Of course. I sold everything. It'll take about a week for the transaction to clear. . . . All right. I miss you too. Bye."

"Take it easy, Jack."

When the conversation ended, everyone fell silent, both inside the house and out. Steve waited a moment to hear if Whitt and Francesca resumed speaking, but they did not. He took off his headphones and motioned for Julia to do likewise.

There was restrained anger in his tone. "Am I imagining it, or did it sound like Whitt had that phony guard kill Ted?"

"You're not imagining it."

"Which means that the whole thing was a setup. Whitt and Francesca must have known Ted would be there. Christ, that means I was just an afterthought in a plot to kill Ted!"

"You were there to legitimatize the break-in."

"God almighty, she's been using me all along, hasn't she? She was so damn smooth! But it was never about me—it was always about her and those other two characters against Ted!"

"Stop blaming yourself, Steve. When you come right down to it, it's always about money. Money's a powerful motive, and it gets a lot of people caught in other people's plans."

"But why Ted, for God's sake?" he said. "I *do* blame

myself. He didn't deserve this. He could be abrasive, sure. Maybe even a little unstable. But the whole jealousy thing, that was Francesca's bullshit. She played us off against each other, feeding Ted and me little half-truths so we'd wind up at each other's throats. Man, the way she set me up was beautiful. I never would've agreed to break into my friend's office if she hadn't pressed all the right buttons."

"She played her part well," Julia agreed. "I don't think you're all that gullible. She must have given an Oscar-winning performance. You were as much a victim as Ted."

"Come on, let's get out of here."

They packed up and drove home absorbed in their thoughts. When he finally spoke, Steve said, "I really fell for her, Jules. You think that maybe, subconsciously, I wanted to?"

"Yes, I do. I think you were ready. She probably saw that at the Christmas party. Women like that are predators. They know what they want and choose their men carefully. Remember, you'd been through a lot. You were perfect."

"So I guess Ted wasn't behind *any* of the crap that happened—not my office charts, not my daughter, and Jesus, probably not Puerto Rico, either. Damn, Francesca's good. Her distress seemed so fucking genuine!"

"She's good, all right. She had *you* fooled."

"I just don't see how she pulled it off underwater by herself. She must've had help."

"You're saying she's not man enough?" Julia said slowly. "If you ask me, she has balls aplenty."

19

"I'm not saying it'll work out, but I want to try," Jared Trent said. "I mean, if that's okay with you."

"What about the blond with the big chest?" Karen Trent asked.

"I told you, that was a mistake. And I'll keep telling you, if you want. I'm not saying let bygones be bygones; I know it's not that easy for you. All I want is a chance. For what it's worth, I give you my word. I've learned my lesson, and I really want it to work out for us."

He even let Karen control the TV remote, which, for Jared, was about as big a concession as there was.

"I'll think about it," she said with a smile. She'd smiled a lot today, ever since Jared drove her home from the hospital. She wasn't used to being doted on, and he was so helpful he was actually getting in the way.

She'd had a long talk with Annie as soon as she was settled in. Annie had a direct, folksy wisdom and didn't beat around the bush. She still thought Karen's husband was a loser, but she was impressed with the way he pitched in when the going got tough. Maybe he was salvageable. Give him another chance, she advised. Watch him like a hawk, but give it a try.

Karen didn't have to think about it long. She'd been given a do-over in life, and she was determined to make the most of it. She felt more optimistic than she had in a long while. She was cancer-free, and her doctors had given her a good prognosis. She still had to weather the chemo, but she felt certain she'd come through that fine.

Everything considered, Karen Trent had done well for herself. The doctors may have given her back her life, but she'd reclaimed Jared's heart herself.

When Steve and Julia reached home, Alyssa was still asleep. Julia checked on her daughter and then joined Steve downstairs.

"What now?" she said. "Isn't it time the police knew what we know?"

"Sure, if we can do it without going to jail. We can't just call and say 'guess what.' "

"What about an anonymous letter?"

"That's a possibility," he conceded. "It wouldn't be my first choice, but it'd probably work."

"What's your first choice?"

"I'd like to go into the police station, find Francesca and her pals sitting there, and say, 'These bastards killed Ted DiGiorgio for his money. Book 'em, Danno.' "

She pursed her lips. "And your second choice?"

"I'd like to have all the facts first. I'm still not sure how everything fits together. Francesca and the boys aren't about to tell me, so I'll have to find out for myself."

She didn't want to hear what he was about to say. "Indonesia?"

"You got it. Okay if I go online?"

"Go ahead."

It took Steve twenty minutes to find what he wanted. Numerous Web sites offered flight schedules, fares, and reservations. Logging off, he found Julia in her bedroom. She'd changed into a robe and was lying on her bed, watching TV. She stared at him and raised her eyebrows in inquiry.

"According to when Francesca said she was leaving, they have to be flying Singapore Airlines. I booked a seat on Continental," he said. "They have a morning flight, twelve hours before Singapore's. It goes around the world the other way—Honolulu, Guam, and Bali. I'll get there way before them, and I can be on-site and gone in a heartbeat."

"What do you hope to accomplish there?" she asked skeptically.

"I want to see the plant, for starters. I want to find out exactly what they did with the coral, and maybe get a feel for their clinical trials. I want to see everything for myself—to understand how and why everything started." He paused. "What? Why are you looking at me like that?"

"I just don't understand why all this is necessary. You already know from personal experience what bastards they are and where they're staying, so why not let the police handle it? I'm sure they could be persuaded to help find this guy Jack, and probably the killer guard, too."

"I guess, deep down, I feel it's important to me to know why," he said. "Sure, we have the puzzle pieces. I'm hoping this trip will help fit them together."

"You're sure that's the only reason? Is it remotely possible you want to confront her at the scene of the crime? Have a little heart-to-heart, get her to confess? Find out what she sees in Jack, and if he's man enough to take her away from you?"

"Come off it, Julia."

"Come here, Steve," she said, switching off the TV and patting the mattress beside her. When he sat down, she placed her hand on his knee. "In case you don't already know, I care about you. Not just as Alyssa's doctor, but as a person. For all your stupid flaws, and God knows there are plenty, I think you stand head and shoulders above any other man I've known, except maybe Jimmy. You're a good and wonderful person, and you certainly don't deserve what happened to you. And I worry about you. I worry that you're so blinded by hurt and hate that you don't see the pointlessness and danger of what you're suggesting." She paused. "And I need you, Steve. *Alyssa* needs you."

"If you're trying to make me feel guilty, you're doing a great job."

"I just don't want to lose you, that's all."

There was an unspoken plea in her worried expression. Steve leaned over and kissed her forehead. Julia put her arms around him and pulled him down to her. Stretching out lengthwise, he lay beside her in silence. Their eyes were closed. She embraced him contentedly, and he stroked her fine hair. Her clinging spoke more of a deep need for warmth and comfort than it did of passion. Steve relished the comforting, and for the first time since his near-drowning, he was able to relax. It wasn't long before they were both asleep.

Sometime during the middle of the night, an inner alarm awakened Julia. She slid out of bed to check on Alyssa. Moments later, when she returned, Steve had barely stirred. She loosened the covers they'd slept on and climbed in next to him. Lying beside him was peaceful and fulfilling. Slumber quickly returned.

They awoke at seven. In the bright light of morning, they seemed surprised to find themselves next to one another. It was evident from their expressions that they both felt slightly embarrassed. Steve sat up.

"Good morning," he said. "I didn't mean to weasel in on your accommodations. Did I keep you up?"

Her voice was husky with sleep. "Not at all, but it was different. I haven't slept with a full-size human since . . ."

"Yeah. I'll go check on your daughter."

After using the bathroom, Julia poked her head into Alyssa's room. Steve was listening to her lungs with a stethoscope. The child's skin was pale and waxy, and her normally bright eyes were flat and lusterless. Julia sat next to Steve and took Alyssa's hand.

"Tired, sunshine?"

Alyssa nodded lethargically. "A little. I don't sleep too good. It's sort of hard to breathe."

"Then just take it easy. We'll go out later." She looked at Steve, who'd put his stethoscope down. "Any change?"

"Some. Let's get some coffee, okay?" He stood up, looking down at his patient. "Can I get you something, kiddo?"

"I'm not hungry."

"All right. Later."

Julia followed him to the kitchen. "I saw that frown. She's worse, isn't she?"

He nodded. "The fluid keeps building up in her lungs. And I think she's in more pain than she lets on. I'll give her a diuretic and increase her digoxin a little. That'll hold her a while."

"How long?"

"Julia, I can't—"

"All I'm asking is, if you're determined to make this trip, will it hold her until you get back?"

"Please, Julia. I feel bad enough leaving her as it is. I promise I won't be gone that long. You want coffee?"

"All right."

While the coffee brewed, they watched the local news. There was another story about Ted's death, this time covering his personal life. He was portrayed as a philanthropic, public-spirited citizen. The story concluded by saying there were still no solid leads. The police were treating the incident as a burglary turned sour.

She poured the coffee. "What time are you going to the airport?"

"The flight leaves Newark at eight o'clock tomorrow morning. I'll get up early to miss the morning rush—say, around four. If the weather's all right, I should be at the airport by six-thirty."

"I don't suppose there's any point in trying to talk you out of this one last time?"

"I know you're worried about Alyssa—"

"Of course I am," she said, "but what I'm saying is, this trip's a wild-goose chase. It won't bring your friend back. If they're shutting things down, Restore-Tabs is a dead issue anyway." Seeing him preparing to object, she raised a calming hand. "Okay, I'm finished. I just had to say it. This is your decision, and I won't interfere. What's that psychological term, where the therapist tries to sum things up?"

"Closure?"

"Right. Maybe this trip will bring you closure and let you walk beyond what happened."

He thought about Francesca and about everything that happened. It was high time to get on with his life. "I hope you're right."

When Steve called Lorraine's house, she answered on the second ring. Although it was late morning, Andie was still asleep. They spoke with more civility than they had in months. Andie was still tired but convalescing well. The doctor had started her on birth-control pills which, given Andie's pregnancy, Steve thought was a good idea. Lorraine stopped taking Restore-Tabs herself, removed all bottles from the house, and strictly forbade Andie to buy any more. Steve was satisfied. Before hanging up, he promised that the three of them would go out to eat soon.

In the afternoon, Julia drove them to Montauk Point, on the easternmost tip of Long Island. Alyssa felt cold, and Julia kept the top of the convertible up. The three of them sat together in the front, with Alyssa and Steve sharing the right bucket seat. She leaned against his shoulder and stared through the windshield. Although it was a relaxed, leisurely drive, Alyssa tired easily. But she had always loved the lighthouse.

The Point's two-hundred-year-old lighthouse stood one hundred and sixty-eight feet above sea level, and at high tide, the surrounding bluffs offered a breathtaking view of the crashing waves below. Alyssa never got enough of the view. Steve and Julia realized this was the last time she was going to see it.

They'd brought along folding chairs and opened them toward the southwest. Alyssa basked contentedly in the sun, whose afternoon rays were strong but pleasant. Steve wondered if, in her awkward teenage way, she was saying good-bye. In no hurry to leave, they stayed for several hours. During the return drive, Julia pressed Steve for details of his trip.

"Do you have a ticket?"

"I downloaded an electronic one."

"What about photo IDs?"

"I have a duplicate driver's license," he said, "and a University ID at the office. I'll pick it up later."

"And your passport?"

He thought about it. "Oh, my God . . . the fire."

"Can't you get one in an emergency?"

"I tried that once for Lorraine. You have to go to one of their main offices in person. I don't think they're open on weekends, and anyway, it's a little late. Christ, how could I forget that?"

For a while, they drove without talking. "So what're you going to do?" she finally asked.

His voice was flat. "I'm not sure. What do you suppose would happen if I showed up in Indonesia without a passport?"

"They'll probably put you on a plane going home. After you got out of jail, that is."

"For the right amount of money, I bet I could buy a black-market passport somewhere."

"On such short notice? Who're you going to call? You'd be better off borrowing someone's."

The trip exhausted Alyssa. She fell asleep the instant they got home. Using the kitchen phone, Steve made several calls to people he thought might have underworld contacts. None could offer assistance at that late hour. He moodily prowled around the kitchen until Julia came in.

"Any luck?"

"Afraid not. One of them said he could help in a few days, but not in twelve hours."

"I suppose that should make me happy," she said, "but I know how important this is to you. Did I ever tell you that one of the reasons I was attracted to Jimmy was because I thought he looked like you?"

"You're kidding, right?"

"Nope. In fact, in some of his pictures, he's you with a mustache." She handed him a passport. "Like in this one."

The U.S. passport had been issued to James Hagen a year before his death, and it hadn't yet expired. Steve studied the photo. Jimmy had more hair than Steve did, and a bushy mustache; but otherwise, there was a distinct resemblance. "You're right, I never noticed."

"You want it, it's yours."

He looked at her. "You sure, Julia?"

"I'm sure Jimmy won't be needing it anymore. Once you're in Indonesia, I doubt they'll check it against the name on your ticket, and if they do, tell them some story about somebody else making the reservation for you. You ask me, you'll easily sail through immigration."

After supper, he drove to the mall for travel items. He'd be traveling light, and he only needed a few changes of clothes. When he was done, he returned to Julia's and composed a letter to the Westchester police. Without identifying himself, he described the sequence of murderous events at Ecolabs.

Reluctantly, he named Francesca. There was no way not to. He also disclosed Robert Whitt's personal involvement, and he said he had a tape implicating them both. He concluded by promising further contact once he had more information. It was a hard letter to write, but Steve felt it was the least he owed Ted. He asked Julia to mail it in the morning.

He was apprehensive about the trip and didn't go to bed until after midnight. He slept fitfully. The alarm awakened him at three-thirty A.M., and he quickly showered and shaved. When he left the bathroom, a towel around his waist, he heard Alyssa call his name. He went to her room and stuck his head inside.

"You rang, mistress?"

"When are you leaving?" she asked weakly.

"Soon. It might be a good idea if I got dressed first."

Her voice had a whiny, adolescent ring. "Do you really have to go?"

He slowly sat beside her and touched her feverish brow. "I wouldn't say it's life or death, but yes. I really have to. But I'll be back real soon."

"I don't want you to leave, Steve."

"My, you learn quickly from your mother. I thought *she* was the only one who could make me feel guilty about this. Look, princess. This trip is important to me, and it's something I have to do. I'm flattered you want me to stay, but that's not in the cards. So you just concentrate on getting your strength back, okay?" He leaned over and kissed her forehead. "I'll be back before you know it."

In the guestroom, he dressed in khakis and a short-sleeve shirt. Everything else, including the small parabolic mike, was packed in one of Julia's lightweight carry-ons. He kept his photo IDs, some cash, and a spare credit card in his pants pocket. Jimmy's passport and outdated driver's license went in the carry-on. He hoped the Indonesians wouldn't check the expiration date on the license. Then he carried everything down to the kitchen.

Julia was already up and waiting with fresh coffee. At the kitchen table, they tried making small talk, but the effort was strained. The fact was that they had already said just about everything. Finally, he looked at his watch and stood up. Julia walked him to the door, where she paused.

"So," she said, hands thrust demurely in her robe pockets. "When's your return flight?"

"It's an open reservation. Once I get to Bali, I doubt I'll be there for more than a couple of days. I'll be back by the end of the week."

"Will you call?"

"As soon as I get a chance. I've left drugs and supplies in my bag upstairs. Just keep an eye on Alyssa and don't worry about me, okay?"

"Who are you kidding?"

They came together for a farewell hug. She clung to him, and when he finally pulled away, he saw that she was crying. He smiled and wiped away her tears.

"Steve," she simply said. Then she took his face in her hands and stood on her toes to kiss him on the lips. It was a needy kiss, touched by fear. "Come back to us," she whispered.

He turned and was gone.

During most of the ten-hour flight to Honolulu, he slept. The Guam leg was somewhat shorter. Rested and alert, he nervously paced about the cabin as the DC-10 crossed the International Date Line. All passengers temporarily deplaned before continuing on to Indonesia. It was then that he understood what Vietnam-era patients described as Southeastern-Asia weather, with its unrelenting, unbearable heat and humidity.

By the time he arrived in Denpasar, Bali, it was eleven P.M. The ersatz passport worked well, and his passage through immigration was smooth. He took his bag outside and flagged down a cab. He didn't have much time to lay over, because the Sulawesi flight left a little before eight in the morning. The driver took him to the Ramada Bintang Bali Hotel, two miles from the airport.

The hotel was American-style with Balinese touches. He turned the room air on and didn't bother unpacking. All he removed from his carry-on was a shaving kit with personal items. After washing his socks and boxer shorts, he hung them up to dry. With the air-conditioning going full blast, the room quickly cooled. He could barely hear the airplanes overhead when he got into bed. Pulling the covers up around his neck, he was soon asleep.

Steve arose at six. He dressed quickly, checked out, and arrived at the airport in ample time. His thousand-mile Garuda Air flight to Manado would stop at Ujung Pandang, and the whole trip would take four and a half hours. As the flight took off from the Denpasar airport, Steve got his first daytime glimpse of Indonesia. The rippled green canopy beneath him was tall and thick and lush, and the jungle soon gave way to the vast Java Sea that stretched across the horizon. Turquoise near the coast, the water slowly became a magnificent royal blue.

In no time at all, the island of Sulawesi loomed up before him, with tall, spectacular mountains just beyond the southern coast. After the plane landed and most of the passengers got off, it took off again for the final leg to Manado.

Once there, Steve took a shuttle bus from the airport to town. He planned to use the small city of two hundred thousand people as a base of operations. But once he was there, he wasn't sure what to do next. The only thing he had to go on was the map in his pocket—Ted's map. At least seven hours of daylight still remained, and he didn't want to waste it. But first, he checked into a hotel.

The three-story waterfront accommodations apparently catered to scuba divers, for diving posters hung throughout the lobby. According to the clerk, most of the guests had just left for afternoon dives. Steve got a room, deposited his carry-on, and returned to the front desk, where the clerk gave him general directions.

Outside, a Mitsubishi cab waited at the curb. After brief haggling, the driver agreed on a price for an all-day rental, not in rupiah, but in dollars. The price quickly doubled when Steve showed him the map. The drive itself would take most of the day, and even if they turned right around once they reached their destination, they still wouldn't be back in Manado until the early morning hours. Steve agreed to the price without further negotiations.

Except for a large central market and quaint horse-drawn carriages, Monado boasted little in the way of urban tourist fare. While Steve relaxed in the backseat, he quickly saw that the area's real attraction was not the city, but the sea. The lure of the water was powerful. His driver explained that the reef system off northern Sulawesi attracted divers from all over the world, and hotels were being quickly built to cater to the wind-and-water crowd.

The urban clutter was soon replaced by mile upon mile of coconut groves. All around, the natural splendor was phenomenal. On the right, the white beaches and sparkling water were mesmerizing, and to Steve's left, the ridges of tall, verdant mountains beckoned, reaching toward the sky. The main coastal highway leading out of Manado was well-maintained. During the long, leisurely drive, Steve was so taken with the scenery that he exchanged few words with the driver. A little after six P.M., they arrived in Inobonto.

The cabdriver stopped in the center of town. Ted's map in hand, the driver spoke with several workmen, who turned and pointed toward the hills. There was an animated discussion, and then the driver returned to the cab.

"These people think they know this place, but they have never been there. It's in the mountains, not far from here."

"Are they sure?"

"Nothing is certain, sir," the driver said, "but they think so. It's about a mile from a factory that blew up this morning. The workmen say the factory was the other mark on your map."

"Good Lord! Blew up? Was it making something explosive?"

"They said it was a coral-processing plant."

Steve suddenly felt a chill. In his gut, he knew *exactly* what kind of coral was being processed, and what it was intended for. "Was anyone hurt?"

"Yes, several people. Do you wish to go there?"

"Not if there's nothing left. Let's go to the other place."

As the cab drove out of town and worked its way into the mountains, Steve now understood what they meant by "shutting down operations." The factory was shut down, all right. No doubt Whitt, Francesca, and her companion had been in touch with locals to do the job before Francesca arrived tomorrow morning. Steve was thankful he'd decided to come early. He'd have a chance to visit the other site before they got to it.

The rising road soon became rutted and narrow. There were no road markers or street signs, but fortunately, there was still ample daylight. Eventually, they reached the small, hidden turnoff. The driver missed it at first, but when he spotted the clearing through a gap in the forest, he backed up. They soon found themselves before a long bungalow.

"A *Bugis* house," the driver said as they got out. "The *Bugis* were great sailors and builders."

It certainly was colorful, Steve thought. Constructed on stilts, it had brightly painted shutters and a gabled thatch roof. It also seemed dry enough to go up in flames at any moment. The front door was closed.

"Think anyone's home?"

"I don't know, sir."

"There's only one way to find—"

He was interrupted by a moan originating inside. It was the unmistakable sound of deep human suffering. His heart beat faster. He hadn't come halfway around the world to tend to the sick, but he couldn't ignore it, either. The driver eyed Steve uncertainly as he started up the steps. With the cabbie bringing up the rear, Steve reached the door and knocked.

There was no answer. Steve knocked again and discovered that the door wasn't locked. When it slid ajar a few inches, he pushed it fully open. Inside, the room was pitch black. "Find out who's there," he said to the driver.

The cabdriver came abreast of him and shouted a few words in Bahasa Indonesian, the national language. When there was no reply, he said something different. This time, the returning sound was the same weak cry they'd heard before. Steve stepped through the doorway.

As light flowed into the room, an odor came out, the fetid smell of decomposing flesh. "Jesus," Steve said. A wave of buzzing flies immediately swept in, attracted by the stench. He took a step forward and let his eyes adjust to the faint light. He spotted overhead lights but no switch. Going cautiously forward, he reached parallel rows of cots and saw, at the far end, some movement.

"I think we should call the police," the driver advised.

"In a minute." Steve warily advanced down the aisle between the cots, gazing from side to side. There was someone in nearly every bed, and they all appeared to be women. He could tell that most of them were dead. Clad in light-weight, filthy gowns, their emaciated faces had hollow cheeks and sunken lids. Most of their jaws were open, teeth bared, and their dry, sightless eyes stared up at the roof. Some appeared to have been dead several days. The buzzing flies quickly settled on their flesh.

"In the name of Allah, what happened to them, sir?"

"Cancer. I think I know what kind, and why. That one over there's still alive."

In the last bed, a woman moved feebly, attracted by the voices. She'd been left in her own filth, and she had a cadaveric look. The stench of urine and drying feces was thick about her. The woman breathed weakly, and her eyes were closed. Steve gently touched her face. The woman responded with slight movement of her head and a gut-wrenching moan. He felt her pulse.

"Forget it," he said to the driver. "I doubt she can survive another hour. There's nothing we can do for these poor people. Let's go."

So this is Bob Whitt's harmless clinical trial, Steve thought. This is what happens when "volunteers" are given up to ten times the normal dose of Restore-Tabs. He walked back to the entrance in disgust, and more than a little angry. Then he remembered he'd left a liter of bottled water in the cab, and the least he could do was make the dying woman a little more comfortable.

Nobody deserved to be left for dead as callously as these poor women had. It was almost as if, like him, they'd been deliberately set up.

"We are going to the police now?" the driver nervously asked.

"You bet we are." Steve started down the building's front steps. "Just stay there while I get something in the backseat. And don't touch anything." As he neared the taxi, he had a feeling something wasn't right. It suddenly struck him how oddly convenient it was for the abandoned clinic to be left in complete darkness. As he grasped the cab's door handle, he turned back and saw the silhouetted driver fumbling on the wall for the light switch.

"Don't!" Steve shouted.

An enormously concussive wave smashed into him an instant before the sound hit. As Steve was slammed against the cab, a roaring thunder exploded about him, nearly bursting his eardrums. Along with the deafening noise, a wave of roiling fire unfolded, barely missing him.

He lay on the ground, stunned, looking up, watching the flames and smoke reach skyward. Dazed, with a ringing in his ears, Steve lay on his back a few more seconds, trying to gather his wits. A low, furnace-like roar reached him. Growing more alert, he turned toward the rumbling noise to see the *Bugis* house completely swept up in an inferno. He rolled onto his stomach and crawled around the taxi like an infantryman. Reaching the safety of the other side, he sat up.

Leaning against the cab, he slowly inhaled, trying to calm his brooding thoughts. He knew there was no helping those inside. It was a blessing for the moribund woman, but not for the unfortunate cabdriver. Steve was angry with the man for not listening to him, but he was also angry with himself.

He'd sensed something was amiss. He should have seen it, or at least been more emphatic with his instructions to the cabdriver. The explosion had been intended for them. Steve figured the lights must have been toggled to a mercury switch that was connected to explosives. What an idiot he'd been! There was no *way* he should travel halfway around the world and leave anything to chance!

Beautiful though it had been, the long house was constructed of little more than wooden poles and thatch. The building quickly disappeared in the crackling flames. As the minutes passed and the fuel was used up, the blaze diminished. When Steve no longer felt heat shimmering over the Mitsubishi, he got to his knees and opened the driver's side door. He noticed that the cabbie had left his wallet and cash on the floor. Steve silently vowed to return them to the man's family. Fortunately, the driver had also left the keys. Steve climbed in, started the engine, and quickly drove away.

By the time he arrived in Inobonto, the sun was setting. The smoke in the hills behind him was barely visible. Steve remembered the route back to Manado, and he also had a map. Just outside of town, he filled up with gas and began the long return journey. He doubted any of the townsfolk had the slightest idea what had happened.

When he reached Manado at one A.M., the city was quiet. The only people out and about were foreigners, mainly American and Australian. He parked the cab in an inconspicuous spot on the waterfront, hoping the cab wouldn't be missed until he'd left town. Retiring to his room, he took a shower and let its relaxing heat seep into him. He was exhausted. His body was sore, and there was an ache in his soul. Everything that happened was so goddamn unnecessary.

He'd learned what he'd set out to. The processing plant where the estrogen-containing coral was refined had been destroyed, and the clinic that housed the victims of the Restore-Tabs trials was smoking rubble. It was all over now. Francesca and Dr. Whitt had won. From New York, she'd tidied up the "loose ends." She would soon arrive to make her payoffs, and then return home to reap the financial rewards. From what he'd overheard, Steve was certain she and the others had cashed in on Ecolabs' skyrocketing stock just before DiGiorgio was killed. In the end, Julia was right. It all came down to something as simple as money.

Still, he felt cheated. Julia had been right about that, too. A part of him still wanted to see Francesca one last time. He wanted her to realize he knew everything. Yes, he wanted to say, you may have gotten what you wanted, but I now understand how I was betrayed, and . . . What? If he were honest with himself, what did he really expect? That, after confronting her, she'd apologize and beg his forgiveness? That she'd admit to having feelings for him and hope they could start over?

He turned off the shower and toweled dry. After all he'd been through, he felt annoyed with himself. He'd been deeply wounded, and yet he still harbored adolescent fantasies about renewed romance. What a self-pitying fool! He'd been given a chance to move on with his life, yet he was still longing for what might have been.

As he got into bed, he told himself to grow up. He wasn't a victim; he'd been a willing participant. The time had come to accept responsibility for his actions. Dwelling on hindsight and resentment was a circular path that led nowhere. Somewhere out there was a future filled with hope and promise. As his eyes began to close, Steve realized it was up to him to live it.

But his last conscious thought was that somewhere out there, there was also a man called Jack.

20

First there came a loud knock, followed by the cry of "Sergeant!" Then, another knock.

Atmosaputro sat up and turned on the light. "Yes?"

"It's Suwarno, sir. I have some information for you. May I come in?"

"The door's open."

It had been a cool night for the region—upper seventies, with a breeze—and Atmosaputro had left the windows open. He heard the police car drive up long before the knock. He slept a lot lately, but he slept lightly. His hand was on the Beretta the instant he saw the headlights shine through the window.

Since his discharge from the hospital, it wasn't unusual for department members to stop by. One officer or another dropped in daily, checking on his progress, offering companionship. He was, in fact, recuperating well. He walked on the beach for hours every day, regaining his strength. He ate well, got a lot of rest, and took his medications. He learned not only to function with one arm, but to use it efficiently. When his family was unable to visit, he spoke with them by cell phone. Most of all, he had a lot of time to think.

Coming face-to-face with death, one questioned what was important in one's life. The larger meaning of things, one's values, direction, and relationships, suddenly became crucial. In this process of internal focusing, if one were fortunate, one came away with greater balance, increased centeredness. And Sergeant Atmosaputro was very fortunate indeed. He came to look at his life in a different perspective, and with greater clarity than ever before.

Yet the sergeant also thought a lot about Jack Buhlman. Atmosaputro had an Asian's concept of what the Japanese called *bushido,* a personal code of honor. He dearly wanted to meet the man again. Fortunately, many people owed him favors. Among them was a high-ranking official in the country's immigration service who promised to keep the American under computer surveillance.

The young policeman entered the bungalow. "I'm sorry to disturb you, Sergeant. We just received a fax for you from immigration in Jakarta. I thought you'd want to see it."

Atmosaputro took the page. "Did you read it?"

"I regret, sir, that I have. It came in on my shift."

"Does it mean anything to you?"

"No, sir," said Suwarno. "This man, Mr. Buhlman. Is he important to you?"

"Oh, let's just say he's an old friend I hoped to see again. If I have anything to report, I'll let you know."

"Yes, sir." He turned to go, but hesitated. "Are you sure everything is all right, Sergeant?"

"Yes, officer. More than ever. That'll be all."

After the policeman left, Atmosaputro studied the fax more closely. According to his contact, Buhlman had arrived the previous morning on Singapore Air, accompanied by an American woman named Francesca Taylor. They listed their Indonesian destination as Java, but airline computers indicated they'd purchased round-trip tickets to Manado. Moreover, the man known as Buhlman matched the height and weight Atmosaputro had supplied, but he had blond hair, possibly dyed, and blue eyes. Finally, if the sergeant wished the man detained, he should reply immediately.

A knowing smile crossed his face. So, my American friend, you have returned. And what murky business are you up to now? Perhaps we'll be lucky enough to see one another again.

There was nothing to keep Steve in Indonesia. His return flight to Newark left at ten P.M., giving him the whole day to get to Bali. It was barely eight in the morning local time. He tried his best to keep busy, for guilty thoughts about the cabdriver kept intruding.

He thought about going to the police, but that would risk getting jailed for carrying a phony passport. He could handle the situation better once he got safely home. From the hotel, he called a travel agent and explained his needs.

The soonest he could be booked on a flight to the Denpasar airport was in the afternoon. Steve took it. Packing his bag, he checked out of the hotel.

Outside, the morning air was fresh and cool, the day bright. He quickly walked the several blocks to the travel office and paid for the ticket by credit card. The memory of the previous evening weighed heavily on his mind. Unfortunately, eager though he was to leave the country, there was nothing to do but wait.

First, he walked to the waterfront and saw that the taxi was where he'd left it, apparently unnoticed. Then he walked to a cafe and lingered over a coffee, watching the Indonesian day unfold. He decided the quickest way to pass the time inconspicuously was by taking a driving tour of the city.

He flagged down another cab and explained what he wanted. This time he didn't dicker on price. In return for the few hours required to keep him off the streets, he was willing to pay what the driver asked. Getting into the cab, he sunk low in the backseat, eyes barely at window level. The taxi drove on.

The cabbie was as much tour guide as driver. In a friendly, engaging manner, he readily explained the city's meager attractions to his disinterested passenger. It wasn't long before the taxi was stuck in thick traffic at a major intersection. Steve furtively glanced at a nearby vehicle.

His eyes suddenly widened, and his pounding heart almost erupted from his chest. Two cars away, another cab was stuck in traffic. In its backseat, two passengers were engaged in conversation. The one nearest Steve slowly turned in profile. It was a face he would never forget.

Francesca.

"Oh, my fucking word," he muttered.

"Sorry, sir?" said the driver.

"Forget the tour," he said excitedly. "That cab, two cars over? I want you to follow it. *Carefully.*"

The driver slowly looked over. "Are they friends of yours, sir?"

"Not anymore. Try not to let them see us."

He couldn't tell with whom Francesca was speaking. He got the impression it was a man, and there was a flash of blond hair. A thousand thoughts raced through his mind, the foremost of which was what was she doing here, right now, lazing the morning away in a Manado taxi? Why wasn't she in Inobonto? Naturally, he knew she'd be somewhere in the area, but if she'd arrived later than he, she should be just settling in.

He was certain she'd have business to attend to, with payoffs and operational shutdowns on her mind. But she seemed relaxed and carefree, having a fine old time. Maybe she operated at a less frantic pace than he did, or perhaps her schedule was less pressing. Or maybe she was simply more comfortable in the company of someone else.

The traffic began to roll, and Steve's driver let the other cab get ahead of them. At that moment, his return schedule didn't seem nearly as important as where Francesca was going. He was glad he'd brought the eavesdropping equipment with him. He knew he was acting like a child, yet hearing what she had to say suddenly seemed like the most important thing in the world.

His cabbie remained a prudent distance behind. Soon the other taxi accelerated through the pack and took the shore road out of town. It was the same route Steve had taken the afternoon before. Concentrating as he was on the vehicle a quarter mile ahead, he had neither the desire nor the opportunity to look at the scenery.

As his contact had indicated, Buhlman now had hair dyed blond. Atmosaputro picked up both vehicles a mile out of town on the coastal highway. For the first time in weeks, his eyes twinkled. This was just the opportunity he'd hoped for. After Suwarno left in the middle of the night, he stayed up planning. If Buhlman was in Manado, he'd find him. Among the city's hoteliers, cabdrivers, and businessmen, he had a network of informers.

Before dawn, the word went out about the recently arrived Americans. Their names and descriptions were supplied. A little after seven-thirty, he got a hit from the desk clerk at the Century Manado Hotel. The two people Atmosaputro had inquired about had checked in two nights before and were now off on a day-trip. A few minutes later, a cop who moonlighted as a taxi driver radioed in that the couple had gotten in his cab and were now headed for the Manado Beach Hotel on the coastal road.

Since he knew where they were going, Atmosaputro stayed well back. It would be simple enough, he thought, to wait for backup and arrest Buhlman when he reached the hotel. Too easy, in fact. The man had astonishing arrogance to think a simple disguise could keep him hidden. He hadn't even used a different name and passport! Was he so convinced Atmosaputro was dead, or did he think his old State Department ID would give him diplomatic immunity?

But, as a former employee, Buhlman had no protection from a charge of attempted murder. Unless the man could work miracles, he belonged to the sergeant. But Atmosaputro wanted to know the bigger picture—why was the couple here now, and what was their business in Sulawesi?

And then there was the question of the second vehicle. The foreign passenger also looked like an American. From the way his cabbie drove, their taxi seemed to be tailing the first. Something was happening that Atmosaputro didn't understand.

But he was determined to find out.

Steve watched the cab ahead turn into a beach resort about ten miles out of town. Francesca and her companion were dropped off at an adjoining restaurant, an alfresco café overlooking the ocean. Steve had his driver stop a considerable distance away. When he saw Francesca being seated at a table, he asked to be dropped off.

Bag in hand, he hid behind parked cars while searching for a good vantage point. There was a generous palm-covered planting bed at the far end of the lot, lush with ferns, rattans, and colorful flowers. He made his way to the thicket and hid in its tall bamboo. Two hundred yards away, Francesca and the blond-haired man seemed oblivious to him. When Steve noticed a third person joining the seated couple, he removed the parabolic antenna from his bag.

He set up the dish, put on the headphones, and concentrated. In the distance, Francesca extended her hand to the newcomer.

". . . A pleasure. Claudia, did you say? You're the nurse

Jack raves about at the clinic." Clearly Francesca, undeniably provocative.

"Yes. I am very glad to meet you. Mr. Buhlman has many beautiful things."

"He doesn't exactly have me, honey. More like a two-way street."

Buhlman? Steve wondered. Was this the man called Jack?

"Street?" Claudia said, puzzled. "I'm sorry, I—"

"Forget it," Francesca interrupted. She removed an envelope from her purse. "We're very happy with the job you've done here, Claudia. Take this. Don't spend all of it here, okay? When are you leaving?"

"This afternoon. There is a direct flight to Manila."

"Claudia's been with the project all year," Jack said.

Steve thought the voice sounded familiar, but he wasn't certain.

"Done a helluva job," Jack continued. "She deserves every penny."

Claudia spoke again. "Thank you, sir. I did not mean to interrupt your conversation before. You were discussing a man?"

Buhlman briefly debated going into details, but Claudia was leaving, and she'd always proven trustworthy. Besides, the subject irritated him. "Not much of a man," he replied. "The latest in Francesca's list of losers."

"Not in every way, darling. He *was* pretty good in bed. Not like you, of course."

"Don't push it, Frankie," Jack said. "All cock and no brain doesn't amount to much in my book."

"He had plenty of brains. He just always felt so damn sorry for himself. God, what a kvetch! 'I don't have feelings, my daddy didn't love me, my fucking wife gave me a hard time about my drinking.' Talk about whiners!"

"Like, 'Get off the cross, we need the wood'?"

"You got it. And such a sanctimonious do-gooder, forget it."

"He's history, now," Buhlman explained to Claudia. "Headed him off at the pass. But he was the luckiest son of a bitch I've ever met."

"How was he lucky?" she asked.

"When he got too close, we decided he should be history. Christ, we tried everything—tying him up with a lawsuit, burning him out, spiking his scotch, you name it. We even got a box jellyfish to sting him."

"How did you do that? Aren't they lethal?" Claudia asked.

The blond-haired man took his time in replying. He casually scanned the parking lot before gazing out to sea. "They're supposed to be, but like I said, this guy's incredibly lucky. As for how, Frankie here can tell you that. I'm going to the john. You guys want something inside?"

"We're good," said Francesca, watching him get up and walk away. A knowing smile crossed her face. "This man Steve was in love with me. He was naive to begin with, but being nuts about me made him super-gullible. Ever have anyone so crazy about you they'll do anything you ask?"

Claudia blushed. "No, I haven't."

"Well, maybe not. But Steve was that way. Jack thought the way we kept setting him up was a little too obvious. But the only thing Jack knows about men is how to kill them. Anyway, Steve and I went down to Puerto Rico for a little diving. Jack had just returned from his last trip here, and he smuggled in the jellyfish and brought it down to Puerto Rico. Steve never saw him. Before one of our dives, I pretended to forget something in my room, and Jack gave me the jellyfish in a plastic bag. I slipped it into my vest and dove with it."

"Did it sting him?"

"Did it ever," said Francesca. "When Steve wasn't looking, I squeezed it out of the bag and put it on his neck. The thing must have been pretty pissed off, because it got him good. But like Jack said, he had fantastic luck. He survived."

Steve could feel his whole face sag. His ears were burning. He felt used, violated. But as painful as Francesca's comments were, he found them oddly satisfying. Although he'd never considered himself particularly naive, he knew he was when it came to her. His feelings blinded him. But, wallowing in self-pity? Well, perhaps he had.

*   *   *

Atmosaputro understood the need for proper concealment. From his nondescript car, he watched in astonishment as the third American blundered across the parking lot into the greenery, making the sort of unintentional commotion Americans were wont to do. He wondered what the man was up to. The question was soon answered when the stranger opened his bag and set up a small parabolic mike and donned headphones.

The eavesdropper obviously wanted information, but for what? And just as obviously, what the man heard displeased him: red-faced and head lowered, the stranger seemed temporarily at a loss. It was apparent from the man's manner that he was unaware of his surroundings, and he was also unaware that Buhlman was now creeping around the edge of the thicket toward him.

Atmosaputro steeled himself. He quickly checked his Beretta, stuck it in his waistband, and cautiously got out of his car.

My turn, Mr. Jack Buhlman. Let's have some fun.

Steve returned his attention to what Francesca was saying.

"I've lived with Jack for years, since I stopped modeling."

"He must be a wonderful man."

"He's not the easiest person to get along with," Francesca continued. "He had a real temper when we first met. See this scar? One day he just popped me, and I've been pretty cautious ever since. But he's calmed down a lot, unless you get in his way. Then watch out."

Steve wanted to hear more, like what her plans were with the man called Jack. But his attention was suddenly diverted to the cold, sharp blade pressed into his neck. Fear like a driven stake plunged through him.

"Frankie's quite a woman, isn't she, Doc?"

When he heard the word "Doc," Steve realized where he'd heard the man's voice before. In Ted's Ecolabs office, Buhlman's tone was just as icy as it was now. And then, like now, he had a knife. Steve's mike hand slowly fell.

Jack pressed a button on a cell phone–size walkie-talkie.

"Frankie, get over here now. You'll never guess who dropped by to say hello."

"Where are you, Jack?"

"Look into the parking lot. Find two vans together, and I'm just to your left of them, in the clump of bamboo. Tell Claudia to stay there." Switching off the transmit button, he pressed hard under Steve's neck, driving him backward into the brush.

"Why call her over?" Steve managed to ask. "Want to humiliate me some more?"

"Humiliation is not exactly what I had in mind. There are a few things I need to know, like how you knew we were here, and who else knows about us. After that, we'll see."

As he crept forward, Atmosaputro saw Buhlman come up behind the unsuspecting American and put a knife to his neck. The sergeant took out his pistol and racked the slide one-handed, chambering a round. The Americans were still too far away for him to hear what they were saying. Winding his way through the palms, he briefly lost sight of them, then picked them up again when Buhlman drew the stranger backward. It was clear that Buhlman was confident of his abilities and his captive was not.

Atmosaputro spent several of his early years in his country's special forces. He was a trained jungle warrior who felt very much at home in the region's hot, steaming forests. Gun ready, he slithered noiselessly through the bamboo, approaching the pair from behind.

He was ten feet away when he heard Buhlman say something about humiliation. Atmosaputro raised the Beretta and sighted along the barrel. Buhlman's head seemed as large as a pumpkin, an easy shot. But as a police officer, the sergeant knew he had to give the man a chance to surrender. And he couldn't simply shout "Hands up!" because Buhlman might slit his captive's throat. He needed to get closer.

Keeping to a crouch, he stole up to the assailant. Occupied with Steve, Buhlman didn't hear him. Atmosaputro put his gun to the back of Jack's skull.

"Quietly, Mr. Buhlman. Release him and put the weapon down. *Slowly.* If you try to use the knife, I will kill you."

For several seconds, Jack didn't budge. He recognized the voice. Then he slowly withdrew the knife from McLaren's throat. When the pressure eased, Steve leapt to safety.

"Funny thing, fate," Jack said. "It gives me a chance to see you again, Sergeant. How's the arm doin'? Losing a hand must be a bitch."

Atmosaputro pulled back the gun's hammer, which clicked menacingly. "The knife. *Now*."

Jack had no choice. He reluctantly dropped his weapon, and when he did, Atmosaputro backed away. Jack cautiously turned around, looking at his captor. "And here I thought *this* son of a bitch was lucky," he said, pointing to Steve. "But he's no match for you. Christ, you must be made of fuckin' nails."

Atmosaputro looked into Jack's hooded eyes. "You're under arrest, Jack Buhlman. Get on the ground, on your stomach."

Although Jack stared directly at the police officer, he detected a glimmer of movement behind him. He realized that McLaren, who now stood off to the side, couldn't see it. Jack allowed himself an inward smile. He knew it was Francesca.

"Listen to the tough guy with the gun. Without it, you're just a one-armed punk. Someone ought to teach you a lesson and grab that greasy hair of yours."

Francesca understood. She leapt forward, arms outstretched, going for the Indonesian's head. Atmosaputro heard the rustling leaves behind him, and Steve now noticed, too.

"Francesca, don't!"

The sergeant whirled just in time to see that the woman was nearly upon him. Jack instantly retrieved his knife. Atmosaputro adjusted his aim but hesitated, unable to shoot an unarmed woman. Instead, he quickly bent under her oncoming arms. Using the stump of his injured arm, he encircled her waist and swung her around. Francesca sailed toward Buhlman, just as he raised the knife.

Jack shoved her body away and rushed Atmosaputro before the officer could raise the gun again. Jack slashed wildly, aiming for the man's good arm. The heavy blade missed the limb, connecting instead with the gun's steel frame and one of the sergeant's fingers. The Beretta flew from the Indonesian's grasp. Steve watched it somersault in slow motion through the air and land at his feet.

Jack slashed again, backhand this time, aiming for the sergeant's midsection. Atmosaputro jerked back, but not before the blade's tip sliced through his shirt. As Jack poised to strike again, Atmosaputro kicked upward as hard as he could. His instep smashed into Jack's wrist, and the knife was knocked away.

Jack grew enraged. With a guttural snarl, he lowered his head and charged the one-handed Indonesian. Atmosaputro, still weakened by his recent brush with death, tried twisting out of harm's way but wasn't fast enough. His fist bounced harmlessly off Buhlman's head before the American's cranium crashed into his chest. The wind went out of him, and the sergeant was bowled over backward, with Jack on top of him.

Atmosaputro snapped his knee up into Jack's groin. Jack groaned, and as he reflexively curled in agony, the sergeant rolled out from under him. Gasping for breath, the sergeant struggled to his knees. Then he got to his feet, trying to clear the cobwebs. But before he could stagger away, a hand shot out and seized his ankle in an iron grip.

Atmosaputro lunged forward, trying to kick free, but Jack wouldn't let go. Struggling to twist away, the sergeant swung around. But he was completely off balance. As he wrenched, Jack yanked. Atmosaputro tripped, and his head thudded heavily into a palm trunk.

"You kicked me in the balls, you little fuck," Jack growled.

Several feet away, the Indonesian lay on his side, eyes glazed. Jack found the knife and rolled its handle lovingly in his palm, a killer's caress. Then he slowly crawled toward the dazed man.

Steve stood unmoving, rooted in place. He felt strangely detached. Part of him was an observer who watched the goings-on with clinical curiosity; another part was quaking in his boots. He glanced at Francesca, who lay face down, unmoving. Then he looked at the gun.

"A guy kicks me in the nuts, I got to repay him," Jack

said as he approached the police officer. "Watch my technique."

Atmosaputro saw him through a fog. His head ached, and he had trouble focusing. But his vision was good enough to see Buhlman grab his belt and tent up his trousers. In the blink of an eye, Jack's knife slashed through the pants at the zipper. What Buhlman had in mind was clear; with his heart in his throat, Atmosaputro feebly swung once more at Jack's head.

Jack swatted the man's arm away, incensed. His eyes blazed, and his expression radiated fury. He instinctively punched at the sergeant's face, striking the man's mouth with the heel of his fist and the butt of the knife. Atmosaputro's bloodied head rolled to the side. Jack eyed the center of the Indonesian's chest as he raised the knife into the air.

As the knife reached its apogee, the air was suddenly split by a thunderous explosion, followed by two more in rapid succession. An irregular piece of Jack's skull flew through the air in a grisly crimson spray, and Jack's body toppled to the side.

Steve slowly lowered the gun. His hands were trembling. As the gunsmoke curled about his face, he looked at Buhlman and saw that the man's wounds were fatal. Beyond him, the Indonesian's lids were fluttering, and the man began to stir. Then Steve tossed the Beretta away and gazed at Francesca.

She lay face down on the ground, quite still. A half-dollar of blood stained the center of her designer top. Steve slowly knelt in the warm, damp soil. He shook her shoulder and softly called her name, but she didn't respond. As carefully as he could, he rolled her over.

He could see that she was still breathing, albeit barely. Her eyes were closed. He took her wrist and felt for her pulse. It was very rapid, very weak. Her entire chest was covered with blood. Ripping her shirt open, he saw the wide, telltale puncture just beneath her breastbone, and the liberal flow of dark blood. The knife had gone completely through her body, severing the aorta.

Her face was deathly pale. With a mounting sense of futility, he tore fabric loose and pressed it hard over the wound. The pressure must have hurt, for Francesca groaned, and her lids fluttered. Her eyes had the opaque appearance of someone in irreversible shock.

"Francesca," he gently called. "Francesca."

Her trembling lips pressed into a moue, and she struggled to speak. "I—"

"Sssh," he soothed. "Don't talk."

All of a sudden her head raised, and she fixed him with a look as intensely penetrating as any he'd ever seen. "Steve," she said urgently, "I . . ."

Just as suddenly, her eyes clouded over and grew cold. Her head fell back, and her jaw went slack. Her final, protracted breath came out as a whistling exhalation. This time, when he checked her pulse, it was gone.

For a long while, Steve looked at Francesca's lifeless face. He felt a conflicting rush of emotions. Most of all, he felt profoundly sad—not so much for himself, but for Francesca and for all those whose lives she affected. But he felt no remorse for his actions.

Sitting on the café's veranda, Steve looked out over the sea from the same seats occupied by Jack and Francesca two hours before. On the other side of the deck, policemen surrounded the nurse. Face in her hands, she sobbed throughout their questioning. The bodies had been removed and taken to the local morgue. Steve wished he were as tranquil as the ocean, but inside, his guts were churning.

The sergeant got off the phone, walked to the table, and sat down. His cuts and bruises had been treated, though his cracked, bloodied lips remained swollen. "Everything's adding up, Doctor. We both had pieces of the puzzle but not the whole picture. Apparently, Mr. Buhlman had been coming here for over a year. He was carrying out the plan of Dr. . . . White, is it?"

"Whitt. Robert Whitt."

"It appears that Mr. Buhlman purchased an old mineral-processing factory, converted it, and refined the coral. A very illegal practice, and there will be many arrests. As you suspected and the nurse confirmed, they tested the refined product here. A Dr. Sayed oversaw the testing. He was found dead near his office not long ago. We considered his

death a suicide, but as it coincided with one of Mr. Buhlman's visits, we will look into the possibility of murder."

"Just check to see if a knife was involved, and you'll
have your answer."

"We will," said the sergeant. "It seems that dozens of
women died in the clinical trials. Their bodies were dumped
at sea, near the reefs. We've found only two, but we are
getting more information about that from the nurse. As for
the refined powder, it went by ship to New York for final
purification. The rest, I believe, you know. What I don't
understand is why. What motive did these people have for
such dark dealings?"

"Sergeant, the way I understand human nature, it's usually sex, money, or power," Steve said, realizing full well
which applied to him. "I think what they always wanted
was money. Dr. Whitt and Miss Taylor worked for Ecolabs,
and Buhlman was a consultant. Between them, they had a
lot of Ecolabs stock. They sold it the day its CEO was
murdered."

"What happens to that money now?"

"That's a matter for the courts. Ultimately, it'll go back
to Ecolabs shareholders. That is, if Dr. Whitt doesn't take
it all out of the country first."

"I've already spoken with the U.S. State Department,"
Atmosaputro explained. "They are contacting the New
York police as we speak."

"Good." He paused, thinking about Alyssa. "I want to
go home, Sergeant. I know there's a lot of paperwork when
deaths are involved, especially if they're foreigners. But do
you think we could get to it as quickly as possible?"

"That won't be necessary, Dr. McLaren. We have all the
information we need. Neither of our countries wants to
make an issue of this. These people were criminals. We
want the matter dead and buried, along with the perpetra-
tors."

"I have no problem with that. Does that mean I can still
catch my flight?"

"I can do better than that," Atmosaputro said, getting up.
"I have you to thank for my life. The people here are also
grateful. We have arranged special transport for you back
to New York, with no need for phony passports."

"Really? When?"

"Right now, if you don't mind. There's a military aircraft leaving for Tokyo's Narita in an hour, and we are holding a seat for you. Do you have other belongings?"

"No, this is it. I'd like to make a call, though."

From the hotel lobby, his call was put through to Long Island, where it was nearly midnight. It took several rings for Julia to answer. She sounded worried.

"Steve, I really need you. How soon can you get here?"

"It's going to be at least twenty-four hours. I'm leaving soon. How's she doing?"

"Not so good, and I'm very worried. I think she's slipping in and out of a coma."

"Did you call Norman Rothstein?"

"I did, but he said unless I admit her to the hospital, there's nothing he can do."

"I guess not," he said with a sigh. "Look, Julia, until I get there, here's what you do . . ."

21

With Atmosaputro's assistance, Steve boarded the Lock-
heed transport in Manado with minutes to spare. When the
flight landed in Tokyo five hours later, luck was with him.
With diplomatic help, he was whisked through customs and
was able to book a seat on United. The late-departing flight
flew nonstop to JFK. Twelve hours later, a little after four
P.M. local time, he landed and called Julia.

Julia sounded frantic. Alyssa was stuporous. When she
wasn't unconscious, she was in a lot of pain. Her daughter
was trying to be brave, but most of her waking moments
were spent whimpering. The medication Steve had pre-
scribed hardly worked at all. Julia was desperate, and there
was an edge of helplessness to her breaking voice. *Please,*
Steve. Just get here!

At rush hour on the Long Island Expressway, Steve
knew it could take four hours to reach Quogue by car. But
as he left the International Arrivals Building, he discovered
an alternative. A company called Island Air offered one-
way helicopter service to the Hamptons for a hundred dollars. An hour later, Steve got off the craft in Southampton
and immediately caught a cab.

It took a while for Julia to answer the door, and when
she did, the strain was evident in her face. The worry lines
around her eyes were now deep furrows. Her old terry robe
looked worn, and there was a stain on the lapel. She hugged
him wearily.

"It's so good to see you," she said, her body slumping
against his. "Come on."

As Steve followed her upstairs, he heard moaning. It was
indistinct, a soft, animal-like sound of suffering. In Alyssa's
bedroom, the shades were wide open, but the room seemed
unusually dark and somber. The old grandfather clock
ticked rhythmically in the corner, counting out the time
remaining. Despite the open windows, the room had an
unwelcome odor: the smell of imminent death.

Alyssa lay at an oblique angle in bed, half on her side,

half on her back. There was a large green oxygen tank behind the bed, and its tubing fed oxygen through nasal prongs. A bag of IV fluids hung from a nearby pole. Alyssa's eyes were closed, and her forehead was damp. She looked pathetically frail.

Steve sat on the bed. When his stethoscope touched her chest, Alyssa's eyes opened. Her customary smile was gone, and her eyes were veiled. She lacked even the strength to greet him. Alyssa appeared to wince, and her eyes closed again. He stroked her fair hair.

"Where's it hurt, princess?"

Just speaking was an effort. "My back," she said in a tired, tiny voice. "It hurts a lot."

"Okay. I'm going to give you something."

"A shot?"

His tone was softly reassuring. "No, sweetie. I'll give it through the IV."

Julia silently lifted up the vial of Demerol from the night table.

"How'd she do on the fifty milligrams?" he asked, taking the bottle from Julia.

"She slept," Julia said. "It made her more comfortable. Of course, it wore off too soon."

"Where'd you get the oxygen and the IV?"

"The Visiting Nurse Service. Dr. Rothstein ordered it."

"Good, that makes things easier for me. Open one of those syringes, will you?"

Julia unwrapped the paper packaging of a three-cc syringe. Steve first drew up Versed, which he administered intravenously.

"What is that?" she asked.

"A tranquilizer. It's mostly used preop." Carefully watching his patient, he saw the tension gradually drain from Alyssa's muscles, and her body relaxed. The tight lines around her mouth disappeared. "How're you feeling, princess?"

"Okay," she said, her voice mellowed by the medication.

"Great. I'm going to give you something else, and you'll probably sleep a little."

He followed the tranquilizer with fifty milligrams of Demerol, giving it slowly IV. Soon Alyssa's head sank into the pillow, and her labored breathing slowed. Her closed eyes seemed at peace, albeit temporarily.

Steve got up and stretched, addressing Julia. "How long's she been in this much pain?"

"Since I spoke to you yesterday. I cannot tell you how hard it was to give those damn shots. I wish you'd been here."

"From now on, I will be. That other chapter's closed."

She looked at him. "Want to tell me about it?"

He did, while slowly pacing about the room, and sparing nothing. There was pain in his eyes, pain tinged with regret. But from his tone, Julia could tell that the months-long nightmare had ended. He'd finally decided to put things behind him and move on with his life.

"So," she said. "You came through unscathed."

"In a manner of speaking. Physically, at least."

As for the emotional part, Julia didn't inquire. "That sergeant sounds like a real lifesaver."

"No question. He was a good guy, and I'll keep in touch with him until the loose ends are tied up."

"Speaking of which, I almost forgot. On *News at Noon,* I saw that Dr. Whitt got arrested."

"Is that right? I didn't realize the cops worked that quickly. I feel better for Ted."

She stared at him pointedly. "And how do you feel for Alyssa?"

He stood behind her and began kneading her shoulders. In the bed, Alyssa slept. Julia's muscles were tightly knotted. "Let's just say I'm glad I got here when I did."

A spasm rocked Julia's body. "God, this drains me. I *hate* having to be so damn strong."

"Then don't be."

"I have to, for her." She hesitated. "How much longer, do you think?"

"Not long, I'm afraid. Today, probably."

Her hand suddenly reached for his, and her voice cracked. "Oh no, not so soon! If only . . ."

"What?"

"If only she were the way she was before this all happened. If only she were ten years old again! If only I'd done something different, protected her somehow."

"There's nothing you could have done, Julia. Absolutely nothing."

"This year, all I wanted was for her not to suffer. And until now, she hasn't. I don't know if I'm ready for this, Steve," she choked, holding his hand tight. "God, I don't want to lose her!"

Steve bent over the recliner. Embracing her from behind, he spoke tenderly in her ear. "You've given her the greatest gift of all, Julia. Through everything, I know you think she's had such amazing strength. And she has. But never forget what you've done for her. To be surrounded by someone as warm, loving, and caring as you . . . How many people can say that?"

"For goodness' sake, I'm her mother."

"No, it's more than that. I think one of the most important things in life is to learn how to touch others with your love, and to allow their love to touch you in return. You've certainly done that, Julia. The way you two have loved each other, she'll live on in your heart, and in the hearts of everyone she's known."

Sniffling, she slowly nodded in numbed silence.

"How long has it been since you slept?" he asked.

"I haven't kept track."

"And when was the last time you took a shower?"

"Am I that bad?" she said.

"Go ahead, relax. Clean up a little. I'm here for the duration."

"All right." She forced herself up and kissed Alyssa's flushed cheek. "I love you, my sunshine."

While Julia bathed, Steve sat in the recliner, gazing out at the trees in the gathering dusk. The low westerly sun painted the leaves with gold, and their dappled tones sparkled when stirred by a breeze. Like the trees, he thought, Julia clearly had the strength. But did he? He now understood what was expected of him, why she insisted he be there when the time came. That time was now at hand.

Alyssa wouldn't last the night. Her heart was rapidly failing, and she was drowning in the fluid that filled her lungs. But far more important was the steadily increasing pain. The intense pain of metastatic cancer was unrelenting. Alyssa might be comfortable at the moment, but her relief was temporary. The merciless agony would soon return.

Steve considered pain to be the degradation of all life. In its most virulent form, it made life not worth living. Alyssa might be gone in hours, but to leave the world gasping and in tortured discomfort was an unnecessarily cruel fate. And an avoidable one. He had not, as some claimed, taken an oath to preserve life at all costs. Rather, his goal as a physician was to help the sick and those needlessly suffering.

His duty clear, he was at peace with it. Before Julia finished showering, he removed vials of the necessary medications from his bag. He reconstituted some and mixed others until their syringes were ready, near at hand. He'd know when it was the right time to administer them. His heart wouldn't let him listen to Alyssa's cries one second longer than necessary.

Julia returned to the room in a new, white cotton robe. Trailing the scent of bath soap, she looked freshly scrubbed. Even in this hour of crisis, she cut a graceful appearance. Steve gave her back the recliner and took a seat on the windowsill, where his back was cooled by the rising breeze.

They were waiting. When they spoke at all, he and Julia talked about simple things like the weather—what a pleasant summer it had been, how enjoyable for Alyssa. But mostly, they listened to the inexorable, muted ticking of the old clock by the wall.

Steve watched Alyssa. Of the many people he'd known who had died, he had never remained at the bedside long enough to observe death's relentless approach. Like an army on the march, death's steady progress was predictable, slowing at some times and speeding up at others. There were moments when Alyssa's expression appeared unusually placid, and then her breathing would turn deep and labored.

Two hours after the last dose of medication, Alyssa groaned. Steve and Julia straightened up with a start. Alyssa's exhausted face twisted, and her fevered head thrashed against the damp pillow. Julia was quickly on the bed, taking her daughter's hand in one of her own, stroking her hair with the other.

"It's okay, pumpkin," she soothed. "I'm here."

"It hurts so bad, Mommy," Alyssa cried. "Why won't it stop?"

Julia fixed Steve with an urgent stare, then put her cheek next to her child. "It will, sweetness. Soon."

"Oh, Mommy . . . Steve?" she called, forcing her head up, eyes widening.

"By the window, kiddo."

"Is it dark out?"

"Yeah, the sun set a little while ago."

Alyssa's eyes blazed, and her gaze was focused. Momentarily lucid, she had the unexpected, mystical clarity possessed by those staring death in the eye. "Is there a full moon?"

He looked through the window. On the horizon, just coming over the treetops, was the moon. "How do you like that? There it is. Big and round and orange, a beautiful full moon. How did you know?"

"I just did." Then her lids narrowed again, and her head fell back onto the pillow. Her next groan had a feral quality, ending in a mournful, extended moan that shook her entire body.

Julia looked frantic. "I'm here, baby! Let me hold you."

Despite her already weakened condition, Alyssa's pain had returned with a vengeance. Tears streamed from her red, exhausted eyes, and she looked like a tortured, inconsolable infant. Her frail arm reached up to hold on, and she clutched strands of her mother's hair. "Mommy, Mommy, please . . ."

Tears streamed from Julia's eyes. She knew she was saying good-bye to her daughter, but she couldn't stand it anymore. "Don't fight it, sunshine; it's going to be okay." To Steve, "You said you'd help her!"

He realized it was time. With trembling hands, he aspirated a hundred milligrams of Demerol from the bottle and injected it through the IV hub. He never before dreamed of doing something with such awesome finality, and prior to taking those last, terrible steps, he insisted that his patient be comfortable.

After the injection, the agonizing seconds slowly ticked by. Finally, Alyssa's sobs ceased, and her breathing slowed. Her glazed and tranquil eyes were not quite closed. Julia

pressed her damp cheek to that of her daughter. She
shushed the child over and over, caressing Alyssa's pale
skin with wispy strokes of her fingertips, just as she'd done
when her daughter was an infant.

"Oh, Mommy, that feels good," came Alyssa's barely
audible voice. "I love you, Mommy."

"Oh, pumpkin, I love you so much!" Julia remained
there a minute more, clutching and caressing her child, until
the drug pulled Alyssa's lids closed. Struggling to keep
from falling apart, Julia swallowed and took a trembling
breath. Giving her daughter one long, last kiss, she pulled
away, her tortured expression chiseled by determination.

Her voice was flat. "I'm ready, Steve," she said. "If you
love her like I do, you won't let her go through that again."

Steve silently nodded, fighting back tears of his own.
The first syringe contained a large amount of the barbiturate
thiopental sodium. Once he was certain Alyssa was unconscious, he would follow it up with succinylcholine and po-
tassium chloride. The latter would still her heart.

He took the first syringe, inserted its needle into the
tubing, and hesitated. What he was preparing to do was
good and right and noble, yet now . . . One final look into
Julia's imploring eyes was all he needed to see. He began
to inject.

Julia stood quivering at the head of the bed. She untied
her robe and shrugged out of it, letting it fall to the floor.
Underneath, her naked skin had gooseflesh. Lifting the
covers, she slid unembarrassed into bed beside her daughter. Cradling Alyssa in her arms, Julia drew her firmly
against her skin, as if the closeness would let every ounce
of warmth and love drain from her into her dying child. As
Steve finished injecting, Julia softly, tenderly sang.

> *You are my sunshine, my only sunshine,*
> *You make me happy, when skies are gray.*
> *You'll never know, dear, how much I love*
> *you,*
> *So please . . .*

Along with her heart, Alyssa's breathing stopped. Julia
shut her eyes tight and clung to Alyssa in tortured grief.

As he looked at mother and daughter, Steve suddenly felt that a piece of him was missing. Yet, in doing what he did, he gave love, the highest form of caring.

It is late evening on a cool night in the Hamptons. In a modest house in a working-class neighborhood, three people are in an upstairs bedroom. The room is quieter now. The only sounds are the ticking of a grandfather clock and the anguished sobbing of a woman who has just lost her only child.

SKEPTIC
HOLDEN SCOTT

DR. MIKE BALLANTINE is a man of science, fact, and logic—until he sees his best friend, the Governor of Massachusetts, obliterated before his eyes. Until a bizarre specter appears before him. Until a beautiful CIA agent named Amber Chen tells him about an executioner emerged from the depths of the Chinese Revolution, bringing to America a murderous art that is part magic, part science, and pure evil. Now, as Mike and Amber desperately try to unravel a mystery of biomedicine and murder, they face the most chilling revelation of all: that the worst weapon ever invented is not a bomb, a missile, or a toxin—it's a ghost . . .

"A truly original thriller—part medical, part paranormal, and totally gripping."   —Nelson DeMille

"Riveting . . . Brilliantly told. The suspense is relentless and builds to an ending that leaves you astounded and wondering why someone didn't think of this before . . ."
                    —Jack McConnel, M.D., cofounder of
                        the Institute for Genomic Research

"Ingenious, fascinating, and thoroughly original . . . SKEPTIC raises the bar for the medical thriller. Holden Scott ventures into exciting new territory."
                    —F. Paul Wilson, author of *Nightkill* and
                        The Barrens and Others